resorting *to* romance

resorting *to* romance

USA TODAY BESTSELLING AUTHOR

JENNIFER SHIRK

Entangled Publishing, LLC
644 Shrewsbury Commons Ave., STE 181
Shrewsbury, PA 17361
rights@entangledpublishing.com

Amara is an imprint of Entangled Publishing, LLC.

Visit our website at www.entangledpublishing.com.

Edited by Alice Jerman and Jen Bouvier
Cover illustration and design by Elizabeth Turner Stokes
Stock art by Ramil Gibadullin/Shutterstock
and fotohunter/Shutterstock
Interior design by Britt Marczak

Trade Paperback ISBN 978-1-64937-650-3
Ebook ISBN 978-1-64937-548-3

Manufactured in the United States of America

First Edition July 2024

10 9 8 7 6 5 4 3 2 1

AMARA
an imprint of Entangled Publishing LLC

For Juliette
I'm so proud of you.

At Entangled, we want our readers to be well-informed. If you would like to know if this book contains any elements that might be of concern for you, please check the back of the book for details.

Chapter One

"Lipstick or no lipstick?"

When her legal secretary didn't respond, Loni Wingate whipped around, her tube of Givenchy matte rouge held tight in hand.

Catherine stood in the middle of her office, shaking her head with an amused expression. "You're going to make partner no matter what you look like, you know."

Loni waved the bright red tube in triumph. "I'm hearing lipstick then." Smiling, she proceeded to apply it.

She turned around, fussing with her blond hair once more. Yes, perhaps she was going a bit overboard on presentation. But she wanted to look perfect. This was the day. *Her* day. What she'd wanted since becoming an attorney and moving away from her hometown in North Carolina and settling in Los Angeles. And if she made partner today, not only would she be the only woman, but the youngest to ever do so at her firm.

Mama would be as happy as a clam at high tide.

She grinned, knowing she was doing her mama proud. In

fact, her mother would have wanted this promotion more for her daughter than anyone else. Loni hadn't thought of her mom in a while, not since her funeral a few years ago. Mostly because Loni tried her best not to. The memories were almost too painful. And, if she were being honest with herself, because she hadn't quite accepted that her mother was truly gone.

"Relax," Catherine told her, coming up to her and laying a hand on her shoulder. "I've been hearing the rumors. You've got a bright future ahead of you, my friend."

A bright future.

The thought of her name on the door made Loni dizzy with pride. She couldn't wait to celebrate with her fiancé, Blaze, who was also an attorney at the same firm. He was going to be so proud, too, especially after all the time she'd put in. Maybe they would have a normal schedule for once and actually spend some quality time together. She was beginning to forget what he even looked like. They could go away somewhere—maybe Sunny Banks.

Er, no, probably not.

Blaze never made it a secret that he thought the little southern town she'd grown up in was...boring. They'd even gotten into an argument over how he'd believed the slow-paced attitude of its residents fueled complacency. Still ridiculous to think about. Bless his heart. But she wasn't surprised that someone as ambitious and driven as Blaze would clash with the charm of small-town southern living. He couldn't relate.

"Plus, the lipstick is a bold power move," Catherine was saying with a wink. "It's so you. Well, that and the Jimmy Choo pumps."

Loni smiled. The lipstick and shoes were her *now*. She glanced down at her new mahogany heels. A fun little early celebratory gift to herself. After all, she'd busted her butt working at Becker, Becker, & Maggio. It was the least she'd deserved after the number of hours she'd put in for them. Not that she minded entirely. Yes, she was a little sleep deprived, a bit pasty from the lack of sunlight, and perhaps she could open up her own pharmacy with the number of herbal supplements she'd been taking for stress, but, all in all, she enjoyed helping clients with their estate planning. She also worked quite a bit on corporate and business contracts as well. She felt as if she was making a difference for people. Such a far cry from what her sisters were doing back in Sunny Banks, running their family resort. Not that she didn't appreciate their hard work and dedication to maintaining their mama's second love—the first being their father. It wasn't part of her world anymore. Not since Mama had gotten sick.

Her office phone buzzed. Too nervous to pick up, she just gaped at it until Catherine wedged her way around the desk and answered the phone for her.

"Yes, Apollonia is right here," Catherine said in her usual professional tone. "Of course. I'll let her know." Then she hung up.

"Who was that?" Loni asked, nerves already sprouting in her belly.

Catherine's smile widened. "The partners want to see you now."

Loni took a deep breath. It was finally happening.

This is not happening.

In the five years she had worked—i.e., *sweated blood*—at Becker, Becker & Maggio, she had always considered herself an up-and-comer. A legal eagle.

Now, she felt more like a pigeon.

The one in the flock that was getting crapped on.

"Honestly, Mark," Loni began, addressing her boss, "I don't know now how that happened." She looked at his laptop again, half hoping that the email he'd pulled up from an upset client would have magically disappeared. She couldn't believe what they were saying, that she had actually sent it. Had she been so tired and overworked these last few months that she had really sent out a document to a client before it was complete?

Mark Becker, senior VP of the firm and someone she'd thought of as more of a mentor than a boss, shook his graying head sadly. "Apollonia—"

Her phone buzzed. Loni's cheeks burned as she murmured an apology. It buzzed again. And then again. And then again.

"Um, hold that thought please," she said, raising a finger to her boss before pulling out her phone and silencing it. She couldn't help but notice that the four texts were from her sisters. Oh God, now was not the time to be held hostage on some random group text with them. She had more pressing concerns than whatever family drama those two were involved in now.

When she finally looked up, Mark sighed. "Apollonia, you've always been a great attorney here, however..." He glanced at the other two partners at the conference table with a grim expression.

Loni closed her eyes. Oh my gosh. He'd followed the "she'd been a great attorney" part with "however" and used her real name and not her nickname. This was triply bad. They were going to fire her for sure. Over something she didn't even remember doing! Could she plead temporary insanity? Sleepwalking? Maybe extraterrestrial abduction?

The man seated to Mark's left—Carson Maggio, who had never uttered more than two words to her since she'd been hired—finally cleared his throat. "We were hoping you'd be the first woman to make partner here," he said gruffly. "I'm sorry to inform you that the committee has had second thoughts now. You made the firm look foolish and unprofessional."

Her shoulders slumped. Not fired. But not promoted. She wasn't sure which was worse.

She'd been working her ass off this year, knowing that there had been an opening for partner, and that it had been rumored she was the potential candidate under consideration. Tears pricked the backs of her eyes as she thought about all the effort she'd put in and how it had all been ruined over one careless misstep. A misstep she firmly believed she had not made.

"Not to mention you haven't exactly been bringing in new clients," Carson added.

Loni stared at him. Maybe she hadn't been bringing them in in droves, but she had just landed a huge account three weeks ago which, in her opinion, counted for a lot more in revenue. She wanted to argue her case—being the good attorney that she was—but she closed her lips when her mom's voice sounded in her head. *Don't waste energy trying to change people's opinion of you. Stay true to yourself, sugar. Never settle for anything less.*

"Apollonia?" Mark said, bringing her attention back to the meeting. "Do you understand our decision?"

"Uh, yes, sir," she croaked.

Mark nodded. He gathered the papers placed out on the table before him and gestured to the door. "Fix your mistake," he said in a dismissive tone.

"Absolutely," she said, then turned on her heels and walked

out of the office as steadily as her wobbly legs could take her. Once she'd closed the office door behind her, she was finally able to breathe again. Oh God, how was she ever going to get back in their good graces? *Could* she get back in their good graces?

Catherine popped her head up from her desk as soon as she heard the door click. "Hey, how'd it go?" she whispered.

Loni shook her head. "I wouldn't exactly call myself the next Ally McBeal."

Catherine gasped. "What did they say?"

Loni glanced around the office. Not that this environment was conducive to gossip-mongering, but she wanted a few hours without everyone knowing she hadn't made partner. There was still a cutthroat edge in the air that she'd not gotten used to since moving here. She motioned to her office, and Catherine automatically stood and followed her in.

Once inside with the door closed, she leaned against her desk and sighed deeply. "For the last twenty minutes, I just got my ass sliced, diced, and handed to me. I obviously didn't make partner, and at this rate, I'm fairly certain I'm lucky to still have my job."

Catherine blinked. "*What?* Tell me everything."

Loni rubbed her head. "Please don't make me repeat it. It was bad enough to live it once."

"I don't understand," Catherine went on, her hands flying in the air as she spoke. "But you've worked so hard. Your billables are impressive. Everything was in place. You were going to move into the corner office, and I was hoping to get yours."

"I know," Loni groaned, walking over to her desk and pulling out her trusted supply of caffeine pills and ibuprofen. She took out two of each, popped them in her mouth, and swallowed them dry. *Bleh.*

"Well, they had to have given you a reason at least." Catherine wrinkled her nose at Loni's medicinal stash and grabbed her a water bottle from the mini fridge in the corner of the office. "And dear God, will you please start taking care of yourself and remember to eat? I have tomatoes that have gone through twelve hours in my food dehydrator that look more nourished than you."

"Whoa, move over Jay Shetty, there's a new life coach in town," Loni said drolly. But she took the water and immediately began chugging. She had to admit, these past few months she hadn't necessarily been treating her body like a temple—more like an abandoned house with a missing doorframe.

Catherine chuckled. "I speak the truth because I love you. Now tell me exactly what they said."

Loni drank some more from her water bottle, then wiped her mouth with the sleeve of her new White House Black Market blazer. Yes, her cream-colored blazer now had red lipstick smeared on it, which would have had the genteel-mannered women back home in North Carolina in dire need of a case of smelling salts. But they hadn't been hardened by LA rush hour traffic—or had the kind of morning she'd just endured.

"They said I sent a draft document instead of the final to a client."

"And did you?"

Loni looked at her friend, hurt that she even asked. "*No.* I didn't. I know I didn't."

"Well, then what's the problem? Tell them it's all a mistake."

"I tried. But what could I really say? The email was there with the draft attached and everything. I don't understand how that could have happened. I have specific files and numbering for each. I know I wasn't finished so I had no reason to send it. Plus, I would have double-checked before signing off. It's sloppy work that is just not me."

Catherine folded her arms. "Wow. You're right. That doesn't sound like you at all. But…I mean, you haven't been getting a lot of sleep lately. You're here after I leave at the end of the day and at the office way before I arrive the next morning. Do you think maybe all that could have been a factor and you *did* send it without really thinking?"

Loni rubbed a hand down her face, perfectly applied makeup be damned. "Honestly, I don't know. But if I did, then I am seriously losing my buttered grits."

Catherine laughed. "Mentioning butter in Los Angeles is sacrilegious. Now I know you're not losing it, because it's already gone."

A light knock at the door had them both sobering fast. Loni just hoped it wasn't more bad news. "Please come in," she called, trying to pull off a professional-sounding tone.

Blaze walked in with his typical no-nonsense stride and immediately came up to her, taking her hands in his. He was classic L.A handsome. Some would say he was borderline "pretty" with his baby blue eyes, short, strategically gelled hair, and smooth-skinned face. He was everything Loni could have wished for, a man who shared the same work ethic and goals, yet someone who also had a sensitive side and seemed to understand the value of thoughtful gestures, like surprising her with her favorite takeout when she'd been working late or texting her in the middle of a workday to ask how she was doing. He was also a true California native, and the sole reason she had moved here from North Carolina after law school. She still couldn't believe her luck that they had both ended up with jobs at the same firm. A true match made in heaven. Just like her parents.

If only they weren't both so busy. She had to admit, with each of them working long hours, a spark between them had died. But she was sure if they could spend more time together, they could rekindle what they'd lost.

"I heard what happened," he said, giving her hands a gentle squeeze.

"Wow, bad news really does travel fast," she muttered.

"Not really," he said, dropping her hands. "I just happened to have needed Mark's okay on a few documents and stopped by his office just now."

Catherine sniffed. "Convenient."

He shot her a look over his shoulder. "Don't you have some filing to do or maybe a particularly bad pot of coffee to make?"

Fire sparked in Catherine's gaze. "Listen, you chauvinistic bast—"

"Cath, please," Loni said, pinching the bridge of her nose. She didn't know why, but her two favorite people in the office couldn't stand each other, and she just couldn't drum up the energy to play referee this time. "Can you two give it a break for one day?"

Catherine glared at Blaze for a beat, then relented. "Sure. I should get back to work anyway. Maybe we can grab lunch. My treat."

Loni smiled, grateful for the kind support. At least she had one friend in this firm. "Thanks. We'll talk later."

She nodded, then slipped out of the office. Once it was just the two of them, Blaze turned to her with a frown. "No offense, but you look terrible."

She rolled her eyes but self-consciously ran a hand through

her blond shoulder-length bob. "You're not the first to tell me that today," she said with a wry smile. "I must look worse than I feel."

"Listen, it probably wouldn't be a bad time to get out of Dodge, so to speak. Take a little vacation. Maybe go to a spa or something. Try and relax."

She let out a laugh. "*You* want to take a vacation now? And to a spa resort? I can't believe my ears." It's like he'd been reading her mind. She'd been trying to get him to take a trip to Laucala Island with her all summer, but he'd always brushed off her pleas under the notion that it would look too frivolous to the firm.

"Oh. About that…" He shifted then, letting out an unsteady breath. "I was thinking *you* should take the vacation. You know, *without* me."

She shook her head, thinking she must have heard wrong. "Wait. We wouldn't be going together? Why not?"

"Well, it wouldn't look good…especially now…" He didn't meet her gaze.

"I'm not sure I understand what you're talking about. What's so special about now?"

He cleared his throat a few times as if he had a giant hairball caught in it. "It wouldn't be good if we went together considering I'm your boss now."

Her head fell back as if his words had slapped her. "*You* got the promotion? Oh my God."

"I was hoping for more of a congratulations."

"Oh, I'm sorry." She shook her head at her thoughtless comment. "Yes, it's wonderful news… Of course. It's just that you didn't tell me you were being considered as well, or that you even wanted it."

He snorted. "Come on, who would turn down an opportunity like that? It should have been obvious I was up for the promotion since we were hired around the same time. And after that mistake you made... I can't help that they gave it to me," he said, his tone turning defensive.

She narrowed her eyes. "How did you know about my mistake?"

He waved off her question with his clean, manicured hand. "Don't read into it, Apollonia. But they confided in me. I knew I was getting the promotion for the last week, but I obviously couldn't tell you."

Loni went cold all over. They were engaged to be married, yet he felt more obligated to the firm—to the committee— than to her. She couldn't believe he'd just said that. She'd trusted him, confided in him. Had barely slept this week. She'd just bought nine-hundred-dollar shoes! And he knew the whole time she wasn't going to get the partnership.

He reached out and fingered the Scotch Bonnet shell that sat on her desk. The one reminder of the years she'd spent playing and shell collecting on the Carolina coast as a child. A reminder of simpler times when she and her sisters would rush back home from the beach for a glass of her mother's freshly brewed sweet tea. Loni had a sudden urge to smack his hand away from it.

"Mark and I were discussing how this all would work between us," he said, still eyeing the shell. "I don't want to be the bad guy in this situation."

Too late, she thought miserably.

"Anyway," he went on, "we were thinking it'd probably be best if you and I took a break from our relationship."

She frowned. "You mean you and Mark think it best you

and I have a break? We're engaged, Blaze. What are you saying? That you can't marry me because you're now my boss?"

He huffed out a breath. "See? I knew you'd take this the wrong way."

"How else am I supposed to take it? Normal people do not take breaks from their engagements. Especially not because their boss told them to! They either get married or they permanently break up. What I'm hearing is that you no longer want to be engaged." Even as she said the words, she couldn't even believe they were having this conversation. They'd been together for years. Had she been that blind? Was she that naïve to believe him when he'd talked about a future together forever?

"It's not that at all. I still want to get married. Just not right now. How can we really afford to get married anyway? The timing is all wrong with the expense of becoming partner. We need to think of our futures."

She scoffed. "You mean you need to think about *your* career. I can't believe you're allowing the firm to get between us like this."

Blaze ran a hand through his gelled hair. She was disgusted when it didn't move a millimeter. "Maybe this was the wrong time to bring all this up," he told her. "I can see that now. You're still feeling raw from being passed over for partner. Believe me, I get that and I'm sorry."

Loni's anger flared. Not getting the promotion was barely the tip of the iceberg. She couldn't believe how incredibly obtuse he was being.

"What exactly are you sorry for?" she asked. "For taking my promotion without remorse and keeping that knowledge from me so I could be blindsided, or breaking up with me after I had found all that out?"

He stared at her for a full minute, his mouth hanging slightly open. "Okay, if you need me to play the villain so you feel better about not being promoted—"

"It has nothing to do with making partner! It's about trust, Blaze. And priorities. You said we were in this for the long haul. You said that you loved me."

He reached out and took hold of her shoulders. "Of course, I love you, sweetheart. That's what makes this decision so damn hard. But our break should only be for a little while. Just a pause. Once we both prove how dedicated we are, the firm won't think anything about us getting engaged again in a few years."

"Get out," she said, surprised at how calm and unhysterical she sounded despite how much she was reeling.

He dropped his arms and had the nerve to flinch. "Loni, are these staged theatrics in case anyone is listening in? Because I don't—"

"Get *out!*" Sweet Mother of all that was Holy, if he didn't leave her sight in the next ten seconds not making partner would be the least of her worries.

He backed up to the door of her office, hands raised. "Okay, okay, I'm leaving. Just know I don't want us to leave it like this. But take some time. Think things through. You'll see how much this all makes sense. I'm still willing to make this work between us."

Not trusting her words, she just pointed to the door. He left and she collapsed into her desk chair, pressing her hands into her heated face. What the hell was she supposed to do now?

Actually, she did know. She twisted the engagement ring off her finger and tossed it down onto her desk as if it had scorched her skin.

She closed her eyes against the sudden pressure of tears. She felt so many things but didn't know what to do with her emotions. They didn't belong anywhere. Suddenly, *she* didn't belong anywhere.

What had happened to her and Blaze taking on the world together? She thought they had had a relationship built on respect and commonality. At least, that's what he'd always told her. Lordy, she'd been a fool to believe his pretty words, to follow him here to California after law school. But Blaze had been so adamant. So sure that this was the place they should settle. His hometown. And she'd gone, blindly. He had said he'd needed her. And she had needed him, too.

Her head hadn't been in the right space at the time. Her mother had just passed away and then her father had announced he was moving to Boston to help run a friend's hotel on Cape Cod. She and her father had had a terrible fight that night. She just couldn't understand why he was leaving to run another hotel when they had their own hotel—the *family* resort—to run.

"Your sisters can look after The Sandy Bottom while I'm away," he'd told her. "They know what they're doing. It was more your mother's baby than anything else, anyway."

Precisely why she thought he should stay. For Mama. But he'd left the day after the funeral. And so had she.

Everything seemed to have changed after the passing of her mom. It was like the heart of the family had been ripped out of its core and they just couldn't patch themselves together no matter how hard they'd tried. Her dad turned so distant, like he couldn't stand to be in the same room with her anymore. Was it any wonder she had grasped onto the first man to show her affection and follow him like a puppy across the country?

She'd kept in contact with her sisters, mostly via phone calls, texts, or shared Instagram memes. But she missed them. And now, here she was. No promotion. No fiancé. No place to live. Quite a record day so far. At this rate, she wondered bitterly if she should even bother looking both ways as she crossed the street today.

Through a salty blur of tears, she reached across her desk to the shell that Blaze had seemed so preoccupied with just minutes before. With a grim smile, she turned it over in her hand, remembering the time when she, her sisters, and her mom went seashell hunting after a storm and had come back with a basket full. Loni had kept this one not only because it was the largest, but because her mother had picked it out of the basket especially for her to decorate. Loni hadn't, though. She liked the simple color and lines of the shell. Wanted to preserve it as it was, just as she did that memory.

She swiped at her eyes. Gosh, she was turning into a blubbering mess. No wonder she wasn't considered partner material. Maybe she did need a vacation. And a nap. And a bottle of tequila. Not necessarily in that order. But she did need to get away from Blaze and figure out not only what the hell she should do next but figure out her life as well.

Remembering the texts from her sisters, she pulled out her phone and saw there were three more messages and a missed call from her younger sister, Marise. She rubbed her temples as she pushed play on the voicemail.

"Loni, I know you must be busy, but we've got real problems here with a capital P," Marise rushed out with an edge of panic in her voice. "It's Daddy. He's gone about as crazy as a dog in a squirrel factory. He's gonna sell the resort. SELL THE RESORT! No discussion about it. I don't know what to do. Kalinda is strangely quiet and well, being Kalinda-like. That's why I need you and—" There was some murmuring and then a loud thump in the background. "Oh, barbecue sauce, Knox," she heard Marise say in frustration. "Sorry, Loni. Work issues. Call me as soon as you can." Then the voicemail ended.

Numb with shock, Loni placed her phone down on her desk. The blows seemed to keep coming today. *How in the world could Daddy even think about selling the resort without discussing it with all of us?*

Yet, maybe this one at least had been dealt at the right time, considering she was just told to take a vacation.

With a decisive nod, she sat back, feeling a weight being lifted from her chest already as she slid her laptop closer to her and began researching flights. She'd make sure she wasn't leaving any loose ends at work—no need to burn any more bridges there. Besides, it was her new *boss's* idea she take this little getaway. Just being a good employee and following orders, after all. Then she'd call her sisters and tell them she had some vacation time coming to her.

Oh, but she wasn't going to a tropical island. She was going to the one place she should never have turned her back on. The one place where she felt the most at peace. To the one place and to the people who needed her most.

She was finally going home.

Chapter Two

"*Twins*, Ian. I can't believe you're turning down twins. What am I supposed to do with the sister now?"

Ian Hollowell finally looked up from the email he'd been composing to a potential builder and gave his business development manager a wry smile. "You're a creative mind, Scott. I'm sure you'll think of something. Besides, I have a date already and I refuse to break it."

He genuinely liked Scott when it came down to the contracts he could draw up on short notice and the relationships he had with big builders in the area, but socially, the guy had the maturity of a fifteen-year-old.

Scott shook his head. "Come on. Break the date and come out with me instead. You can't be serious about this woman."

"How would you know?"

"Dude, because you're *The Predator*. Not exactly the kind of guy marriage-minded mamas want their daughters bringing home to them. Besides, we've known each other for, what, a few years now? And I've never seen you go out with a woman more than seven times."

Ian blinked. *Was that true?* Seven dates? He hadn't realized his regimented work life had spilled over into his love life as well. Although he had to high-five his subconscious—it wasn't a bad rule of thumb for him to follow. Seven dates seemed like a reasonable limit. Enough time that it wouldn't label him superficial yet not so much time spent together where attachments could be made, and hearts broken. Of course, he'd always been very upfront with the women he had dated. He'd respected them and enjoyed them but preferred to do all that without the commitment part. Emotional attachments had a way of killing an otherwise perfectly pleasant relationship.

Ian went back to his email and hit send. "Are you sure about that number?"

"Pretty sure," Scott said with a shrug. "Give or take a date. So, what gives with this one? Don't tell me that cupid stung you in the ass this time and you finally found love."

Ian smirked. Like that was even possible. Love was not a word allowed in his personal dictionary since he doubted it was even ingrained in his personal DNA. "Since when are you so preoccupied with my love life?"

Scott grinned. "When it starts hurting *my* love life, obviously."

"Maybe you should focus more on work. Like yours truly."

Scott scoffed. "Hey, it wasn't my fault that The Planning and Zoning Board in that little New Jersey beach town was such a force to be reckoned with. Damn, they really didn't like you coming in and buying up their land there."

Ian gave him a look. "I like how you blame me. As if you're not part of this company, too."

"Ah, but you make a better villain."

Ian rolled his eyes. He wasn't so much a villain as he was a sap. Because now he was stuck with all that land that the town didn't want him to develop—especially into boutique hotels or what the townspeople call oversized homes. Which happened to be Ian's specialty.

"Well, take your pretty face down there and see if you can change their minds," he told Scott.

"I will. Tomorrow. After my date."

Ian glanced around Scott to see through the glass door of his office. Speaking of dates. The woman he'd been waiting for was chatting it up with his secretary. With a grin, he shut down his computer and stood, signaling Scott to leave as well. "Sorry, dude. My dinner date has arrived."

"Oh, I gotta see this." Scott craned his neck and then frowned. "You're blowing me off to have dinner with your grandmother?"

Ian chuckled. "For your safety, I'm not going to tell her you said that. She happens to be a friend."

Scott shook his head. "You're ruining the illusion. In my mind your date was going to be Megan Fox."

Ian grinned. "Come meet her anyway." He walked over to the door and threw it open. "Hey, Pam," he said, greeting her with a smile. I thought Joe would be joining us, too."

"Darling," Pamela gushed. She walked up to him, no doubt leaving a wake of her favorite perfume, Chanel No.5, and planted a light kiss on his cheek. "I told Joe to wait for us downstairs. You know those southern types. His legs move like he's walking through molasses."

Ian grinned at the older woman. "This is my friend Pamela Dubois," he said to Scott. "We met when I was in Cape Cod last year and bought those old condo units by the fishing pier. After seeing me four days in a row eating lobster rolls and fries at the same restaurant, she finally came over and began lecturing me on the high fat and cholesterol content I was putting in my body."

Scott extended a hand. "Well, hello, Pam. Scott Simpson, Ian's right-hand man. A pleasure to meet someone who cares so much about our colleague's health."

"Well, somebody needs to look out for Ian. But truth be told, I was really trying to get the attention of the man Ian was having lunch with that day," she said with a wink.

"Did it work?" Scott asked.

She fluffed her hair a bit. "Of course it did. And Joe and I are still together." She turned her gaze to Ian and smiled. "Actually, we're *all* still together, aren't we?"

Ian nodded, feeling forever grateful and damn lucky to have gotten two good friends as well as role models out of that visit to the south shore—especially this late in his life. But better late than never. "Went to Cape Cod to see about a property and came back with it and two parental figures. Like it or not," he added with affection.

Pam reached out and lightly patted his cheek. "You like it. Although maybe I've been slacking in my motherly role— Joe and I should visit more often. I was just having the nicest conversation with Amy, here," she said, gesturing to his young assistant. "Ian, you promised me you had cut down on the caffeine. She says you walk across the street three times a week for a six-shot latte called The Big Papi. Shame on you."

Scott snorted and Amy had the good graces to turn beet red as she mouthed *sorry* from behind Pam.

"You both are so fired," he said to them without any heat, then led Pam to the elevators. "Come on, before I have to let any more employees and their big mouths go."

Pam frowned. "Don't blame them. And what kind of name is that for a coffee, anyway?" she said, pressing a bright pink manicured finger on the down arrow.

Ian placed both hands on his chest as if suffering in pain. "Ouch. We're in Boston. If you don't get the Red Sox reference, then I regret to inform you that you're going to have to move out of the state."

"Hmm... Funny you should say that," she hedged lightly.

"Oh? Are you really thinking of moving? I thought things were going well with Joe." The elevator *dinged*, and they walked in together.

She bit her red-lined lip, appearing to be smothering an impish grin. "Things are going well. In fact, they're going extremely well. Sweetie, we had planned on telling you at dinner, but... Oh, why not now?" She raised her left hand in front of his face and fluttered her fingers. There was a two-karat diamond solitaire sitting on her ring finger.

Ian swallowed; a rush of happiness and shock coursed through him. Engaged again at sixty-five years old. Imagine that. Ian couldn't picture ever wanting to commit and get married, let alone twice in one lifetime.

"Congratulations, Pam," he said, reaching out and wrapping his arms around her.

The elevator *dinged* again, and the doors slid open.

"Well, if this just doesn't dill my pickle," came a southern male voice from outside the elevator.

Ian and Pam broke apart to face Joe Wingate, standing there in the lobby, holding a single long-stemmed red rose. He gave them a wide smile, looking elated, if not a bit fidgety in his tan suit and baby blue tie.

"Joe, we're going to have to work on your northern slang," Ian said, holding out his hand with a grin.

Joe handed the flower to Pamela, dropping a light kiss on her cheek, then wrapped him in a hug of his own. "Son, I'm going to take this as a neon sign of approval for our engagement."

Joe was a burly-looking man with the manners and disposition of a true southern gentleman, always calling him *son* with utmost affection and genuineness. A welcoming contrast from Ian's real father.

"I couldn't be happier for you both," Ian said truthfully.

Pam laid a hand on Ian's arm. "I hope you don't mind, but we have some things we need to discuss with you. Exciting things."

"More exciting than your engagement?"

Joe winked at Pamela and pulled her close. "Not half as thrilling as that. Business dealings. Uh, a property you might be interested in."

Ian grinned, rubbing his hands together. "I'm already interested."

The good humor on Joe's face slipped a notch. "Righto, but, ah, there is a bit of a delicate situation with it. Although, one I feel you'll have no trouble handling for us."

Partly intrigued and partly concerned, Ian nodded as he pulled out his phone. "Well, then. First things first. Let me start by calling us an Uber."

Ian ordered appetizers and a bottle of champagne for their table. At Joe's insistence, he and Joe had a standing dinner reservation at Ocean Prime once every two months for the last few years. Then, when Joe began dating Pam, she would join them as well. It was a rare constant in Ian's life, because Ian had no real family of his own now.

Once their waiter had poured their champagne, Pamela reached for her glass with an excited squeal. "I'm so happy to be celebrating our engagement with you, Ian," she said, raising her glass in the air.

"Maybe we'll be celebrating yours next," Joe said with a wink.

There was no way in hell that was ever going to happen.

However, Ian politcly smiled and raised his glass to theirs. "I'm very happy for you both," he told them. "You may not have been each other's first love, but how very special to be each other's last."

"That's lovely." Pamcla sniffed and lightly blotted the corner of her eyes.

Joe nodded, then took a sip of his wine. "Thanks, son."

Son.

As many times as Joe had uttered the endearment, it still sounded foreign to Ian's ears. But he supposed Joe was the closest thing he had to a dad. His real father—who wasn't much of one while Ian was growing up—had been an alcoholic, who devoted much of his life to bouncing in and out of hospitals and rehab programs up until about eight years ago when he'd had a DUI accident and ended up taking not only his own life but that of his wife as well.

His mom had deserved better than to be dragged down that vicious cycle. If only she hadn't been so blinded by love for his dad. She would be alive and would have seen that her son had needed her, too.

Now, Ian needed no one. He had gotten used to being alone, sometimes even preferred it. Sure, he had friends, and women, but when he met Joe, something changed in him. Joe seemed to take an interest in Ian that went beyond business or what Ian could do for him. Joe even gave him some guidance when Ian started working in business development. Turned out Joe had given advice that Ian would never forget. Because of that, Ian could almost trust again.

Almost.

But not quite. He was just shy of allowing anyone in too close, friendship or otherwise. Especially not in the romance department. That's where his emotions shut down. He apparently didn't have the bandwidth to deal with emotional attachments. The kind of crazy codependency he saw and had to manage with his parents' love had drained him and now a steady relationship was something that Ian wouldn't—*couldn't*—even touch with the tip of his brand-new wingtips.

Joe clasped his hands together and placed them on top of the table. "Let's talk business before the wine arrives," he suggested.

Joe was someone Ian respected and liked, but Ian also admired a man who could get right to the point. Another plus in Joe's favor. "Sure, Joe, what's on your mind?"

"With Pammy and I getting married and what have you, I've decided it best to completely sever ties with some property I have back home in North Carolina. An old hotel and resort."

Ian lifted a brow. "And you want my company to acquire the property?"

"Yes. I know you'll take care of that area. It's a real nice hotel, son. A real vacation resort kind of property. Sits not far from the beach in the Outer Banks. Figured you could develop it into whatever you like, though."

Beachfront property in North Carolina. Yes, please! Ian's

mind was already churning with ideas. He'd always had a passion for real estate and rose up the ranks fast at Hollavest, a development company specializing in state-of-the-art residential homes around the country including New Jersey, Montana, the Carolinas, Pennsylvania, Nantucket, and most recently, Costa Rica. In fact, he'd helped grow the company so quickly, his boss had nicknamed him "The Predator"...which Scott had appropriated for Ian's approach to his love life as well.

Ian had a nose for business, but he wasn't a fool. "What's the catch?" he asked.

Joe chuckled. "No catch, son."

Pam elbowed Joe in the side. "Joseph..."

When Pam elbowed Joe again, he added, "Okay. Not a catch as much as a fly in the ointment. Technically, three flies."

Ian shook his head, wondering how they could start talking about a hotel and end up talking insects. "Three...*flies*?"

Joe grinned. "My three daughters. Although my middle one might be more of a hornet than a fly. Spittin' image of her mother in looks and personality," he said with a little shake of his head. "They might all give you some flack initially, but in the end they'll come around."

Ian sat back and weighed the potential conflict this situation could create for Joe—not to mention for himself. He wasn't so sure any property would be worth the money or hassle three young women could garner him. "Maybe a better idea would be to put the hotel up for sale with a local realtor," he suggested.

"Tried that. No bites. Personally, I think they're more loyal to my daughters and haven't even tried to sell it." His tone changed, matching the hardened line of his mouth, and surprised Ian. "I really want that property gone."

"Why, if you don't mind me asking?"

Joe looked down at his clasped hands. "Too many memories. Now that I'm getting remarried, I want to move on, and my daughters need to move on, too. Also, I need the money."

Ian glanced at Pam, trying to get a clue into what her thoughts were. As much as he appreciated the sole chance at acquisition, something didn't sit right.

Pamela leaned over and reached for his hand. "Ian, we know you can get this done for us. A fresh start for everyone is best. Plus, I really think this will be good for you."

He arched an eyebrow. "Good for me how?"

She smiled gently. "You check out the resort and see if the property makes sense for your company and any builders you know, and you'll get a little vacation out of your stay. Joe has been telling me all about the town. It sounds heavenly. You work so hard all the time. You should enjoy yourself for a change."

"Real quaint down there," Joe added. "You'll be getting the best of the season, too. September is beautiful. Still warm enough to swim and take advantage of all the water toys you can get your hands on, but the tourist crowds are slightly thinned out because of back-to-school time. Living in New England, I'm sure you'll be interested in the town's seafood fest. Plus, you'll get to meet my girls. I know you're not true family, but you are like a son to me. Consider it a family initiation," he said with a chuckle.

Ian didn't like the sound of an initiation, but the getaway was mildly attractive. More importantly, the growing company he worked for could certainly use the added investment to its portfolio. He could already think of at least two capital partners he could contact if the area showed promise and the zoning checked out. But something about mixing business with friendship had him pressing the pause button a little longer.

"Please, Ian," Pam said. "This would mean a lot to us if you could just go down and check it out. See what you could do with the property if you took it off Joe's hands. Sort of a wedding gift to us."

The hopeful looks in both their eyes had him relenting. Joe was obviously a motivated seller. And if the property looked good, he'd be an effing hero to his boss, Raj. What was Ian so worried about? It'd be like a child refusing a free ice cream conc. Plus, he'd always wanted to visit the Outer Banks.

"Fine." Ian smiled at the both of them. "I'll take a look," he said, picking up his menu. "I just need to finalize a few things tomorrow and then I'll jump on the next plane to…" He laughed at himself. "I don't even know where I'm going. What's the town's name?"

"The town is called Sunny Banks," Joe said, giving him a fond glance. "I'll text you the info. And of course, I'll be sure to give my girls a heads-up as soon as we're done with dinner. Remind them that they're to give you a proper southern welcome."

Ian lifted his brow. "Do they really need the reminder?"

Joe's smile dissolved. "You don't know my daughters." His posture then straightened, and he gave Ian a hearty slap on the back. "Hey, don't look so glum. You'll see. Once they find out you're a friend of mine—and considered family of sorts— everything will be as smooth and as sweet as homemade peanut butter pie."

Ian managed to return the older man's smile as he picked up his menu again. Little did Joe know that his words did not give him any comfort at all.

Especially because Ian hated peanut butter.

Chapter Three

Loni slept the entire flight. She was obviously more overworked than she'd realized.

After securing a convertible rental car and the largest iced cold brew coffee she could get her hands on, she took her time driving into town. It was almost September, but still so much warmer than Los Angeles. The sun was shining and as she drove with the top down, she'd almost forgotten how sweet fresh air could smell and feel in her lungs.

Not that she didn't love where she was living. She genuinely liked the LA scene. The energy. The constant motion that made her feel as if she not only had a purpose in life, but there was nothing else on earth she should be doing with that life.

But this, she thought, seeing the fishing boats and array of coastal cottages along the bay, this was what she didn't know she needed right now. To slow down. A grounding of sorts. Her mental health had already markedly improved just knowing she'd see her sisters soon. They'd help her figure out what to do about Blaze. *If* she wanted to do anything about him. She was too numb to think or feel much of anything with regard to their relationship at the moment.

She'd alerted Marise via text as soon as she'd landed and that as long as there wasn't any of the usual tourist traffic, she'd be in town around three p.m. Marise had said Kalinda was already planning a welcome home dinner of all her favorites: pulled pork, grits, and buttermilk pie. Enduring the chatty person at the airport gate terminal would be worth the trip just for that meal alone.

Kalinda was a wonderful cook, who ran a café called The White Squirrel, which happened to be the only dining choice offered on their hotel premises. The restaurant was quaint, which basically meant "no frills." Locals touted it as one of their best and finest establishments among the glitzier chain restaurants that had sprouted up in their small town over the years. Mainly because Kalinda understood the hard-and-fast rule of southern cuisine that most newcomers did not: that barbeque was a food and not an event, and that people from their particular Carolina town were darn serious about it. The last time Loni had decent barbeque was at her mother's funeral. Just thinking about those close-kept family recipes that Kalinda was still using made her mouth water and miss her mother even more.

Gosh, what would her mother think about the mess she'd created in her life? Loni had just had the worst fight with a man she'd been with for five years and she hadn't even managed a good cry about it yet. Maybe she was too cold and detached. That served her well in her career, but obviously wasn't a glowing attribute in the romance department. Had she inadvertently ruined her relationship because she'd been too preoccupied with making partner?

Loni turned left at the surf shop where she'd gotten her first wet suit as a child and drove until she came upon The Sandy Bottom Hotel. Her stomach did a little nosedive as she placed the car in park and blinked at the building her family had owned since before she was born. If she were being completely honest, she'd have to admit the hotel looked a bit weathered. Not terribly embarrassing, but obviously not what it had been when she was younger. Was this something that had happened recently, or had it looked like that when she'd been home for her mother's funeral? Maybe she was so distraught with grief she hadn't noticed. Regardless, she was still reeling over the news that Daddy was willing to sell it.

She shook off the wave of disappointment that had enveloped her and stepped out of the car. Marise, who must have been watching from the window of the corner office, came running down the steps.

"You made it!" she shouted, launching herself at Loni. "This is going to be great. The sunshine sisters back together again."

Loni squeezed her tight, then pulled back to get a better look at her sister. Marise was just shy of twenty-four—practically a baby—and still as smiley and adorable as she was when she really was a baby. Sunscreen and freckles were the only things Marise ever wore on her face, and with her long, curly blond hair, she barely looked the age of twenty.

"You should come out to visit me more," Loni told her, admiring how pretty her sister was. "Those California girls have nothing on you."

Marise chuckled, flipping her hair off her shoulder and batting her eyes. "So true. And you...you..." Her hazel eyes traveled up and down Loni and her smile faltered. "What the heck happened to you? You'd make a vampire look like he'd spent time in a tanning bed."

Spoken as bluntly as only a sister could, Loni couldn't help but still grin at her. "I do work in an office in the city, if you recall, so I don't get to the beach much." Meaning she'd gotten to the beach once this year.

Marise took Loni's face in her hands. "If Mama saw you looking this peaked, she'd take to spoon-feeding you collard greens."

"I happen to like collard greens."

"Ah, so that's the real reason why Mom liked you best," came a voice behind them.

Kalinda stood grinning down at them from the top of the hotel steps. Her ash-blond hair was gathered high on her head in a messy top knot bun, and she wore her usual restaurant uniform of tattered white jean shorts that showcased her tanned legs, and a peach apron that bore the emblem of a white squirrel her mother had drawn and designed herself back in the day.

"Marise is right," Kalinda said, coming up to her and giving her a hug hello. "You do look pale and skinny. Don't tell me you caved into some LA fad diet or something."

Loni glanced at her Apple watch. "Gee, back in town for exactly six minutes and already you two have teamed up on me." To be honest, she didn't really mind it one bit. Although she'd never let her sisters know that.

Marise slung an arm around Loni's shoulders good-naturedly. "Six minutes? I can't believe we waited that long. We must be slippin' in our old age."

Kalinda grinned. "If *you're* old, I've got one foot in the coffin. Come on, Loni. Made a fresh batch of sweet tea that I've been guarding from Knox all day. Please have some so both of us can be put out of our misery."

Sweet tea! Yes! Loni thought she'd died and gone to southern heaven. Oh, how she'd missed such a simple beverage. She found it such a strange phenomenon when she'd first moved away that no one in California drank the stuff.

"Tall glass, plenty of ice," Loni said, turning back to her rental car.

Marise grabbed her hand and tugged. "No, no, honey, Knox will grab your luggage and put it in your room. We gave you Mom and Dad's suite since it has a mini kitchen."

"You didn't have to turn down guests who may have wanted it. Despite my Los Angeles lifestyle, I'm still pretty low maintenance. I would have taken any room."

Kalinda snorted. "What guests?" She made a sweeping gesture with her right arm of the sparse parking lot. "We don't exactly have people beating down our doors. Only half our rooms are occupied right now."

Loni frowned. Technically, the summer season was coming to an end, but tourists should continue to pour in well into the end of October and sometimes, if the temperatures were still mild, even into Thanksgiving time.

"Is there competition in the area?" Loni asked, letting a seed of worry plant itself in the back of her mind. "Is that why Daddy is so keen on selling?"

Kalinda shrugged, leading them into the side entrance of the restaurant. "No, unless you count all the VRBOs that have popped up over the last several years."

"It'll be fine," Marise said brightly. "I've got some ideas already in the works. Big plans. Huge return on investment type stuff."

Kalinda rolled her eyes. "Business majors."

"Hey, I straightened out our books, didn't I?"

"Thank heavens for that. Culinary school only took me so far."

As Loni took a seat on a stool by the stainless-steel counter in the restaurant's kitchen, she felt a twinge of guilt begin to take root in her core. Even though her father spent most of his time in Cape Cod, she'd assumed he would still be helping run the business as he normally had done. But for some reason, it seemed to have fallen all on her sisters' shoulders.

"Is there anything I can do?" Loni asked.

"Yes, there is." Kalinda took out three tall glasses and filled them with ice. She then reached into the refrigerator and pulled out a large pitcher of sweet tea. She set it on the counter next to several canisters of Moravian sugar cookies. "You can help yourself."

Loni had lost her appetite as soon as she'd realized the hotel could be in trouble, but she did pour herself some tea. For some reason she didn't like being cut out of the family business even though she was the one who had technically cut herself out of it by moving away. The hotel was still part of all their heritage.

An older woman wearing the same peach-colored apron as Kalinda walked into the kitchen. "That's a wrap and I'm outta here," she announced, untying her waitress apron. She tucked her dark hair behind her ears. "Hey, did y'all see what I did there? That's a wrap for the day and it was also one of the lunch specials!"

Kalinda chuckled. "You're a regular Jeff Foxworthy." She motioned to Loni, sitting before her. "Hazel, this is our middle sister, Apollonia. She lives in California and is here on vacation."

Hazel's brown eyes warmed as she stepped closer to shake her hand. "Oh, howdy, dear. Wow, you sure are spittin' images of each other. And wowsa, but Apollonia is simply a beautiful name. Just gorgeous. I definitely won't forget a name like that."

Loni smiled, having heard similar comments from people before. "Thank you and so nice to meet you, too."

Hazel nodded. "Well, I'll see y'all tomorrow, ladies. And nice meeting you, Olivia," she said with a wave.

Once Hazel had left, Marise stepped up to Loni and placed a hand on her shoulder. "Don't mind her, *Olivia*," she said unable to suppress a laugh. "Hazel is a real sweetheart. She may screw up a lot of orders, but the customers don't seem to mind."

Kalinda jerked a thumb at herself. "Uh, the cook actually minds."

"Well, the restaurant is your venue," Marise said, grabbing a cookie. "You need to handle Hazel and train her better if you're not happy with her."

Kalinda sighed. "I've got enough on my hands with Knox and Lucille, since you won't deal with them properly."

Marise shrugged. "I feel I serve better as the 'good cop' in our working relationship."

"Wait." Loni began rubbing her temples. "Who's Lucille?"

"She's head of housekeeping and guest relations," Marise said with a wave of her cookie, leaving a trail of crumbs on the counter.

"Lucille *is* the housekeeping and guest relations," Kalinda pointed out. "She fills in when Marise goes missing at the check-in desk, too."

"Temporarily." Marise narrowed her eyes. "You know, your negativity is stifling."

Kalinda raised her hands. "Since when is the truth called

negativity? I'm simply a truth teller."

Marise looked at Loni. "Do you see what I have to deal with here? She's mean. And just because she's older doesn't mean she's wiser. I know exactly what I'm doing with my staff. Tell her, Loni."

Loni thought about her life in California versus what she was dealing with now. Maybe it had been a mistake to leave after all...

Marise snapped her fingers in front of Loni's face. "Hey," she said, in a softer tone. "Are you okay?"

Kalinda pulled up another stool and sat down. "Yeah, Loni, are you really here using your vacation time to help us or is something else going on? You're not even arguing with us or taking sides. You come here all pale and stiff. I have to admit it's freaking me out a little."

Loni managed a small smile. "I..." *I'm fine is a lie.* I'm okay *would be stretching it and* I'm on the verge of a mental breakdown *would be a definite cause for alarm.* "I—I just needed to see you both in person."

"We haven't even asked you about Blade," Marise said, topping off all their teas.

"*Blaze*," Loni corrected out of habit. Her sisters never remembering her fiancé's name had annoyed her in the past, but now she couldn't help but feel a little glad he was so easily forgettable to them.

Kalinda nodded. "Right. Blaze. We should probably get his name right since he'll be part of the family soon enough. At least one of us is in a healthy long-lasting relationship."

Healthy long-lasting relationship? Loni's heart sank as her eyes welled up with tears.

Marise quickly grabbed her hand. "Oh, sugar, what's the

matter? Did we say something wrong? I swear on Mama's sweet potato pie recipe that we will never mess up his name again."

"No," Loni said, grabbing a napkin and dabbing at her eyes. "It's not that. Although it is a bit disconcerting that you can never remember his name. But it hardly matters now. I... We broke up." She paused. "Sort of."

Kalinda folded her hands on the counter and leaned in like a judge about to pass sentencing. "Honey, what exactly do you mean by you *sort of* broke up? Is this a California thing or something?"

She looked at her sisters, feeling helpless and just as confused as they seemed. "No, but we had a terrible fight and it does have to do with why I'm here. It's kind of a long story."

Marise stood and went over to one of the corner cabinets of the kitchen and pulled out an ornate glass bottle filled with clear liquid. She came back and set it down on the table with a thud. "The restaurant is closed, and Lucille is manning the front desk. We've got plenty of time."

Kalinda blinked at the bottle as if she couldn't believe it had been in her kitchen without her knowledge. She pointed. "What is *that*?"

Marise caressed the bottle in a loving gesture. "Just a friend's homemade gin."

"Oh Lordy, moonshine?" Loni groaned.

"Nothing at all like moonshine," Marise said with a trace of defensiveness. "This is completely legit and legal since it's not made in town. And it's pure gin, not whiskey."

Loni shuddered. She and gin had a love/hate relationship ever since college. "Is it any good?"

"It's very smooth and has a nice flowery finish without being so strong that you can't mix it with say...sweet tea," Marise said, pouring some in each of their glasses. "I thought you'd like to sample it. Besides, seems like we could all use something to take the edge off."

Loni wasn't going to argue there, no matter her feelings on gin. "How do you know so much about gin? Or any alcohol for that matter? This is a dry town."

Marise gave a little shrug. "My, er, uh, friend is very knowledgeable about this kind of stuff. I just found it interesting is all. Can't I have interests that go beyond running this hotel?"

Loni and Kalinda shared a look. Marise seemed a little sensitive about the gin comment, but Loni wasn't going to read too much into it. Her sisters were under a lot of stress with the hotel and Loni didn't want to add to it by asking more questions. Marise obviously didn't want to answer them even though Loni was definitely more curious about Marise's so-called "friend."

Once Marise had finished pouring the tea over the gin, they all raised their glasses and clinked. Loni was the first to take a sip. She had to admit, the gin was extremely smooth, and it complimented the tea nicely, just as Marise had said it would. "Really good," she said. "I'm impressed."

Marise beamed. "I'll tell my friend."

Kalinda took a healthy sip and swallowed. "Yes, not bad at all. But let's get back to the matter at hand. What happened with Blaze? Did you two have trouble settling on a wedding date or something?"

"Hardly, especially since there's not going to be a wedding date. At least… I don't think so. The problem is he seems to care more about his job than me."

"I'm sure it is hard to find quality time together with the hours you both work," Marise said. "And well, Blaze is kinda arrogant, but I do think he loves you. In his own way…"

Loni bit her lip. "Yeah, I guess. But engaged people don't keep secrets from each other, right?"

"What kind of secrets?" Kalinda asked with a hard frown.

"Blaze knew I wasn't going to be offered partnership and he was, but he didn't tell me until it was a done deal. I can't help but feel betrayed by that. That he cared more about them than me."

Marise shook her head. "That was really a crummy thing to do."

Loni sighed, dropping her head onto the steel island. "And then he drops the bomb on me that we should take a break."

"A break from what?" Marise asked. "Working together?"

"No," she mumbled into the counter. "Our relationship. Or maybe both, since it was his idea I get away. Blaze also said it wouldn't look good to the partners if we were involved right now since he's now my boss."

"But you're engaged," Kalinda said flatly. "Isn't that already being involved?"

Loni sighed. "That's what I said. I was just so upset by that and not making partner, I couldn't think straight. I just packed up and came here."

"Jeez of Nazareth," Kalinda moaned. "Men. I'm so sorry, Lon."

"Men are the worst of the worst of species," Marise agreed, taking another sip of her drink. "Our father unfortunately is included in this sentiment. I mean, first wanting to sell the resort and now this other thing."

Loni lifted her head off the counter. "What? What do you mean, and now this *other thing*?"

Kalinda and Marise exchanged surprised glances.

"What?" Loni insisted, not liking how they both immediately clammed up on her. "Did I miss something else? Tell me what's going on."

After a few beats, Kalinda huffed out a breath. "Well, I'm just surprised Daddy hasn't told you yet. He called and spoke to me and Marise about a week ago. Maybe you were busy with the whole partnership thing..."

Loni brushed a tear that had escaped her right eye. Guilt suddenly overwhelmed her. She *had* been busy. But really, when was she *not* busy? Daddy had called and left a message, wanting her to call him back. It hadn't sounded urgent. She should have made time to call him back. But ever since their mother's funeral their relationship felt strained and awkward.

"What *else* has he done?" Loni asked, letting her lawyer imagination get the best of her.

Kalinda reached for more tea, and Marise looked away.

"For land's sake," Loni said, slipping into her southern accent as she did whenever she was upset. "What is it? Is there more to the story as to why he's selling the resort? Embezzlement? Blackmail? Tax fraud?"

Marise shook her head. "Worse."

"Worse?" Loni cried, already thinking of a few attorneys she knew who could take her father's case—whatever that *case* may be.

With a snort, Kalinda smacked Marise in the arm. "Marise stop being dramatic. You're scaring Loni. I know you're upset, but honestly, it's not as bad as all that."

"It absolutely is," Marise insisted, folding her arms like she did when she was six and about to have a tantrum. "Daddy's getting married to a woman we haven't even met yet!"

Loni blinked, feeling suddenly winded at her sister's announcement. "*Married?*" she whispered.

How can that be? Her mom had only been gone five years.

She and her dad had been high school sweethearts. The love of each other's lives. It was one thing to date. But wasn't it too soon to even think about marriage?

Marise nodded solemnly "Yeah," she breathed. "Married. And I think he wants to sell the hotel to pay for the wedding."

Chapter Four

After Marise had given her the keys, Loni stormed to her suite. Their father was getting remarried. *Remarried.* And they didn't even know the woman! What was going on with everyone right now?

But to be honest, Daddy had never been the same after Mama was diagnosed with cancer. He'd grown distant. Guarded. Distracted. Loni had thought it was because his heart had been broken—in the midst of losing the love of his life so early when they had hoped to spend their golden years together.

What happened to that sweet and sensitive man? The man who'd shown her how to paddle board and bait her first fish. He and Mama were everything to her, everything she wanted in her own marriage. It was a slap in the face to their mother's memory that their father was getting remarried to a woman none of them had even met, but to even consider selling their family resort—her mama's love! It was cold. It was unforgivable. No, it was more than that...

It was mutiny.

She flopped down on the bed and immediately took out her cell phone. The slight buzz from the gin only fueled her fire more as she scrolled down to her father's number and punched the call button.

"Apollonia," her father answered. His warm tone sounded foreign, something she hadn't remembered hearing from him since before her mother's diagnosis. "I'm so glad you're calling me back."

"I'm not so sure you're going to be glad." She paused and took a breath. "How could you?"

"Hell's bells," he groaned. She heard him sigh and mumble something else to someone in the background. "You've been talking to your sisters already, I assume."

"Yes. But it would have been nice if you had talked to me directly."

"I tried, darlin', if you recall. Several times. Wanted to speak to you first actually, knowing how much you love that old termite condominium of a hotel."

"It is *not* a termite condominium. Mama would put a frying pan to your head for saying such a thing. It's lovely and homey. And it's in— Well, it looks…it looks…pretty fine okay."

Gah. Was that really the best she could say in the hotel's defense?

He snorted. "Pretty fine okay isn't worth much in the real world. It's time to part ways with it."

She gasped. Hearing those words come directly out of his mouth felt like a knife in her gut. "Daddy, no," she whispered. "Please. You can't. It means too much to us." *Too much to me.*

"Does it now? Honey, instead of talking to me about this, maybe you should talk to your sisters about the hotel."

"I have, actually. For your information, I'm here with

Marise and Kalinda now."

"You're *what?* Ouch," he cried, sounding like he bumped into something from a sudden movement. "What do mean you're with them now? In Sunny Banks?"

"Of course, in Sunny Banks," she repeated. And why on earth was he sounding so upset about that fact? "I'm staying at The Sandy Bottom to be exact. You know, Mama's *pride and joy* and the one thing that's been a source of lovely family memories for us that *you* want to sell as fast as a hot knife through butter."

Her dad surprised her by chuckling. "Well, well, it's nice to know you still have some southern heritage left in you and you haven't converted completely to Californian, no thanks to that fancy fiancé you have. I suppose Blaze is there with you, too."

Loni rested her head against the wooden headboard and closed her eyes. "No, Daddy, he's not."

"Well, Sunny Banks is too hard for city boys to love."

She held in a sigh. Apparently, *she* was the one too hard to love. It was draining always coming in second to the men in her life. Attention was hard to come by with her mom as well. The curse of being second born. As a result, Loni had always tried to be a little more driven, to be the funnier one, had even tried and gotten the fancier college degree. But even after all that, the person Mama had asked for on her deathbed had been Kalinda, not Loni.

"It's not that, Daddy. Blaze just couldn't get away from work," she said, glad to be able to say something partly true. She didn't know why she felt the need to keep her breakup with Blaze a secret just then. Probably had something to do with her father not being entirely open about his own relationship with this woman to which he was supposedly engaged. A little tit for tat.

"I don't care what his excuse is. That boy should be with you," he said, his tone growing firm. "Doesn't sit right with me that he can stand to be away from you for any length of time. You'll be getting married soon after all."

"Apparently, so will you."

Her father paused a beat. "You'll like her, Apollonia, once you meet her. She's real sweet. We have a lot in common, like playing golf and going to wine tastings together."

Golf and wine tastings? Eww. Who was this man? She didn't remember her father doing anything like that with her mother. But then again, her parents had been young and raising three rambunctious little girls and running a hotel.

"Plus, she's a widow, too," he added softly. "We have a mutual friend. Practically a son to both of us. He's good people, too. That's exactly why I'm having him come down there to check out the hotel for me. His name is Ian Hollowell."

Loni swallowed against the rising bile in her throat. "I'm sorry, but who is this Ian Hollowell and why exactly is *he* the one checking out *our* hotel?"

"Technically, *my* hotel." Her father cleared his throat. "Ian works for a development company. Works all around the country. Pammy thinks it's best that Ian be the one to handle everything."

"Really," she said flatly. "And what else does *Pammy* say about what we should do with *our* family resort?"

"Now, Apollonia, I don't like your tone. I just want Ian to have a look at the property and see what could be done with it. Don't go putting your cornbread in the oven so soon. Nothing's been signed or set in stone."

She heard the implied "yet" in his voice and bit down on her tongue. "You mean his company would just come and maybe spruce up the hotel a bit? Is that all?"

"That, or they could decide to develop it into something else. That's the point of being a developer. They can rehab an existing structure or start from the ground up where an entirely new structure can be built in its place."

Yeah, probably develop it into over-priced condos. Or something really depressing like... a Glamour Shots. She shuddered.

"No," she blurted. "I veto this idea. Sorry, Daddy. I can't let you sell. Marise and Kalinda will be behind me on this, too."

"Well, I hate to remind you ladies but what you do or don't want doesn't mean a hill of beans. I own that hotel and if I want a developer to take a look at it and the area, then that's exactly what I'm going to do. He'll be arriving sometime tomorrow or so. I expect you and your sisters to welcome him with open arms regardless of what he'll do with the property. Like I said, he's a good friend and practically family, so you better behave and show him some true southern Wingate family hospitality."

Loni fumed in silence. He was treating her like she was twelve. Why didn't he care about their mother or what his daughters wanted? It was only her southern upbringing and respect for her mama that had Loni biting down on a retort that wouldn't further her cause. But heck, if her father wanted his good ole' boy buddy to have a proper southern welcome, she was fairly sure she could come up with one—even if hers might be a bit rusty.

"Apollonia," he said sternly, "do we understand each other?"

"Yes, Daddy." She smiled, already mentally preparing her version of a southern welcome to Sunny Banks. One she was sure she could enlist her sisters' help with. "I believe we finally understand each other perfectly."

. . .

Ian had debated on whether or not to give his friend's daughters a courtesy call before arriving at their hotel. But in the end, he felt it was always best to have an upper hand in negotiation situations such as these. Arrive stealth-like. They didn't call him The Predator for nothing. That way he could casually see how business was conducted and check out the land without the ladies buzzing around in his face and getting in his way. Joe had mentioned that all three daughters happened to be in town now. Lucky him. Marise, Kalinda, and...*Apollonia*? Really, Joe? What happened to simple names like Mary or Sarah?

Truth be told, Ian wasn't holding out much hope for this property of his. If in-town realtors weren't touching it, there had to be good reason. He had done a little research on the plane. Sunny Banks was considered a dry town, meaning no alcohol served or sold. Not exactly conducive to the luxury hotel market partnerships he'd forged over the years, who typically liked to put upscale restaurants in them. Without a liquor license or even the ability to bring your own, he was sure they would give this area a hard pass. However, he gave Joe his word he'd take a look to be sure and see what could be done. Plus, he didn't mind getting a free room out of the deal and figured he might as well enjoy all that the hotel and Sunny Banks had to offer.

Unfortunately, as soon as Ian pulled his rental car into the parking lot of the hotel, he already knew there wasn't much he could do with the old place. The dull, blue trim around the gray siding, which might actually be white and not gray, wasn't exactly screaming "first-class resort." Although the one thing it had going for itself was the location. What a view. It was perfect, practically steps from the ocean, so he was pretty sure they offered a wide array of water-based amenities. Not a bad selling point. He supposed some vacationers would like the charm of its simplicity, too. But considering how sparse the parking lot was, he could only assume most were not so charmed as one would imagine.

He stepped out of the car and gazed around the property some more. There was an ice cream parlor and several gift shops within walking distance. He wondered if they would be willing to sell their property, too. Then he actually might have quite a worthy investment. Good old Joe...

"*Helloo!*" a woman called out.

Ian turned in her direction. She stood waving from the glass double-doors that had a big WELCOME sign overhead it as if he'd miss where he should be heading otherwise.

He grabbed his suitcase from the back seat and walked up to her. The woman had black hair with copper streaks in an extremely stylish pixie type cut. She appeared to be in her forties and of African American descent. Obviously not one of Joe's daughters.

"I'm Lucille," she said brightly. "Welcome to The Sandy Bottom where it wouldn't be a true vacation unless your bottom got sandy."

Ian inwardly flinched at the thought, yet somehow managed to keep his smile in place. Maybe southerners enjoyed that kind of thing. "Uh, hi, Lucille. My name is Ian Hollowell. I'm a little early for check-in, but I was hoping my room might be ready now."

Lucille's brown eyes widened a bit. "Oh, um, I'm sorry. Did you say your name was Ian Hollowell?"

Ian nodded, hoping with all his might the woman never indulged in any card games. Her poker face needed some serious work.

Lucille glanced over her shoulder. "I see. Well, I, um, don't think your room is quite ready yet..."

He tilted his head. "Are you sure? Maybe you want to check your computer first. You do have a computer system, don't you?" He peered at her closely.

"Oh, heavens yes," she said, clutching at her hotel staff lanyard. "We're old-fashioned in a lot of ways but not *that* antiquated." She sent him a nervous smile and continued to stand there, blocking the door.

He frowned. "Are you going to let me pass?"

"Oh, of course. Ha!" She paused and glanced behind her again. "Um, sure." She stepped aside, holding the door open for him.

The cool air of the air conditioning was a welcoming relief. The lobby was clean but had a metallic seashell wallpaper that was probably considered stylish and chic back in... Maybe the 1980s? A fresh-faced woman with curly blond hair stood behind the front desk, beaming at him. She had a nice smile and eyes like a Kewpie doll. Very cute, although perhaps a little young to be considered his type. Not that he was particularly looking for a woman here, anyway. And based on the name he saw clearly printed on her lanyard, she was not even in the same hemisphere as his type.

Marise Wingate.

From what Joe had told him, she was the youngest of his daughters. So much for him catching the sisters off guard.

"Hey, y'all," she said in greeting. She motioned for a burly-looking guy with dark skin and a beard wearing a beaten baseball cap to approach the desk. "Knox, please take this gentleman's bag for him. I'm sure he's exhausted from traveling, especially in this heat."

Knox's thick brown hand reached out, but Ian held onto his carry-on. "No, really, it's fine," Ian told Knox. "I've got it."

"I ain't gonna steal it," the man said gruffly. "That only happened one time, but I honest to goodness thought that family was really giving me their luggage."

"Who the heck makes a mistake like that?" Lucille asked with a snort.

Knox rested his knuckles on his hips. "For your information, miss rocket scientist, the husband had clearly said for me to *take it*. Duh."

"*Duh* is right," she murmured, rolling her eyes.

Marise quickly cleared her throat. "You guys," she whispered in warning. Then she glanced up at Ian with a glowing smile. "Um, anyway, how may I help you?" she asked.

He smiled and held out his hand. "Ian Hollowell. Nice to meet you."

Her friendly smile faded, and she did not shake his hand. "Oh, yes, uh, hi." She quickly picked up the phone instead and spoke into it. "Code red," she blurted.

Ian blinked. *Code red?* He glanced at Lucille who had her arms folded as rigidly as a bouncer, and the wide-eyed look of someone waiting for a drug bust to go down. *Ah*...and then he suddenly got it. *He* was the "code red."

Interesting. But also a tad worrying.

Another blond-haired woman suddenly emerged from the back office. The woman wore a yellow sundress that fell over her curves like a snakeskin, and she tossed her hair off her shoulders like she was a contestant on *America's Next Top Model*. A small smile tugged at her red-lipped mouth when she looked at him, and that's when Ian almost forgot his own name.

Hell, he'd bet most men would have taken one look into those ocean-blue eyes and forgotten how to breathe. *Damn.*

"Ian Hollowell," she said pleasantly, coming around the desk to greet him. "Our daddy said you were coming to visit us. My name is Apollonia Wingate, but you can most certainly call me Loni seeing as you're such a *good friend* of our daddy's. Believe me when I say that we are happier than an ol' dog layin' on the porch chewin' on a big ol' catfish head to have you with us."

Marise snorted a laugh but quickly raised her hand to cover her mouth. "Oh, yes, um, ditto." She looked about to laugh again, but a cross look from her sister had her sobering fast. "Ain't this just the berries to have you here," she mimicked, her southern drawl suddenly becoming as pronounced and as thick as Loni's. "I'm so sorry if I was rude to you when you first came in, Ian. I'm Marise Wingate. Daddy mentioned you were coming, but I just wasn't expecting you so soon and to be so... um, so..."

"Fine as a frog hair split four ways?" Lucille interjected.

Loni wrinkled her nose. "I wouldn't go that far."

Lucille grinned. "*I* would."

Loni shot the woman a warning look. "Lucille, why don't you get our new friend and guest a glass of sweet tea? This Yankee looks positively drenched from all this southern heat. I made a fresh batch in the back refrigerator. There are some mason jars on the counter, too. Have it delivered to his room as soon as possible." She turned her pretty blue eyes back his way and wrapped her neatly manicured fingers around his arm. "Come with me, sugar. It would be my honor as a Carolinian and a Wingate to show you to your room personally."

Ian bit back a grin as he allowed himself to be led away.

He wasn't sure what game the sisters were playing, and to be honest, he didn't really care at the moment. There were worse things to endure than the company of an attractive and obviously clever woman. However, something told him that Joe hadn't adequately prepared him for what he was in for with his daughters.

Chapter Five

Ian Hollowell wasn't exactly what Loni had expected in her father's new BFF. She certainly wasn't expecting him to be quite so...*fine* as Lucille had put it, or so young either. She'd guess he was probably just a few years older than herself. No wonder her father thought of him like the son he never had. Or most likely wanted. Another thing that grated on her nerves about Ian—as if usurping her family's property wasn't enough.

"Nice place you have here," Ian told her as they walked the few short steps to the second floor. There was a spark in his eyes as he glanced around the hotel, yet the man had a cautious reserve to his stature, which probably came down to being a by-product of the northeast. Boston, Daddy had told her. Although in the few words Ian had spoken, she hadn't detected any kind of accent.

"Have you been to Sunny Banks before, sugar?" she asked, laying on her own southern accent a bit thick even by Carolina standards. But no sense in showing her dislike for the man overtly. After all, she had promised her father she would welcome his friend. And so, she would. As well as make the man's trip as *memorable* as possible.

He glanced over at her with a slow smile. Almost predatory. "I haven't had the pleasure until now," he said, his tone smooth and deep. "*Sugar.*"

She gulped when she felt a low pull in her stomach. How annoying that she would find him mocking her fake accent somewhat appealing. Gah. The humidity must be clogging her good sense.

"Well, you're in for a real treat," she said, stopping in front of his room. "Although, I guess I should really apologize in advance."

"Apologize? What for?"

She pulled his room key out from the front of her dress, noting with smug satisfaction that his eyes had lingered a little longer than necessary there, and waved the card in front of the sensor. "We have quite a lot of renovations going on at the moment. Since the summer season is ending, it's really the perfect time to start painting because we can keep doors open to air out the rooms." She propped the door open to allow him entrance. "This was unfortunately the only room available for you."

When Ian walked in and visibly blanched, she had to fight back the laughter that wanted to spring up from her throat.

Ian dropped his carry-on onto the twin rollaway bed, which was in the center of the room and placed his hands on his hips. Loni wasn't sure she could be so bold as to call it a "room." It was more like a closet, with no windows and an even smaller bathroom attached to it. Marise was kind enough to have Lucille put a seashell bedspread on the mattress and even bring in some fresh flowers to cover up the musty smell. Too bad the flowers appeared to be wilting from the heat and lack of air circulation already.

He turned and gave her an incredulous look. "You're kidding."

She summoned her most surprised expression and placed a hand over her heart for good measure. *Julia Roberts eat your heart out.* "My stars, you don't like it?"

"What exactly is there to like?" he demanded. Heading over to the bathroom, he looked in and frowned even harder. "That shower is so small, it'd be easier for me to soap the sides of it and just spin around."

She wanted to point out to Ian that the shower—well, everything here in the room—appeared small, because he was also freakishly tall. Loni had always felt her own height of five foot nine had served her well with commanding attention and intimidation in the courtroom, but standing next to Ian Hollowell, she definitely lost that edge. Not that she was daunted. She'd faced tougher adversaries across meeting room tables. And she was just getting started.

She glanced toward the ceiling. *Mama, forgive me for I am about to sin.*

She let out a fake chuckle. "Oh, you are so hilarious, sugar."

"I wasn't trying to be funny, Loni. Aren't there any other rooms available?" He sniffed the air. "Did something die in here?"

"Oh heavens, no." Honestly, she had no idea. However, she wouldn't bet her law degree on it. "The room just hasn't been used by anyone in ages. I'm sure the smell will go away once it's been aired out a bit."

"A bit? Is that southern slang for *years*?" he deadpanned.

Loni lowered her eyelashes as demurely as a Scarlet O'Hara

wannabe. "This is all so troubling. There's nowhere else we can put you at the moment. I was a little afraid you Yankees were soft, so I did call around to a few of the bed and breakfasts in the area. They're all booked, too." She added a *tsk tsk* and a shake of her head for good measure. "But I'm sure you won't mind this room so much seeing how my daddy comped your stay and all," she said, lacing her tone with more sugar than her sister's sweet tea.

Ian looked as if he wanted to argue more or perhaps wring her neck—she couldn't be completely sure—but after a moment, he relented. "You're right, Loni," he said pleasantly. "Your dad *is* allowing me to stay as a guest for free. This room will be more than fine."

Really? "Wonderful," she said, clasping her hands together.

"Knock, knock," Lucille called, walking in with a tray of sweet tea and cookies. She stopped where Loni and Ian were standing and looked around for a place to put the tray. When she didn't see anything adequate—since there was nothing adequate—she gently placed it on the bed.

"Hey, did something die in here?" she asked, wrinkling her nose.

Loni gave the woman a tight smile. "That will be *all*, Lucille."

Lucille eyed Ian from head to toe, then waggled her eyebrows. "Are you sure that's all?"

"*Yes*," she ground out. "I'm sure Marise has other guests for you to attend to."

"Yeah." She sighed, then glanced up at Ian again. "If you need me for anything, just dial extension 448. I'll be here faster than green grass through a goose."

Ian grinned as he pointed to his head. "Already committed

that image and number to memory."

Unfortunately, we all have. Loni cleared her throat. "*Goodbye*, Lucille."

Lucille took her cue, albeit reluctantly, and once she was out of the room, Loni picked up a glass of tea and held it out for Ian. "I bet you could use a refreshing glass of our famous sweet tea. My sister Kalinda makes it especially for all the incoming guests. Helps introduce them to the true Carolina culture."

Ian took the tea from her hand. "Heard about this stuff but never had it."

"Oh, it's a real treat. My personal favorite, too. The recipe is my mama's. *Everyone* just *raves* about it."

Obviously, thirsty, Ian lifted the glass to his lips and took a large swallow. Once the tea hit his tongue, his eyes bulged slightly then he managed to swallow. "That's uh...sw-sweet."

Oh, she was sure it was sweet. Three times the amount of sugar in a normal recipe sweet, to be exact.

Oops.

Loni treated him to a smile just as sugary. "I'm so glad you like it. There's plenty more where that came from, too."

Ian quickly held up a hand. "I'm good. Thanks." He placed the glass back down on the tray. He glanced around again, running a finger around his polo shirt collar. "Tell me this room has air conditioning at least."

She let out a light laugh. "Why of course it does. It was just turned on so y'all might have to give it some time." *Meaning a week. A month tops.*

More oops.

"Well, I'll let you unpack and freshen up," she said brightly. "We unfortunately don't serve dinner at the hotel but be sure to stop by The White Squirrel Café in the morning. My sister Kalinda will prepare a real special breakfast for ya."

"Can't wait." He smirked. "But for some weird reason I do feel the need to remind you that it is unlawful to place strychnine or ground glass in foodstuffs of any kind."

While she normally appreciated sarcasm, she ignored it *and him* and turned to go. "Don't let the bed bugs bite," she couldn't resist adding with a little wave. "But seriously, watch out for bed bugs."

Ian jumped away from the bed. "There's bed bugs?"

"Oh no, no. We fumigated last week. Should be all clear now, but you can never be too sure. They're tricky little buggers." She stopped at the archway of the door and grinned. "Y'all have a nice evening."

Loni had the satisfaction of hearing a string of curse words come from Ian's mouth as the door closed behind her.

"You're positively evil," Marise said, marching into Loni's suite with Kalinda following behind her. "But I love it."

"Why thank you," Loni said, pouring them all some wine. "But as far as I'm concerned, I did everything Daddy wanted me to do. Ian Hollowell got a warm southern welcome." She chuckled and offered them both her leftover French fries from the takeout she'd ordered earlier. She had changed from the sexy little sundress she had on—specifically to welcome Ian—to shorts and a light tee hoodie. She had already washed her face and was in complete relaxation mode even though it was only eight o'clock in the evening. It was her reward to herself for handling Ian's welcome so masterfully.

Kalinda folded her arms, casting her a dubious look. "A

southern welcome? You actually put him in the old storage room."

Loni nibbled on a fry. "What's wrong with that? It's a room. A *free* room, I might add."

Marise snorted. "Not much of a room. We never put guests there before."

"It has a bathroom," Loni insisted. "What more could he want? I mean, besides a window, A/C, and hot water."

The sisters busted up laughing.

Kalinda was the first to get serious. "Daddy is going to kill us when he finds out what we did to Ian."

Loni sat down on the sofa in the small sitting area of her suite and propped her feet up on the coffee table. "I'll handle him."

Marise grinned. "Well, well. Didn't take you long to move on from Blaze to Ian, now did it? Good for you, honey."

Loni quirked an eyebrow. "I meant I'll handle *Daddy*. Not Ian."

"Maybe that's for the best," Marise said, biting her lip. "I'm pretty sure you would have had to wrestle Lucille for him anyway."

Kalinda snatched a fry off her plate and popped it into her mouth. "I didn't think Lucille liked men older than her."

"She doesn't," Marise said. "This guy, Ian, has to be in his mid-thirties. Tops."

"Cute?" Kalinda asked, sounding suddenly interested.

Loni folded her arms. "*No.*"

Marise made a face. "Correction. What our dear Apollonia means to say, is no, Ian Hollowell is not cute, because that description is far too pedestrian a word for him."

Kalinda squinted as she chewed. "Hmm…so one to ten,

what is he?"

"Sixteen," Marise blurted.

Kalinda's eyebrows shot up. "Is he *really* that good-looking or is he just tall?"

Loni couldn't help but grin. "He's both, unfortunately."

Kalinda eyed Loni with a shrewd look. "All that and you still put the man in a closet? You are cold, Loni."

Loni frowned at her sister's words. The reminder of how emotionally deficient she was—for lack of a better term—stung and also reminded her of her failed relationship with Blaze. "I had no choice," she said, sitting up and grabbing her glass of wine so fast, she almost spilled some on her shorts. "Ian Hollowell needs to go back to Boston or whatever other city he wants to buy up. Plus, you should have heard Daddy, talking about Ian like he was his precious baby boy."

Marise almost choked on her wine. "Oh my Lord, are you actually jealous of Ian?"

Loni didn't want to admit it out loud and certainly not to her sisters, but yes, maybe a small part of her was jealous of Ian Hollowell. It goaded her that their father would listen to an outsider—a *man,* for that matter—and not consider the thoughts and feelings of his own flesh and blood. His own daughters.

"Don't be ridiculous," Loni scoffed. "Just something about the man rubs me the wrong way."

Marise smiled. "If Lucille were here, she'd say the man could rub—"

"Can we just *not* go there, please?" Loni asked, exasperated with everyone's fixation on Ian's attractiveness. "Let's not forget the real reason Ian is even staying in our hotel. Daddy actually wants the man to buy it out from under us. All our memories of Mama, what she loved here, will be destroyed, and for some reason, Daddy couldn't care less. If you ask me, *he's* the cold one."

Marise sat down next to Loni. "It is really sad to think this place could be wiped away." She gazed around the suite. "I used to love to stay and live here in the summer when we were little. It was like we were on a twenty-four-seven vacation."

"I know. I still have a seashell in my office from when we used to go and walk the beach with Mama."

"It was an almost daily ritual," Marise said on a sigh. "What on earth did she do with all those shells? We must have collected a houseful every summer."

Kalinda poured herself some more wine. "Mama donated some to the local library for their children's programming and the rest she gave to Angela for her craft fair designs."

Marise blinked. "Really? I had no idea."

"There's a lot of things Mama did that you two don't know about," Kalinda said, walking over to the slider doors that led to a small balcony.

"Like what?" Marise asked.

"Things," Kalinda said stiffly.

Loni leaned her head on Marise's shoulders. "There's a lot of things we did that Mama didn't know about, either." She chuckled as she thought of one time. "Remember the weekly bonfires? We snuck out to make s'mores with the guests and Marise's hair caught on fire."

Marise elbowed her in the ribs. "That's because you held your roasted marshmallow too close to my head."

"No, Kalinda bumped my elbow and—"

"Is there really any point in trying to fight Daddy?" Kalinda interrupted from where she still stood by the balcony.

Loni popped her head up, thinking she must have misheard

her sister. *"What?"*

Kalinda whirled around to face them with a steely expression. "Look at us. What real threat do we pose to this Ian Hollowell? Like Daddy has said over and over again, *he* owns the hotel so he can do as he wishes with it."

Loni blinked. Kalinda had been the closest to their mother so her words were the last thing Loni had expected to hear from her. But even if Kalinda was suddenly getting cold feet, Loni was determined to stay strong for all of them. "I told you I would handle Daddy," she reminded her.

Kalinda shook her head. "How are you going to handle Daddy, Loni? Or even Ian for that matter? Let's see, how long are you here for exactly, until Friday? And just what are Marise and I supposed to do after that?"

Loni was speechless. But her sister was right. She hadn't really thought that far out beyond her vacation stay. Daddy and his new fiancée were scheduled to arrive just before she left, too, and she had no idea how long Ian planned on staying. In her optimistic mindset, she had sort of hoped she could make Ian's life so miserable that he'd leave by the end of the week. But what if that didn't happen?

"I'm sorry, Kal." Loni let out a rush of breath. "I guess I've been a little emotional lately because of Blaze and didn't think that far out. Honestly, I was just trying to help."

"Yes, help. Help for how long?" her sister went on. "At the end of the week you're just going to leave us again. Just like you did after Mama died. It's bad enough Daddy left us on our own to go run that Cape Cod pet project of his. And now all of a sudden you want to play rescuer?"

Loni sat up, running a hand through her hair. "I—no, I wasn't going to just—" *Leave you.* But wasn't that exactly what she was going to do? Stay for a few days, try to block her father's friend from wanting the hotel, and then go back to her life in California. Whatever kind of life that was left there for her, anyway.

Marise clapped her hands together several times to get their attention. "Enough you two. Loni *was* trying to help and I for one appreciate it." She turned her big, round eyes toward Loni. "But maybe you could get some more time off? Just a few more days. In case we need it. Being short on help and then with The Beach Bash coming a week after that, we could sure use all the hands we have available."

"What's a Beach Bash?" Loni asked.

Marise grinned. "Our little idea to bring more visitors not only to the resort, but to Sunny Banks in general. We're going to host a type of vendor and craft show. Some of it will be on the beach and some of it will be in the actual hotel. I've reached out to a few restaurants, too, who said they'd come and showcase a few of their food specialties. The jazz club at the high school even said they'd come and play for free."

"Wow, sounds great," Loni said. "That's a lot to take on, though."

"I know. Plus, Daddy's bringing Pamela down here this coming weekend. I think Kalinda and I could use all the reinforcements we can get for as long as we can get them. Maybe by then, we can all formulate a plan to convince Daddy not to sell." She cast a meaningful look at Kalinda. *"Together."*

Kalinda folded her arms, raising an eyebrow at Loni as if to say *Well, what will it be?*

Loni swallowed. She glanced between her sisters, banking down the guilt and the worry that she wouldn't be able to get the time off she would need. But she couldn't let her sisters down.

She had to try. "Okay. I'll see what I can do. No promises," she quickly added.

Marise and Kalinda nodded. "In the meantime, what do we do about Ian?" Marise asked.

"Well, we stick to the original plan," Loni said. "At least, until we can come up with a better one. He strikes me as a country club kind of guy. I bet he'll get so disgusted here with us and our "lack of culture" that he'll be on the next plane to Boston by sundown tomorrow." *Hopefully.*

Marise grinned. "We can get Knox to give him a massage."

"I smell a lawsuit in the making," Kalinda grumbled.

"Oh, hush," Marise said, waving her comment off. "He's totally licensed. Well, pretty sure he's licensed."

Loni raised her hand when Kalinda's mouth opened. "I'll make sure he's licensed. However, you should know that I invited Ian to stop in at The White Squirrel tomorrow for breakfast." She raised her eyebrows and waited.

Kalinda blinked. "So?" Then it seemed to dawn on her. "Oh no. You want me to sabotage my own food?"

Loni placed her hands together in a prayer pose. "It's for the greater good!"

"To ruin my reputation as a chef?"

"Oh, who's Ian going to tell?"

"Believe me, the culinary world is a small world," Kalinda grumbled.

"Kal, do it for Mama," Marise said in a pleading tone.

After a few long beats, Kalinda flung her hands up in the air. "Fine. What exactly do you want me to do?"

Loni shrugged. "Anything you want. Except poison him," she added. She didn't deem it necessary to share that Ian had already suspected they would try that.

"Gee, thanks for clarifying." Kalinda rolled her eyes.

"This is so much fun," Marise said, bouncing up and down. "I sure hope it works."

Loni threw an arm around Marise and grinned at Kalinda, feeling more upbeat about the situation. "Are you kidding? With the three of us banded together, Ian Hollowell doesn't stand a chance."

Chapter Six

Loni surmised she'd overindulged in wine last night because her head was pounding.

But then she actually heard the pounding. *Bam, bam, bam.*

Her eyes sprung open and she glanced at the time. It was 6:30 a.m. Who could be banging on her door at this hour?

"Loni, get your ass up," Kalinda whispered heatedly through the door. "It's an emergency."

Emergency? Loni immediately tossed the covers aside and jumped out of bed. "What happened?" she demanded as she threw open the door. "Is Daddy all right? Did something happen to Marise?"

Kalinda rushed in, rubbing her temples with both hands. "They're both fine. This is a hotel emergency." She turned and faced Loni. "Hazel might have broken her foot."

Loni slumped against the door, grinding a fist into her eye. "Who's Hazel?"

Kalinda threw her hands in the air. "You met her when you arrived. She called you Olivia. She's my only waitstaff since

Yolanda is in Tennessee visiting her mom until Sunday."

Loni remembered the woman now and nodded. "Okay."

Her sister gave her an incredulous look. "Okay? No, everything is *not* okay, Loni. Hazel took a misstep off her ladder. She's at the ER now."

"Oh no. Do you want me to go to the hospital with you?"

"No, I want you to take her place."

"How can I take her place?" Loni said, giving into a yawn. "I don't have a time machine." She scratched her head as she made a beeline for the coffee maker.

Kalinda stepped in front of her, blocking her path. "No, but you can take her place this morning and waitress for me. *Please*," she whimpered, throwing her arms around Loni.

That woke her up. "Wait. What? B-but I'm on vacation."

"Vacation *smation*. You said you were in this with us. I can't get by with just one server. I definitely need two. Mornings are a bear here. I'm stretched as far as I can go. Did you tell your office that you needed extra time off yet? Because—spoiler alert—we now need you more than ever."

Loni tried to clear her brain fog to keep up with her sister. Everything seemed to be happening at warp speed. "Um, yeah, I emailed them last night. Believe me, I'm totally going to try and be here for you guys. In everything else *but* this. I mean, don't be ridiculous, Kal. I can't waitress."

"Of course, you can. What, did law school erase your memory of all other prior jobs you've held? I mean, you've waitressed before."

"Um, yeah, like when I was *seventeen*."

Kalinda snorted. "Oh, please. It's like riding a bike. But the bike has a flat tire. And the chain is also rusted."

"Very encouraging."

"You've got this," Kalinda said, taking Loni by the shoulders and giving her a little shake. "Besides, you wouldn't want Ian to see the café in disarray, would you?"

"Hell, no," she automatically snapped. And it would be her luck that Ian would take her up on her free breakfast offer and then see the chaos Kalinda would be dealing with being short on help. He'd probably rejoice in it, too. The swindler. Well, not on her watch.

"Okay, I'm in," she told Kalinda. "Whatever you need me to do."

"Have I ever told you that you are hands down my favorite sister?" Kalinda stepped back and reached into the bag that was slung over her shoulder and pulled out an orange tee shirt. She flung it at Loni, who wasn't fast enough so it hit her square in the face. "Report at the café in thirty minutes."

"Do I have a choice?" Loni grumbled.

"No. But I'll have plenty of hot coffee waiting for you."

Loni sighed. "Have I ever told you that you're *my* hands down favorite sister?"

Kalinda walked over and opened the door. "Try and remember that later this morning."

. . .

Ian couldn't remember the last time he had such a horrible night's sleep.

He turned on his side for the eighty-second time. The bed—or as he had begun referring to it as, the "back twister"—had springs that poked him in various angles every time he'd begun to breathe. The temperature felt close to one hundred degrees in here, probably because it had been some old bank vault that they'd converted into a "room," and, dear God, he could only hope the reason he'd itched all night was psychosomatic and not because he actually had bed bugs.

Damn that woman.

Southern hospitality his ass. Loni may have sounded and looked like a Southern belle, but the only thing pretentious about her was her name. Apollonia Wingate. No, she wasn't fooling anyone with that phony southern accent of hers and that all-too-innocent batting of the eyelashes. One look into those baby blues of hers and he could tell the woman was one hundred percent shrewd. Don't get him wrong, he'd always admired women with brains. He liked a woman with a sick sense of humor, too, which she also had to have in order to put him in this room with a straight face. Kudos to her. Too bad those characteristics only added to her already way too attractive allure. Because Loni Wingate not only wanted no parts of him but was also hell bent on driving him out of town on a rail—and most likely a spiked one.

Giving up on the pretense of sleeping, he kicked off the sheet and stood. Heading to the bathroom, he gave his bare chest a once over for any red welts or bite marks, just for good measure. All clear. At least he was starting the day off on one positive note.

Once he came back out and reached for his jeans, his cell phone began ringing. He saw it was Scott and picked it up.

"Yo, man," he said, glancing at the time. "You've got your nose to the grind a bit early. Trying to win brownie points with the boss?"

Scott chuckled. "If I was really trying to win brownie points, I would have let you sleep in and enjoy your vacation."

Ian took a look around his postage-sized area of the hotel room and smirked. "This is hardly what I would call a vacation."

"I had a feeling you'd say something like that, hence the early morning phone call. Raj had a brief Zoom meeting with Denali Construction yesterday. They know you're down in North Carolina and already seem interested. They want first dibs on any property you acquire down there."

Ian dragged a hand down over his face. Jeez, that was fast. He wasn't even aware his boss knew he was looking at the resort. "I haven't even had any time to assess the property or even the area." He hadn't even had a cup of coffee yet.

"I know, I know. But you understand how these things work sometimes. Just thought I'd give you a little inspiration this morning. No need to thank me. Unless of course, you make a wad of money off this deal, then you can thank me with the many faces of my favorite green presidents."

Ian smirked "Understood. Anything else you'd like to report or request?"

"Yeah..." There was a pause. "So, what do Joe's daughters look like anyway?"

"Good grief. You should hear yourself."

"What?" Scott protested. "It's a healthy male question to ask. Joe's a decent-looking guy. In my experience that translates to having hot looking daughters. So, in the interest of science at least, I'm curious to learn if they are in fact hot or not."

Ian took a seat on the edge of the bed, amused and also partly annoyed at the inner workings of his business partner's mind. It was just too early to entertain this crap. "And what are you going to ask next, if I got their Snap or not?"

"Hey, I didn't know you were on Snapchat."

"I'm not." His tone was flat.

"Oh. You didn't answer my original question."

"That's because I'm hanging up now."

"That means they *are* hot! You lucky dog. I swear you get—"

"Bye, Scott." Ian ended the call.

Shaking his head, he tossed his cell on the bed and contemplated his next move. If Denali Builders was interested, he'd bet his Alfa Romeo that others would be interested, too. This could mean serious money. Money their little development company could use right about now, especially after the investment fallout in New Jersey. He'd be a friggin' hero if he could make that happen.

Ian would have to play it cool, though. Not seem too eager to the sisters. In his business, these dealings were like playing a real-life game of chess. And what he loved about his job more than making money was the chase.

First things first, though. He'd shower, then head down to the White Squirrel Café and meet the third sister. Perhaps the best approach to this situation would be the old divide and conquer method with the women. He'd have a better idea once he took them up on their offer of a free breakfast. Then he could see exactly what he was up against and begin to plan out his tactical warfare.

That's of course if they didn't try and poison him first.

• • •

As soon as Marise saw Loni walk into the restaurant she ran over to her. "Oh, thank God, you're here," she said, grabbing her by the arm and ushering her over behind the counter.

The café was crowded—more so than Loni had expected. No wonder Kalinda was so desperate for her help. However, the atmosphere was more lively and friendly than chaotic. Country music played in the background and the place smelled of a heavenly mixture of bacon and coffee.

Loni had to admit Kalinda did a wonderful job with the restaurant. She loved the charm of the white eyelet curtains and the fresh flowers on each table.

"Kalinda and Duke are up to their elbows in gravy and biscuits today," Marise said, wiping her forehead with her forearm.

Loni pulled on the front of her tee shirt, which fit a bit snug around her chest. "Who's Duke?"

"The fry cook." Marise took off her serving apron and wrapped it around Loni's waist. "He's a doll. Plus, you'll absolutely love his chunky monkey pancakes."

"I was hoping to love his coffee."

Marise snapped her fingers. "Oh yes." She pointed to two full pots behind her. "Help yourself. You're going to need the energy."

Loni frowned. "Why does everybody keep saying that?"

Marise patted her on the shoulder. "We just know how you are, honey."

"What is *that* supposed to mean?"

Kalinda chose that moment to pop her head out of the kitchen window. "Table six," she shouted. She saw Loni and smiled. "Oh, thank God you're here."

"Everybody keeps saying that, too." Loni poured herself a hot cup of coffee and immediately took a sip. "Oh, God. The best coffee I ever had."

"I think Duke adds cinnamon to the grounds," Marise said, smiling. "Or pixie dust I'm not sure."

Loni chuckled. "Whichever it is, it's delicious."

Kalinda walked out of the kitchen with a towel over her shoulder and a notepad in her hand. "Thanks for filling in, Marise, until Loni arrived. Here," she said, handing the pad to Loni. "This is yours. The specials today are baked apple pie oatmeal, a veggie bomber omelet, and s'mores pancakes."

Loni's stomach rumbled. "They all sound amazing."

"They are," Kalinda said proudly. "I wrote a little cheat sheet for you in your notebook. You have sections one and three. The other server over there is Dana. She knows you're new and will help you. Other than that, make sure the coffee is flowing. I have a hostess coming in soon and she'll help you both bus tables."

Loni felt exhausted already, but she put on a confident front. "Okay, I'm on it."

"Great," Marise said cheerfully. "I'll check on you girls later." She winked at Loni. "Oh, my, look who your first customer is."

Loni turned and was expecting Ian, but instead she saw Roy Bennis. In a tiny way, she almost preferred Ian. Roy owned one of the two surf shops in town. They all went to high school together, although he was a grade older than Kalinda. Roy was a sweet guy but didn't quite have the ambition and drive that Loni found attractive in all the other men she'd dated. She and Roy had gone to his senior prom—as friends—but unfortunately, Roy made it uncomfortably obvious he wanted more. She hadn't seen him since her mama's funeral, where he'd stuck by her side like white on rice.

"Oh...great," Loni said flatly.

Marise chuckled. "Good luck." Then with a light wave goodbye, she filtered out of the café.

Kalinda slapped her lightly on the back. "Be gentle with him."

"You know, I'm tired of you two thinking how heartless I am. I can be sensitive to the feelings of others. Growing up, who was the one who cried during *The Lion King*?"

Kalinda nodded. "You're right. Just so you know, there are tissues under the register."

"I won't need them."

"But Roy might."

Loni sighed, then with determined steps walked over to Roy with a bright—albeit forced—smile. "Hey, Roy, so good to see you."

"Loni, wow." Roy ran a hand over the top of his damp blond hair, then leaned in to kiss her on the cheek. "I heard you were back in town. Man, you're prettier than a pumpkin."

Loni ignored the enthusiasm in his tone, especially since she wore very little makeup and had her hair in a ponytail and picked up a menu. "You here for breakfast?"

"Yup. I'm here most mornings." He leaned in and grinned. "Of course, if you're working here now then I guess it'll have to change that to *all* mornings."

Loni shook her head. *Why did she think it was a good idea to come back here?* "Don't," she told him pointedly.

"Don't what?" He seemed confused.

"Don't get any ideas about you and me. I just broke up with my fiancé and I'm only here for a week, Roy." Maybe a few days more at best. She'd need to check her email after her shift and see if the firm had responded to her request for more time off. It wouldn't look good to them, but at this point, she had nothing left to lose. And as she saw it, her sisters needed her more.

"That's okay. I'm a fast worker," he said, waggling his eyebrows up and down.

"Roy!" She rolled her eyes. "I told you back in high school, it's never gonna happen."

He made a disgruntled face. "Still in the friend zone after

all these years? Come on, sugar, we're not kids anymore. I'm a successful businessman," he said, puffing out his chest.

She arched an eyebrow at him. "Congratulations."

"Look, I just want to have dinner with you to catch up on old times. You can tell me all about your fancy lawyer job and your fancy California condo. Just as friends."

She took a breath. "Really?"

"No."

Loni had to laugh. Then she saw movement and glanced behind him. There was a line of people forming, waiting to be seated. "Roy, I don't have time for this. You're causing a log jam."

He stuck out his bottom lip. "Have a heart, Lon."

She gave up and turned away, hoping he'd follow her to his table. He did.

She slapped his menu on the table. "I'll take your order in a few."

"Hurry back," he called behind her.

Good grief. Ten minutes on the job and she was practically getting harassed. She managed to seat a few more people, then rushed over to grab coffee refills for her section and check on the other diners. Luckily Dana seemed to be a seasoned pro.

Kalinda came out of the kitchen carrying a tray of breakfast pastries that were so symmetrical in shape, they barely looked real. "How are we on coffee?" she asked Loni.

Loni placed one of the pots back on the warming plate and picked up the second one and gave it a little shake. "One coffeepot is definitely kicked. And Roy Bennis is someone I would like to kick."

Kalinda chuckled. "Unrequited crushes are the worst. Leave the poor guy alone. He's a good paying customer. Plus, he gives all our guests at the hotel half price surf and paddle board rentals."

"I'm being totally nice. And I'm happy to report that he hasn't shed one tear. So there."

"The morning is young." Kalinda's eyes narrowed as she surveyed the restaurant. "Any sign of our *code red* yet?"

Loni quickly grabbed a napkin and dabbed her forehead. In her dealings with Roy and the frenzy of the café rush, she'd forgotten Ian could potentially show up. "I haven't seen him. He's probably lurking around outside checking the foundation while we're here busy servicing the customers."

"Checking the foundation? That doesn't sound like such a bad thing." Kalinda grabbed two breakfast plates Duke had placed on the counter window and handed them to Dana.

Loni snorted. "Of course it's a bad thing. Because he's doing it for nefarious reasons." A customer came up to the register, and Loni rushed over to ring them up. When they walked away, she turned and saw Kalinda eyeing her with a small smile.

"What?" Loni asked, checking her hair.

"Oh, nothing." Her sister bit her lip. "Well, that's not true. You should look at yourself."

Loni glanced down at her tee shirt. Dang it. There was a coffee stain down the middle already. She grabbed a napkin and began dabbing at it.

Kalinda lightly punched her arm. "Not literally look at yourself, you ding dong. I meant, look at you working here. It reminds me of better... Well, it's just nice having you here. Sisters really are the little bit of childhood that you can never lose." Her eyes glistened but she blinked them away. "Anyway, thanks for listening to my TED Talk," she said with a chuckle.

Loni chuckled, too. "If you're trying to say thank you, then you're welcome."

"I guess I was." Then Kalinda pointed to a table of four people giving them a megawatt death stare. "I also wanted to say get back to work," she whispered.

Loni saluted her. "Aye aye, Captain Cook. See what I did there? Hazel's jokes must be rubbing off on me."

Kalinda blessed herself. "Lord have mercy. We can only pray her waitressing skills don't rub off on you, as well."

Chapter Seven

When Ian walked into the café later that morning, he was surprised to see it so busy. All these people here couldn't possibly be...*guests* staying at the hotel, right? And if not, where could all these people have come from? And why?

A young, college-aged woman with chin-length brown hair carried a pot of coffee across the room and then signaled that she'd be right with him. He was also surprised, although not disappointed, to see Loni working at the café. She looked a bit different today. Gone was the fake southern Jessica Rabbit ensemble. Today, with her less than pristine white sneakers and hair pulled up in a sloppy high ponytail, she was more natural and less...*bedazzled*. But damn, if she didn't wear that look just as well. And it further annoyed him that he couldn't keep his eyes off of her.

Nope. Don't go there, Hollowell. There were plenty of pretty fish in the sea. No need to grab a fishing rod for this one who happened to have the teeth of a piranha and who also happened to be the daughter of his friend.

After Loni handed someone a to-go cup of coffee and rang them up, she turned toward him as if realizing he was still looking at her. He tried to ignore the stab of awe in his chest when her gaze met his. She'd somehow gotten prettier since the last time he'd seen her. Hell, she'd also gotten grumpier. For someone who had extended the invite to breakfast in the first place, she sure didn't seem happy that he actually showed up. But he had to give her credit for immediately catching herself and offering him up a wide, dazzling—if not completely fake—smile.

"Good morning, Ian," she said, with her accent and batting eyes back in full force. "Sleep well?"

Her tone suggested that she knew he hadn't.

"Slept like the dead," he lied.

"It's a shame you didn't stay dead." She gave a light laugh. "I mean, because I'm sure you could use the rest after all that traveling."

"Ah, ah, ah," he said, waving his forefinger in front of her cute, turned-up nose. "Remember, that doesn't give you permission to try and kill me."

Her eyes went wide-eyed innocent. "I have no idea what you could mean by that, sugar." She grabbed a menu and waved him to follow her.

He did. And also tried to ignore the sashay of her hips in those jean shorts which seemed to be painted on her backside with perfect precision strokes. Add that to the list of reasons he needed to figure out if this deal was worth the trouble and hightail it out of here as fast as he could.

"Here we are," she announced, stopping at a table at the far end of the room. "Very private."

It was private for sure. Ian also couldn't help but notice that the table was wedged in a corner right by the kitchen—and that it hadn't been wiped down yet.

"Excuse the mess," she said, flicking some crumbs aside. "We've been super busy today, as I'm sure you can see. This café is a complete and total gem to this town."

Ian nodded. "The food must be good."

"The best. Everyone would be up in arms to see this restaurant *and* the hotel disappear."

He sat down, trying not to be amused at her overt messaging. "Yes, I clearly see that. But like the old saying goes, nothing is irreplaceable."

Her blue gaze turned to ice. "Well, I can see sentimentality has no place in your line of work."

"Sure it does, but it never lasts long and never interferes with business decisions. Rule number one: emotions have no room in contracts. You should know that, Loni. You are, after all, an attorney. Though perhaps…one who hasn't made partner yet?" he guessed.

Her lips parted and a deep flush crossed her cheeks.

Ian had wanted to take a small jab at the woman—a little payback for everything she'd done and said to him up until now—but her facial expression combined with the way her posture suddenly went rigid, told him he may have hit below the belt.

"How dare you," she seethed.

An apology automatically rose to the tip of his tongue but someone calling Loni's name had both their heads turning in that direction.

A tall woman, appearing to carry the same blond and beautiful Wingate gene, rushed up and threw her arm around Loni. "Oh, hello," the woman said, smiling down at Ian while keeping Loni in a full-on death grip. "I'm Kalinda Wingate. I run The White Squirrel Café. You must be Daddy's friend, Ian Hollowell."

"I am," he said pleasantly.

"Well, any friend of Daddy's..." She held out her hand.

He couldn't resist tossing a smirk at Loni before he shook her sister's hand.

"He's hardly a friend," Loni muttered.

Kalinda tightened her hold on her sister. "Nonsense. Everyone in the South is a friend."

Ian sat back, crossing his arms. Well, this was certainly interesting. It was like watching an episode of good sister/bad sister play out before him. He wasn't sure what to make of it. But he might be able to use this difference to his advantage. Plus, since Kalinda ran the restaurant, he felt a hundred times better about not being poisoned.

He grinned up at the sisters. "Yes, I certainly appreciate the hospitality you both have been showing me. I'll be sure to mention it to Joe when I see him."

Kalinda gave a slight frown. "Oh? Do you plan on staying until Daddy and Pam come down this weekend?"

Ian wasn't planning to stay more than four or five days but seeing the sheer horror on Loni's face had him reconsidering a longer visit. "Maybe. I'll have to check my schedule."

"Oh, that's interesting," Kalinda said, tipping her head to the side.

"Why would me not staying be interesting?" he asked.

Kalinda shrugged. "It's just that Alex Winters is in town."

Ian blinked. "Alex Winters?" he asked slowly.

"Yes," Kalinda answered, a sly smile hovering over her lips. "He was at the zoning board meeting last night." She looked up, tapping her chin. "Something about wanting to build a parking garage downtown. Thought maybe he was a friend of yours is all."

Ian stared at her. Alex Winters was no friend. In fact, he just so happened to be a direct competitor. And something about the way Kalinda's eyes narrowed so shrewdly told him that she already knew both those things about him. What kind of game were these women playing? And more importantly, what the hell was Alex thinking of doing to the downtown area? Ian had thought Alex was tied up with the Florida real estate market which was currently booming but completely overpriced for Ian's tastes as well as pocketbook. There was no way Ian could let a guy like that get market dominance here without further investigation. He'd have Scott put out some feelers on that right after breakfast.

Ian sat back, assessing the sisters in a new light. "Thanks for the tip, Kalinda. You're right. Maybe I will stay a little longer. It's always nice to see an old friend."

"Lovely," Kalinda said brightly. "Isn't that lovely, Loni?" she said, giving her sister a little shake.

Loni gave her sister a cross look. "Why absolutely. Imagine that Ian actually has more than one friend. I can't think of anything lovelier." Her southern tone was as sweet as honey but if her gaze were any icier, he'd have an icicle hanging off the tip of his nose.

He chuckled despite himself.

"Well," Kalinda said, clearing her throat, "has Loni told you about our specials yet?"

Ian cocked his head, pinning his gaze to the woman in question. "Why no. Loni hasn't yet. Please enlighten me. I'm eager to learn why this place is such a gem to the town." He knew he was being a jackass to her. But her needling him and the little southern-belle-heroine game she was playing brought out the worst in him. Plus, to be fair, she *had* started it.

Loni licked her unpainted lips and he wanted to kick himself for being immediately drawn into staring at them. "We have a baked apple pie oatmeal, s'mores pancakes, and a delicious veggie bomber omelet."

"Any cheese in the omelet?" he asked.

"This is the south, honey," Loni said with a roll of her eyes. "We put cheese in anything edible."

He handed her the menu. "I'll have the veggie omelet—hold the cheese then."

Loni placed a hand over her heart. "You monster," she breathed in mock shock.

Ian grinned, but before he could respond, Kalinda clasped her hands together. "Wonderful. You won't even miss the cheese. All the vegetables are super fresh. I grow them myself in my little garden on the property."

Loni looked at her sister, her expression growing soft. "In Mama's garden?" she asked in an almost reverent tone.

Kalinda nodded. "It's not quite what she had, but it fits the need we have here."

"I saw it," Ian told them. He'd wandered around the hotel grounds before stopping at The White Squirrel. The garden was hard to miss. It was amazing, even to a city boy like himself.

Loni placed a hand on her hip. "You saw our mama's garden? When exactly did you see it?"

He shrugged. "It's a nice morning so I took a walk before breakfast." He looked at Kalinda. "The garden is very impressive."

Kalinda smiled. "Thanks."

Loni's eyes narrowed at him. "Oh, really? You were just taking a walk or were you sizing up the property?"

"Loni," Kalinda warned.

Ian held up both his hands. "Yes, guilty as charged," he said lightly so Loni wouldn't fling a cup of coffee in his face, or worse stab him with a fork. "As you both are perfectly aware, that is the sole reason I'm here. I'm not trying to hide that. It's my job to have a look around to see if anything here sparks interest in our company. The garden just happened to grab my attention while doing that."

"Oh?" Loni said, crocking a hand on her hip. "By chance, anything else around here *grab* your attention that I should know about?"

Yes, he thought, enjoying how pretty she looked when her cheeks flushed with anger. *Very much so.*

A little *too* much so.

He met her gaze directly. "Believe me, *sugar*, if anything here sparks my interest, you'll most assuredly be the first to know," he said, with a small grin.

Ian had the satisfaction of seeing Loni's cheeks go redder and the fire he'd seen in her baby blues when he'd first walked in, flickered even higher. He was definitely not doing himself any favors goading her like this. What was wrong with him? He was usually more in control when dealing with prospective sellers. But there was something about the middle Wingate sister that got under his skin and prickled and burned. Like a bed bug.

Dear God, please don't let it be bed bugs…

Kalinda cleared her throat and quickly grabbed Loni's elbow. "Well, that is so good to hear."

"So nice meeting you, Ian! I'll put your order in and Loni

will bring you out some coffee in a jiff. Enjoy your time here. We'll try to make it as memorable as possible." She pulled her sister away with some effort, which was a good thing. Kalinda must have sensed—as he did—that Loni might have taken a swing at him, otherwise.

Not that he'd blame her. Perhaps, he was playing the villain role up just as much as Loni was playing up the Southern belle routine. He couldn't help himself. If nothing else, it was doing a good job of keeping her at a distance until he figured out what could be done with the property.

After all, Ian had never let a woman distract him from business in the past. And no matter how attractive or spunky the woman was, he certainly wasn't about to start now.

. . .

"Why are you being so nice to him?" Loni demanded once they were back in the kitchen. She was still fuming at Ian's brazenness. The man seriously had the audacity to flirt with her.

As if!

Not to mention the comment about her making partner...

Duke, the fry cook, froze as he was cracking an egg into a bowl. He was an attractive guy, not pretty or GQish but he had an interesting face all the same, one that seemed to imply that he played as hard as he worked. "Kalinda is being nice to a man?" he asked gruffly. "What man?"

"Ian Hollowell," Kalinda replied.

Duke raised a dark eyebrow. "You were being nice to the enemy?"

"Ah-ha!" Loni exclaimed. "See?" she said, pointing at Duke. "*He* gets it."

Kalinda threw her hands up. "All right. Everybody calm down." She pinned a sudden curious glare at Loni. "Although, you have some nerve being upset at me. I saw the way you were looking at Ian. What's up with that?"

She blinked. "What? Y—you heard what he said to me. And for the record, I was *not* looking at him. *He* was looking at me."

"Well, whoever was looking at who definitely gave me the *uncomfies.*"

Loni huffed out a breath. "The man was just trying to throw me off balance." Which was, Loni realized with dismay, exactly what he had done. But she knew his type. One hundred percent career driven. Heck, she was engaged to that type. She was not going down that rabbit hole again.

Kalinda snorted. "If the rosiness of your cheeks is any indication, I'd say it worked. You were off balance and slightly stammering. If I didn't know you better, I'd think you had some sort of crush on the guy."

"Oh, please," she grumbled. "Like I would be interested in someone like *him.*"

"Right," her sister replied drily. "Because young, intelligent, handsome businessmen are such a huge turnoff. *Ewww.*"

Loni poked Kalinda in the arm. "Hey, I'm the insensitive, sarcastic one in the family. Not you. *You're* supposed to be the stubborn, organized one. But now you're acting like a pushover, especially regarding Ian. Maybe you're the one with the crush."

Duke frowned. "Kalinda has a crush?"

"I was only being cordial to Daddy's friend." Kalinda grabbed a plate from Duke and added a heaping scoop of hash browns to it. "Don't deflect. Besides, it's all part of the plan."

Loni and Duke exchanged skeptical glances. "What plan?" she asked. "You didn't tell me you had a plan." She pointed to herself. "*I* had the plan. Make Ian's stay here as miserable as possible, so he leaves. The end."

Duke scratched his chin then nodded. "That's a damn good plan."

Loni smiled and made a show of tidying her hair. "Why, thank you."

"Hey, you stay out of this," Kalinda snapped at him.

Duke shrugged and went back to beating his eggs.

Loni pointed at her sister. "But no, your plan is apparently treating Ian like he's Prince William. And then you went and told him about Daddy coming home this weekend and about some friend of his named Alex Winters. Why don't you just change the name of the hotel to Ian's Place, order him his own Sleep Number bed, and save everyone the time and trouble?"

Kalinda placed the plate in the window for Dana to pick up and rang a bell to signal to her. "Loni, relax. Don't you see, it's much smarter to be cordial to the man so his guard slips. That way when he's least suspecting, we swoop in for the kill."

Loni thought about that a bit. Her sister may have a point. Plus, she really liked the sound of swooping in for the kill, especially with regard to Ian.

"Okay, what's the rest of this so-called plan?" she muttered.

With a small grin, Kalinda pulled open the refrigerator door and took out a bowl. "This is the next part," she said, placing it on the counter.

Loni glanced down and then back up at her sister. "Vegetables? You plan on boosting his immune system or something?"

"Ha-ha," Kalinda said drily. "These are not just any vegetables. I grew long-hot peppers this year. And they are smokin' hot, if you get my meaning."

"Yeah, I almost choked on the fumes alone when I was cutting them up," Duke added from behind them.

"Precisely," Kalinda said proudly. "Which will make them the perfect addition to one veggie bomber omelet—hold the cheese."

Loni laughed. "And here I thought I was the insensitive one. You are practically the southern version of Maleficent."

Kalinda patted herself on the back. "Yes, I have my dastardly moments."

Duke smiled at her sister. "Kalinda has quite the green thumb, too. But then again, there's not much she can't do."

"Aww, thanks, Duke," she said, giving his arm a light pat. "I appreciate that."

Loni noted that Duke's tanned face turned a shade darker as he went back to cooking his omelet. She had to wonder if Duke saw her sister as more than a boss and friend. Kalinda, ever oblivious to what was going on, went over to the window to look out into the dining room.

"Dana needs help. You better get back out there," she told Loni.

Loni nodded. "Right. His Majesty Ian is probably wondering where his coffee is."

Kalinda cocked a hand on her hip with a resigned sigh. "Just stick to the plan," she grumbled.

"I'm trying. It's just that he annoys me so much," she said with an exaggerated pout. Worse than that, he seemed to sense those feelings and was going out of his way to irritate her further.

Her sister took her by the shoulders and pointed her in the direction of the dining room. "Pretend you're in a courtroom. Work your stoic attorney magic on him." She gave her a slight push.

Considering how well she'd been doing as an attorney, she felt the need for other options. But Kalinda was right. She couldn't let Ian Hollowell rile her up. He'd think it a sign of weakness. She needed to have the upper hand.

"What if that doesn't work?" Loni asked.

Kalinda grinned. "Channel your inner Kate Middleton, of course."

Loni chose to ignore that little remark and, with an inward eyeroll, went back to check on her tables. She picked up a check from one and noticed the hostess had seated another table of hers. Sheesh, she thought practicing law was challenging! Her calves were already aching, and she knew she had to be emanating a strange aroma of sweat, bacon, and hibiscus.

Taking a deep breath, she made her way over to the coffee machine. Before picking up the pot, she allowed herself a glance Ian's way. Mistake. He was looking straight at her, leaning on the table, his chin in his hand. He'd obviously been watching her the entire time. He then chose to grin broadly and give her a little wave with his free hand.

Lordy, that man could piss off the Pope.

Loni had a feeling that sweet Princess Kate wouldn't flip the bird to a practical stranger from across the room, so she chose a more refined response—even though it practically killed her— and sweetly flittered her fingers back at him.

Mama always had such an easygoing way about her and could handle the crowds and people in such a smooth manner. If she were living, she'd know how to handle someone like Ian Hollowell. Of course, if Mama *were* living, there'd be no Ian Hollowell in the picture. There'd be no talk of selling the property at all. And just like that, the thought of losing the hotel felt like Loni would be losing not only a piece of her mother, but a piece of herself. She'd barely felt whole since her breakup with Blaze, and she just wasn't sure who she was or what she wanted anymore—except this hotel. The only home she'd ever known. That was one thing she definitely wanted, and she'd do just about anything to keep it.

Kalinda rang the bell on the kitchen serving window, and Loni looked over. She pointed to the omelet she'd set down and winked.

Ian's omelet. Loni could only hope Ian didn't have a spicy food tolerance. Kalinda seemed pretty confident, though. They must be some peppers. Loni took the coffee pot with her as she walked over to grab the omelet plate.

Ian was staring at his phone as she approached. She carefully set the plate in front of him and filled his coffee cup. "Can I get you anything else, sugar?" *Bottle of antacid? One way airplane ticket to Point Nemo?*

He put down his phone, then inspected his breakfast as if he were expecting it to jump out at him. "I don't think so. This looks surprisingly good."

She bit her tongue at the slight about her sister's food and smiled tightly. "It *is* good. I'm sure you'll find it full of, um, flavor." She glanced over at the entrance and, seeing Marise standing in the doorway, waved. "*Enjoy...*" she purred, then went to check on another table.

Loni barely got another cup of coffee poured when she heard Marise gasp.

"Is anyone a doctor here?" Marise shouted, waving her hands frantically. When no one responded, she pointed toward the corner of the restaurant. "Help! He's choking!"

He? Loni spun around. Ian's face and neck were red as a fire engine. His hands were clasped around his throat and he was gagging and—goodness!—he did in fact appear to be choking. Oh God. She took comfort that he wasn't turning blue—at least not yet. What had they done? She rushed over to his table along with Marise and two customers who were dining nearby.

Marise immediately slapped him on the back, which didn't seem to help and if Loni wasn't seeing things, only served to annoy him. "Get him something to drink!" her sister ordered.

Ian gasped more and nodded.

Grabbing the closest liquid to her, Loni immediately poured more coffee into his cup.

Ian frowned and shook his head.

Seriously? He's going to be picky at a time like this?

"He don't need no liquid," said the burley customer, hovering around them. "He needs this." The man shoved Marise aside and then threw his beefy arms around Ian's middle and began thrusting his forearms up and down Ian's chest like he was churning butter.

"Oh yes," Marise said, clapping her hands. "Good thinking, Darin! His color looks better already."

Kalinda came rushing over with a pitcher of water. "Crikey, he's not choking! It's the peppers! He needs water." She grabbed Darin's wrist. "Stop trying to do the Heimlich, Darin, you're going break his ribs."

Loni let out a relieved breath when she saw Ian's eyes widen in agreement. People around them in the restaurant were on their feet now, and in between the commotion, she heard someone yell that they were calling 9-1-1.

Darin had yet to drop his arms, so struggling to get out of his grasp, Ian threw his elbow up and knocked the pitcher out of Kalinda's hands. All of the water splashed up and then down onto Ian's face like a scene out of *Flashdance*, soaking his chest and lap.

"You're all crazy!" Ian spluttered hoarsely, wiping crushed ice out of his shirt collar.

Darin crossed his tree trunk arms and frowned. "Well, holler fire and save the matches," he grumbled.

"And whatever the hell you just said has just proven my point, buddy," Ian declared hotly. He then grabbed a napkin and rubbed it down his face. Turning, he waved the damp napkin at Loni and her sisters. "*You* are even worse. That omelet nearly singed my trachea."

Kalinda and Loni exchanged guilty looks. Loni didn't know much about cooking, but she did learn something about it today. Apparently, it *was* possible to make a dish *too* spicy. Huh.

He stood and flung the napkin down on the plate. "Thanks again for the great southern hospitality," he spat. He stormed off and the rest of the customers in the restaurant parted like the Red Sea for him to pass. For a brief moment, as Loni glanced around the concerned and confused faces of some of the lingering patrons, she felt a stab of guilt over what she and Kalinda had done. Their "prank" scared a lot of people and more importantly, could have really harmed Ian.

"Well," Kalinda said, dropping napkins on the floor to wipe up the water, "that certainly did the trick, didn't it?"

Loni brushed at her sweaty bangs, then picked up the discarded omelet. "Yeah, I'd bet anything he's packing his bags as we speak." Which was exactly what they all wanted. Perfect, actually.

So why was she feeling so uneasy about it now? That is… besides the fact that she was an attorney and could smell a lawsuit a mile away.

Kalinda made the rounds to various customers, letting them

know that everything was fine. Just a joke gone bad. Luckily, most went back to eating, although some, Loni noted, had left during the excitement without paying.

Face flushed, Dana came over with a roll of paper towels and handed them to Marise. "What did y'all do to that fella?" Dana asked. "He seemed madder than a squirrel in a sack."

"Kalinda put a bunch of her long hot peppers in his omelet," Loni said, realizing how childish it sounded now.

Marise let out a long whistle. "Whoa. Duke told me they were five and half-alarm-fire hot peppers."

Loni gave her a sardonic grin. "Based on Ian's response to them, I'd say that description was on point."

Dana shook her head. "Damn, y'all *are* crazy."

Loni had to admit, again, that that description was on point, also.

Marise slapped a hand against her forehead. "Sweet sugar, I just thought of something else we need to worry about."

Loni inwardly flinched. What else could possibly go wrong today? She dropped into the chair behind her and looked up at her sister. "What?" she asked tentatively.

"Do y'all think Ian will give us a poor Yelp review now?"

Chapter Eight

Ian ignored the slacked-jawed stares of the people loitering by the front desk as he stormed his way back to his so-called hotel room. His entire shirt was drenched and cold and clung to his chest as if he were microwaved in plastic wrap and... Dammit, his mouth was still on fire from the two bites of omelet he'd eaten.

No doubt in his mind. The Wingate women were completely certifiable.

Joe certainly had his hands full with them. No wonder he needed help in dealing with this property. However, Ian's next suggestion would be a crisis hotline.

"Ian!" he heard across the lobby.

Dear God, please don't let this be another welcoming committee bearing a bouquet of fire ants.

He stopped and warily turned around. Lucille was rushing over to him, her eyes round with concern. "What happened, honey?" she asked, taking in his soaked attire. "Did y'all fall into the pool or something?"

"No," he said flatly. "I was just enjoying one of your typical Carolina breakfasts."

The woman scratched her head. "Here? At the White Squirrel Cafe?"

"Is there another place to have breakfast around here?" *If so, that would have been nice to know!*

Lucille cocked her head and thought for a good minute. "Well, no place good. At least, not for breakfast. But I am partial to Top of the Muffin at the corner of Jackson Street. They have the best—"

"Muffins?" he supplied impatiently.

She shook her head. "Babka."

That did it. They were *all* crazy. Was it something in the water? In the air? Well, he wasn't about to stay a minute longer to find out. He'd had enough of this place. Enough of these people! He'd explain to Joe. He could send Scott instead. Yeah, let his partner suffer the brunt of this town. Who knows? Maybe Scott will have better luck with these people.

Ian gave Lucille a tight smile, already dreaming of being dry and sitting on the next flight out of here. "Thanks. I'll keep that in mind next time I visit." *Which won't be in this lifetime.* He turned back in the direction he came from.

Lucille grabbed his arm. "Wait. Does that mean you're leaving? So soon?"

Hell to the yes. "I'm afraid so. Not that it hasn't been a dream." *Or better yet, a friggin' nightmare.* He gently pried her bony fingers from his wet sleeve. "Now, if you'll excuse me, I need to change into some dry clothes before I can do anything else."

"Do you need any help?" she blurted.

He gave her a look.

"Er, I mean, help with your luggage. I can get Knox for you. Or if you'd rather, I can come and get your luggage." She waggled her eyebrows, then added in a staged whisper, "It's the personal service we give here at The Sandy Bottom."

Ian wondered how fast he could be at the airport.

He patted Lucille on the back of the hand. "I think I'll be fine, but if I need anything, I have your extension memorized," he said, pointing to his temple.

She sent him a dreamy smile. "Just ring and I'll be at your service."

He slowly backed away. "Yep. I'll be seeing you." *From a high-powered telescope at best.*

"I hope so!" she called out.

Not trusting his luck with the elevator, Ian took to the stairs and ran up the one flight. He knew he was letting Joe down, but things were just too wacky here. Obviously, the sisters were hell bent on opposing him at every turn. Maybe if Ian were lucky, he could hold off his investors until Joe fought this battle himself.

Ian was composing in his head what he would say to Joe as he approached his room but stopped when he saw a white plastic bag hanging off the door handle.

What now?

He truly hoped it wasn't actually fire ants this time, but he took it as a good sign when the contents didn't appear to be moving. Slipping it off the handle, he took a peek. A delicious aroma hit his nose before he could even see what was inside.

Food.

And not just any food. Heavenly, otherworldly food. His stomach made a noise that would have had a grizzly bear running for cover. He brushed aside some of the paper. There was a wrapped biscuit filled with egg and bacon, a chocolate chip muffin the size of Plymouth Rock, a small container of fresh fruit, and a bottle of orange juice.

Huh. He glanced around, but the hallway was silent and empty. Was this some sort of peace offering? Or was this whole set-up with the omelet a test that he somehow... *passed*?

Too hungry to question it further, he drew out his key card. But then something shiny by his foot caught his attention. He bent down and picked up the object. It was a dangle earring in the shape of a shooting star. He'd seen this piece of jewelry before. His mind drifted to its owner, and he had to smile.

Loni.

Well, well, maybe she wasn't as heartless as she first tried to appear. Not one to look a gift horse in the mouth, he let himself into his closet of a room and emptied the contents of his breakfast down onto his bed. After taking a small bite of egg and not detecting a bit of spice or—*thank you, Jesus*—poison, he housed the rest of the sandwich.

Much better.

He tore off his wet shirt and shorts and put on some dry clothes. Feeling slightly more human, he sat down and considered his next move. First off was Alex Winters. He took out his tablet and sent an email to Scott, asking him to dig up what he knew about Alex's company and why they were in North Carolina. Then, he decided to Google some information for himself.

Nothing too noteworthy. Although Kalinda was correct when she'd mentioned that Alex had been at last night's zoning meeting. He'd apparently given a proposal to the board about why the downtown should change the zoning to allow for extra parking. There was even a picture in the local paper of Alex holding an architectural rendition of the garage he'd like to build. The parking garage would be where the police station and municipal court now stood. He'd advised moving and building a new police station closer to the fire department. A few council members were there and liked the idea.

Ian tossed the tablet onto the bed with a loud curse. Alex-mothereffing-Winters was the bane of his existence. The one man who picked up the pieces of Ian's costly mistake years ago and had been capitalizing ever since. Strange that Alex somehow knew Ian was in Sunny Banks. He was probably hoping to fix another mistake of his and gain the upper hand in the industry. Well, not this time. Never again. Alex was not going to be moving in on *his* territory.

Wait. His *territory?*

Ian frowned, rubbing his face tiredly. Wasn't he just about to get on the next plane to Boston? No, *run* onto the next plane to Boston? And now, just because Alex Winters was sniffing around Sunny Banks, it suddenly was "Ian's territory"?

Yeah. Pretty much. But that's how the game was played, and Ian wasn't going anywhere until he knew if the rules had changed.

Wondering what to do next, he leaned his head back and stared at the ceiling. That's when he noticed a ceiling tile out of place. He shouldn't be surprised since this seemed more of a storage room than an actual guest room. He hadn't noticed it yesterday—probably because he was more concerned about bed bugs—but now he became worried about some other kind of critter coming through the ceiling.

With a sigh, he sat up and climbed onto the bed. The tile could probably just slide back into place. He reached his hand toward the ceiling but as he shifted the tile straighter, he felt some paper in the way. Not just paper. He grabbed for it and realized it was a stack of letters.

After correcting the tile, he jumped off the bed, letters in hand. He glanced through them. Huh. They looked to be some old love letters from Joe to his wife. The question was why would anyone stick them in the ceiling of a closet? He'd give them to Loni. Maybe she'd know.

He glanced over at his half-eaten food. The Wingate sisters were obviously trying to make amends with this little breakfast do-over. Maybe there was a chance they all could come to an agreement after all. He was definitely going to stick it out a little longer here. There were too many reasons to stay, and each was getting more and more interesting.

He would go down to the lobby and thank Loni personally for the food—and for extending the olive branch. Then he'd extend one of his own by giving her the letters. Hopefully, then, he'd find out what was really going on with this change of heart of hers.

Right after, of course, he finished the rest of his breakfast.

• • •

Kalinda took pity on Loni's fragile feet and was worn down by the mega amount of complaining she'd done, so once the breakfast rush—the busiest time of the day for them—had died down, she let Loni drag herself back to her suite.

Loni smelled like a deep fryer and was in dire need of a shower. Unfortunately, that thought brought the breakfast incident with Ian to mind. She still felt bad about what they had put him through, but she couldn't help chuckling just thinking about him getting doused with all that water. Her mama had always been up for a good prank, and if she had seen that display, she would have split her sides laughing.

Of course, it was only a matter of time before she heard from their father about it. And that was a phone call she was not looking forward to receiving.

Right on cue, her cell phone began ringing.

Fudge. It obviously hadn't taken Ian long to contact her father to complain. But Daddy was just going to have to come to terms with the fact that when she and her sisters said they didn't want to sell, they meant business. She stepped into the suite, closed the door behind her and pulled out her phone.

However, it wasn't Daddy. Blaze was calling her.

Her heart rate kicked up, but more from nerves than excitement to hear from him. She had hoped to hear from him sooner. She thought he would have told her he'd been a fool, that he was sorry and that he missed her and then beg her to come home and start afresh. But that hadn't happened. Now, coolly staring at his name on her phone, she had to wonder if she even wanted him to call at all. Mama always said things happened for a reason. Maybe her not hearing from Blaze was the sign she'd needed to reevaluate her relationship with him or at least give them the time in order to do that.

"Hi, Blaze," she answered, sliding out of her sneakers.

"Apollonia." His tone was curt and all business. If she'd entertained for one brief second that he might have been calling to apologize and reconcile, she was dispelled of that dream quickly enough.

"We received your email," he went on without emotion. "The extra time off you've requested unfortunately won't be a problem."

Her jaw almost dropped. "Really? Thank you. I—" Wait. *Unfortunately?*

"It's not as good as it sounds." He continued, "We're not

giving you the time off because of your request. I'm only saying it won't be a problem because you've been placed on probationary leave by the firm while we evaluate your performance."

"*What?*" Her head began to throb. *What had been that bullshit saying about things happening for a reason?* "Why, Blaze?"

He let out a drawn-out sigh as if he were dealing with a troublesome child. "You know full well why you would be placed on that kind of leave."

"Spell it out for me," she said between gritted teeth.

"There's been an ethical complaint made against you here at the firm. Therefore, we would like you to step away while the disciplinary committee here investigates the claim. As a courtesy for your service, we have yet to inform the ABA until the end of our own investigation. But if these matters prove to be true, you will most likely risk being fired or worse, disbarred."

Complaint? Investigation? Disbarred? Now she was at risk of losing her job? "I don't even know what you're talking about. Who would complain about me?" She flopped down on the chair next to her and held her head in her free hand.

"I'm afraid until the investigation is complete, we are not at liberty to say yet. Just know salary and medical will be untouched until then."

Sheesh, thank goodness for that! "So, what am I supposed to do in the meantime? I can't defend myself against these claims?"

"Of course you can. Once the committee deems there is in fact a case." He sighed. "This was my recommendation, Lon. I felt considering the recent mistake you made and in light of your sudden departure, it would be best for your mental health to have the paid leave."

Instead of helping her refute the claim. "Wow, thanks."

"You're welcome," he said in all seriousness. "Listen, Apollonia." His tone grew uncharacteristically soft. "I'm concerned about how we left things."

Her heart cracked a fraction. Oh, wow, he sounded as if he missed her. Maybe Blaze wasn't as totally career-oriented as she thought, and he really did care about her. Had she judged him too harshly? When they had first started dating, he'd been so thoughtful, so sensitive. Maybe he hadn't changed that much.

"Are you?" she asked warily, not knowing what she'd say if he asked for a second chance.

"Well, of course. There are a lot of rumors circulating."

"What kind of rumors?"

"That you've been messing up at work because of your hormones and that's why you left town all of a sudden. Are you...*pregnant*?" he asked in a horrified whisper.

"No, I'm not pregnant," she spat. "Gee, thanks for your concern. However, if you recall, the reason I left town was because *you* suggested I take a vacation after you swooped in and got my promotion." ·

"Ah. I can see you're still upset about that. Well, now that you're in North Carolina, this leave really is the best thing for you."

"You mean, the best thing for *you*."

"Don't be ridiculous. I have to take over your clients while you're away. Like I already don't have a full plate to contend with. Which is another reason I needed to speak with you today. I can't access your computer. Did you change your passcode or something? I need it, otherwise I'll have to call IT and that will take forever."

Her limbs went limp, and her mind was in a fog. She had the

potential to lose her license to practice law and here Blaze was worried about the hassle the IT department was going to give him. Of course, she had changed her passcode to her computer before she'd left! *Duh*. She may have been accused of being sloppy and unprofessional, but that didn't mean she was stupid. She still couldn't believe she'd sent those contracts before they were finished. Just to be on the safe side, she wanted to prevent anything like that from happening again while she was away, especially since the time stamp on that email had been during normal business hours.

"Well, I need those files," he told her. "Mark has court today so I can't ask him for access."

There had been only two other people who had access to her computer passcode and could have gotten into her computer email. Blaze and Mark Becker. She couldn't imagine being sabotaged by her mentor and refused to believe her own fiancé could be so calculating. But just a few short days ago, she wouldn't have imagined herself sticking one of her Daddy's friends in a closet-sized room with no air conditioning and then trying to singe his taste buds off with an omelet full of long hot peppers.

"I'm not giving you my passcode," she said tiredly, rubbing her forehead.

"Apollonia." His tone was reproachful. "You're being unreasonable. Remember, we're all working for the same team."

Were they on the same team? Once, she would have wholeheartedly agreed. Now, she didn't know anymore. Wasn't even sure she knew *him* at all. Loni couldn't remember a time that she wished her mother were alive to give her some advice more than right now. Her mother was, after all, the one who'd encouraged her to follow her heart and Blaze across the country when he'd asked her to.

And just look where that had led.

She closed her eyes, feeling the exhaustion of the morning settle on her like a weighted blanket. "I have my laptop with me. I can email you anything you might need."

Blaze was silent for a moment. "Fine," he huffed out. "I was hoping not to trouble you, but if you prefer it this way then that's the way we'll do it." There was a pause. "By the way, what did you tell your family...you know about *me not being there with you*?"

Loni gave a disconcerted laugh. "I told them the truth. That we had a fight. I had hoped you were calling to apologize."

"I'm not going to apologize for my promotion."

She rolled her eyes toward the ceiling. He really was that clueless. "I have to go, Blaze. I'm very busy."

"What could you possibly be doing down there that's so important? Attending the NASCAR Hall of Fame?" he snickered.

"For your information, I've been helping Marise and Kalinda with the resort."

"No offense, Apollonia, but I hardly think your sisters need your kind of help, unless they're in some sort of legal trouble. You're a damn good attorney despite the recent mistakes you've made. You'll see, by the end of the week. That's not part of your world anymore no matter how much you like to pretend it still is."

She couldn't believe he was saying these kinds of hurtful things to her. But of course, in a small way, maybe she needed to hear it. He was right. She could barely handle serving food today. What real value could she be to the hotel or her sisters? Sure, they'd managed to chase off Ian Hollowell, but for how long? And what if Daddy sent someone else in his place? Blaze was right, there was no legal way she could prevent the hotel from being sold. It was as though everything Loni had touched was turning to vapor before her very eyes: her relationship, her career, and soon, even the hotel.

"Are you quite finished?" she asked, rubbing her eyes.

He let out a breath. "I really don't mean to be so blunt, honey. Look, take this time for yourself and enjoy your sisters. I'll work on things with the other partners. Like I said, I'm sure it's all a misunderstanding. We'll get you back here where you belong in no time. Just...hold tight for a bit."

She swallowed past the lump in her throat. It was nice to hear that someone was finally looking out for her wants for a change. "Okay," she whispered.

"Good. And now that we understand each other again, how about giving me that passcode, huh?"

"You're unbelievable."

"You're only making things more difficult for yourself here. You not trusting me is going to be seen as you not trusting all the partners."

She allowed his words to hang in the air a few beats and sadly realized that she didn't trust him—not anymore—and that this was not the path an engagement should ever begin on.

"You're absolutely right," she agreed. "Goodbye, Blaze."

"Loni, wait. Your job isn't the only thing on the line now. You hang up on me and we are officially through," he warned. "Do you hear me?"

Loud and clear.

Without further thought to his threat or the consequences, she clicked the end call button.

Chapter Nine

With Loni's earring in his pocket and letters in hand, Ian was feeling in much better spirits about staying as he made his way back to The White Squirrel Café. The restaurant wasn't nearly as crowded as it was earlier this morning—although he'd probably scared off most of them—but there were no signs of the woman he was looking for. He debated going back into the restaurant and asking the hostess if she'd seen Loni, but then he caught a glimpse of that shiny blond hair through the café window. She had her cell phone up to her ear and appeared to be heading toward the beach.

It was a beautiful, sunny day so he couldn't blame her for wanting some downtime there. There'd been a hell of a lot of excitement already this morning, but he had yet to check out the beach. Ian had always enjoyed living near the water in New England, however, the north couldn't really compete with the stunning white-sand beaches of the Carolinas. He'd bet the ocean temperature was much more palatable even for this time of year as well and wished he'd changed into his bathing suit instead of just shorts and a tee.

Careful to avoid being seen by Lucille, Ian turned and skirted out of the café and into the lobby. Blending in with a family of four walking by, he followed them out the side door that led to a patio area. The swimming pool was a decent-size rectangle with sun-faded lounge chairs positioned toward the water. A red and white SWIM AT YOUR OWN RISK sign leaned against the lifeguard chair. Not that anyone was currently in the pool. Most of the vacationers seemed to be heading out toward the beach, too, armed with their towels, umbrellas, and beach bags. Taking an educated guess and heading in the opposite direction of the crowd, he soon saw Loni sitting alone on the sand. She was still on the phone and was staring straight ahead into the ocean as she spoke to whomever was on the other end.

But he knew something wasn't right even before he saw her tears.

"I don't know, Catherine," he heard her say. "Just see what you can find out for me. I feel like I'm being undermined at every turn. I can't even access my voicemails over there." There was a pause. "That's true. Right, deep breaths. Okay, thanks. I'll call you tomorrow."

Loni ended the call, then swiped at her eyes in frustration or maybe anger. He couldn't tell from this distance. He probably should have gone and changed into some board shorts and pretended he'd never seen her out here. Yet, he trudged on, his feet having a mind of their own until he stood behind where she sat. Yes, he was probably the last person she'd want seeing her cry, but he couldn't turn away now. Plus…for some reason, he couldn't get rid of the feeling that she needed him. At this minute anyway. Growing up with an alcoholic father, Ian knew firsthand the full weight of helplessness, even loneliness, and what it could do to a person's soul. He couldn't help him—or his mother for that matter—but maybe he could help Loni.

He shook off the unpleasant chill of that memory and dropped down beside her.

Loni jerked at the shock, then realizing it was him, she let out a groan. "Oh, jeez, when it rains it pours," she mumbled, drying her face with the sleeve of her shirt. "What are you doing here?"

"I thought we already covered that."

She shook her head. "I meant that I figured you'd be on the next plane back to Boston or perhaps your hometown of *Hades*."

He casually leaned back on his elbows and closed his eyes, so he wouldn't be tempted to stare at her tear-stained face. "I thought about Hades, but I heard it's hot as hell there this time of year."

She let out a reluctant sounding laugh. "I can see why my father likes you."

"Because of my solid character, incredible work ethic, and steadfast loyalty?"

"I was going to say your childish sense of humor."

Ian nodded solemnly. "Your dad *is* my best audience." He opened one of his eyes and regarded her closely. Despite her hardened expression, she still seemed vulnerable to him. "Are you okay?" he asked gently.

She let out a long, drawn-out sigh. "That's a good question."

"Anything I can do to help? I, uh, kind of heard you on the phone."

"Wonderful," she muttered.

"Hey, I happen to be a great problem solver. My mom used to call me the fixer." At the time, when his mother had told him that, he took it as a compliment. But after years of therapy, he discovered that it was less of an innate characteristic and more of a learned coping skill because of his upbringing: a need to take care of everyone and everything around him. In his life, when his father was drinking and his mother was checked out, somebody had to.

"You can't fix this," she bleakly told him.

"Try me."

She shook her head, still gazing out onto the water. "Please don't try to be my friend."

"Wouldn't dream of it. We're like ice cream and olives."

She looked at him. "Ice cream and *olives*?" she asked incredulously.

He shrugged. "Two things that don't mix. Plus, I already have plenty of friends."

"I'm sure you do. My father being one of them." She cast him a side-glance. "Although, if you want one more, I'm sure Lucille is more than willing to be your number one BFF."

"Yes, I'm quite aware. Subtlety is not her strong suit." He shuddered.

"Well, don't get any ideas of trying to get into my pants, either," she said, jabbing a finger into his arm. "I'm taking a break from men."

"And trying women?"

She rolled her eyes. "I'm not looking for *any* kind of relationship."

"It's kismet then, because I don't *do* relationships. In fact, it's been recently pointed out to me that I never date women more than seven times in a row."

"Really?" she blinked. "On purpose?"

"No. Just seems to work out like that." Although maybe

deep down inside he knew it was his subconscious triggering his protective mode. He'd never seen or been a part of a healthy long-term relationship in his life. He didn't have much of an example to follow. "Whacked" would be the best description his neighbors or friends growing up could say about his parents' marriage. The odds were that whatever messed up genes his parents had were most likely passed on to him. Feelings didn't register with him. Even now, the thought of "love" had his chest tightening as if it were in a vise.

Loni was staring at him, but to his surprise her gaze was not mocking or even disgusted. Things he was used to seeing from people. No, her gaze held sympathy. He shifted uncomfortably.

She looked away, remaining silent with her brows furrowed as if she were trying to do a math problem in her head. "I've been put on a probationary leave from my law firm," she finally said. "The kicker is, I was accused of doing something I know I didn't do and now it's under investigation."

He couldn't say what he was more stunned about: Loni being put on probation at work or her confiding in him about it. But the fact that she did share that information with him was somewhat humbling to him.

"I'm sorry to hear that, Loni. But I think you should hold on to the confidence that if you didn't do anything wrong, then you have nothing to worry about."

She let out a mirthless laugh. "Well, I'd think that too but law can be just as cutthroat as business."

"Does Joe know about this? Is that why you're here in Sunny Banks?" *Is that why you were crying?* Ian almost preferred it was the reason for her tears and that it didn't have anything to do with him or her worrying about losing the hotel.

She bit her lip. "Daddy doesn't know. But that's not the

only reason I'm here." She sent him an accusatory glare. "Of course, it appears my timing couldn't be better. I won't let you talk Daddy into selling this resort."

Ian ran a hand through his hair. Normally, he could not care less about being the bad guy. Business was business. But dealing with this woman was just...*different*. Somehow. "Look, for the record, Joe asked me to come here. I didn't approach him. I may not know your dad as well as you do, but he really is a decent guy and I believe he wants what's best for you. All of you."

"Right." She shook her head. "That's what you think, but as far as I'm concerned, it's all part of the clown show. Another man wanting what's best for *him* yet telling me it's best for *me*."

Ian wanted to know what other man she was referring to, but more alarming than that, he was curious to know if that man was still around in Loni's life. But, really, why the hell would he care about that? The reason had to be because he only wanted to understand her better to try and help. It was in his nature. A trait he picked up, trying to keep what was left of the family together for so many years.

Liar, accused his kicked up heart rate. *You like this woman.*

He cleared his throat. "Uh, speaking of clown show, I can't help but notice that your Loretta Lynn accent has suddenly disappeared. S*ugar*," he added to drive home his point. "Could my Yankee aura have had that much of an unwanted effect on your southern upbringing?"

She sent him a sheepish grin as she wiped a stray tear from her cheek. "Don't flatter yourself," she said without any heat. "My accent thinned out pretty fast when I went away to college, otherwise I would have stuck out like—"

"Pineapple in potato salad."

She let out a chuckle. "Something like that. Plus, it's hard enough to be taken seriously in the courtroom as a blond woman. Add a southern accent and you might as well be invisible."

Ian had a hard time imagining anyone ignoring someone as intelligent as Loni, but then again, he wasn't in her shoes.

"I may have been laying it on a bit thick," she went on, "so you'd think I was stupid and naïve." She turned and cocked her head at him. "I guess you didn't need my southern accent to figure that one out pretty quick, huh? Especially after everything I've done to you."

He frowned. "Loni, I never thought you were dumb. But you must think *I'm* the naïve one if you thought I'd fall for your act."

"You mean you didn't?"

He grinned at the disgruntled look on her face. "Not for one second. An A for accent, but you get a B for acting skills. I had a feeling you wanted me to underestimate you."

"Hmm…I feel even more foolish now." She picked up some sand in her fist and began letting it sift through her fingers like an hourglass. Appearing deep in thought, she watched the grains for several moments until her palm was empty. "You know, Marise was the actor in the family anyway. She landed the lead in three of her high school plays."

"If it's any consolation, her acting was the worst of the three of you."

She cracked a smile at that. "Strangely enough, that *is* a bit of a consolation." She drew in a deep breath, turning to look at him again. "I guess since you're being somewhat nice to me, I should say I'm sorry about your room. And the whole bed bug scare. And the lack of air conditioning. Sort of sorry," she added with a wink.

"And sorry about the pepper thing?" he prodded with a grin. "My tongue may need reconstructive surgery."

She bit her lip. "Oh, yeah, *really* sorry about that one. Definitely not one of my better moments. But you should have seen yourself." She chuckled, raising her hand to cover her mouth. "Oh my gosh, that guy Darin squeezed your chest like a tube of toothpaste."

"Let's not relive the details," he said drily.

"Are you sure you're not hurt?"

"Physically, I'm fine. Although, pretty sure my pride will need about six to eight weeks of rehab. Tack on another three months of mental health therapy and I'll be... What would you say down here? Fit as a fiddle?"

"We would say *fine*, but I'm glad to hear you'll survive." They smiled at one another, then after the briefest hesitation, she looked away. "What's that?" she said, pointing at the letters clenched in his fist.

Ian looked down at the letters, almost completely forgetting about them. "Oh, right." He held them out to her. "I found these in my room and thought you might like to have them. I think they're love letters from Joe to your mom."

A small gasp escaped her lips as she took them from his hands. "Oh my gosh, thank you. How sweet of Daddy to keep them after all this time. These are—" Her face fell as she read one of the letters.

"What's the matter?" he asked. "Hard to picture that your mom and dad were once in love like that?" For Loni's sake, he hoped they weren't *too* personal.

She shook her head, still looking at the letter. "No, it's just that these are..."

"These are...*what*?" Ian prompted.

Loni glanced up with a puzzled expression. "Not from my daddy."

"What? Those letters aren't from Joe?"

She held one of the letters out for him.

Ian took the paper from her limp fingers and combed through it. "Who's TJ?"

Loni rubbed her forehead. "I-I don't know. Daddy's full name is Joseph Elmer and Mama certainly never referred to him as TJ in his entire life."

"Okay, no big deal. So your mom saved some old love letters from a high school sweetheart."

Her chest rose and fell on a shudder. "No, Ian," she said softly. "Look at the date."

Ian's shoulders dropped when he saw 1998 on the postmark. There was no return address. He glanced at Loni whose face had grown extremely pale.

"Hey, now," he said, dipping his head to look her in the eye. "Let's not jump to conclusions. Remember, counselor, we don't have all the evidence yet. We have time to figure this out. We haven't even read everything that's in those letters yet."

He didn't want to examine why he had used the word "we" as often as he had just then. But she looked so lost, and he had a sudden need to alleviate at least one part of the hellish week she seemed to be having.

"Hey," Ian said again, his gaze searching. "Are you going to be okay?"

She swallowed. "Yeah," she said, forcing a smile. "It's fine. You're right. No need to get worked up yet. Maybe it's all a misunderstanding."

She glanced around then as if trying to regain her surroundings. "I guess I should go and see if my sisters need me for anything." She brushed the sand off her legs and stood.

"Are you sure you're going to be okay?" he asked, quickly getting to his feet.

She looked out at the ocean waves a few beats before answering. "For now. I guess I should at least thank you for that."

"Thank me for what?"

"For making me forget half my problems, even though you're practically the cause of the other half of my problems." She waved a hand in front of her face, but he didn't miss the flicker of gratitude in her eyes. "I'm sure I'll see you around."

"Wait," he called out when she turned to go.

She stopped and looked at him expectantly. "What?"

Yeah, Ian, what? He didn't know. Just... He didn't want her to go. Not yet anyway. Then he remembered her earring. Reaching into his pocket, he pulled it out. "I believe this is yours," he said, presenting it in his palm.

She looked down at it, then back up at him. "That's not mine."

"It's not?"

"Nope."

He glanced at it again. "Are you sure? I could have sworn you had on earrings with little stars on them yesterday."

She folded her arms, a half smirk on her lips. "That's very observant of you to notice my earrings, however, I must sadly inform you that I wore earrings with little dangle crescent moons. Not stars."

"Oh." He frowned, scratching his chin. This really wasn't adding up. "So...you didn't come by my hotel room today?"

She threw her head back and laughed. "Oh, heck no. Why on earth would I do *that*?"

"I...I don't know. I guess it does seem kind of funny to ask." He ignored the bruise her words and laughter had caused to his apparently fragile ego and redirected his thoughts. So, Loni *wasn't* the one who left him the breakfast, which didn't quite add up. He'd wondered if all the sisters were on the same page with regards to selling the hotel and now, he definitely knew they were not. Which meant he had an ally here. There was a good chance to work this deal out after all. However, ally or no ally, he still had one hurdle yet to overcome.

And that was Loni.

When she turned to go one more time, he tried again. "That's it?" he asked her.

"Excuse me?"

"No more pranks?"

Her brow shot up. "You *want* to be pranked now?"

"Hell no," he blurted, his hands in the surrender position. He didn't think he could survive any more of the Wingate family humor. "But I can't believe you're just going to let me be and do my job. It seems out of character for you."

"Well, I tried to get in the way of your job, but as you can see," she said, gesturing to him with her hands, "you're still standing here. Epic fail."

"So you're just going to give up then?"

She blinked. "You want me to fight you more?"

Ian leaned in closer to her then, close enough to catch a feminine scent of flowers and lemon and had to fight to stay focused. "I was, uh, thinking more of a truce than a fight."

"A truce," she said slowly, as if dissecting its meaning. "Absolutely not." She whirled around and began walking away again.

Damn, this woman was as stubborn as they came. "I just

want two more minutes of your time," he called to her.

She stopped but didn't turn around right away. Finally when she regarded him, she looked more put out than interested. "What do you have in mind?"

"Show me why this place is worth saving."

She snorted. "You've got to be kidding. That's your idea of a truce? I'm not helping your cause, Ian, if that's what this is all about."

He wanted to smile because she was so damn smart and quick-thinking, but he was afraid she'd think he was mocking her. "How do you know it wouldn't help *your* cause?"

Loni just stared at him, so he could tell that had her thinking. "I don't," she said quietly. "But I don't trust you, and I don't see what good it will do either of us."

"If you can convince me, maybe I can convince your dad."

"Really?" She narrowed her eyes at him. "You would do that?"

He shrugged. "If it made sense." Of course, Ian didn't have the heart to tell her that nine times out of ten sentimentalities *didn't* make sense. But he didn't want to see her leave looking so defeated after the day she'd had. With Loni's help, he'd have a much better idea of the land and area. Plus, a cease-fire with her meant he'd be more likely to have a pleasant, undeterred stay and have less of a risk for any more of the sisters' pranks.

At least, one could hope.

"And..." he added. "If you ever need or want to investigate who TJ is, I may be able to help you with that, too."

After a few beats, she gave him a curt nod. "Okay. I guess I can do that. But no funny business," she quickly added.

"Don't worry," he said, crossing his heart. "I never mix funny with business. It's a philosophy I live by. It goes with the whole no-mixing-of-emotions-with-contracts philosophy I also happen to live by."

"I'm serious," she warned.

"Me, too," he warned back.

Loni let out a sigh. "I somehow doubt that. So would our meetings be more of a morning or afternoon thing?"

"Would you prefer to draw up a formal contract?" he asked in mock seriousness.

"No," she said, oblivious to his teasing. "That's all right. I don't suppose that will be necessary."

When she looked down her nose at him, he was caught off guard with the urge to smile again. He kind of liked seeing this no-nonsense side of Loni—realized he liked this as much as the family loyalty side—and could imagine her being a thorough attorney. Plus, she certainly wasn't hard to look at, either. He'd love to see her in action.

In the courtroom! his brain clarified when his body parts began to spring to life. He had an interest in seeing her perform as *an attorney in the courtroom.* Jeez, he had no idea why his brain was veering off to *bowchickabowwow* land all of a sudden. Hadn't Loni just told him she was taking a break from men?

"Well, that's a relief," he said with a half laugh. *What were we talking about again?*

"There's just one more thing." She bit her lip. "I would prefer no one know about our little informal agreement."

"Ah." He nodded, rocking back on his heels. "You don't want your sisters knowing you're consorting with the enemy?"

She bristled. "It's not just that. I don't want to tell them about the letters yet. Until we know more. Until then, I prefer that we keep our meetings as brief and professional as possible. And this little agreement of ours will become null and void if I find out you are holding anything back from me about the sale of the hotel. Understood?"

"Understood," he agreed, holding out his hand for her to shake. When her arms remained at her sides, he cocked his head. "What? This is a business deal. Let's shake on it." When she continued to stare at his hand, he warily asked, "We *do* have a deal, right?"

"Temporarily," she amended as she placed her hand in his.

Her grip was warm, her fingers slightly gritty from handling the sand. Heat traveled up his arm, as if there were lights being turned on one by one, and he dropped her hand in an instant.

He coughed into his fist to hide how shaken he was. "Okay, then. So...when do we start this southern conversion of yours?"

"Tomorrow."

"Why tomorrow?" he asked, embarrassed how whiny he sounded. *You're Ian Hollowell*, he reminded himself. *The Predator. You're the one always in control of business.*

"Ian?" Loni asked, "Did you hear what I said?"

He shook himself out of his pep talk, feeling as if he'd lost control of the situation again. "I'm sorry, what did you say?"

"I said we're meeting tomorrow so it'll give you time to buy a wetsuit."

He frowned when he caught her trying—and failing—to hide a smile. "And why would I need a wetsuit?"

"Because we're going surfing tomorrow morning and although the water temperature is fairly warm, you'll get chilled because of the cooler air temperature. Have you ever surfed before?"

"I've seen the movie *Soul Surfer*. Does that count?"

She let out her smile then, a real honest-to-goodness smile and it was like sunshine bursting through a rain cloud complete with a full-on rainbow tied at the end.

"It does *not* count," she said, shaking her head. "Meet me here at seven. I saw the wave report and they're predicting nice clean waves tomorrow morning. At least waves *you* should be able to handle, anyway. I would rest up to be on the safe side. And don't eat any strange-looking omelets," she tossed over her shoulder as she walked away.

Disquieting thoughts began to race through his mind, and it took him almost a full minute to get moving. She did it again. She turned the tables of his negotiation on him. Ian wasn't sure how the hell that happened, but for a brief moment, he wondered if enduring another death-defying pepper omelet would have been the easier option than what she had in store for him.

Chapter Ten

The next morning Loni was surprised to see Ian in board shorts, a long-sleeved tee, and flip-flops already waiting for her in the lobby. As she suggested, he had a shorty wetsuit with him that was draped over his arm. He stood tall and straight and looked amazingly refreshed despite the accommodations she knew all too well that he was staying in. The corners of his mouth kicked up as soon as he saw her and a jumpy feeling awakened in the pit of her stomach.

Loni still wasn't so sure of what to make of Ian. The whole wanting to get to know the town better didn't sit right with her, but she couldn't quite dismiss him as the barracuda she once thought he was, either. She appreciated the help in going through her mama's letters. Plain and simple, Ian had been kind to her yesterday. And funny, too. He was much nicer to her than she deserved. She had needed someone to talk to—a friend—after that horrendous phone call with Blaze. She still couldn't believe she'd hung up on him! What had gotten into her? She had officially ended her engagement and had potentially thrown her already jeopardized career completely out the window and hadn't looked back. She should really be spending time getting her resume in order instead of spending time with Ian. Loni's only hope right now was that her friend Catherine could be her eyes and ears for her at the office while she was back home. Maybe there was still a chance she could salvage both the resort and her job. Blaze was a lost cause.

Loni walked up to Ian. "You're here," she said for lack of something better to say.

"Did you really think I'd bail on you?"

No. She didn't think that in the least. Ian Hollowell definitely seemed a man true to his word, which was why she was going to pay careful attention to whatever he said to her from this moment on.

She shrugged. "I don't know you well enough to answer that," she half lied.

His grin widened. "Hopefully we can rectify that."

"Easy, lover boy." She placed a hand over his chest—which was totally the wrong thing to do, because his chest, even through the tee shirt, felt warm and solid and well…very male. "I'm immune," she lied. *Ha!*

"Then why are you still touching me?"

Loni realized with a start that she *was* still touching him. Dammit. She pulled her hand back in a huff. "Just making sure you know the boundaries."

"And reminding yourself of those boundaries in the process?"

Damn him. "Let's go," she said tersely. "I told Kalinda I'd be at the café by eight-thirty."

He glanced at her attire of jean shorts and tee shirt over her bathing suit. "Where's *your* wet suit?"

"Roy has one waiting for me if I need one."

His brows lifted. "Roy?"

"Roy Bennis. He will be your surf instructor."

"But I thought you were going to be my instructor."

She laughed. "Just because I know how to surf doesn't make me a teacher. Roy has a surf class going on right now and is doing me a personal favor by allowing you to join in on it." *And keep you completely distracted.* "For free I might add."

"What a prince," he muttered.

Loni was about to tell Ian that Roy really was a nice guy, but the fact that Roy seemed to still be sporting a crush on her probably did influence his generosity a tad bit. "Don't worry. I'll be with you every step of the way." She put on her sunglasses and opened the door. "Come on, Moondoggie."

He followed her out. "What's a Moondoggie?"

"Seriously?" She stopped and gave him a dubious glance. "You're older than me so I figured you would have at least heard of that reference." When he shook his head, she continued. "My parents used to be big fans of the old movies, especially surf movies like *Gidget* with James Darren. Moondoggie is Gidget's boyfriend in the series."

He gave her a rakish grin. "Oh. In that case definitely call me Moondoggie."

She laughed. "I wouldn't get ahead of yourself. Let's see if you can actually surf first."

They walked past the pool area and down the path toward the beach. Roy had about seven teenagers in his class. All the surfboards were on the sand and the kids were lying on their stomachs on them, pretending to paddle.

"Hi, Roy," she called with a wave. "Here's one more student for you."

Roy glanced over his shoulder and Loni caught his frown when he looked at Ian. But he waved back and jogged over to them.

Loni pointed to Ian. "Roy, this is my...um..." Who was Ian exactly? He wasn't necessarily a friend. *My guest? My enemy? My* frenemy *who I happen to find extremely attractive?*

"Ian Hollowell," Ian finished for her, sticking out his hand to Roy.

Roy shook his hand but appeared to be sizing him up. "So whatcha y'all doing here, Ian Hollowell—just on vacation in our good ole town?"

"Among other things," Ian said.

Roy stepped closer to Loni's side, his frown growing harder. "What *other* things?"

"Surfing!" Loni blurted, grabbing Roy's arm lightly and noticing his bicep wasn't half as beefy as Ian's. "Ian wants to learn to surf like a real local. Remember? You said you'd do me this favor?"

Roy turned to her, and his tone softened. "Yeah, of course I remember. Anything for you, Lon. You know that."

She smiled, trying to strike a balance between politeness and gratitude so he wouldn't read anything more into it. The last thing she wanted to do was feed his crush. "Do you have a surfboard for him?"

"Yeah, I got an extra soft board for you. Y'all can join the others over there," he told Ian. "We'll go over paddling methods and how to stand up on a surfboard in the sand before we take you out on the actual white water."

"Sounds easy enough," Ian said pleasantly.

Roy snorted. "Yeah, we'll see, Kook."

Ian took a step forward, almost getting right in Roy's face.

"Who are you calling a *kook*?"

"Easy, big fella," Loni said, getting in between them and pushing Ian back toward the other surfers. "It's just surf slang."

Ian's stance relaxed and she dropped her arms. Sheesh, time was ticking, and it was way too early in the morning to be dealing with Roy's jealousy and Ian's ego. "Roy is just joking around with you," she explained. She pinned a hard gaze at Roy, showing him that she meant business. "Weren't you, Roy?"

"Yeah, I like to kid around," Roy grunted, looking ironically ill-humored for someone who was supposedly joking. "It's a southern thing. You wouldn't get it."

"Wonderful, Ian accepts your apology!" Loni blurted. She grabbed Ian's hand and began pulling him away. "Oh, look, I see your board over there. Come, Ian."

"What's his problem?" Ian whispered heatedly to her as they walked over to the empty surfboard on the sand. "Am I still being hazed or something?"

"No hazing. You must just naturally bring it out in people."

"Ah." Ian glared back at Roy. "Old boyfriend then?"

She huffed out a breath. "We went to high school together. Roy's practically a brother to me. Since you're a stranger, I'm sure he's just being protective as most brothers would be. It's a southern thing."

"Hmm," he grumbled.

When they reached their spot, Ian immediately took off his tee shirt and dropped it to the ground despite the comfortable lower seventies temperature. Loni's gaze traveled over Ian's muscular chest and for the briefest of moments, she had the urge to reach out again and explore the texture of all that tanned, smooth skin. A Mount Olympus of muscle.

Loni swallowed hard. Not the kind of thoughts she wanted

to be having at this time of day with this kind of man.

"And what exactly is a kook anyway?" he asked, with a roll of his shoulders.

She forced her gaze away from his chest. "Oh, uh, it basically means someone who has an exaggerated perception of his/her surf skills. Like I said, it's a very common term to use. Roy was just teasing you."

Ian looked doubtful but dropped to his knees and began copying the moves of the other surfers.

"Make sure you keep your back arched and your elbows high for maximum drive," Roy called out to them, walking to the front of the class again.

"I'd sure like to elbow him," she heard Ian mutter.

Loni did her best to hide her smile and moved to stand back a little while Roy demonstrated the next part of the lesson: the pop-up technique. She had to admit, Ian was taking the lesson in stride, considering he was the oldest of the group and Roy wasn't exactly the most patient of teachers with him. But Ian had an athletic physique and natural sure-footed balance that would most likely do him well when actually out in the ocean. Plus, for a city guy, Ian sure looked the part of a surfer. Damn him.

The corner of his lips tugged when he looked up and caught her watching. "What do you think? Moondoggie material?"

Loni wrinkled her nose at him. "Not quite yet," she lied but couldn't help approaching him again, just to see his form of course.

His gaze fell to her mouth, taking its time finding its way back up to her eyes. "When do you think I'll be Moondoggie material then?"

Was this more than flirting? Lordy, it'd been so long since anyone had flirted with her she barely recognized it. She stopped herself. *Flirting? With Ian? What was she doing?* She quickly took a step back. "You're goofy-footed," she blurted.

Smooth, Loni.

He frowned. "Excuse me?"

She pointed to his stance. "It's more natural to stand with your left foot in front, but you're standing with your right foot forward. That's called being goofy-footed."

"Is that bad?"

"No," she said with a laugh. "It's whatever feels most comfortable. I'm actually goofy-footed, too."

"Well," he said, grinning down at her, "I feel much better then to be in such good company."

"Let's go, Yankee!" Roy called to him. "Put your leash on. We're heading out to the water now."

Ian leaned down and murmured in her ear, "What the heck is a leash?"

She pointed to the strap attached to his surfboard. "Attach that Velcro strap around your right ankle. This way if you fall off, you won't lose your board." *When* you fall off, she mentally corrected. She could only hope to witness that, too.

He did as she said, and she couldn't help but admire the way the muscles in his back moved as he bent down and fiddled with the leash. Yes, she seemed to be a glutton for punishment, but she figured there was no harm in looking as long as she wasn't touching—as tempted as she was.

"You coming, too?" Ian asked her when he stood back up.

She shook her head. "Nope. You're on your own."

"You're leaving me already?"

"Wouldn't dream of it." She pulled out her cell phone from her back pocket and waved it in front of him. "I do need to go to the café soon, but this needs to be documented first. Wouldn't want you to forget your whole North Carolina experience." Plus, a picture or two of Ian getting hit in the head with a surfboard would just about make her year.

He surprised her then by reaching out and tucking a strand of her wind-tangled hair behind her ear. "Oh no, you're mistaken about that. I won't need any pictures to remember this at all."

We'll see about that.

Loni muttered some foul words to herself as she made her way back up the path to the hotel. Ian didn't fall off the board once. Surprisingly enough, he took to surfing like he was born and bred at the beach. Where did he get such great balance? Watching him surf made her yearn to get in the ocean herself. Maybe she'd have time to try some real waves with him this week.

Take him out surfing with me? She almost stumbled forward. What the heck? Oh no. The whole point of the surfing lesson was to knock him down a peg, wear him down until he was too sore to move and completely distract him from snooping around the resort. But that didn't appear to be happening. *She* was the one getting distracted instead! She certainly was *not* going to help him enjoy surfing even more and she definitely didn't plan on spending that kind of time alone with him.

Enemies, she reminded herself. *Enemies, Loni.*

"You-hoo! Is that you, Apollonia?" She heard someone call.

Loni turned and saw Angela Canter, her parents' friend and longtime neighbor. Angela was a stylish woman, who still wore her platinum blond hair in a chin-length bob. She was probably close to seventy by now, but still held a youthful figure that she attributed to many years of beach yoga. The woman was practically a second mother to Loni and her sisters and was a complete sweetheart to her family, sending over meals weekly when their mom was undergoing chemo.

"Hi, Mrs. Canter," Loni said, giving the woman a warm hug.

"Oh, honey, please call me Angela. You're too old to be calling me Mrs. Canter and more importantly, I'm way too young," she said with a chuckle.

"Of course," Loni said, smiling. "I forgot, *Angela*."

"I didn't know you'd be visiting now. You should have called."

"Yeah, well, it was kind of a spur-of-the-moment decision," she said feebly, thinking of the mess she was in with her job and Blaze and the hotel on the brink of a new owner.

"Is your handsome boyfriend here, too?" she asked, scouting the beach for him.

"Uh, no. He's partly the reason why I'm back visiting. We broke up."

Angela's brows lifted. "Well, if that don't make my bladder splatter, I'm not sure what would surprise me more. He was a dear the last time I met him, if not a little tightly wound. But you seemed happy together."

Loni sighed. "Yeah, I guess seeming happy isn't quite the same as truly being happy."

"Amen to that," she said, patting Loni's shoulder. "Never settle. Besides, a pretty and intelligent woman like yourself won't be alone for long."

"Oh, I'm not looking," she protested. "A little alone time

is exactly what I want for the time being." Her mind drifted to Ian and the sexy way he had looked at her before carrying his surfboard into the water and Loni wondered if her nose was growing.

Right then and there, Loni made a promise to herself to avoid him the rest of the day. No sense in taking this so-called truce too far.

Angela took her hand in hers. "Now tell me, how's your sweet daddy doing? I haven't seen him around these parts in ages."

The idea that her father was not only keeping a distance from their town and sisters, but also someone who had been considered a good friend, additionally concerned her. "I suppose he's doing all right. I'm not sure if Marise or Kalinda has said anything to you yet, but um, Daddy's engaged. To be married," she added as if it needed further explanation.

Angela startled a little. "Oh no, I hadn't heard. Well, that *is* surprising but not unexpected."

She shot Angela a look. "Why is it not unexpected? Did my mama and daddy have marriage problems?"

The memory of the letters and that mysterious TJ suddenly loomed large in her mind.

Angela chuckled. "Honey, calm down. Your parents set the gold standard for wedding vows. Everybody in town knew that. Plus, they had the magic of the resort behind them as well. They firmly believed the resort granted good luck to those who honeymooned there. I'm just saying that your daddy is a handsome man. He should find love again. It's wonderful news."

"Is it?"

"I can see maybe not so much on your end," Angela said

with a sympathetic smile. "How do your dear sisters feel about it?"

"Pretty much the same as me." Although maybe Loni had taken it a bit harder of the three. As much as she wanted to see her father happy, how he went about announcing it and everything tied to his engagement just didn't sit well with her. Plus, it was hard to imagine anyone ever replacing her mama. But now, with these love letters Ian found, Loni didn't know what to think anymore.

"Well, speaking of marriage, don't forget my Ansley is gettin' married next year. She's decided to have the wedding here in Sunny Banks, too."

"That's fantastic. Now, I'm looking forward to it even more." Ansley and Marise had been in the same grade in school and had been the best of friends since ninth grade. Loni wouldn't be surprised if her sister was in the wedding party.

Angela bit her lip. "I sure do hope Kalinda feels the same way."

"Kalinda? Why wouldn't she...?" Then it hit Loni. "Oh, I see. I guess that means Clarke is coming back to Sunny Banks for the wedding?"

Angela nodded slowly.

Lord, have mercy on everyone's souls then. Kalinda and Clarke had started dating in high school and were together for as long as Loni could remember. Their relationship had endured through college, even after Clarke went out of state and Kalinda remained in state at Purdue University for her culinary major. The two of them had talked about getting engaged right after graduation. Then something happened. Without warning, Clarke ended things. Loni had been away at her own college at the time so wasn't privy to what was going on then. She still didn't know what exactly happened, only that Kalinda had been devastated and even demanded the family never bring up Clarke's name again.

Loni and Angela stood in silence for a few moments. "I guess Kalinda knows?" Loni asked, already guessing she did since Marise and Ansley were still close.

"Yeah, she does."

Loni blew out a long breath. That sure did explain her sister's unusually surly attitude. Loni had just thought it was the stress of Daddy and the hotel.

"But Kalinda seems to be right as rain with it all," Angela explained. "She always was the mature one of you three."

Mature? Loni wanted to tell Angela all about Kalinda's "grown-up" idea to shove extra hot peppers in a man's omelet without him knowing, but it would only warrant further explanation as to why Loni's equally "mature" response was to readily agree to it.

Loni gave a noncommittal shrug. "Kalinda has her moments."

"Oh, and, honey," Angela said, squeezing her hand, "you can rest assured that I'll be telling everyone coming into town for the wedding to stay at The Sandy Bottom."

Loni's stomach dropped. If only she could be sure The Sandy Bottom would still be in existence by then.

Angela frowned. "Darlin,' what on earth has you looking paler than a pearl in an oyster?"

"I'm surprised one of my sisters hasn't told you already."

"Told me what?" she asked, clutching the neckline of her blouse.

"Daddy recently told us he wants to sell the hotel."

"What?" The woman jammed both hands on her hips. "Your

mama would be spittin' fire if she heard that kind of talk."

"That's exactly what I told him! But he just refuses to listen and even sent this grim reaper big shot developer to come and check out the property so he can buy it, bulldoze it, and make all his builder friends rich in the process."

Just saying it out loud made her angry with Ian all over again. And even more angry with herself for getting sidetracked by that hot surfer body of his.

Angela gasped. "Don't you worry, we'll set your daddy straight and send that no-good developer back to where he was born."

"Oh, thank you, Angela," she said, squeezing her hand. "I knew I could count on you."

"Loni!" she heard a male voice call out. Loni knew it was Ian even before she had turned her head. The surf lesson was apparently over already, and he was walking back up to her— still shirtless and dripping wet in all his glistening tan-skinned virtue.

"My, my," Angela said, growing flushed and then fanning herself with her hand. "Who is that fine-looking gentleman? Don't tell me he's your new beau."

"Not a chance," she murmured. "Not even close. *That*, uh, happens to be the developer Daddy sent."

A shadow of a smile crossed Angela's lips as she turned back toward Ian. "Honey, if that's true, y'all are in trouble and going to Hell in a handbasket."

Wonderful. Because *that* was exactly what Loni was afraid of.

Chapter Eleven

Ian brushed his wet hair off his forehead and picked up his pace to where Loni stood with an older woman at the start of the boardwalk. Surprisingly enough, Ian had a good time in Roy's surf class despite their initial rough start. Ian had even managed to stand up on his board a few times and ride some short waves onto the shore. Best yet, he'd managed not to look like a total *kook*.

Roy even shook his hand at the end of class and took down his cell number. The instructor told him that the hotel had some free surfboards he could use whenever he wanted so he could practice, and Roy had also said he'd text him when there was an offshore wind and the waves were clean.

Whatever that meant.

"Hey," he said now, smiling up at Loni. He liked how the sun shone on her light blond hair, giving it and her an almost ethereal glow. He gestured to his body, dripping wet from the many times he fell off his board. "I forgot a towel." Thank goodness that although the air was cool, the sun was already baking hot.

Loni frowned as her gaze traveled the length of him. "Right. I should have reminded you."

With the appreciative way Loni was looking at his body, Ian was glad she hadn't.

The woman next to her cleared her throat, and Loni startled as if she'd forgotten the woman was even there. "Oh, uh, Angela Canter meet Ian Hollowell. Angela was our neighbor growing up. You both are friends with my daddy."

"Charmed," Ian said, taking the woman's hand in his. "What is it about this southern air that makes the women around here so beautiful?"

Loni snorted when Angela preened.

"So happy to meet any friend of Joe's...and Apollonia's," Angela said, taking his hand cautiously so as to not get water on her.

"We're not friends," Loni cut in. "We're acquaintances."

When Angela's brow rose, Ian added, "Friendly acquaintances. It's the next phase of our relationship."

"There's no *relationship*," Loni said, back to being annoyed with him.

Angela cleared her throat, failing to hide her amusement. "So, I hear you've got some big plans for The Sandy Bottom."

He glanced at Loni's guilty face before answering. "No plans yet, ma'am."

Angela eyed him as if she was trying to decide whether to believe him or not. "Well, for what it's worth, you should know The Sandy Bottom is practically a historic landmark. Lots of famous people vacationed here. Back in the eighties Dionne Warwick even stayed for a weekend. It was all the buzz in town then."

Loni's eyes widened. "Wow, I had no idea."

Ian narrowed his eyes, now wondering whether to believe Angela or not. "Any pictures to back that up?" he asked.

Angela seemed amused at his question. "Honey, you can go down to the library and look up the articles for yourself."

He definitely would. But he'd probably just google them. And ask Joe about it, too. If he decided to take on the property that kind of information might skew public opinion on whether the hotel should remain or if something else could be built in its place.

"Interesting history," Ian remarked casually. "But I'm still just trying to get an idea of the area as well as the property."

Angela raised a thin eyebrow at him. "And you were doing that in the ocean?"

Ian frowned. "Huh?"

"How did you enjoy your surf lesson?" she asked him with a grin.

"Oh. It was great." He made an exaggerated move of gazing out along the beach. "Figured it couldn't hurt to get in a little R and R. I could totally see myself getting used to the culture down here."

"I wouldn't get *too* used to it," Loni shot.

Angela chuckled. "If you like it so much, Ian, you should come by my house and check out all the seashell gifts I've been making to sell at The Beach Bash next week. Maybe you'd want to pick up a little souvenir for your...girlfriend?"

"*Angela*," Loni admonished.

"What?" the woman asked in exasperation. "Sorry. The man could certainly pick up a souvenir for his boyfriend as well."

Ian grinned. "No boyfriend or girlfriend, ma'am." He cast a

side-glance at Loni and she blushed.

"Excellent," Angela said brightly, "then you can pick a souvenir for yourself. But you better come soon. Word of mouth is spreading, and I can barely collect shells fast enough to meet the demands of my orders."

"I'd be happy to go seashell collecting for you," Loni offered. "In fact, I'd love to. I haven't done that since I was in grade school with my mama."

"I'll help, too," Ian blurted, then froze.

What. Did. He. Just. Say?

Seashell collecting?

Did he really just offer to do that? Ugh. Now look what the south had made him do. The Predator was turning soft. Before he knew it, he'd probably be creating poems about love and downloading Joni Mitchell songs to his music playlist.

Loni clearly thought the same. She shook her head, giving him a glare to end all glares. "You don't have to do that, Ian. I'm sure you've got better things to do with your free time. Much. Better. Things. Perhaps even a trip to the library, as Angela suggested."

"Nonsense, sugar," Angela said, touching Loni's shoulder. "It's too lovely out to be cooped up in a library. If Ian wants to take a beach walk with you and help you collect shells, you should let him. It'll save me even more time with the two of you. The baskets can get so heavy, and Ian looks as if he has some capable arms."

Ian raised his bicep and flexed it for good measure. "Yeah, seashells can get heavy, Loni. It'll be good exercise for me, too. Wouldn't want these babies getting flabby on me."

"Child, something tells me your body doesn't know what the word flabby is," Angela crooned.

Loni folded her arms with a pout. "I hardly think seashell collecting will keep you toned."

"Then think of it as adding to my North Carolina experience," he quipped.

Angela clapped. "Oh yes. The shells you'll see on this beach will knock your breeches off. Or at least, Loni should be so lucky if that happens..." she murmured, giving Loni a wink.

Loni threw her hands up. "Fine, you can come. Best time to collect is low tide."

"When's that?" he asked, hoping it would be sooner rather than later.

"Tide is going out the rest of the day," Angela offered. "Probably mid to late afternoon would be best."

Ian saluted them. "I'll be ready. I'll just bide my time doing push-ups in my room until summoned."

Loni rolled her eyes, then glanced at her phone. "I'm going to be late," she said, not looking entirely as happy with the prospect of spending the afternoon with him as he was. "I need to go help out at the café. See you both later." Then with a quick wave, she jogged the rest of the way up the path and into the hotel.

"Be careful today on your walk, sugar," Angela told him once Loni was a good distance away.

He dragged his gaze away from Loni's retreating figure and looked at the older woman with some confusion. "I had no idea seashell collecting was so dangerous around here," he said with a sardonic grin.

"No, it's not, sugar. But you mess with my girl or her hotel, and you'll be seeing trouble worse than if you had your pockets full of fish chum in a sea of tiger sharks."

Ian swallowed hard. The woman's tone was sweet as honey,

but the fierce mama-bear spark in her eyes left him in no doubt of such consequences. *Southern women...*

"Are we clear?" she asked pointedly.

And although Ian was unclear about what exactly was going on between him and Loni and how it affected the sale of the hotel or his relationship with Joe, he understood this woman's warning and was smart enough to know that she wouldn't let him leave until she had some kind of answer from him.

"Crystal clear," he murmured.

• • •

Loni didn't know what was making her rush faster to the café: her need to get away from Ian or her fear of Kalinda's wrath if she showed up too late to work. Most likely a combination of the two, and as a result she almost knocked Marise into a wall as soon as she reached the café doors.

"Hey, slow down, speedy," Marise said, bracing herself against the doorway. "Lose track of time or something?"

Loni tucked her tee shirt in the front of her shorts and glanced up in alarm. "Huh?" she asked. Did Marise know where she'd been? Had her sister seen her? "Wh-what do you mean? Why would I lose track of time?"

"I saw you on the beach earlier," Marise said, giving her a crafty smile. "I thought you and Roy were just friends." She wagged her eyebrows up and down suggestively.

Loni almost collapsed in relief. "Ha! Me and Roy. Right. I guess you caught me."

Marise nodded. "I thought so. All that denial didn't fool me one bit. Daddy always said you were the book smart one, but I'm the one who could rival Agatha Christie."

"Oh, yes. That's for—"

"I mean some people would automatically think you and Ian were a thing, for example."

Loni blinked. "Um, think what?"

"Some people might think you and Ian had something going on, because he was down there on the beach, too. But that would be considered one of those red herrings in a mystery novel."

Loni felt nauseous. "Red herring?" she murmured.

"Yeah, that's a clue that's—"

"I know what a red herring is!" Loni snapped.

Marise huffed out a breath. "Well, gee whiz, you don't need to get all huffy about it, miss know-it-all. All I'm saying is that you and Ian together is way too ridiculous, especially with the way you've been torturing him, and I thought you might find it funny that Lucille asked me if you had a thing for him."

"Lucille?" Good Lord. Everyone seemed against her. *Take a breath, Loni.* Really, why was she so nervous? She shouldn't have anything to hide from anyone.

Shouldn't being the key word there.

Marise chuckled. "I know. Crazy, right? Lucille told me Ian had planned to go back to Boston yesterday, but something or *someone* must have changed his mind. She weirdly automatically assumed it had to do with you."

"Th-that *is* crazy," she spluttered. "I want him gone as much as everyone else does. Why would I want to encourage him to stay?" Loni suddenly felt the pangs of an oncoming headache.

Marise nodded. "That's what I told her."

"That's what you told whom?" Kalinda asked, coming up alongside them.

"Nothing," Loni blurted. "We're just talking nonsense."

Kalinda arched an eyebrow. "Well, it can't be too

unimportant if you're standing here talking about it when you should be helping me wait tables."

"I was just telling Loni that our plan didn't work," Marise told her. "It looks as though Ian isn't leaving."

Kalinda glanced at Marise, looking more curious than unhappy. "Really? He's staying, huh?"

Marise shrugged. "That's what Lucille said. One minute he was all set to pack his bags, the next he was taking a surf lesson. Weird, huh? I thought that pepper omelet of yours was the absolute cherry on top."

Loni felt her cheeks grow warm. "Well, uh, maybe he couldn't get a flight, so he just decided to stick it out."

"That could be it," Kalinda agreed. "Weekend flights get booked pretty quick."

"We'll just have to think of more ways to torture the man," Marise said with a sly grin. "Itching powder in his bed sheets, anyone?"

Loni laughed. "I'm not against that idea." Besides, it's not as if she promised Ian that she wouldn't still try to get him to leave.

"Whatever you guys decide is fine," Kalinda said, giving the "one more minute" sign to Duke. "I'm out. By the way, did your firm give you the extra time off you asked for? Hazel can come back to work, but she can't get around too well. I figured I'd just stick her on counter service and the register."

Loni averted her gaze. "Oh, yeah, they did. Um, got at least two weeks. Maybe longer." *Unfortunately.*

"Wow, you are clearly selling yourself short as an attorney," Kalinda said in awe. "You must have a lot of pull over there. Lucky for us you're on our side."

When Marise and Kalinda happily high-fived each other,

Loni decided to just let them believe what they wanted about her work situation. Besides, they all had enough to deal with and she didn't want to add another thing for them to worry about. She'd figure out what to tell them about her job when the time was right.

"I ran into Angela," Loni said, trying to change the subject. "She told me about Ansley's wedding." But when Kalinda's face fell, Loni realized her slip in reminding her sister about Clarke.

"Oh, I'm so glad you saw her," Marise gushed. "Angela asks about you all the time. Did she tell you that sometimes she comes and hosts wineglass painting classes for our guests?" Marise went on as Kalinda stiffened. "They're very popular with the guests, especially when the weather isn't cooperating. In July, she was teaching everyone to paint sea turtles. I thought it might be fun for her to do a class for all of Ansley's bridesmaids and paint something wedding related on the glasses. We could make it a wine party. Doesn't that sound fun?"

Kalinda glanced away. "Yeah. Sounds like a blast," she murmured. "Angela must be thrilled that *one* of her children is getting married and in Sunny Banks, too, since the other one seems to be so dead set against it. It'll be the event of the year, I'm sure."

Loni and Marise exchanged concerned looks. "Hey, I'm sorry," Loni said, resting a hand on Kalinda's back. "I didn't mean to bring up the wedding."

Kalinda smiled tightly. "No, relax. It's no problem. I am happy for Ansley. Everyone should know that I have nothing against her or Angela. Clarke is the dickweed and just because Ansley happens to have an asshat for a brother, it doesn't mean you can't talk about her or the wedding or the fact that said asshat is coming back to town to attend it. It's all *fine!*"

Well.

Loni couldn't speak for Marise, but she, for one, was never assured that everything was *not* fine more than that very moment.

"Whew," Marise said, sounding unconvinced as well. "Glad to hear it."

Kalinda pointed to a young couple, holding hands, who had just walked in and were standing by the PLEASE WAIT TO BE SEATED sign. "Let's go. I can't afford to get dragged into talking nonsense with you two." Her gaze darted to Loni. "You coming?"

"I'm right behind you," she said.

Kalinda stormed off, grabbing two menus, and immediately seated the couple at Loni's station.

"Me and my big mouth," Loni muttered. "She'll be a pleasure to work with all morning now."

"Well, that sinks it," Marise stated decisively. "We're taking her out tonight."

Loni snorted. "Oh, really? Where exactly do you want to take her? There are no bars in Sunny Banks. Unless the dry laws have changed while I've been away."

"No. Unfortunately. Not yet. But I know a place," Marise said, rubbing her hands together. "There are some good spots that have opened up in the surrounding towns. Let me just make sure Lucille can cover tonight and then the rest is easy."

"I'm not so sure about this."

Her sister gave her a quizzical look. "I'm even more sure now. We *all* could use a night out before Daddy arrives. Think of it as therapy—only wearing stilettos," Marise said, throwing an arm around Loni's shoulders. "Come on. The three sunshine sisters raising some hell again. What do y'all say?"

Loni smiled. They hadn't referred to themselves as the sunshine sisters in a long time. Their mother's love of Sunny Banks inspired her to give her daughters names that reflected the sun in some way or meaning. Her name, Apollonia, meant "belonging to Apollo" the god of the Sun.

Still, Loni wasn't exactly in the mood to go out, not with so much on her mind regarding the hotel, Blaze, her job, and those damn letters. But poor Kalinda. She definitely needed a little cheering up, and who knew? Maybe Kalinda would even meet someone, which would be just the thing to get her mind off of Clarke. Plus, getting out of town sounded like the perfect solution to Loni's recent preoccupation with Ian.

"Sure." Loni grinned and hugged her sister back. "As they say in Napa, wine not?"

Chapter Twelve

Before Ian could set foot in the lobby, Lucille was at his service with several towels in her hands.

"Oh my," she said, her eyes roaming his chest, "Loni said you'd gone surfing and forgot a towel, but this is a bigger treat than I'd expected."

As flattered as he was, Lucille eyeing him up didn't quite have the same effect on him as when Loni had done it.

He gave her a tight smile. "Appreciate the towel," he said, reaching for it.

She pulled it out of his reach. "Oh, of course, we can't have you parading around here all bare-chested and wet and all... well, *you*." She let out a giggle that was far too young sounding for someone her age. "Allow me to dry you off, sugar."

Ian jerked back. "Just a towel is fine, Lucille."

She pouted. "But I'm trying to give you exemplary service."

Unfortunately, *that's* what he was afraid of.

Ian held out his hand. "Look, you're doing fine work, but all I need is one towel. Nothing else."

"Fine." Lucille handed it to him with a large sigh. "You Yankees are about as fun as an army of ants at a picnic."

He smiled. "Exactly why it would never work between us."

"Is that the reason or does it have anything to do with a certain blond catchin' your eye?"

Ian stopped drying himself off and looked up. "What?"

Lucille lightly shoved him. "I've seen the way you look at our Loni. Boy, you are asking for trouble. She ain't ever going to look at you twice while you're entertaining buying this hotel. You're lucky she didn't drown you already."

"I don't understand why I'm the bad guy here. Joe is the one who wants to sell. I'm just the middleman." *Keep telling yourself that*, Ian thought. *Who hopped on a plane instantly at the sound of a good deal?*

"Maybe." Lucille folded her arms. "It doesn't help that you're an outsider. People in this town remember Loni's mother, Sandra Wingate. This hotel helped their businesses grow. That's not something people here take lightly."

No, Ian suspected that much to be true, especially in a small town the size of Sunny Banks. But that didn't mean that Ian's company couldn't develop the land into something that would bring in even more business to the area. "Joe has to realize what the town would think about him selling."

"I'm sure he does, which is why he hasn't had the guts to show his face here and decided to let you be the sacrifice," she snickered.

Ian shrugged. Joe was a mild-mannered man. Probably didn't have the heart to face his daughters or the town even though it would be the best for everyone all around. "Joe knows I can take it. I have a knack for leaving emotions at the door in situations like these."

Lucille narrowed her eyes, which were filled with skepticism mixed with humor. "Even if Loni can't?"

"Why does Loni care so much about this building?" He shook his head. "I mean, it's just a bunch of bricks and wood."

Lucille gave him a sympathetic smile. "Sugar, this is more than that to the girls. It's a home. But for Loni, especially, it was a refuge."

"What do you mean?"

"Never easy being the middle child. The poor thing had a heck of a time getting any attention as I recall. I think that's why she believes that old superstitious yarn her mama spun on this place."

"Superstition? Joe never mentioned anything like that."

"That's because he never believed in the power the resort had on love for anyone who stayed here." She shrugged. "Although, hard to argue with facts."

"Facts? You mean like it could be true? Are you actually saying this hotel has some kind of spell on it?"

She patted his arm. "That's something you're going to have to dig out of Loni. Not my hotel. Not my place to tell."

Ian frowned, wondering if he was reaching the point of no return with Loni with his false pretense of trying to help her. He was out of his league when it came to family or emotional ties—and especially superstitions.

Lucille laughed. "Relax, Ian. No one is sending you to the guillotine. Not yet anyway."

No, but in a way, it felt like that's exactly where he was headed. But as much as his inner alarm bells were ringing, he still planned on meeting Loni at the beach this afternoon. He had a job to do after all, and there was still a chance she could listen to reason and understand why her father wanted to sell.

He looked at Lucille with new interest. "How long had you known Joe's wife?"

"Sandra? Oh my, I guess, at least thirty years. Sweetheart of a woman. Devoted mother and wife. She and Joe seemed to have it all until the cancer diagnosis. Such a shame."

Ian didn't comment. Obviously Joe and his wife did not "have it all" but no one—not even their own daughters—was aware of it. "Thanks for the info, Lucille," he said, heading toward the steps. "Oh, and the towel."

"Anytime. And I do mean *any time*," she added with a saucy wink.

. . .

After her shift, Loni picked up two baskets from Angela that she used for collecting shells and walked back to the hotel. People were still sunbathing on the beach and there were a few men surf fishing in front of her family's cottage which was right next door to the hotel. Living so close to The Sandy Bottom came in handy when there was an emergency, or her parents were needed on site for anything. Loni and her sisters had always loved being able to use the hotel swimming pool after school when the weather turned hot, and they had considered many of the workers there like extended family. But more than anything, Loni enjoyed seeing her parents work side by side, laughing, sharing ideas. The hotel brought out the best in their relationship. At least, she *thought* it had. Whatever had happened in the past, Loni supposed it was a true testimony to what Mama had always told her about the good luck the old place brought to those who honeymooned there and how marriages had lasted. As silly as it sounded, Loni had even hoped she and Blaze could spend a few days of their honeymoon here—for luck.

Too late to be needing any luck now.

"Loni," Ian called from the boardwalk, interrupting her thoughts with his rich, deep voice.

She looked up and held in a sigh. Every time his gaze met hers, her heart turned over in response. Why, oh why, did Ian Hollowell have to be so attractive? Was she that much of a glutton for punishment? Did she have a fetish for bad boys or something?

Even still, Loni couldn't help but appreciate the way his long-sleeve tee stretched across his broad shoulders, and she even liked the way he stood there, waiting for her, like he half expected her to rush into his arms where he'd sweep her up and whirl her around.

Gah. Like *that* would ever happen in this century.

Loni took her time approaching, then held out one of the baskets for him. "Here ya go, Little Red Riding Hood."

Ian took the basket and grinned. "How do you know I'm not the wolf?"

Oh, you're definitely one of those... So nice of him to remind her.

"Let's head north," Loni told him, ignoring his question. She refused to fall into those flirty little Venus fly traps of his again. She was going to be all business this afternoon. Collect shells. Check. Give him some stats on North Carolina beaches and wildlife. Check. Deposit him to his closet-sized hotel room without so much as a handshake goodnight. Check and double check.

Ian caught up to her and walked in companionable silence for several beats. "So," he finally said, "what kind of shells does Angela want for her crafts anyway?"

Loni also appreciated how Ian was determined to keep their arrangement all business, too.

"Well, scotch bonnets are the ones you'll see most." She bent down, picked one up and held it out in her palm. "But really, whatever shells we can find that are relatively clean and intact, she can use. There should be some good ones on the wet sand over here," she said, leading the way.

Ian went off and began collecting some on his own. Loni had to admit, it was refreshing to see him take collecting shells so earnestly. Plus, he looked kind of cute with his basket slung over his wrist. Blaze went shell collecting with her once but got bored after the first five minutes and went bodysurfing instead. She had been a little hurt by his actions, especially since she thought it would be nice to just spend some time talking but decided it was too small an instance to make an issue out of it. However, next time—if there *was* a next time with a different man—she *would* make a big deal out of it.

Ian came over to her, holding up his basket with a grin. "Look what I found."

Loni glanced inside his basket and gasped. "Those are lightning whelks," she said, picking one up and admiring it in the sun. She hadn't seen shells that size since a tropical storm when she was a teen. Hundreds of shells had washed up on the beach. She and Kalinda had made pretend phones out of them, acting like they were calling Harry Styles and Niall Horan to invite them to a surprise birthday party for Marise.

"So, let's see," Ian said, his tone playful. "I'm good at surfing and now shell collecting. Maybe I was a North Carolinian in a former life."

"You should be so lucky," she said with a laugh.

"I'm feeling pretty lucky right now." Ian's eyes sparkled

with amusement.

"Well, you're not going to get any luckier," she said with a smirk. "Remember? Taking a break from men."

"Yes, but I don't recall you specifically saying what your feelings were toward a man-child with trust issues," he said, referring to himself.

She laughed. Damn him. Handsome *and* funny were her kryptonite.

Ian's gaze dropped to her mouth as he took a step forward. "See? I'm harmless."

Part of her wanted to believe that but he wasn't the only one with trust issues on this beach. And right now, she definitely didn't trust Ian in the romance department any more than she did in the business department. Although she was desperately tempted.

Remember, we don't trust this guy.

"We better keep moving," she told him, whirling around in the opposite direction. "Angela isn't going to be happy until these baskets are full."

Ian followed next to her. "Have you looked at the rest of those love letters I found?"

"A few." She glanced at him. "I even tried to look through the guest booklets to see if I could match up the initials with any guests staying around that time."

"And?"

"And," she huffed, "it's like putting together an all pink puzzle."

He chuckled. "I told you I'd help you with that."

She licked her lips, torn between wanting his help and not wanting to spend so much time with him. Plus, there was the trust issue. "I'll let you know."

Ian cocked his head at her and seemed to understand her need to change the subject. "So, you and your mom collected shells together a lot when you were growing up?" he asked.

The wind kicked up and she fought to keep several strands of her hair from flying into her mouth as she spoke. "Yes. My mama adored the beach. She loved Sunny Banks and well, anything to do with it and the sun."

"Ah," he said, snapping his fingers. "That's why you and your sisters have the unusual names."

"Unusual?" She shot him a cross look but then had to smile. She couldn't really argue with that. She and her sisters *did* have unique names. All throughout school, they barely needed to use their last name. They were the Cher, Sting, and Madonna of their time.

"Sorry," Ian offered. "I meant that I'm guessing your mom wanted you girls to have meaning to your names."

"Yeah, my mama did everything with passion and meaning, including naming us and even begging my daddy to buy this hotel after they had their honeymoon here." Stopping in front of a bed of shells, she bent down and sifted through a few broken ones until she found a few beauties. She carefully placed them in her basket and stood.

Ian cocked his head at her. "Your parents actually honeymooned at the hotel and then decided to buy it?"

She chuckled at his dubious expression. "It's not as horrible as you think. I think it's quite romantic. My parents didn't exactly come from money. Each of them grew up about an hour from here, but wanted to enjoy the beach scene after they were married. They both fell in love with the place. Mama, wanting to stay close to the water, convinced my daddy to purchase it as an investment. The rest was history." She bit her lip. "Or more like, the rest *will* become history, when the hotel is demolished. That's why I have to try and change Daddy's mind."

"Lucille mentioned that the hotel was a refuge to you growing up."

She rolled her eyes. "Lucille has a wild mouth," she grumbled.

"And don't forget, wild hands."

She tried to hold back a laugh and it came out like a half snort, half choke. "It keeps her young."

Ian smiled back. He then surprised her by reaching out and catching her hand in his as they continued to walk along the beach. And even though her head was telling her to take her hand back, that he was still the enemy, something entirely different going on inside her kept her hand exactly where it was. What was wrong with her? She'd thought herself immune to Ian Hollowell. She hated to admit it, but she was genuinely affected by this man.

"I never had any kind of sole refuge place," he told her. "My dad was an alcoholic who just couldn't keep sober for very long, as much as he did try. Binge drinker was what my mom had explained to me. He wouldn't drink when he had to show up for work then on his days off, he'd spend them drunk. Eventually, he couldn't control the cycle. The cycle controlled him, and he started to miss work. I hated seeing him that way and my mom always trying to get him to stop. Sometimes I'd hang out at a friend's house, sometimes the library, when I could. Wherever I could go to get away."

"Wasn't your mom concerned about where you were?"

"Sometimes." Ian's mouth took on a faint, wry curve. "When her sole focus wasn't on babysitting my dad."

"How long did that go on?"

"Seemed like forever. But as soon as I was eighteen, I got the hell out of there. Never heard from either of them again."

Loni blinked. Ouch. No wonder Ian always left his emotions out of business and personal matters. And no wonder he had problems with relationships past a certain number of dates. An alcoholic's home could be unpredictable. She'd once read children of alcoholics grow up afraid to let their guard down fearing something bad could happen. She knew now that he wasn't kidding when he'd told her that he had trust issues. He never had the experience of a happy home—or even just a home. It made her feel a little sorry for him, and more than a little surprised that he would even share that with her.

"I can't imagine what that must have been like," she said feebly. Despite the imperfections, Loni and her sisters had nothing but special memories of her parents, the resort, and her homelife in Sunny Banks.

He grinned, puffing out his chest. "I think I turned out all right."

She smiled back. "TBD. But I guess no one's life is perfect. Even though I had two sisters, I often struggled with loneliness. When my sisters and I were in high school, Kalinda was always involved with her boyfriend, Clarke, and Marise was involved in high school theatre. I had my books and my mama. Whenever I felt in limbo or lost, Mama asked me to help around with the hotel. I don't know, it may sound stupid to you. But she gave me a purpose here that I'm very grateful for."

He shook his head. "I don't think it's stupid. I think your mom was pretty intuitive. But you're an attorney now. You don't need the hotel to give you a purpose anymore."

No, she supposed she didn't need the hotel in that way. But The Sandy Bottom meant much more to her than that. And being back now made Loni realize even more that it gave her something infinitely dearer than her job in California ever could: home and family.

"Sometimes people need more than a purpose," she told him. "They need love, even just a symbol of it." She had once thought she had both with Blaze. But there had been times, she had tried to open up to him and they couldn't quite connect. Looking back now, she may have confused their shared ambition as love.

Ian scratched his head. "I'm sure you had a lot of great memories together here, but maybe that's why your dad wants to sell. He's getting remarried and maybe—"

"Maybe he wants to forget my mama? You don't know if Daddy knew about Mama's affair and even if he had, they obviously worked things out and their marriage became stronger."

"I guess. But sometimes it's easier to block emotions than deal with them."

"And block your own family in the process?" she said through gritted teeth. "Is that what you're saying?"

"No. Well, yeah. But not—"

"That's a horrible reason to sell." She pulled her hand from his and stopped walking. "Not that you would understand, Mr. Unemotional. My daddy is barely even in town anymore. I don't understand why he would even care so much when Kalinda and Marise are running things here."

Ian set down his basket on the sand and then ran a hand through his hair. "Loni, the place needs updating. If things continue as they are, the hotel could decrease in value. If I were to buy—"

"Just stop right there," she said quietly.

"Please, listen to me." He took a step forward, making a motion to reach for her again, but she jerked away.

"No," she said, proud at how calm she remained. "I think we're done."

He glanced at their half empty baskets. "But we still have room for more shells."

She shook her head. "We're done with everything. Shell collecting and this ridiculous truce. I don't know what I was thinking, trying to get you to understand how I feel."

"Look, you have to understand where I'm coming from."

"Don't bother explaining." She picked up both their baskets. "I'm done wasting my time. I can take you surfing and seashell collecting all you want, but now I see it doesn't really affect you, does it? You're just going through the motions."

She stormed off, more angry with herself than Ian. After all, she was the one who allowed herself to be duped by him.

"Loni, I was only trying to help. I still am trying to help."

Loni stopped walking and before she knew it, a mirthless laugh bubbled out of her throat. "Right. Help. Well, *sugar*, go find yourself another southern sucker to help."

Chapter Thirteen

Loni hadn't anticipated going out for any nights on the town when she'd packed up to come home. The only sundress she brought with her seemed a bit too fancy for what was most likely going to be some dive bar her younger sister, Marise, had suggested. Most of the things she now owned were fine for a big city, but here, she'd stick out like a clown at a funeral. Working with what she had, Loni pulled out her white capri pants and decided to pair them with a strapless peplum top she'd borrowed from Kalinda earlier in the day.

Now, after the scene on the beach with Ian, Loni was glad they were all going out tonight. A little more bonding with her sisters and a little less bonding with Ian was definitely in order. She was so stupid to think she could convince him to change her father's mind about selling the hotel. After their argument today, she now knew Ian was only out for Ian. Period.

Loni had just hoped…

What was it that she'd been hoping for? Obviously, any interest Ian had in her beyond acquiring the resort was a pipedream. *For the best,* she reminded herself.

The last thing she needed was another relationship hot off the heels of her last one. But still…every time she looked around this suite, walked around this hotel, she was reminded of what was lacking in her life.

When her cell phone rang, Loni tossed the capris onto the bed and went to pick it up. Speaking of her old life…

"Hi, Catherine," she said, checking the clock on the nightstand. "What are you doing calling at this hour and on a Friday?"

"I'm on my way out now," she said, sounding out of breath. "But this couldn't wait until Monday."

"What couldn't wait?"

"I heard the two Beckers talking today." She took another breath. "And I heard Mark Becker tell Blaze that you were rude to clients."

"*What?*" The phone began to tremble in Loni's hands. She lowered herself to the bed behind her. "Are you positive?"

"I heard what I heard."

"Did Blaze defend me?"

"Not that I heard. You need to come back to defend yourself."

Loni felt a momentary panic. It was too soon. Daddy hadn't arrived yet and her sisters still needed help. "H-how can I come back? I'm on temporary leave. Catherine, look at it from their perspective. What real evidence do I have? It's his word against mine at this point. And because I sent out that email by mistake, I'm definitely looking the least credible at this point."

Catherine was quiet for a moment. "I guess you're right. This is so messed up. But I would call Becker on Monday. Try to explain yourself. It's just not fair. I'm so sorry."

Loni could hardly believe it herself. Blaze wasn't even

helping her. He had warned her if she'd hung up on him that he'd have her fired—but the betrayal still cut deep. How could she have been so blind? They truly had been happy together. She had to wonder why she was so unworthy of loving relationships with the men in her life. First Daddy and then Blaze and then Ian.

Ian?

She frowned at herself. Why on earth would she lump *Ian* onto that list?

"Hello?" Catherine said into the phone. "Are you still there?"

Loni shook herself. "I…yeah, I'm still here. I guess I'm just…shocked."

"I hear that. I'm sorry I had to be the one to tell you this."

"No," she said, rubbing her forehead, "I'm thankful it was you." There was a knock at her door. "Um, look, I have to go."

"Okay. But you'll call Becker on Monday?"

"I will. Thanks. And if you hear anything else, let me know." After Loni hung up, she rushed to the door.

Marise stood there, striking a pose in the doorway with a hand on her hip and the other behind her head. Her hair, which flowed past her shoulders, was curled in a beach wave fashion. She wore a hot pink tube top with white jeans and as promised, pink spikey heeled shoes. A large white tote was slung over her shoulder.

"How do I look?" she asked, batting her eyes. "Just so you know, I'm not looking to cause fatal heart attacks in the men in our vicinity tonight, just a teensy bit of heart failure."

No doubt her sister would be causing heart attacks tonight. "You look great," she said, numbly turning away.

Marise closed the door behind her and followed her in.

"Hey, what's your problem? And you're not wearing heels. Why aren't you dressed yet? I told Kalinda we'd meet her in the lobby in ten minutes."

Not wanting to make tonight about her, she forced a smile. "Sorry. I got tied up on a call from work."

Marise grinned. "Well, in that case, you're forgiven. You're my idol."

"Why?"

"Because you're out there in the world, doing what you love. I'm so jealous."

Loni frowned. She hardly would call herself "out there" and right now, she was not loving her job at the firm at all. "Don't you like running the hotel?"

Marise walked over to the mirror hanging on the door and smiled into it, checking for lipstick on her teeth. "Sure, I do, but sometimes I want a little more. Maybe even a little creativity. Wouldn't it be cool to add a banquet room to the hotel?"

"Wow, yes. Have you talked to Kalinda about that?"

Marise turned to her with pursed lips. "No. She's always busy. Plus, she's been just so hard to talk to ever since Mama passed."

Loni nodded. She'd noticed it, too, but had attributed it to her breakup with Clarke as well. "Okay, listen, maybe after a few martinis, she'll loosen up and we can broach the topic together."

Marise sent her a grateful smile. "That would be awesome. But if you don't get ready really quick, Kalinda will get tired of waiting and fink out on us for sure." She pointed to Loni's bare feet. "And don't forget the heels. It's part of group therapy. You should see Kalinda's red pumps. It'll give you shoe envy for a week."

Loni chuckled. "Sorry, I didn't pack any."

"I had a feeling." Marise reached into her oversized bag and pulled out a pair of gold, four-inch pumps like a magician pulling a rabbit out of a top hat. "That's why I brought a spare."

When Loni had envisioned a night out with her sisters, she pictured a bar with two pool tables and that country line-dancing. Instead, she got a much more modernized place called Big Daddy Kahuna's that was about twenty minutes away in a nearby shore town. The bar/restaurant had a fun, luau vibe, complete with two bars—one inside and one on the beach, with tiki torches around the outside high-top tables. Popular music played in the background, but a live band was scheduled to go on at ten p.m.

"How did you find this *splace*?" Loni yelled over the crowd and music. Good grief, she'd already had two lemon drop martinis and was already slurring her words. Maybe she should have eaten more. Marise had ordered a bunch of appetizers, but Loni had been so worked up over her conversation with Catherine, that all she could swallow was one BBQ rib and two nacho chips.

Marise winked at the dark-haired bartender who had been giving her sister bedroom eyes ever since they'd walked in, then turned to Loni. "Some friends of mine know the owner." She took a sip of her drink and sighed in appreciation. "They make the best pink gin martinis," she said, swirling the grapefruit rind with her pink nail.

"What's with you and gin drinks all of a sudden?" Kalinda asked. "You were always a wine spritzer kind of girl before."

Marise flipped her blond curls off her shoulder. "My tastes

have matured." She suddenly grabbed Kalinda's forearm. "Ooh, speaking of mature, there is a super-hot guy checking you out right now."

Kalinda made a face. "Eww. Mature? Does he have gray hair?"

Marise laughed. "No, I said mature, not old."

"What's your idea of mature?" Loni asked, searching the area for the man. "Fifty?"

Marise shook her head. "No, like thirty."

Kalinda rolled her eyes. "Oh, well that's perfect then. We can share walkers," she said drily.

Their server came over to them with another round of drinks that Loni hadn't remembered ordering. "Wow, I guess I need to catch up," she said, picking up her half-filled glass and finishing her martini.

"You need to slow down, killer," Kalinda said, moving Loni's drink out of her reach.

"These are from the guy on the left of the bar," the server said, placing each new drink down in front of them. "He said he's infatuated with the blond here."

Marise shoved Kalinda in the shoulder. "Told you that guy was into you."

"We're *all* blond, ding dong. How do you know he isn't infatuated with you or Loni?"

"You mean the senior citizen?" Loni asked with a giggle.

The server looked over her shoulder. "Nah, he looks about thirty-five to me," she commented before heading to the next table.

Loni busted up laughing. Everything was so funny. Oh, how she needed to laugh like this. She wrapped an arm around each of her sisters and squeezed. "I love you guys."

"This isn't good," Marise muttered, her cheek pressed hard against Loni's. "Loni's tipsy already."

Loni pouted. "No, I'm not."

"We saw you when you went to the restroom. You can barely walk," Kalinda said with a laugh.

"No, I think those are the shoes." Marise pointed. "My feet are smaller than hers."

Loni nodded. "True dat. But the shoes are super cute." She reached the newly delivered martini and dragged it on the table her way.

"Wait," Kalinda said, leaning in closer. "Don't drink it. What's the protocol in situations like these? If we drink these drinks, do we have to invite him over?"

Marise cocked an eyebrow at her. "Wow, I can't believe you're so inexperienced for being the oldest."

Kalinda's lips twisted. "I was in a relationship for most of my young adult life. Men didn't send over drinks while I was with Clarke."

Loni winced. She and Marise were fumbling this night badly. They were trying to distract Kalinda from thinking about Clarke, not bring him up. "I think we can just say thank you," she said, mouthing her thanks and waving at the guy.

"Oh, gosh, she's going to encourage him," Kalinda muttered, covering her eyes.

Marise huffed out a breath. "Good. You need to meet someone. Or at the very least get laid."

"I do not want to get laid by some random guy at a bar," Kalinda replied haughtily.

"What about a guy you know?" Marise asked.

"I'm not sleeping with Ian, either."

Loni's mouth fell open. "Who said anything about *Ian*?"

Oops. Did she screech that?

Both of her sisters looked at her. "I was talking about Duke," Marise said, slowly like she was explaining to a child. "Duke is very sweet on our Kalinda here."

Kalinda made a face. "No way."

"Way," Loni countered. "I picked up on it the other day. It's beyond obvious he's lusting after you. If Duke were a cartoon, he'd be drawn with the heart eyes and tongue sticking out the side of his mouth for sure."

"Roy's lusting after Loni and Duke's lusting after Kalinda. It's not fair. How come nobody ever lusts after me?" Marise grumbled.

"I don't know," Kalinda said, nodding her head in the direction of the table at the far end of the room. "Isn't that Sheriff Brennan over there?"

Marise glanced behind her and scowled. "Ugh. What's *he* doing here?"

"I'd say lusting after you," Kalinda offered with a grin.

"That's not lust. I swear Ford always thinks I'm up to no good. He's been treating me like I was twelve ever since… Well, ever since I was twelve!" she said, throwing up her hands in exasperation.

Loni held in a laugh. When Ford Brennan was a teenager, he had worked at the hotel for a few years before he'd entered the police academy. Loni remembered him as a kid who kept to himself, probably more out of shyness than unfriendliness, with sharp angles in his cheekbones from being so underweight. However, Loni had to admit, the now grown-up police officer had filled in quite nicely and had become a rather attractive man.

"Ignore him," Marise said, scowling. "I'm more interested

in getting Duke together with Kalinda."

"But Duke *works* for me," Kalinda protested.

Marise shrugged, grabbing a nacho. "One in ten couples in the U.S. say they met at work."

"Duke and I will never be a couple."

"Well," Marise huffed. "Not with that attitude. But I guess I can see where it could get sticky since he is such a good employee. It's just as well. I think your first suggestion is much better. Ian is the more perfect rebound guy for you."

Loni's attention perked up. What the—? *Ian and Kalinda? What was happening?*

"How do you figure that?" Kalinda asked, not bothering to hide her amusement at her younger sister's dating advice.

"Because," Marise said simply, waving around her nacho chip, "it would just be about the sex. You know the old saying, keep your friends close and your enemies closer. And even better, is you'd probably never see him again after this week."

"That's crazy!" Loni blurted. She grabbed Kalinda's hand. "You can't possibly sleep with Ian. Duke is a much better option for you."

Kalinda and Marise traded a mystified look.

"What?" Loni asked, not able to look them in the eyes. "What's wrong?"

Marise sucked in a breath. "I can't believe it. *You* have a thing for Ian Hollowell?"

Loni shook her head. "No! I don't. I wouldn't. *I can't.*"

"Oh my," Kalinda groaned, sliding her drink over to Loni. "She definitely does."

"I don't." But even to Loni's own ears her protest sounded weak. "I mean, he's the enemy. It's crazy, right?"

Kalinda cocked her head. "Not all that crazy. He's pretty

cute. You're on the rebound. Add in the forbidden fruit thing and it brings a whole other level of spiciness to the situation."

"B-but he's heartless," Loni said, folding her arms. "He doesn't care about our family's legacy of the hotel. And he's a womanizer. Do you know he never dates a woman more than seven times?"

"He told you that?" Marise laughed. "*Seven* times? What happens after eight?"

Loni shrugged. "Turns into a pumpkin?"

"More like turns into a committed man," Marise said with a smirk.

"I like the honesty," Kalinda announced decidedly. "No BS. It's refreshing. And as far as him wanting to buy the resort... well, that's really on Daddy, now isn't it? Not Ian."

Loni supposed Kalinda had a point. Ian had said something similar to her, but she hadn't wanted to listen at the time. "But Blaze and I just broke up. Isn't there some kind of rule that you should wait at least six months?"

Kalinda shook her head. "You should wait as long as it feels right. No one is going to judge you. And if they do, screw 'em."

"But only figuratively, not literally," Marise added. "Unless they look like Ian."

"Well, I don't think I'm ready," Loni said. "And even if I were, it wouldn't be with someone with relationship issues or someone who wants to convert our family resort into a pile of dust. I want what Mama and Daddy had. A true loving, committed relationship."

But even those words sounded a little hollow to her, remembering the letters.

Kalinda snorted. "I have to pee," she announced. Then she hopped off the stool and strode in a none-too-straight line to the restrooms.

Loni frowned at Kalinda's retreating back. "She sure is sour on love ever since Clarke broke up with her."

"I know. I think she wants love again deep down but is afraid to look for it."

Loni knew exactly how that felt, even to the point where Loni was thinking something was seriously wrong and unlovable about herself. But being back at the resort gave her a sense of peace and contentment. And an understanding about herself and her priorities. She could lose love, but she couldn't lose the hotel, which was why she had to fight to keep it.

"Well, I can see why Kalinda is so gun-shy," Loni said reflectively. "Mama and Daddy had a high benchmark, right?"

Marise nodded. "You know it. Everybody in town wanted a marriage like our parents."

Loni let out a relieved breath that she wasn't seeing what she wanted to see in her parents' marriage, any more than her sister. "Yeah. Seems like I'm just as doomed as Kalinda to find love as well, which is another reason why I'm in no hurry to jump back into the dating pool."

"Oh honey, one bad apple doesn't mean a piece of the pie can't still be tasty."

Loni threw back the rest of her martini. A mistake since she was already feeling more drowsy and less giddy now. "What are you talking about?"

"You and Kalinda both need to dust yourself off and get back on the horse."

She squinted at her sister. "I thought we were talking about apple pie. Now you're talking about horses?"

"I'm talking about you and seeing other men."

"No, absolutely not," she said, setting her martini glass

down with more force than necessary. "My instincts are terrible when it comes to men. I was even crazy enough to think that even Ian had a heart with regard to buying our property. Boy was I wrong. In fact, we had a fight earlier today over the resort and I'm more convinced than ever that I never want to see or speak to him again."

Marise looked up, her eyes widening. "Well, uh, that might be an issue."

Loni frowned. "Why?"

"Because he just walked in and I'm quite sure he's already spotted you."

Chapter Fourteen

"Hell's bells, I've got to get out of here," Loni muttered, wondering if she could make it to the exit without being seen.

"No way," Marise countered hotly. "He's the one who should leave. You were here first."

Kalinda returned and flopped back down next to Loni. "Who should leave?"

"Ian," Loni groaned.

Kalinda shifted to look behind her. "Oh, yeah, there he is. Huh. Ian doesn't seem to be with anyone."

Loni hated the fact that she was secretly thrilled Ian hadn't managed to find a woman while he was on vacation here. *Not* that *she* was interested. She massaged the bridge of her nose. "He's not coming over, is he?"

"I *am* coming over," a male voice interjected. "In fact, I'm already here. Ta-da!"

With alarm, Loni looked up and into the grinning face of Free Drink Guy.

Oh, this was turning into a horror show of a night.

"Hey, there, sugar," the guy said, tipping his chin to Kalinda. "Thought I'd bring you another drink, personally this time."

Marise folded her arms. "Dammit, I knew he liked Kalinda," she grumbled.

Free Drink Guy held out a martini for her, and when she didn't take it, he sloshed it down in front of her. "Mind if I sit?"

"Yes," they all said in unison. Then Kalinda picked up the drink he'd brought and handed it back to him. "That's very kind of you, but I'm not interested, and I think I've had enough alcohol for the night."

The guy looked at her like she'd spoken another language. "Enough alcohol? Says no one ever," he said with a laugh. "Am I right?"

"Well, we're saying it," Loni said, taking charge. She already had had enough of this guy. He was being too pushy. Plus, the glazed eyes and his slightly soured beer breath were making her uncomfortable.

Free Drink Guy turned his glassy eyes her way and smiled. "Don't worry, my friend over there thinks you're as cute as a button, too, but was too shy to come over. His name is Pete and I'm Kevin."

Marise threw her hands up in the air and pouted. "See? This is what I was saying. No one is lusting after *me*."

"Shh," Kalinda admonished. "We're leaving now anyway."

"You can't *grow now*," Kevin slurred. "Not until you have one drink with me."

Loni stood. "No, we're leaving now," she said, pushing the drink away as he tried to set it down again. Unfortunately, someone was passing behind him and his hand jostled. As if she were watching it happen to someone else, Loni saw the entire contents of the martini glass spill onto her chest.

Gross. And the perfect ending to this nightmare of a night. Loni pulled at her blouse, which was now plastered to her skin. People turned in their direction, some with faces of shock and some with distaste. No doubt she and her sisters were all now collectively lumped into the "bunch of sloppy drunks" category.

Marise grabbed a fistful of napkins and shoved them at her. "Here ya go, Loni. I don't think it will stain."

"No worries. I'll buy y'all another drink," Kevin said, swaying slightly.

Kalinda shook her head. "Why? So, you can dump it on my sister again?"

Kevin's face turned red. "I didn't dump it. *He* was the one who spilled it." Kevin pointed in the direction of another guy, who was tall and brawny with a dark beard down to the center of his chest. "Yo, you gonna pay for that?" he called to him.

The Bearded Guy turned and shoved Kevin in the chest. "You gonna make me?"

Kevin shoved back, and they got in each other's faces.

"Hell's bells," Kalinda muttered. "Let's flag down our waitress before a fight breaks out."

"No man has ever gotten into a fight over me, either," Marise lamented.

Loni wanted to shrink into a hole. She was soaked, smelled like a distillery, and already had the makings of a hangover. Then out of the corner of her eye, she saw Kevin swing at Bearded Guy and the boisterous crowd got rowdier with some already taking sides in the fight. Then the bouncers appeared out of nowhere, along with Sheriff Ford Brennan.

The arguing ensued and more people pushed through the crowd. Suddenly, Loni felt a gentle hand on her back. She bristled and was about to tell the person off, but her words died on her tongue as she looked up into Ian's concerned gray eyes.

"Loni," he said, his gaze swiftly taking in the situation. "Are you all right?"

She looked down at herself, and her cheeks heated. Her blouse had become nearly transparent. "Just a little wet."

"Come on, I'll take you home." He looked at her sisters. "I'll take you *all* home, if you want."

"Great," Marise said, popping out of her seat.

"Not so fast," Sheriff Ford said, turning to her sister. "I want to ask you a few questions here first."

Marise let out an audible groan. "Of course of all the people here tonight, you have to question *me*."

Kalinda waved Loni and Ian off. "You guys go ahead. I'll stay with Marise. We'll pay the bill, then catch an Uber."

"Are you sure?" Loni glanced at the detective. His gaze was focused solely on Marise. "Maybe I should stay."

Marise shook her head. "Go on. No sense in you staying all wet and uncomfortable just because Hercule Poirot here has made it his life's mission to torture me," she said, jerking her thumb in Ford's direction.

Ford flashed Marise a sardonic smile. "If trouble didn't seem to follow you around, Miss Wingate, I wouldn't have to torture you half as much as you seem to think I do."

Loni grabbed her purse and Ian began to guide her through the crowd. Once they reached the parking lot, she stopped and turned to him. "You know, I can call an Uber for myself. You should go back in and enjoy your night."

Ian shrugged. "Who said I was enjoying my night?"

"Well, maybe you will. You only just got here."

The corners of his mouth kicked up. "So you *did* notice me walk in."

"No. Technically, Marise noticed."

He folded his arms. "Do you want to argue with me or do you want to go home?"

A soft breeze hit the front of Loni's shirt and she let out a shiver. "Home, please."

He nodded then took her hand, leading her to his fancy rental car. Once she was inside and buckled in, he turned to look at her. "I want you to know that I honestly wasn't stalking you or anything. It was a complete coincidence I came to this bar tonight."

"Lucky me," she muttered. She tilted her head back and closed her eyes, giving in to the effects of the alcohol she'd consumed tonight.

"Have it your way then." Ian chuckled as he started the car. "Although, I have to say, I'm glad I showed up when I did."

Despite their fight earlier, she was glad, too.

• • •

Loni was quiet the whole drive back to the hotel. Although Ian had suspected it was because she'd fallen asleep and not because she was still mad from this afternoon. He'd been completely truthful about how glad he was that he'd shown up when he'd had. Ian had noticed the Wingate sisters as soon as he'd walked into the bar. Hell, he wouldn't have been surprised to learn that half the male population there had noticed them. Their physical beauty was one thing, but the women also had a natural, fun openness that seemed to be a magnet for attention as well.

Ian had no plan on infringing upon an obvious sister-bonding girls' night. Besides, he didn't need to see Loni's face to know that he was not a welcome sight, especially after their fight. He knew as far as Loni was concerned, he was still the enemy.

Instead, Ian sat down at the beach bar, observing them from afar. He'd only been looking for a drink, since—being a dry town—it was impossible in Sunny Banks, and maybe a bite to eat. Lucille had given him two recommendations earlier in the day. It was just dumb luck he'd chosen the same one as Loni and her sisters.

After about ten minutes, Ian had thought about getting up and leaving. Why torture himself, after all? But when he'd seen the two men approach the sisters' table, Ian knew he wasn't going anywhere. And when that drink landed on his woman, it took everything in his power not to go over and start the brawl himself.

His woman.

He'd never felt such a protective nature toward a woman before. Had never even thought such a thing before. It went against his nature. It went against his relationship "rules." Everything about it was so...*not* him, and a warning chill raced through him as he pulled into the near empty hotel parking lot.

Loni fluttered her eyes open as soon as he cut the engine. "I don't feel good," she mumbled.

"Let's get you to bed." Despite her current physical condition, Loni still landed him a contentious look. *"Alone,"* he amended.

Ian opened the car door for her and helped her out. Unsteady on her feet, she readily fell into his chest. He wrapped his arms around her slight frame to keep her from falling and froze. Damn, her skin was soft. And even through the scent of vodka and lemons, she smelled heavenly.

"Uh, we should keep moving," Ian said, gruffly, putting his

left arm around her shoulders and tucking her into his side. He guided her up the steps and into the hotel lobby. He said a prayer of thanks that Lucille was not manning the front desk at the moment and that he and Loni could slip up to her room relatively unnoticed. He led her toward the elevators.

"You're going the wrong way," Loni murmured.

His lips twitched. "How would you know? Your eyes are barely open."

And just like that, she turned her big blue eyes up at him. "I'm on the bottom floor." She pointed toward the pool area. "I've got my parents' suite all to myself."

"Of course, you do."

Through a little more direction, he found her room. Still leaning against him, Loni dug into her purse and pulled out her key, which he promptly took from her hands and opened the door for her.

"Here we are," he said, walking her inside with her head pressed against his shoulder.

Loni turned and faced him, wrapping her arms around his neck. She looked up at him, her eyes soft, and his pulse kicked up a notch. "Thank you," she said quietly. Then she raised herself up on her tiptoes and her mouth came down on his, easing him into a gentle kiss.

The kiss stunned him, just for a small moment, as her tongue touched his, and he was reminded of how much he had wanted her ever since they'd first met and she'd begun her Scarlett O'Hara impression.

Ian was the one to pull back and end the kiss first. However, he kept his arms around her still unsure if she was too drunk and unsteady on her feet.

"I'm sorry," she said, blinking up at him.

"I'm not."

"No, this is wrong." She finally stepped away from him. "I shouldn't take advantage of you like this."

A huff of laughter escaped him. "*You're* the one who's been drinking."

She shook her head. "No, I'm the one coming off the bad breakup. I'd be using you." She cocked her head and seemed to rethink her words. "On second thought, maybe I should use you."

Ian was torn between amusement and worry. "Well, just to settle misconstrued feelings on the matter, if you're looking for rebound sex, I'd be perfectly happy to volunteer my services. But maybe you'd like to tell me about your breakup so I can gauge if I am truly being used or not. For example, scale of one to ten, how bad of a breakup was it?"

"Seven. No, eight." Loni bit her lip, closing her eyes. "Seven."

"Seven is bad, but in my opinion leaves just enough room for a backslide. Sleeping together would definitely be a bad idea for that reason alone."

"There's another reason?" she asked, flopping down on the bed and struggling to take her shoes off.

"I'm afraid so." He bent down on one knee and unbuckled the strap of her heels for her. "The alcohol ratio between us is uneven and therefore it's an unfair playing field. And although I did not create the rule surrounding that, I adhere to it most unwaveringly."

Once Loni kicked off her heels, she began rubbing her feet. "Thanks again." She paused. "You're not what I expected you to be."

Ian stood then took a seat beside her on the bed. "I hope

that's a good thing."

She continued to eye him through squinted lids. "I don't know if it's a good thing. It's definitely an interesting thing."

"Loni, I just want you to know that I won't force the issue if your dad changes his mind about the hotel. You *can* trust me."

"I hope so. I trusted Blaze and look where that got me."

"Blaze, I assume, is the ex?"

She fell back against the bed with a sigh. "Unfortunately. We were engaged."

Ian said nothing, although he was a little surprised Joe had never mentioned that one of his girls was going to be married. Perhaps Joe had more insight into Loni's relationship than she had.

Settling into the conversation, Ian leaned back, too, with his hands resting behind his head. "Did he cheat on you?" he asked, keeping his voice sympathetic.

"Worse."

Worse? He shifted to lift his head, so he could see her face. Mistake. She gazed up at him with those dreamy blue eyes and soft mouth of hers, and if it were any other circumstance, if the timing was better, he would have most definitely kissed her again. "What did he do?" he asked instead.

"Remember when I told you that I was being set up at work?" She looked away, closing her eyes. "Well, someone told my boss that I've been rude to clients and my ex-fiancé who should know me better than my own family didn't even come to my defense. He's allowing my reputation to go up in flames. I'm just so shocked. But I think the fact that I misjudged *his* character hurts more than anything."

Ian blew out a long breath. He'd heard some wild stories in his life—had even seen a few—but this had to be among his top three. "Good riddance then."

"I guess. But now I could lose my job. Maybe even my license. I talked to HR and they're still doing an investigation. But I feel I'm on the losing end because Blaze only seems to be worried about himself and Blaze's dad is good friends with one of the partners. So I'm kind of already on the outs. I don't know what to do. Part of me feels like I should go back to LA and part of me feels I'd be letting my sisters down if I left, ya know?"

"Being an only child, no, I don't know. I've only ever fended for myself. But I find it hard to believe that your sisters wouldn't understand."

"But I already disappointed them once. I left them to take on the resort by themselves after Mama died. I wasn't even around that much when Mama was undergoing her chemo. I tried to be around, but it was hard being across the country. And Mama was so adamant that I didn't take too much time off of work, so I didn't. She wanted me to succeed. And I wanted to make her proud. Now look at me."

He heard her sniffle, and his chest tightened. "I'm sure you did make her proud. You're a strong, intelligent, beautiful woman. Blaze took advantage of that and used you to advance his own career. I think that speaks volumes to how talented you really are."

Loni didn't respond right away. "He was the longest relationship I ever had. I really thought he'd seen me for me. Liked me for me—what I was, not what I could do for him."

"Well, an asshole is an asshole."

She laughed. "Or I was just blind."

"Hey, much better to find this out about his character now instead of marrying him and finding out too late. Some women aren't as lucky as you," he added, thinking about his mother.

"Yeah," she said after a pause. "I guess I was lucky. I wonder if it had anything to do with the hotel."

"The hotel? You think it brought you luck?"

Loni let out a little yawn. She was definitely tipsy—and completely adorable. "I do think it's lucky," she said. She settled on her side, then, tucking her hands under her chin like a child. "This hotel is special. Mama always said it was." Slowly she closed her eyes. Before falling asleep, she whispered, "In fact, I think it's magical."

Chapter Fifteen

Loni awoke the next morning with a headache the size of the Smokey Mountains. Her bladder screamed at her, and as she sat up, she noticed with alarm that she wasn't alone.

Ian Hollowell was in her bed.

Sweet Moses, what on earth happened last night? Nothing too particularly interesting since they were both fully clothed. But she remembered kissing him, maybe even trying to seduce him. Lord have mercy. There was a fight at the bar. A spilled drink or two. And what the heck did she say?

She was pretty sure she told him about her job. About Blaze. Ugh.

That might have been all, but it was enough to have her cheeks catch fire all the same.

Loni gently slid out of bed and padded to the bathroom. Once she finished, she washed her hands and face, then finger-combed her hair. If she *had* done anything embarrassing last night, at least she was going to look somewhat presentable while facing up to it.

When she re-emerged, Ian was still asleep, face down on his stomach. Leaning over the bed, she tentatively jostled his shoulder. "Ian, wake up."

He didn't budge. But she was pretty sure he was breathing.

Loni tried again, using both hands to shake him. "Come on, Ian, you need to get out of here."

Before she could register what was happening, Ian's hand snaked out and grabbed her wrist, pulling her down onto the bed. He rolled over, pinning her beneath him.

"Good morning," he said, smiling down at her.

Damn, he was glorious with those sleepy gray eyes and bedhead. "Don't 'good morning' me," she said, giving his chest a half-hearted shove. "What are you still doing here?"

With an audible groan, Ian rolled off her. "You know, you were *so* much nicer to me when you were drunk."

She scowled. "How *much* nicer?"

"Not as nice as you fear," he said, his tone thick with amusement.

She blinked. "Then why didn't you leave?"

Ian stacked the pillows behind his head, then gave her a look. "You've seen my room, Loni. This suite is way better than what I have. I actually got a good night's sleep for the first time all week."

Her room. Not *her* had him staying. She didn't want to unpack right then and there why that stung so much. "Well, I hoped you enjoyed it, Sleeping Beauty, because this is the last you'll be seeing of this place. It's not a good idea...us being together."

"But you have this huge suite all to yourself. And I promise I'll be a perfect gentleman—if that's what you want. Come on, have a heart, Loni."

Loni was tired of people thinking she was heartless. She wasn't. In fact, she felt a lot of things—especially when it came to Ian. But that didn't mean it was a good idea to have him under the same roof—or even in the same bed as her. "Look—"

Loni's words died when she heard a knock at her door.

"Loni," she heard Marise say. "Are you up? Let me in. I need to talk to you."

Loni stifled a gasp. "Get in the closet," she whispered.

Ian's eyes widened. *"Seriously?"*

She tried to shove him off the bed, but it was like trying to move hardened concrete. "Yes, I'm serious. My sister can't see you here. Especially in my bed." She shoved at him again.

"Why?" he asked with a laugh. "Would we be compromised and forced to marry?"

"Of course, n— Wait," she said, peering at him closely. "Do you actually watch *Bridgerton*?"

Ian averted his gaze and shrugged. "Maybe."

Good grief, could this man get any hotter? But *Bridgerton* or no, she needed him out of here. She tried moving him again. "Ian, please. I can't have you complicating my life with my sisters right now." That's all she needed—her sister seeing their enemy in her bed.

Ian must have heard the desperation in her voice, because he finally gave her a short nod and stood up. "Where do you want me?" he said with a sigh.

A loaded question, but she pointed to her bedroom closet. "In there. Hurry," she added.

Ian dragged his feet into the closet, then whirled around. As he raised a finger, he looked about to say something, but she slammed the door in his face before he could argue with her. As petulant and cute as he looked right now, it was not the time. Sheesh!

Loni rushed over and opened her door. Her sister stood with her arms folded and eyes narrowed to slits.

"What on earth took you so long?" Marise said, standing on tiptoes to look over Loni's shoulder.

"I, uh, had to pee." Loni stepped out of the way to allow her sister to enter.

Marise shot her a dubious look. "Couldn't you have let me in first?"

"It was an emergency," she said, glancing over at the closet door and making sure it stayed closed. "Um, why are you here anyway? Something going on?"

"Yeah, I wanted to tell you—*warn* you—that Daddy and Pamela are here. They're staying at the cottage and unpacking right now."

Loni swallowed. "They are?" A feeling of dread washed over her. But she knew she had to meet her father's fiancée sooner or later. "What's Pamela like?" she couldn't help asking.

Marise shrugged. "Not as horrible as I expected. She's actually quite nice."

"Nice?" Loni wasn't prepared for that. She wanted Pamela to be a combination of Cinderella's stepmother and Voldemort with just a dash of Cruella for good measure. If that were the case, it'd be easier to hate the person who was at least partially responsible for persuading her father to sell their hotel.

"Yeah, she is. Anyway, Daddy wants all of us to meet them for lunch by the pool at twelve fifteen," Marise told her. "Kalinda's already preparing a bunch of his favorites."

Twelve fifteen? That didn't sound like Daddy, either. What was with the odd time? But at least it would give her enough time to get ready and mentally prepare for battle. "Got it.

Anything else?"

"Yeah." Marise's gaze slowly traveled to Loni's bed. "Do you always sleep on both sides of the bed?"

Loni glanced over her shoulder. Sure enough, the bed—with its four dented pillows and ruffled coverlet—definitely looked as though more than one person had slept there. "I, uh, had a restless sleep last night."

Marise raised an eyebrow. "I'll say. With anyone in particular? Like maybe a certain hunky evil developer?"

Loni inwardly cringed and prayed Ian was not listening through the closet door. "Nope. Ian brought me home and I went straight to bed." *Pretty much.*

Her sister rolled her eyes. "Sheesh, Lon. You sure know how to waste a good drunk night out." She headed back toward the door. "It's depressing to think that Daddy is the only one getting laid in this family right now."

An image flashed in Loni's mind, and she wanted to vomit. "Ugh. Let's make a pact to never speak of Daddy's love life again, okay?"

Marise chuckled. "Agreed. And don't worry, we'll change Daddy's mind. See you later," she called, walking out.

Loni bolted the door after Marise for good measure, then rushed over to the closet and threw it open. "Coast is clear." She blinked when she noticed Ian had a necklace in his hands. "Have you been going through my things?" she asked, making a reach for it.

Ian pulled the necklace above his head. "Not so fast. I don't think this is technically one of *your* things."

"What are you talking about? Anything here belongs to me."

"Not where I found this. You said this was your parents'

room? I think it was probably your mom's."

Mama. The idea of having a new personal item of her mother's made her almost weepy with joy. "Let me see." Ian held out the necklace to her. "Where did you find it?"

He jerked his thumb behind his back. "There's a little patch of carpet that's cut out. When you forced me in here, my foot snagged on it, and I stumbled into the hamper. When I bent down to see what I tripped on, I noticed I had kicked up the rug and there was a jewelry box shoved underneath."

"So, you just took it upon yourself to look through personal property?"

He ran a hand through his already disheveled hair. "Loni, give me a break. I didn't know how long you were going to keep me in here. What else was I supposed to do?"

Guilt stirred inside her. She shouldn't be taking her feelings out on Ian. But the fact that her mother kept the letters told her that something wasn't right despite her parents remaining married. "You're right. I'm sorry. I guess I'm stressed having to meet up with Daddy and Pamela."

"They've arrived already?"

"That's what Marise came by to tell me. We're having lunch today on the pool patio." She cracked a smile. "Daddy's smart enough to hold this little meet and greet with everyone in public."

Ian stared down at her intently as if he saw through her bravado. "Well, maybe I can just so happen to stop by the pool around lunchtime. Create a buffer. If you want a little extra moral support, that is."

"Yes, I'd like that." She was surprised by just how much she liked the idea. Having Ian there could potentially ease the tension in the air between her and her father. She looked up and shot him an impish grin. "Probably not much of a sacrifice, since it seems you can't stay away from me."

"You're right about that." He raked her with a blistering look that had her cheeks bursting into flames.

As if to prove that point further, Ian leaned into her then, and his mouth sealed against hers in a long, fluent kiss. She answered it, letting herself fall into him as she drank in the sweetness of his lips and tongue. When he finally eased away, she gazed up at him unsteadily.

"What was that for?" she asked.

The corners of his mouth quirked. "Call that a little extra moral support from me."

. . .

Ian's mind was at odds with itself as he walked back to his room. He was making a mistake getting so close to Loni. He'd even promised her he wouldn't pressure her father to sell. What had he been thinking?

This, he thought grimly, *was exactly why I avoid personal entanglements, especially in business.*

There was no room for emotion. He needed to evaluate the hotel based on cost and return on investment, decide if he could gather enough interest and capital to move forward, then pounce or walk away. Period. He couldn't let personal feelings confuse his judgement.

Interestingly enough, when he arrived at his door, there was a serving cart parked in front of it with a carafe of coffee and a metal domed lid over a plate. He stopped in front of it and carefully lifted the dome. There was a fruit cup with a warm, homemade biscuit, whipped butter and...a copy of the hotel property plans.

What the hell was going on here?

Placing the dome back down, he took one more glance around, then opened the door and wheeled the cart inside. The site plans would definitely be useful. But who would give this information so readily? Joe? He doubted it, Joe had just got into town. Certainly not Loni. She'd rather sever her own head than help him in any possible way to buy the hotel. Most likely it was one of her sisters, whoever had left him breakfast before, which made this whole situation all the more precarious. But he'd take it and move forward with what he had.

Ian poured himself some coffee and even though it was a Saturday, he knew Scott was just as much a workaholic as himself, so he decided to call him. His partner answered on the second ring.

"You bored with your vacation already?" Scott said in greeting.

Ian chuckled. "It's not quite a vacation but I can't say I'm bored."

"Interesting. Anything to do with one of Joe's daughters or perhaps all three? Please say it has to do with all three."

"It does."

"Yes! I knew it! The Predator is back!"

"Not in the way you think."

Scott groaned. "You're killing me here."

"Can you get your mind out of the gutter for five minutes? I have the site plans of the hotel. I'm going to scan them on my phone and then email them to you."

"Nice work. Those plans will help us maximize the use of available land. I'll take a look at them and make sure there are no environmental or infrastructure concerns. I've been checking out the zoning laws over in Sunny Banks, too. What's your take on the tourism? Not sure what direction we can market this yet."

"Just relax. I'm working on that. Plus, once I talk to Joe this weekend, I can get a better handle on his seriousness to sell and what a sale would look like to the community."

"How it looks to the community?" Scott said "community" as if Ian had said the word "feces" instead.

Ian rubbed the back of his neck. "Well, yeah. I want to see how the community views this potential project, too. There might have been some celebrities who stayed here. The town seems to be proud of that little rumor—if it's true. And if it is true, it's a pretty cool reason to try and revitalize the hotel."

"Yikes," Scott murmured.

Ian picked at his biscuit. "What do you mean by that?"

"It means you need to cut out the sweet tea and come back to Boston. *Now.* You don't sound like you. You sound like a caring human. It's weird."

"How is it weird?"

"Because you initially said high-rent condos. That's what I've been pitching to our builder friends. You changing your mind like this is bad for business—and our jobs. Raj might even skin us both alive."

Ian rolled his eyes at the mention of their boss. He would handle him if and when the time came. "Ridiculous. Raj loves me because business always comes first in my book."

"You better hope it does."

"Is that a threat?"

Scott sighed. "No. A friendly reminder that my ass and reputation are just as much on the line as yours. This is a great opportunity, Ian, yet you're moving slower than the Big Dig construction. The Predator I used to know would have overstepped me and had business meetings already set up to discuss options. Hell, you definitely would have had more than just site plans by now. You would have secured finances."

"I'll get to it," Ian ground out. "This is supposed to be my vacation, remember?"

Scott paused, his tone softening. "All right. I'm sorry if I'm up your ass about this, but after that last deal that bombed, I'm a little paranoid. And Alex Winters is not only proposing a parking garage in the Sunny Banks downtown, but a small airport as well. If that happens, you better believe your sweet ass that there will be an influx of people. People needing a place to live. We need this to work."

Right. Ian knew that. Real-estate investment wasn't without its risks. And their company had taken a big hit several months ago when they had underestimated their costs and decided to use a different builder on a project they'd financed. But before renovations started, he and Scott had a gut feeling Denali Construction was overcharging so they went with the recommendation of a friend and hired someone new. Big mistake. That decision nearly sent them to bankruptcy. It also ruined their relationship with a fantastic builder. A builder that Alex Winters then scooped up and has been working with ever since. This property could be their chance to right that wrong with them and also make some much-needed money.

"Understood," Ian said. "I'll get you those plans as soon as we hang up."

"Hey, if you're having a problem, do you need me to come down there and run a little interference for you?"

"I don't need a babysitter," Ian snapped. He took a deep calming breath.

He could fix this. He always fixed things himself. Everything was lining up fine. All he needed was more time. Once he talked to Joe and made sure all involved were square. No sense getting worked up over it.

No room for emotions.

"I can handle things here myself," Ian said in a more calmed tone. "I can handle this resort acquisition myself, and I can sure as hell handle Loni Wingate."

Scott went silent for a moment. Then he let out a long breath and finally said, "I'm not going to argue with you anymore. However, I do find it interesting and even more concerning that you only mentioned one of Joe's daughters. Remember, it's all fun and games until the contract is signed."

Then Scott promptly hung up.

Chapter Sixteen

Loni was grateful Kalinda had closed the café this weekend to prepare for Daddy and Pamela's arrival. It gave Loni a chance to go through her mother's letters before she had to meet everyone for lunch. She'd originally promised Ian she was going to wait, but there had to be an important reason as to why her mother kept those letters hidden and she just couldn't hold back any longer. Besides, it was much better to have her mind focused elsewhere and not on Ian—and how perfectly wonderful he'd taken care of her last night and even this morning. And it was much better than thinking about how much her heart had been involved in that kiss they'd shared.

Loni sat down on her bed and spread the letters out before her. She picked up one that seemed to have the earliest date and took a deep breath.

My dearest Sandra,

It's only been a day and I already miss you terribly. When will I see you again? Tell me when would be a good time to call you. I need to hear your voice, or I'll go crazy.

Her cheeks burned as she read on. She didn't have to get to the third letter to have every reason to believe that Mama and this *TJ* were involved in a love affair like she'd originally suspected. The intimate words written were meant for only two people, and she felt like a Peeping Tom. She suddenly felt ill-equipped to undertake this secret alone.

Oh, Mama, she thought miserably. How could she have done this to Daddy? To us? All this time she'd thought her parents had the perfect marriage. The best relationship. Apparently, Loni wasn't only blind to her own love life. Daddy couldn't have had any idea what had been happening right under his nose. Kalinda and Marise would be devastated to learn this as well. Was it better they never find out? Maybe she should put the letters back where Ian had found them. Mama obviously made a mistake and then chose to stay with her family, it was probably best to forget about them.

She gathered the letters up in her arms and headed for the closet. Dropping to her knees, she searched for the panel of loosened carpet that Ian had told her about and pulled out the jewelry box. The necklace Ian had found was a pendant in the shape of the sun. Gazing at it made Loni's chest ache. Sandra Wingate loved the sun so much she made sure each of her daughters had a name that was in some way derived from it.

The necklace wasn't familiar to Loni. But maybe she never noticed her mother wearing it before. Or perhaps, it didn't belong to Mama at all. The necklace could be something that belonged to Marise or Kalinda. She put it in her pocket and decided she'd at least ask them about it.

...

When Loni walked into the main office, she found Marise surrounded by Lucille and Knox.

"You were supposed to reserve a table by the patio," Marise was telling Knox.

"That's exactly what I did," Knox said, scratching his beard. "Put a big ole sign on it and everything."

Lucille folded her arms, a smug look on her face. "And how did you secure the sign to the table, genius?"

Knox's brows furrowed. "Secure?"

"It blew away," Lucille said, throwing up her hands. "Now, there are no tables left. A family of five took the last one."

"You reckon I should kick them out?" Knox asked, rolling up his sleeves. "I'll do it in a heartbeat. Mark my word."

Marise pinched the bridge of her nose. "No, no, don't do that. We should be thankful there's even a crowd at the pool as there is. I know Daddy wanted to impress Pamela, but maybe we can just have a private lunch in the café."

Loni stepped farther into the room. "Impress Pamela?" All eyes turned toward her. "What's to impress? She doesn't even want this hotel."

"Well, we don't know that for sure," Marise said diplomatically.

Loni snorted. "Of course, we do. Why on earth would Daddy be selling otherwise?"

Lucille grabbed Knox by the back of his shirt. "Let's go, Big Guy. Maybe we can figure something else out by the pool area. I think we have high-top tables in one of the storage rooms."

Marise clasped her hands together. "Oh yes. That would be perfect. It'll have more of a party atmosphere."

"Right," Loni muttered. "Because there's *so* much to celebrate."

"Oh, hush," Marise said to her, waving Knox and Lucille off. "Thanks, guys. I'll come help you in a bit."

Once they were alone in the office, Marise turned to her. "Your panties are twisted tighter than a lasso rope. What's going on? It can't be just because of Pamela."

Loni sighed. "No, it isn't." She pulled out the pendant and held it out to her sister. "I found this in my suite. I don't remember Mama wearing anything like this. I thought maybe it was yours or maybe Kalinda's."

Marise fingered the pendant almost reverently. "It's beautiful," she breathed. "I've never seen it before. But it's something I'm sure Mama would have worn if it was hers." She looked up. "Have you asked Kalinda about it?"

"Asked me about what?" Kalinda said from the doorway. Her sister wasn't wearing her normal White Squirrel Cafe uniform today. She wore a pretty pink sundress with white flowers and white strappy sandals. Her hair was up as usual, but she had curled a few strands to frame her face. Aside from last night when they had all gone out, this was the nicest and happiest Loni had seen her sister look all week.

"You look pretty," Marise commented with a sly smile. "Trying to impress Duke?"

Kalinda frowned as she walked into the office. Searching her desk, she snatched up a file and held it close to her chest. "I told you I'm not interested in Duke. Besides, I'm keeping Duke way too busy preparing our lunch for him to notice what I'm wearing."

"Believe me, he's noticed."

Kalinda rolled her eyes. "Can't I just enjoy having the café closed and wearing some normal clothes for a change? I don't want Daddy worrying about me."

Marise pointed to the folders in Kalinda's hands. "Do you want me to take care of those for you so you can check on the food?"

Kalinda clutched the folders tighter. "No, I'm good. In fact, I was just going to take them to the shredder."

"Well, I can do that," Marise said, holding out her hand.

"No, I'll do it." Kalinda seemed unusually irritated by the attempt at help, which she seemed to try to deflect by turning to Loni. "So, what did you want to ask me?"

Loni hesitated, then held up the sun pendant again. "Do you recognize this necklace?"

Kalinda froze when she glanced at it. "No," she said, and averted her gaze as if she couldn't bear to look at it.

Loni narrowed her eyes. "Are you sure?"

"Yes, I'm sure," Kalinda snapped, smoothing down the front of her dress. "Who would wear that? It looks cheap."

"It does *not*," Marise protested. "It's lovely. I'd wear it in a heartbeat."

Kalinda snorted. "Until it turned your neck green. Where did you find that thing anyway?" she asked Loni.

"I found it in my closet," Loni said, giving the pendant one last look before stuffing it back into her capri pants pocket. "Maybe Daddy bought it for Mama and never had a chance to give it to her before she died." Although Loni doubted Daddy would have hidden a necklace under a patch of carpet. Now that she thought about it more, the necklace was looking more and more like it could have been a gift given to her mother from this TJ.

"Maybe," Kalinda said, in a calmer tone. "But I hardly think now is the time to ask Daddy about it. You'd only bring up sad memories for him, when this should be a happy occasion."

Kalinda had a point, but for Loni, this was hardly a joyous time. Nonetheless, she'd gotten nowhere trying to find information about the pendant and wondered if she should mention the love letters Ian had found. However, seeing how agitated her sisters—especially Kalinda—now seemed, maybe it was better to wait another day.

Marise checked the time on her phone. "I better go check on Lucille and Knox." Her gaze swung to Kalinda. "Need any help with lunch?"

Kalinda shook her head. "Nope, Duke has it all covered for me."

Marise chuckled. "I bet he does."

"I'm paying him well for his effort," Kalinda pointed out. "Get your mind out of the gutter."

"Too late," Marise said, grinning. "My mind has taken up permanent rent space there."

Loni took a deep breath, too much on her mind to find amusement in her sisters. "Okay, I've got to go," she said, glancing with uncertainty at her sisters. "I guess I'll see you both at noon?"

"Twelve fifteen," Marise reminded them.

"Whatever," Kalinda said. "Let's just try and get through lunch with as much decorum as possible."

"Hey, why did you look at *me* when you said that?" Loni asked. "I can play the part of the perfect Southern belle as much as you guys." *Although if Ian had been here, he might have begged to differ.*

"If you know you know." Kalinda grinned. "And let's make a pact to not bring up the hotel this afternoon, either."

"What?" Loni pressed her fists on her hips. "No. Veto. I will do no such thing. We need to talk him out of selling before it's too late."

Marise placed a calming hand on her shoulder. "Lon, I agree with Kalinda on this. I don't think we should bring the hotel up in front of Pamela. This involves the immediate family. And right now, she's not family. Not yet, anyway."

Loni's shoulders slumped. Since when did her little sister become so reasonable? "Fine. I promise *I* will not bring up the sale of the hotel...today."

Kalinda and Marise nodded, both looking satisfied with her answer. Which was perfect. Because if Ian showed up at lunch as expected, she'd bet good money the topic would be brought up automatically without any assistance from her.

And if that did happen, well, Loni made no promises after that.

Lucille and Knox had decorated the pool area tastefully with several high-top tables placed close together with white tablecloths tied around the center legs with gold ribbon. Small glass mason jars with several stems of fresh flowers sat on the center of each table. The wind was light, and the sun was shining. A beautiful September day to be outside enjoying the weather. Still, Loni was grateful for the sun umbrellas that were strategically placed along the area. The humidity combined with her nerves had her already feeling hot and clammy, and she was sorry she hadn't worn a tank top instead of the cotton blouse she'd chosen instead.

"There are my sweet girls," Joseph Wingate said, his voice warm and booming. He strode out onto the patio, a petite woman with short, wavy hair that was dyed an unnatural strawberry blond color trailed behind him.

"Daddy!" Marise said, rushing over and throwing her arms around him.

Kalinda came out a side door, carrying a tray of bruschetta, and gave him a sunny smile.

Her father looked a lot healthier than when she'd seen him last year. His coloring looked good, too, which Loni attributed to all the golf playing he'd said he'd been doing with his new fiancée. Loni hung back a moment, allowing her sisters—who seemed much happier to see their father and vice versa—to greet him first.

After a few beats, Loni placed her sweet tea down on the table and, with a deep breath, forced her legs to move toward her father.

His brown eyes widened when he gazed down at her. "Loni, you look paler than two ghosts having a snowball fight in the middle of a blizzard."

She forced a smile. "I've been told that."

He held out his arms. "Well, it's good to see you." And before Loni knew it, she was wrapped in a cocoon of his sturdy arms, making her feel as if she were ten years old again. She wished she could feel this way around him always.

Daddy pulled back first and finally motioned to the woman standing behind him, nervously twisting the strap of her handbag. "I want to introduce the love of my life, Pamela Dubois. Pammy, these are my lovely daughters. Kalinda, Marise, and Apollonia."

Pamela gave them all a guarded, if not kind, smile. "I'm so happy to meet you all. Your father talks so much about you. All I hear is what a wonderful cook Kalinda is and how creative Marise is."

Loni didn't fail to miss her omission from Daddy's glowing

praise of his daughters. He'd often overlooked her as a teenager, but Loni had hoped becoming a successful attorney as an adult would have garnered some overdue attention. Apparently not.

Marise—ever the sensitive one—placed a hand on Loni's shoulder. "Don't forget how smart Loni is, Daddy. Not to mention the prettiest," she told Pamela proudly. "Loni has the closest resemblance to our mama more than any of us."

Pamela's smile faltered slightly as she looked at Loni more closely. "Oh? Is that right?"

"Can I get anyone a drink?" Kalinda interrupted, grabbing a wine bottle from a nearby ice bucket. "I have some champagne here."

"Oh yes," Pamela said, sounding relieved. "That sounds absolutely perfect."

While Kalinda opened the bottle and began pouring the wine, their father gazed around the patio area. "The place looks clean at least," he said, giving the pool a critical eye. "How was business this past summer?"

Marise bit her lip. "Not bad. It's tough competing with the VRBOs in the area."

He nodded. "True. The hotel I'm managing in the Cape took a bit of a dip in profits this past season, too." He elbowed Pamela, playfully. "Not that this little lady knows troubles like that. Her gift shop is thriving down there."

Loni forced a shallow smile to her lips, trying to be on her best behavior. "You own your own business?"

"Yes," Pamela said, her face becoming more animated as she talked about her store. "It's a combination souvenir and gift shop. I named it The Seagull. I'm hoping to eventually have a website where I can sell items online as well. Seems to be the thing to do nowadays if you want year-round income."

Joe nodded, wrapping an arm around her shoulders. "Pammy here is a very savvy businesswoman. She knows a lot about investments, too, and has been advising me."

Loni frowned. She didn't have to guess how much Pammy knew and what exactly she was advising her Daddy to do.

Joe then looked at Marise. "You still involved in that winery, honey?"

Loni's mouth dropped open. Her sister hadn't mentioned anything about being involved in a winery. Although, Loni supposed she had her own secrets she hadn't shared with her sisters so really wasn't one to talk. "What winery? You can't have a winery in Sunny Banks."

Marise took a glass of champagne from Kalinda and passed it to Pamela. "Uh, no. I had mentioned to Daddy about opening up a winery with some friends a few towns over. Sounded like a good investment. But we couldn't get zoning for it."

"Oh, that's too bad," Pamela said. "Your father said you were working on designing a label and everything."

Marise shrugged, her cheeks growing pink. "That's me, always putting the cart before the horse. But I might have something else in the pipeline soon. Fingers crossed."

Loni had to wonder if this was what Marise had mentioned to her when her sister had said she wanted to do something with the hotel that was more creative. Marise had majored in marketing in college. She'd always been the artistic one, whether it be in acting or other creative endeavors she was dipping her toe into, like the winery.

After everyone had received their glass of champagne, Daddy raised his in a toast. "To new family," he said, smiling down at Pamela. "And new opportunities."

Loni drank in silence. Everyone was complimenting the

wine, but to Loni, it might as well have been battery acid. She was trying—really trying—not to have a sour attitude and be on her best behavior for her sisters' sake. But the added "new opportunities" comment made her think he was talking about selling the hotel—*not* Marise's interest in wineries—and it formed a cold knot in her stomach.

Just when she thought about begging off lunch because of a sudden headache, Ian came walking out the hotel doors. He was wearing navy shorts and a white linen shirt with the sleeves rolled up to his elbows that accentuated his newly acquired tan. Damn, he was striking, sexy with a quality of self-assured attractiveness.

"My two favorite people," he said, smiling as he kissed Pam and shook hands with her father. "Glad I was able to be down here for your arrival."

Marise folded her arms, grinning. "Yes, Ian, we're so glad you were able to stay as well. Weren't we, Loni?"

Loni caught Ian's amused gaze, then cleared her throat. "Uh, of course. The more the merrier."

Joe's eyebrow went up. "Glad to see you girls respected your daddy's wishes and were hospitable to my friend here."

"More hospitable than you know," Marise quipped, and Loni lightly kicked her ankle.

"Absolutely," Ian agreed. "Joe, from day one of my arrival, your daughters have impressed upon me their tenacious desire to treat me to the culinary delights of the South and to the most generous of accommodations you have here. All, might I add, with manners rivaling the Queen of England herself."

Loni looked away and rolled her eyes. Ian sure knew how to drive home a point.

Pamela gazed at Loni and her sisters with newfound

fascination. "How wonderful of you girls." She beamed up at Joe. "See, sweetheart, you had nothing to worry about. They don't mind you selling the resort to Ian at all."

Loni swung her head back so fast, she thought she might have whiplash. "Uh, no, actually. That isn't true. Not even close."

"Loni," Kalinda and Daddy warned.

"No," Loni said, shaking her head. "No, Pam brought up the resort first. Maybe we all should just clear the air on this right now."

"Oh, here we go," Marise groaned, raising her glass and taking a huge gulp of wine.

Pam brought her hand to her mouth. "Oh, dear."

"You know," Ian said, smoothly taking Pamela by the arm, "the beaches here in North Carolina are so different from Cape Cod. Would you like to see for yourself? I know a great spot we can walk down to. I took surf lessons there the other day."

Kalinda grabbed the champagne bottle again. "*That,*" she said, pouring herself more wine, "sounds like a fantastic idea."

Joe glared at Loni, then gave a stiff nod. "Go on, honeypie. I'd like a word with my girls alone for a moment anyway. I'll come get ya as soon as lunch is ready."

Pamela allowed Ian to guide her away and down to the boardwalk.

Loni put down her drink and wasted no time. "Is Pamela the one trying to convince you to sell the hotel, Daddy? Be honest."

Her father ran a hand down his face. "Loni, stop trying to point the blame. Pamela has nothing at all to do with me wanting to sell."

"Well, I'm just trying to understand what's going on here, and why you won't listen to reason. Marise and Kalinda feel exactly as I do." She looked at her sisters and widened her eyes at them, silently asking for some moral support.

"Loni's right, Daddy," Marise said, jumping in. "This is Mama's sanctuary. We need to preserve it. And just what would we all do for jobs if you sell?"

"I had planned on taking half of the earnings as an investment in a hotel in Cape Cod. The other half would be split between you three," Joe said. "Kalinda could easily move her restaurant and you, my dear, should find your own passion, because I know for a fact, it's not here."

Marise's eyebrow shot up. "That's so not true. We're planning our first ever Sunny Banks Beach Bash next weekend in partnership with the town Chamber of Commerce. It's going to be great. You'll see. And I do have other things in mind for this hotel, if given the chance. I'm just waiting for my investment to kick in then just you watch." Marise bit her lip, then helplessly looked at her sisters.

Loni didn't know what else she could say, either, but found it disconcerting that Kalinda was so strangely quiet. She just stared out onto the dunes, sipping her wine as if wrestling with her own thoughts.

Loni huffed out a breath. "Do you hear what we're saying, Daddy? I really wish you'd reconsider. I think Mama would think it selfish of you not to."

Her father's gaze flared with burning, reproachful eyes, which had Loni taking a step back. "You watch what you say, darlin'. One thing your mama could *never* accuse me of is being selfish." He sighed. "But I hear your concerns and I understand your love and dedication to this place. To show you how unselfish I can be, I'll make a deal with you all."

Loni and her sisters looked at one another, hope hanging

in the air.

"You said something about some beach party you're putting together?" Joe went on.

Marise frowned. "It's more than a party. It's going to be a huge event."

He nodded. "Right. Well, if you can channel all this passion for the resort and manage to make it more profitable by the end of the month with this so-called *event,* then I won't sell."

Loni felt the pressure in her chest instantly lighten. To be replaced with a different kind of anxiety.

"You're not exactly giving us a lot of time," Kalinda said, folding her arms.

"We can do it," Loni blurted. *Somehow.*

"We can?" Marise asked, nibbling her lip.

"Yes." Loni took each of her sister's hands and squeezed. "We'll figure it out together."

Joe straightened his tie, then pulled his sunglasses out of his shirt pocket and put them on. "Good. Now, if y'all are done here, I'm going to go join my fiancée."

Then he turned and walked off toward the beach.

Loni quietly let out the breath she'd been holding. It wasn't exactly the resolution she'd wanted, but at least there was a fair chance of them keeping the resort.

Kalinda finally placed her glass down. "I'll go check on lunch," she blurted, already heading for the hotel entrance.

Marise turned to Loni. "Jee whiz, Loni, there are areas in the hotel that need paint touch-ups, restaurants still need to be contacted, and maybe we need to create some extra social media posts to help get the word out."

Loni continued to watch her father walk down the boardwalk until he disappeared behind the dunes, her mind churning. "We can make a list of what needs to be done and we'll split the tasks. Don't worry."

"Daddy sure got his skivvies in a jam when you called him selfish for selling the hotel," Marise said. "Do you think he's just on edge because Pamela's here or do you think it's something else?"

"I'm not sure," she murmured.

Loni couldn't concern herself with Daddy's mood at the moment. At least, he was willing to compromise. Right now, the only thing on her mind was The Beach Bash and making it a success. Because it might very well be the resort's only saving grace.

Chapter Seventeen

The next morning, Loni showed up at the café thirty minutes before opening so she could have a few words with Kalinda in private. But when she walked into the kitchen Duke was already there heating up the grills.

"Morning," he said, dipping his chin as he turned on the coffeepot.

"Hi, Duke. Have you seen Kalinda yet?"

He jerked his thumb over his shoulder. "In the storage room."

"Thanks." Loni walked back there and found her sister sorting through boxes of napkins. "Hey," she said to her.

Kalinda peered up, body language stiff. "Hey."

Loni took a step farther into the room. "I, uh, wanted to talk to you about lunch yesterday."

"What?" she said, pulling out an armful of napkins. "Were you hoping for vegan pulled pork? Isn't that what you Californians prefer?"

Loni huffed out a breath. "Look, I can see you're upset

at me. And I'm sorry for bringing up the hotel, but you heard Pamela. I couldn't let her get away with thinking we were just going to roll over to her whims."

"Maybe it's not Pamela. Maybe it is Daddy's idea, like he said."

Loni fumed. She refused to even entertain such a notion. "Oh, come on. It seems awful sudden."

Kalinda shrugged. "Not so sudden. Daddy wants the money to invest in another hotel."

"I can't believe you're okay with this. I thought you felt like I do. Like Marise does. I thought you were as invested in this place as we are."

Kalinda looked away and placed the napkins down on the desk behind her. "I do. I love this place. However, Daddy just seems…"

"Heartless?"

Kalinda shook her head. "Unsettled. I felt a little sorry for him."

"I know it must be hard for Daddy to be back here. It's hard for me, too. But that's still not enough of a reason in my opinion." Loni gave her sister a hard look. "Would you really open up another restaurant somewhere if Daddy sold?"

"I would try. Honestly, Marise could even manage it for me if she wanted. We would land on our feet. I'm convinced Daddy would make sure of it. So, no need to worry about us. I'm sure you'll be plenty busy once you get back to the law firm."

Loni leaned against the shelving behind her. "Yeah, about that… I may not have a job to go back to."

Kalinda frowned. "What do you mean?"

Loni then told her about Blaze, the email, and finally, about being under investigation.

"Hell's bells," Kalinda murmured. "Why didn't you tell us sooner?"

"I figured you had enough to worry about."

"Loni," her sister said, throwing her arms around her. "You never have to worry about burdening us. That's what family is for. Does anyone else know yet?"

Loni hesitated. "Just Ian."

Kalinda's eyes widened. "Ian? The so-called enemy?"

"He caught me in a moment of weakness."

"That seems to be happening a lot." Her eyes narrowed. "What's really going on between you two?"

Loni sighed, thinking back to their shared conversations and then even to their kiss. "I don't know. Nothing. But I like him. *Really* like him," she amended when Kalinda shot her a sardonic smile. "How messed up is that, though?"

"I've heard worse."

Loni shook her head. "I suppose, but after being betrayed by Blaze I feel like I'm setting myself up for that to happen all over again. I mean I don't know if Ian is truly into me for me or because he's just out to get the hotel and have it go as smoothly as possible. My feelings are all over the place and it's just so hard to—"

"Trust?" her sister finished for her.

"Yeah, trust." She and Blaze had it all. On paper at least. She'd thought her parents had it all as well. How wrong she was. How could she really trust her instincts anymore?

"Well, maybe, I'm not exactly the person to ask about trust and relationships," Kalinda admitted. "Not that Marise is much better. She's never even been in a relationship."

"Lucky her," Loni muttered.

"But if I was one to give advice," Kalinda said, "I would

say, you can't compare Blaze to every other guy you meet. I kind of always got the impression that Blaze was an ass, but I overlooked it because you seemed happy. As for Ian, well, he's just doing his job. Aside from that, he seems like an okay kind of guy."

Loni laughed. "A ringing endorsement if I ever heard one."

Kalinda grinned. "Coming from me, it is. Plus, if he really is friends with Daddy, he has to have some admirable qualities. Therefore, I'd like to believe he likes you for you. That and because you're a pretty great person. And beautiful as heck, with gorgeous sisters I might add."

"Yeah, well, Ian likes women in general. He hasn't made that fact a secret. But I'm a relationship girl. A monogamous relationship kind of girl. I don't think I have the energy for a casual fling."

"I hate to admit that our younger sister is sometimes wiser than us, but maybe that's exactly what you do need now. Light and fun. No strings and commitments. Sheesh, you just got rid of the old ball and chain," Kalinda said, her eyes twinkling. "And I like Ian, too. Although not quite in the same way as you do. And personally, I think he'd be insane not to fall for you."

Loni tilted her head. "Aww...thank you. You're not as cynical about love as I thought you were."

"No, I am." Kalinda turned and picked up the napkins again. "For *me*. For you on the other hand, maybe it's worth a shot. And like I said, if it's not meant to be long term, at least you went into it willingly knowing that. It's empowering when you think about it."

It was scary when she thought about it. However, she'd already gotten out of her comfort zone and taken a risk. She'd come to North Carolina and was on the brink of losing her job in the process. But she had no regrets about that now. Most times the things you regret aren't the paths you choose but those you don't choose. The things you don't experience. The people you don't get to know. And when you begin to worry about your choices, those are the times you just need to take a leap of faith. Unfortunately, she had more pressing concerns at the moment.

"So, what can I do to help with The Beach Bash?" she asked.

Kalinda cracked a smile, then pulled out a slip of paper from her shorts pocket. "I was hoping you'd ask."

Loni took the paper and began reading down the list. "Let's see... I can call to confirm the vendors and email them instructions on set-up time and where to park. No problem. And I can definitely—" She looked up in surprise. "You want me to paint?"

Kalinda shrugged. "The chairs around the fire pit area could use some sprucing up. Oh, and the floorboards in the lobby are so scuffed. I'd hire a painter, but I couldn't schedule one in time and with money being tight..."

"Say no more," Loni said, waving off her excuses. "Like I said before, I'm here to help my sisters as much as I can while I'm here. I'll get to the calls today and the painting tomorrow right after my shift at the cafe."

Kalinda chuckled. "You don't have to do it all, Loni. Marise and I will help you."

"No, it's fine." Loni folded the paper and slipped it into her own pocket. "I prefer to stay busy. It'll keep my mind off of my troubles in California."

"And keep your mind off troubles with a certain developer," Kalinda pointed out.

Well, Loni certainly hoped so.

•••

Ian had gotten up early and did a little bit of work before meeting Joe for a 9-hole round of golf. Scott—a man of his word and eager to make the acquisition happen—had already promised Denali Builders the construction work, and also had looked at the zoning. Turned out, he was right. Their best bet and return would be to create some fantastic luxury condominiums on the land. People would most likely snap them up like caramel corn, either for their own use or to rent to tourists, which would be plentiful if Alex Winters went through with his addition of more parking for shopping and the proposed airport. Either way, Ian was sure the locals would come to see that the change would be equally good, if not even better for the town. Convincing Loni, however, would be another story.

Despite the brief tenseness with his daughters over selling the hotel yesterday, Joe seemed to be in good spirits during their golf game. And afterward, Joe was happy to show Ian around the area.

"You're a little rusty on your game," Joe said, driving them back to the hotel. "And that backswing of yours." He let out a low whistle. "Not getting out as much, huh?"

Ian chuckled. "No, sir. I don't have time for much outside work."

"Oh?" Joe gave a skeptical side-glance. "Well, then maybe you should stay a little longer down here and take a proper vacation. Maybe even one of those horse and carriage rides through the downtown that are so popular with the tourists."

"Actually, I'm thinking of staying through next week to do some work. If it's okay with you. Seems like Sunny Banks has some promising real estate growth in its future." He was sure his boss would have no problem with him staying longer than intended, especially while Scott did some investigation with the site plans he'd given him.

Joe grinned. "It's fine by me. It's the approval of the women you need, though."

Ian planned on asking them to extend his stay this afternoon, although he didn't think it would be too much of a hardship on the hotel. He doubted many guests would be waiting for the accommodations he'd been staying in and he'd certainly pay for the extended time. "I'm sure I can convince them."

Joe chuckled. "Maybe. But they'll probably want you to stay only to rub it in your face."

"Rub what in my face?"

"The BBQ Beach Bash is this weekend. If it's a success, I told 'em, I'd reconsider my stance on selling."

Ian stilled. This was news to him. No wonder the women were in such a frenzy painting and reaching out to vendors. But could they really pull off such a miracle? Doubtful, so he wasn't too worried. However, he was only just beginning to realize that the one thing he could never underestimate down here was the Wingate women. He needed to stay longer for that reason alone.

"I hope you plan to come either way," Joe added.

Ian thought of seeing Loni again and smiled. "Yes, I do."

"Fantastic. You haven't had true barbeque until you experienced North Carolina barbecue. Kalinda's a great cook, that one is. Marise has her moments, too. Better baker, though."

"What about Loni?" he found himself asking.

"Apollonia?" Joe snorted. "Cooking is the one thing she did *not* get from her mother. She got everything else, though. Beautiful, and book smart as anything. But can't boil water to save her life. Probably why she's so skinny. Just like her mama."

Ian couldn't help but hear the derisive tone in his words and wondered why he was so hard on his middle child. Loni was a wonderful woman—smart, loyal, funny. He still had a hard time believing what her asshole boyfriend did to her. But thank God, she was done with him. Loni deserved someone special. Someone who... Someone who could give her the very best of a loving relationship.

Too bad that someone couldn't be Ian.

Joe shook his head. "Damn, she's just as stubborn as her mother, too. I'd forgotten that. Apollonia's even gone and rallied her sisters with her to save that damn hotel, too. If I didn't know her better, I'd swear she'd Super Glue her hands to the front desk like one of those climate change activists."

Ian smiled. He wouldn't put it past Loni to do something like that, either, which was why he decided now was the time to confront the elephant in the room. There was no choice. His boss was already assuming the hotel sale was a done deal. If Ian didn't act now, he could let down a lot of people and ruin his company's reputation. "When it comes down to keeping the hotel in the family, yes, Loni certainly is tenacious."

"Like a dog with a bone."

Ian cleared his throat. "And *has* she succeeded in changing your mind?"

Joe was silent for a moment, which made Ian sweat even more than the Carolina humidity. "Not yet," he said gruffly. "This hotel always seemed like a thorn in my Achilles heel. I was hoping Pammy and me could completely bury the past and start fresh. But being back here... Seeing how it brings my girls together. There were a lot of good times there, too."

"What would you say if I told you my company was very

interested in your property. We'd pay a fair amount. I'm looking to make money but I would never shortchange you, Joe."

Joe waved that thought away with a wave of his hand. "I ain't worried about that." He huffed out a breath. "Look, Ian, I don't mean to jerk your chain on this. But I gave Apollonia my word that I would at least think twice on selling after I see what they do with this event of theirs this weekend and that's what I'm going to do."

As much as Joe's words concerned him and threatened the operations of his company, he knew what Joe was up against with Loni. Ian would just have to wait the weekend out and do his best to show both Joe and Loni the pros of selling to him. As soon as they got back to the hotel, Ian would tell Scott the situation, along with the news that he was staying a few more days. Ian didn't look forward to that. To quote Joe, Scott was going to be madder than a snake married to a garden hose. But he'd make good use of his time and take another look at the downtown. Maybe there were some potential properties there as well.

Ian nodded. "It's okay, Joe. I think I know Loni well enough now that I wouldn't want to break a promise to her, either." He wouldn't want to do anything to cause her further upset. She'd taken her mother's letters better than expected, but he knew they had to be weighing heavily on her. Part of the reason Ian only wanted to play half a course with Joe was because he wanted to get back and check on her. He'd promised to help her sort through the files to see if they could find whoever TJ was.

"You like my daughter, don't you?" Joe's tone was more a statement than a question.

"I like *all* your daughters," Ian hedged. "You did a wonderful job raising them. What's not to appreciate in three strong, independent women?"

"Damn, you're a good salesman." Joe laughed. "But I can tell when a dog's caught scent of a rabbit. Sorry, son, I would let this one go. It ain't gonna work between you two."

Ian turned to look at him, surprised he was that transparent. "I thought you liked me."

"I do. But I like my daughter more. As difficult as she can be at times," he added under his breath. "And Apollonia wants the fairy tale. The prince, the carriage, hell, even the castle. So, that's what she should get."

"And you're telling me I'm not the prince, I'm the frog?" Ian didn't know why this discussion with Joe was irking him so much. Everything Joe was saying was true. But that didn't mean he wanted to hear it told to his face.

"You're more like the horny toad."

Ian couldn't help but be amused. "And you *are* sure you like me, right?"

Joe laughed. "Like I said, I do like you. You're a good man. But I also know you. I don't want my daughters settling and making the mistakes I did, thinking you can change a person. Because you can't," he said bitterly. "People are what they are and if you try to make them what you want, all that happens is you both end up miserable."

Ian had a feeling Joe was talking about his marriage. But Ian knew that from his parents' marriage as well. His mother should have accepted the fact that his father did not want help with his alcoholism and walked away. Instead, his mom struggled, argued, and screamed at her husband, hoping he'd change. In the end, nothing changed except they both ended up miserable and paying the ultimate price with their lives.

"Yeah, I get it," Ian murmured. He needed to heed Joe's

warning. Ian had been upfront with Loni about his views on relationships, he had no business starting something that was obviously going to end badly for her.

"Good," Joe said, slapping Ian's thigh in a friendly yet firm manner. "As you often say, never let emotions into the boardroom. Wise words, my friend."

Ian gritted his teeth. Yeah, that rule always served him well in the past. He just had to hope it wasn't too late for him to follow it.

• • •

The next day, the crowd at the café had thinned out significantly after one o'clock, so Loni left early to finish the painting that needed to be done around the resort. First thing she wanted to tackle were the Adirondack chairs that would be used around the firepits for The Beach Bash. Then maybe while they were drying, she'd take a look at Mama's garden and see if she could weed it a bit, too. Kalinda obviously had enough on her plate with the café and couldn't tend to it as much as it needed.

Marise had already done some light sanding and applied the primer earlier in the morning. Now all Loni had to do was apply the paint. Easy peasy. She could knock this out in no time. She swirled the white paint a few times with her paint brush then proceeded to apply it to the chair.

"You're applying it too thickly," said a familiar voice behind her.

Loni didn't need to turn around to know she'd find Ian there, probably smirking at her with his all-too-handsome grin. Oh no. There was no way she was going to let him distract her today. She was a woman on a mission. This Beach Bash was going to be the success of all successes, so help her.

"Go away," she said, continuing with her broad paint strokes.

"Why? I'm just trying to be helpful."

She sighed. The man was as annoying as a fly at a picnic. "You're not being helpful. You're being...*distracting.*"

Ian seemed to savor that information. She even had the impression it pleased him.

"Seriously," she said. "I need to get this done. It's for Friday's Beach Bash, if you must know."

"Ah. In that case..." Ian squatted down next to her and pointed. "See? The paint is too thick. You're not going to get a nice even finish."

Loni finally looked over at him and was sorry she had. He had his swim trunks on with an unbuttoned shirt casually thrown on over his nicely sculpted bare chest. Unfortunately, that very nice chest was joined to a very nice set of abs. She jerked her eyes away and his grin grew as if he knew she had not only just checked out his body but liked what she saw.

She scowled. "Look, Picasso, I just started painting. It will be nice and even when I'm finished."

Ian glanced up, shielding his eyes from the sun. "You know painting in extreme temperatures can affect the drying time and maybe even the adhesion of the paint."

Loni rolled her eyes. She doubted Ian would be this "helpful" if he knew The Beach Bash would have a direct effect on her father's decision on selling the resort. "Thanks for the tip, but the temperature is fine and it's a fairly dry day, too."

"You're still not painting even."

"I don't remember asking for your advice."

Ian reached for her brush, but she jerked it just out of his reach. "Hey, what do you think you're doing?"

"I'm going to show you the proper way to paint."

She snorted. "I don't need your help."

"Apparently you do. Here," he said, making a grab for her brush again. He managed to take hold of the handle but she wasn't about to let go. They wrestled back and forth with it until finally Loni abruptly let go and the brush went flying, hit Ian's chest, then plopped to the ground.

Loni took one look at the giant white smear on Ian's pecks as well as the specks of paint on his neck and chin and busted up laughing. "Oh, look, Mr. Perfect, it's not quite even," she said, gesturing to the paint on his skin.

He quickly grabbed the brush again and held it up like a weapon. "You're right. It's not even. You could use a coat, too," he said, waving the brush toward her face.

She screamed and jumped up. Ian followed and began chasing her around the chairs with the brush. "Ian, I swear," she shouted as she ran, "if you so much as lay a drop of paint on me, I'll—"

He caught her by the wrist and pulled her into his chest. He dangled the brush several inches above her, and they grinned at each other, their chests rising and falling in labored breaths. Then Loni felt a change in the air. Her gaze locked with his and her breathing slowed. Their faces were so close, and she realized that without very much movement at all, her lips could easily reach up and touch his.

"You'll what?" His voice was soft with just a whisper of hoarseness to it.

She swallowed, her legs suddenly feeling a bit shaky. She didn't have an answer to his question. But to be honest, she wasn't sure she could answer any question at the moment. Their bodies were barely touching but she felt the heat of him, nonetheless. His gaze then dropped to her lips and her mouth went dry in anticipation.

"Ice cream!" a voice called out. "Get your ice cream!"

The spell or whatever had just passed between them broke—thank goodness—and Loni took the opportunity of her regained senses to grab the paint brush from his hand.

"Want some ice cream, Miss Loni?" A boy Loni had only met a few days ago was standing by them, a cooler chest clutched to his chest.

"Hi, Samuel," she said, walking over to him, grateful for the interruption. Samuel was probably about ten or eleven years old and regularly sold ice cream on the beach all summer and after school while the weather was still warm. Marise had told her he was saving up for a new bicycle that his family couldn't afford.

An ice cream wouldn't exactly cool her down from what just transpired a few moments ago with Ian, but it was the perfect distraction that she and Ian both needed. Plus, she really wanted the boy to earn that bike. "What do you have today?"

"Let's see." The boy slid the little cooler chest he had around his shoulders and opened it up. "Chocolate covered bananas, ice cream sandwiches, and vanilla ice cream in a waffle cone."

"I'll take the ice cream cone."

Ian came to stand at her side. "Hi," he said to Samuel when the boy looked up.

Samuel narrowed his brown eyes. "You don't look familiar. Are you here on vacation?"

Ian glanced at Loni before answering. "Sort of. My first time here."

Samuel nodded as if he approved. "It's nice here. My mama says this resort is the best resort in North Carolina."

Ian's brows went up. "Oh? Why does she say that?"

"Because these ladies are the nicest. And they always buy my ice cream, too. I almost got all the money I need to buy my bicycle now. Then my mama can borrow it when she goes to work."

"Those are good reasons," Ian said with a slight frown. His gaze then traveled to Loni. "And you're right. These ladies are the nicest."

Loni chuckled. "His standards are obviously questionable."

Ian shook his head. "I don't think so. But I guess this means that I should buy an ice cream, too," he said, reaching into the pocket of his swim trunks. "I'll take the ice cream sandwich."

Samuel held out the sandwich, but shook his head when Ian attempted to pay. "No, sir. My mama said I need to be *hospital* to visitors."

"Hospitable," Loni corrected.

Samuel frowned. "That's what I said. Hospital. So, I will give you an ice cream for free to welcome you to Sunny Banks."

Loni grinned. "Wow, Samuel, I have no doubt that in a few years you'll be mayor of this town."

Samuel grinned. "Oh no, Miss Loni. I want to be an astronaut." He took her money and closed the lid of his freezer and attached it back around his shoulders "Mama is waiting for me at the end of the block, so I need to go."

"Tell your mama, hello," Loni said, unwrapping her ice cream. "Come back tomorrow and I'll make it worth your while."

"Okay, cool," the boy said, waving goodbye. "See you both tomorrow."

Once the boy walked down the beach a bit farther, Loni took a bite of her ice cream and then turned to Ian. "Your ice cream is going to melt," she said, pointing to his still wrapped ice cream sandwich.

Ian frowned at his ice cream sandwich. "That was really nice of that kid."

Loni smiled, amused at how dumbfounded Ian seemed to be at receiving something that had no strings attached. "Spoiler alert, people here in Sunny Banks are really nice."

"But it's more than that. He needs money to buy a bike for not only himself but his family. I'm a stranger. He could have charged me double and I would have never known."

Loni took another lick of her ice cream before the heat of the sun had it running down her fingers. "Yes, and Sam will get his bike—especially with the good karma he's creating. You have to remember this is Sunny Banks. People don't use each other for their own gain here. It's a rarity and certainly refreshing from Los Angeles."

"From Boston, too."

"Well, not everyone can see the charm," she muttered, thinking of Blaze. "But I think of Sunny Banks as one big, happy family."

"Family," he repeated as if the word was foreign to him. But maybe, she realized with some sadness, it *was* foreign to him. He obviously had parents who had let him down and had chosen their addictions over him. Over family.

"That concept must be tough for you to fathom," she remarked, eyeing him closely.

"What concept?" He finally began to unwrap his ice cream, and once he had removed the paper, he took a large bite.

"Choosing people over business."

He stopped chewing and pinned her with an annoyed look. "Loni, me wanting to buy the resort has nothing to do with choosing business over people."

Oh, but didn't it? She was finally starting to understand

the inner workings of Ian Hollowell's mind. He always chose business over people. But not because he was necessarily a bad person, but because that's what he knew. It's what he was taught. People in his life had never chosen him. But she decided to keep that analysis to herself. She had let him take enough of her time away from prepping for the Bash. If it went well enough, Ian wouldn't be able to choose The Sandy Bottom at all.

"We'll see about that," she said, turning back to her painting.

"Do you need any help painting?" he asked, making her freeze in her step.

To say she was surprised at the question was an understatement. "I don't need any help being told how to paint, if that's what you mean."

Ian looked down at his ice cream. "No, I meant I could actually paint with you. If you want. Two hands are better than one."

"Technically, it would be four hands. And why on earth should I accept help from you?"

"Well, for one, you're good at math but you're a lousy painter." He grinned. "And two, maybe you inspired me with all that karma crap."

She couldn't help but laugh. "Come on, then."

Come on, then?

Well, shoot, why not let Ian help? Having the enemy help you with his own downfall would only make the victory that much sweeter, right? Besides, maybe she could learn a thing or two about painting from him. Plus, he was good company and—so help her—she kinda liked having him around, despite the threat he posed to her family's business.

A revelation she chose to ignore as they set out to work together.

Chapter Eighteen

On Thursday morning, the first thing Ian saw when he logged into work was an email from his boss, Raj. It was short and to the point.

Close the deal ASAP.

Well, Raj knew what he wanted, that was for sure. But easier said than done. Ian needed Scott to run interference for him for just a bit longer. There was just no way the sisters could magically change Joe Wingate's mind on selling, no matter what the man promised his daughters with their Beach Bash efforts. Ian just needed to wait it out.

Scott was not enthusiastic about Ian's request. As Ian had expected, the text exchange between him and Scott was not pleasant. He had to hand it to his partner, though. Ian had no idea how creative Scott could be in using the F word. A rare talent that Ian hoped he wouldn't have to experience again for quite some time.

But Scott had made a promise to Denali Construction and Denali Construction had been burned by Scott and Ian before—largely because of a mistake that Ian had made—so the last thing he needed to do was drop the ball on them again. The company Ian worked for, Hollavest, was already getting a bit of a reputation for reneging on deals and that was something Ian couldn't afford to escalate, or he could potentially lose his job.

Thinking he better make some more headway, he was just about to go and search out Pamela and Joe when there was a knock on his hotel room door. When he opened it, he was surprised to find Loni. She still had her White Squirrel Café tee shirt on from waitressing this morning, and her hair although worn up in a ponytail, looked about as limp as a wet noodle. Still, he'd never seen her look more adorable.

"Hi," she said, giving him a tentative smile. "I just got off work and ran into Daddy. He told me you two went golfing the other day."

Ian folded his arms. "We did."

"You never mentioned it when you were helping me paint the chairs. Did he say anything about the resort?"

"Nothing. Except..."

"Except?"

"Except that he was going to think about it some more before making any decisions because he promised you he would."

Her shoulders visibly relaxed as she let out a long breath. "Oh, thank goodness."

"What did you think would happen? That I would get your dad alone, twirl my mustache, and convince him to sell?"

Loni flushed as she let out a light laugh. "No, no. Of course, not. You don't even have a mustache for heaven's sake. Not that you wouldn't look good with one." When he just continued to stare at her, she threw her hands up in defeat. "All right, that's exactly what I thought. Sorry."

Ian shrugged. He supposed he'd think the same thing if he were in her shoes. Not too long ago, Ian would have done everything in his power to make this deal go through. But now, with Loni, the situation was quickly becoming vastly different, and he hardly recognized himself anymore. He shook himself, remembering his boss's terse email. No, now was not the time to let emotions into business. There was too much at stake.

"Is that all you came here to find out?" he asked with more gruff than intended.

Loni's eyes widened. "No, actually. I came here to see if you wanted to come to Angela's with me."

"Why?"

She looked over her shoulder, then lowered her voice. "I read through Mama's letters and finally found that TJ's first name was Tom. I thought I would show them to Angela and see if she remembers anyone by that name. She was closer to Mama than anyone."

He slowly nodded. "Probably a good idea. But maybe I'm not the one to bring. You should tell Kalinda and/or Marise and bring them instead."

The hurt look in her eyes almost had him relenting, but Ian needed to pull back. He was too close to her, to her family, and he couldn't think straight or even remember the real reason he came to this town in the first place. And he couldn't let it impact his job.

"I tried to tell them. I really did. But I want Angela's take before I try again. To be sure I'm doing the right thing."

"I can't." *I shouldn't.*

"Oh." She gulped and looked away. "Sure," she choked out. "I should have realized you'd probably be busy. I'll go myself. It's no big deal. You're right. I shouldn't have asked you." Then she whirled around and began heading back toward the stairs.

Begging her with his eyes to come back, Ian watched her leave for a few seconds and then called her name. Dammit, he knew he was making a mistake, but he was incapable of putting the brakes on at this point. And going to Angela's wouldn't stop him from buying The Sandy Bottom, would it?

Loni turned around. "Yeah?"

"I'll go with you."

A smile bloomed across her face. "Really? But you said—"

"I say a lot of things." And she looked so broken, so desperate for answers. If he could help her in this way maybe it would ease the burden that was on his conscience over buying the resort out from under her.

She took a tentative step closer to him. "Are you sure? Because I don't want you to feel obligated."

"Are you trying to get me to change my mind?"

She laughed. "No. And thank you. You're...a good friend."

He blinked because that's all he could do.

"What? Isn't that what we are now?" she asked, frowning.

Friend. Ian tried the word out for size in his brain. He wasn't sure he'd ever been friends with a woman before, aside from Pamela. But Loni was different than any other woman he'd met. She made him laugh, and he liked her heart. When she committed to doing something, he could tell that she gave all 100 percent of herself to it, even when things got tough. And even when she wouldn't directly benefit. A trait that was rare to find these days—at least in his circle. So if friendship was what it took to be a part of her life, then he supposed friendship was what he'd take, even if there was a part of him that wanted slightly more. It was for the best—for both of them.

Gazing into her hopeful blue eyes, the corner of his lips tugged. "Yeah, I guess we are."

. . .

Loni had changed out of her waitress uniform and put on a navy tank top with white shorts which she thought made her legs look quite long and tan. Not that Ian had bothered to notice. Or even glance at her. Yes, he was acting perfectly nice and even had changed his mind about coming with her to Angela's, but he still seemed a bit restrained—distant—as if he'd completely forgotten they had ever kissed. Not exactly what her ego currently needed after her breakup with Blaze. However, she was a mature woman. If Ian just wanted to keep her in the friend zone, that was perfectly fine with her. She'd accommodate his wishes perfectly because she wanted exactly the same thing.

Sort of.

Besides, she had enough on her mind with her mother's letters. Not only did they trouble her, but who knew how her sisters would react once they'd learned about them, too.

Loni adjusted the tote bag she had slung over her shoulder, and once she and Ian had reached the front porch of Angela's house, she rang the doorbell.

A dog started barking, then the door swung open. "Welcome, welcome," Angela said, waving them in. "Don't mind Lovey here." She glanced at Ian and her brows went up. "Oh, and, congratulations, I see you two have advanced from the friendly acquaintance stage to the actual friends stage."

You got that right, Loni thought sardonically, but she kept her mouth wisely shut for once.

Ian grinned. "Slow progress is still progress. I hope you don't mind Loni inviting me."

"Not at all," Angela said, closing the door behind them.

Loni reached down and allowed the dog to sniff her hand. It was a cute little thing with black wavy hair and white paws. It couldn't have weighed more than ten pounds. "I didn't know you got a dog."

"Oh yes." Angela bent down and stroked the dog's fluffy neck. "It got kind of lonely here once my husband passed and then your mama."

Ian tentatively held out his hand like he'd never been around animals before. "Does she bite?"

Angela chuckled. "Oh, heavens no. Although I bet if provoked, she could give a stranger a good nip."

Lovey sniffed Ian's hand, then gave it a gentle lick before jumping up on its hind legs and pawing his thighs.

"She likes you," Angela said approvingly. "Ever have a pet growing up?"

Ian's expression grew stony, and he shook his head. "My, uh, parents weren't the type."

Angela clucked her tongue. "Too bad. Animals, like friends, are like the family you get to choose. Lovey here is the sweetest companion and so smart, too. Watch this." She clapped her hands to get the dog's attention. "Who wants a treat?"

The dog jumped up and barked.

"Who wants to stay home and snuggle all day?" Angela asked next.

Lovey wagged her tail and barked again.

"And who thinks Jason Momoa is hotter than a firecracker in hell?"

The dog howled and then began to run around the room.

Loni laughed. "The dog obviously belongs in Mensa."

Angela grinned. "Precisely." She led them to the kitchen in the back of her cottage while the dog still raced around the house. The room was painted in a sunny yellow and had a large window that overlooked the water. She had boxes of shells on the floor by the table and ribbons and a hot glue gun were sitting on the table. "Don't mind all this. Trying to get my wreaths ready on time for the craft show this weekend."

Ian walked up to a row of her finished wreaths that were lying on the kitchen island. "These are nicer than I expected," he told her. "You could be selling them in gift stores, not just craft shows."

Angela's face brightened. "Why thank you, sugar. That's what your friend Pamela said as well."

Loni frowned. "Pamela? You've met her already?"

Angela gestured for them to have a seat. "She and your daddy came by bright and early this morning before he went out golfing." She picked up a pitcher and poured them each some tea. "I have to say, honeypie I found her delightful with a capital D."

Ian nudged her with his elbow. "I told you."

Loni sat back and chewed the inside of her cheek. It's not that she didn't think Pamela was a perfectly nice woman—on the outside. But she couldn't shrug how odd it was that Daddy was listening to her more than his own daughters. Seemed like Pamela had an ulterior motive. "I'm reserving judgement for now."

Angela let out a tinkling laugh. "Honey, we all know that your judgement on that woman has come down fast and furious like a seagull on a French fry."

Busted. "Perhaps slightly," she conceded. "But Pamela is not the real reason we're here." She opened her tote bag and pulled out a handful of letters, then placed them on the table. "We found these hidden in the hotel. They're written to my mama. We also found this." Loni pulled the sun pendant necklace out as well.

Angela's gaze traveled over the necklace appreciatively. "It's very pretty."

Loni held up the necklace near the window and watched as the center gem caught the sun's rays and twinkled like a shooting star. "So, you don't remember Mama wearing it?"

"I don't, I'm afraid." Then Angela picked up one of the letters and began reading. "Oh, my," she breathed.

Loni and Ian looked at one another. "So I guess this means you didn't know my mother was having an affair."

Angela set the letter down, looking visibly shaken. "As God is my witness, I did not."

Loni let out a long breath. For whatever reason, it did make her feel better that she hadn't been the only one in the dark. "I'm surprised she didn't confide in you. Do you have any idea who TJ could be? I figured out from one of the letters that his name was Tom."

Angela shook her head. "No. But maybe this Tom was a guest at the hotel."

"Did she ever say she was unhappy in her marriage to Daddy? In her life with us?"

"No. Not really. I mean, she had little bouts of depression here and there. We'd share silly little dreams of running away to Europe, doing something out of character like work for a touring company in Italy and maybe take on a lover or two. We'd laugh and it always seemed to bring her out of her funk.

But I always thought it was just wine talk. At least, it was for me. I guess you never know what someone is truly going through."

Loni shook her head, grateful when Ian placed his hand over hers and squeezed. "I know things like this happen in real life, but it's just so hard for me to believe this about Mama. She and Daddy always seemed so happy, and they gave me the best memories here because of that. The best example of marriage."

"Your mama was very devoted to your father. And obviously he was just as committed to her. The way your daddy took care of Sandra when she got sick was borderline Mother Theresa and Mark Wahlberg mixed together."

"Yeah, I guess that's true," Loni said, thinking how her father had tended to her mother through the worst of her chemo.

"Don't take it so hard," Angela said. "Obviously nothing happened because of it, which is a blessing. In fact, I'm sure your daddy and mama staying together even had something to do with the hotel. A lot of long-lasting marriages resulted from that old place. This was another example."

"Oh, come on," Ian said with a snort. "You don't believe that the hotel has some kind of magic to it, too, do you?"

Angela gave a noncommittal shrug. "That's an awful lot of coincidences if it isn't. And heck, if your mama made a mistake maybe it was the hotel that set her straight again. Because I know she wouldn't do anything to hurt her family."

Loni sniffed, feeling the pressure on her chest lift. She needed to hear those words. Believe that good things still came from her childhood home. "Thanks, Angela. Do you think I should tell Kalinda and Marise about the letters?" she said, gathering them back into her tote.

"Oh," Angela said, raising a hand to her chest. "They don't already know?"

Loni shook her head miserably. "I didn't have the heart. I felt it would hurt them." *It certainly crushed me.*

Angela picked up Lovey and set her on her lap. "Well, honey, I've always felt that a secret at home is like broken shells under the tide. You think you're going to have a nice swim and then all of a sudden you cut your foot and need ten stitches."

Ian looked from one woman to the other and then quirked an eyebrow. "Um, translation for the northerner here, please?"

Angela's troubled expression relaxed into a small smile. "Better to tell them the truth. Then they can have their water shoes ready."

Loni and Ian barely exchanged any words as they walked back to the hotel. Ian was being his usual casual, matter-of-fact self, while Loni was preoccupied with thoughts of how she was going to bring the topic of the letters up to her sisters.

Once they reached the boardwalk steps that led up to the pool area, she turned to him. "Thanks for coming with me today," she said, lifting a hand to her eyes to shield them from the sun. "I probably could have gone myself, but it was nice to have the support in case I chickened out."

Ian's gray eye crinkled in amusement. "I would venture a bet that you've never chickened out of anything in your life. But you're welcome. I know this isn't easy for you to deal with, especially because you can't ask your mom personally about any of it. But from my experience with my mom, I learned that good people still make mistakes."

Loni nodded. "Thanks. *Again,*" she added with a grin. She pulled out her phone and checked the time. She really wanted to go over the guest booklets again in search of Tom, but her favorite boutique would be closing in a few hours, and she had nothing to wear to The Beach Bash Friday night. "Well, I better let you get back to…whatever you were doing." She turned on her heel to leave.

"Where are you rushing off to?" he called out. "Hot date?"

She turned back and cocked her head. "Would that matter to you?"

He took a few steps, closing the distance between them. "Only if your date was hotter than me." He then smacked his forehead and laughed. "Oh, wait. That's impossible. So, no. It doesn't matter to me."

Loni bit down on a smile. "Okay, I guess I'll see you around then."

"Wait." His voice rose in surprise. "So you *do* have a date?"

"Only with myself. I hadn't planned on staying this long here so I wanted to see if I could pick up a few more outfits downtown before they closed."

Ian clasped his hands together. "Perfect. I love shopping."

"Said no man *ever*," she said with a laugh. "Besides, I feel bad for already taking up enough of your time today."

"What if I said I *liked* you taking up my time. Very much. And as long as you want to take." His gaze roved and lazily appraised her. He then seemed to catch himself and cleared his throat. "Uh, I mean, as friends. Or more than friends. Or whatever you feel comfortable with," he added hastily. "You know I'll be heading back to Boston soon."

Loni bit her lip and thought about what Kalinda had said moving forward in a relationship as long as both parties were upfront and honest about what they were willing to invest. Blaze had lured her in with verbal promises but had never fulfilled them. And here was Ian, with his self-admitted flaws, trying his best to warn her so her emotions wouldn't get tangled up, and she'd get hurt.

It was strangely alluring.

"Well, this is a coincidence," she said. She held out her hand to him and when he took it, it was like an electric current had opened between them. "I happen to like you taking up my time as well." So much so that she was about to throw caution to the wind and try to spend whatever time they had left, together.

Chapter Nineteen

Ian meant for his words about spending time with Loni to be taken lightly, but truth be told, he did enjoy spending his time with her. And if he was being even more honest, he'd even admit he enjoyed spending time in Sunny Banks as well. Why else would he have been talked into a horse and carriage ride in the middle of an eighty-degree sunny afternoon?

"The last time I'd taken one of these rides, it was with my mom," Loni said with a sigh.

Loni wasn't looking at him as she spoke. She was gazing out at the downtown with a nostalgic expression, a light breeze blowing her blond hair against her cheek.

"First time in a carriage ride for me," he told her.

She turned to him and grinned. "A virgin, huh?"

"Yes," he said, patting her hand. "Thanks for being gentle with me."

She chuckled, gently elbowing him in the side. Then her smile faded just as quickly as it came and she seemed to grow pensive again.

"You talk about your mom a lot," he said without thinking.

She shrugged. "Yeah, I guess I do talk about her a lot. I just miss her so much. Sorry."

"Don't be sorry. It's...nice to have the memories that you have." Much better than any of the memories he currently held onto of his family.

She turned her probing blue eyes at him. "I know you had a difficult upbringing, but you must miss your parents. I mean, don't you have some good memories of them?"

His chest grew tight and he suddenly had difficulty taking a deep breath. He wasn't used to talking about this. Didn't *want* to talk about this. The only person he'd ever confided in about his parents was Pamela, and even then, it wasn't extensive. Just enough to keep people near but still at arms' length. A safe distance.

He was about to make a snarky remark—a joke about how his memory was so bad he couldn't even remember if he brushed his teeth this morning—so they could laugh and he could easily change the subject. But before he could open his mouth, Loni reached out and took hold of his hand, silencing him. As if reading his mind, she gave his hand a gentle squeeze as if to say, "don't deflect." It was such a simple movement, and if she were any other woman, that would have been exactly what he would have done. Deflect.

But apparently, Loni wasn't just any other woman.

"I miss the times my dad was sober," he finally said, staring at their joined hands. "When I was fortunate, those times would coincide with my birthday and he would go all out—buy the best baseball equipment, gift cards to my favorite gaming stores, and he would drive forty-five minutes out of his way to this Italian bakery just to get these chocolate cannolis I liked."

Loni's expression grew soft and they exchanged smiles. "That's a nice memory," she said, moving her thumb soothingly over the top of his hand.

"Yeah, it was nice. My mom was happy then, too. And it was great, while it lasted. But that was the problem. It never lasted. Something would set my dad off and he'd go and binge drink again. When that became the pattern, and I was older, I eventually told him the best gift—the only gift I wanted—was for him to never drink again."

"What did he say?"

"He said he would try." He snorted. "Maybe he did try for all I know, but failed. Or I wasn't as important to him as alcohol was."

"Oh, Ian, trust me when I say that love isn't always expressed in the ways we need. Just because he struggled with an addiction doesn't necessarily have to diminish the love he had for you or your mom."

He huffed out a breath. "Now you sound like Pamela."

Loni's eyes widened. "Pamela knows about your parents?"

"Yeah. She's been a good friend to me practically a mother. Although, I'm sure she'd prefer being called an *aunt*."

"Well, I think I'm liking Pamela a little bit more now," she mused. "That she was there to tell you that you're not alone, and show you there are people who care about you and want to support you. That's important. And for the record, if you ever need someone to talk to about this, I'll listen, too. I find the more I talk about my mom, the good times, the better I feel about her loss—and whatever happened between her and my dad."

The carriage finally came to a stop after making a loop around downtown. Surprisingly, Ian's mind was clear and he felt as if a weight had been removed from his chest and shoulders. He had actually shared something emotional and hadn't been struck by lightning. Imagine that. He half wondered what other sorcery Loni was capable of.

She let go of his hand and pointed to a storefront called The Little Ole Miss. "Oh, look, something else that makes me feel better."

He hopped out onto the street and then extended his hand to help her step down. "And what's that?"

"Shopping, of course."

Watching Loni shop, he soon found out, was an experience all its own. She wasn't one to spend hours in a dressing room, trying on 90 percent of a store in one outing. She was quick and decisive, shooting down salesclerks who attempted to get her out of her style comfort zone with the diplomatic dodging of a White House Press secretary.

After about twenty minutes, Loni had settled on a red sundress—which looked amazing on her—three tops and a pair of strappy high-heeled sandals. She approached the cashier with all her clothing and the woman nodded approvingly.

"Great choices," the woman commented, snapping her chewing gum. "Good thinking bringing your boyfriend in, too. After all, he's the one that's gonna be looking at ya all night, right?"

Loni blinked, then glanced at Ian. "Oh, him?" she said, pointing as if there were other men in the store. "He—"

"Loves everything you chose, honey," he said, stepping up to the counter. "But then again, you look absolutely stunning in anything. And in nothing," he added with a wink.

The cashier nodded with a wide grin. "Oh my stars aligned in heaven, this one's a real keeper, sugar," she told Loni with the seriousness of a priest in confessional.

Loni lightly patted his cheek. "He is a keeper for sure. In fact, he said this whole purchase was his treat because he's such a lucky man." She turned fully to him, a wicked gleam in her eyes. "Didn't you say those exact words, sugarplum?"

Ian wasn't surprised that Loni had outsmarted and out joked him once again. She was quick on her feet. One of the many things he'd admired about her.

He grudgingly pulled out his wallet. "I don't quite recall those exact words, but anything for you, boo bear."

"Great, honey bun buns," Loni said brightly. "Maybe throw in that sunhat, too, then. Oh, and that gold shell bracelet. And maybe those pink flip-flops. Size eight."

Ian threw her a deadpan look. "Christmas is coming, dear. Maybe you should leave me something to buy you," he muttered.

Loni smothered a laugh as the cashier beamed. "Oh, if you two aren't cuter than two June bugs on a peach tree," the woman said, taking Ian's card and completing the sale. She placed Loni's items in a bag and then handed it to him. "Y'all come back here real soon. End of season sale is next weekend."

Loni snapped her fingers. "Darn. Sorry we'll miss that."

"I'm not," he murmured, heading to the door, before she decided to throw anything else on his tab.

They stepped outside the store and Loni began to roar with laughter. "Oh my goodness," she wheezed. "Your face. It was even funnier than when you ate that pepper omelet."

Ian grinned back, enjoying how beautiful she looked when she was so happy and carefree—even if it was at his own expense. "Well, then I'll chalk up this spending spree to entertainment costs for the day."

Loni immediately sobered. "Oh no, I didn't mean for you to actually pay for my things. I'll write you a check when we get back to the hotel."

When she went for her bag, he yanked it out of her reach. "Nope. No deal. This is my treat, *boo boo bear*."

"Ian," she warned.

Ian opened the bag and looked in. "Then I guess I'll just keep what I bought for myself here."

Loni held out her hand. "Fine. I'll accept then. But only because I really want to make Marise jealous with those shoes."

Ian chuckled and handed her back the bag. "Good. Seeing how red's totally not my color, this is the best possible scenario for both of us."

Loni rolled her eyes. "Thank you."

"You're very welcome. Any other shopping to do?"

Loni glanced around the row of small boutique stores along the street. "No, I think that's it. No need to increase your credit limit," she said with a wink.

"Great, now where'd we park?"

Loni pointed. "We're over by the bank building."

"Bank?" That rang a bell. Scott had sent him a list of potential sellers in the area the other day and one of them was the owner of that building. He glanced at the old building on the corner that had to have at least eight floors to it.

"It used to be a bank, back when I was in high school. Now, the bottom floor is a thrift and consignment shop. The other floors house the local newspaper and a financial planner, I think."

"Nice building." Despite being known for buying up land and building new, Ian still had an appreciation for historic buildings. Based on its looks, it had to be about a hundred years old. His mind was already churning with ideas to modernize it. He was extra glad he'd gone shopping with Loni now. He'd text his secretary and see if she could set up a meeting with the owner, since he'd be in town a little while longer now. With the info he knew about the airport and added parking garage, he could get a head start over a lot of developers.

"Why Apollonia Wingate, is that you?" A crusty voice behind them interrupted his thoughts.

Loni whirled around. There was an older gentleman with white thinning hair and a long beard that rivaled Santa Claus, sitting on a bench along the main sidewalk.

"Oh, Henry," she said with a laugh, "I didn't see you there. How are you?"

The man folded his newspaper and set it down beside him. "Still living," he answered with a wink. "Just celebrated my eighty-third birthday last month."

Eighty-three? Ian schooled his surprise. The man looked well past a hundred and three in his opinion. "Happy birthday," he offered.

Henry's gaze turned to Ian and his expression soured. "Who are you?"

Ian smiled and stuck out his hand. "Ian Hollowell. I'm a friend of Loni's."

Henry didn't take his hand. Just gave him a short nod and a grunt, then turned back to Loni. "Heard you were helping out with your family's hotel."

Loni nodded. "Yes, for a little bit anyway."

"Nice to see you young people hold onto tradition for a change. We all loved that place as much as your mama did."

Loni glanced at Ian. "See?"

Henry squinted at Ian. "You've got something against resorts, boy?"

"No," he said, the same time Loni said, "Yes. Ian works for a development company that would like to buy the resort from my daddy."

The man grunted. "Heard about you."

Ian's brow rose. "Bad news travels fast."

Loni nodded, then leaned in and whispered toward Henry. "Not only that but Ian wants to tear the hotel down."

"What?" The old man slapped his knee and then spit on the ground. "Over my dead body!"

Ian highly doubted it would be a long wait.

"The big decision is up to Loni's father," Ian said. "That's out of my hands, I'm afraid. But if the sale should go through, well, my company would carefully investigate all possibilities but, in the end, we won't do anything that would upset the town. We only want to capitalize on its growth potential that would benefit everyone."

Henry folded his arms with a glare. "That's the biggest bunch of Yankee bull crap I've ever heard."

So much for his diplomatic skills working in this town. Maybe he was losing his touch. Or the people of Sunny Banks were a more formidable opponent than he'd first judged.

Loni grabbed Ian's arm and tugged. "We'll be seeing you, Henry. Come by the café and Kalinda will have a cinnamon bun with your name on it."

Henry pointed at Loni, glaring at Ian. "Now, *that's* how you pacify an old man."

"You mean all I had to do is buy him a doughnut to get him to like me?" Ian grumbled on the way to his car.

"Well, that and leave the hotel alone. Quite simple really."

Ian frowned. He wished it were that simple, but he had his own interests to protect as much as Loni's and the town's.

"I am sorry for throwing you under the bus back there," she said when they finally reached the car.

"No harm done." Without thinking, Ian reached out and wrapped a strand of her hair around his finger. "I can handle the Henry's of this town if need be." *The Loni's of this town were something else entirely...*

"It was unfair." Loni let out a sigh, leaning into his touch. "I don't want to fight with you, Ian."

"Me either."

"Good."

"I'd like to kiss you instead."

Loni startled, her big blue eyes widening. "Oh, I..." She looked around nervously. "Uh, that's not a good idea."

"Why not?"

"Well, for one, I shouldn't even be seen talking to you. You're the enemy."

He grabbed his chest in mock pain. "Harsh. I much prefer *friendly adversary.*"

"Whatever." She rolled her eyes. "The point is we don't want the same things."

Ian hid a smile. "I'm pretty sure we do." At least *one* thing.

Her cheeks colored slightly. "I'm pretty sure we don't," she said, but her tone sounded unsure.

Ian stepped closer to her but hesitated, giving her a moment for her brain to catch up with her body. When he saw something flicker in her eyes, he gave in and gently lowered his mouth to hers. She immediately kissed him back with a force that surprised him as one of her hands went to the nape of his neck, massaging.

This, he thought, feeling drugged as he traced the soft fullness of her lips with his tongue. This was more than mere desire. It was like a longing so deep in his soul that he'd do anything to quench it. He wanted nothing more than to take her to bed right then and there, do what he'd desired to do since he'd first met her. However, the last thing Ian wanted to do was hurt her.

He pulled back slowly, trying to keep his breathing under control.

She looked up and sent him a dazed smile. "Okay, you're right," she breathed. "I guess we do want the same things." She bit her lip. "Maybe you can even show me a few more of those things when we get back to the hotel?"

It took all the willpower in his body, but he shook his head. "No...well, only if you're sure."

Loni stood up on her toes and pressed a brief kiss to his lips. "I am," she said, heading to her side of the car. "But let's use my room. It's way nicer."

Loni was fairly sure Ian broke several speed limits and might have even run a red light heading back to the resort. And it still hadn't been fast enough in her mind. They were giggling like teenagers as Ian took her by the hand and led her up the steps of the hotel, where she was suddenly hit with a dose of reality and panicked.

"Wait," she said, pulling him back.

Ian looked stunned. "*Wait?* I just did speeds I didn't even know a Toyota could do and now you say wait? What's wrong?"

"Um, nothing." She bit her lip, then glanced around. "We, uh, just shouldn't be seen walking in together."

He arched an eyebrow. "Ah. Can't be seen sleeping with the enemy?"

She ignored his perturbed tone. "Here. Maybe you go in first," she said, opening her purse and pulling out her room key. "Let yourself in and I'll knock when I get there. I promise I'll be five minutes behind you."

He took the key grimly. "Is this really necessary, Loni?"

"Yes, please," she said, giving him a light push through the door. "I'll make it worth the extra effort," she added with a smile.

He flashed her a grin and then wasting no time, he spun around toward the door. "See you in five!"

Once Ian disappeared inside the hotel, Loni hung outside for a few minutes and once she figured it was safe, she picked up her shopping bag and walked into the lobby. It was just her luck that Kalinda had emerged from the back office and began waving her over as soon as she saw her.

"I've been looking for you," her sister said, glancing down at the bag in Loni's hand. "Were you downtown?"

Loni smiled and held up her bag. "Guilty. I needed something for The Beach Bash."

"Nice, because that's exactly what I want to talk to you about."

She glanced toward the back hallway that led to her suite. "Um, can it wait?" she asked, thinking of Ian.

Kalinda huffed out a breath. "No, it can't. Listen, I wanted to know if you emailed The Beach Bash flyer that Marise created to all our past guest contacts?"

"I did. On Sunday. Marise told me The Chamber has already gotten lots of calls. It sounds like people are excited about it."

Kalinda smiled. "Great. Hey, just so you know, I've decided

to close the café early tomorrow. I have pies to make for the Bash and I want to make sure I'm available to help direct the vendors. What do you think?"

"Sounds great." Anxious to get to Ian, Loni made a motion to leave, but Kalinda blocked her way with her arm.

"Not so fast," Kalinda said, seeming amused at Loni's impatience. "Even though the café will be closing early, I still need you to help me with the pies. Can you come to the kitchen a little earlier, like around eight tomorrow morning?"

"If you let me leave right now, I'll be there at seven."

Kalinda laughed. "Sheesh, hot date?"

Loni felt herself flush all over. "Why would you say that?"

Kalinda tilted her head. "It's a joke, Lon."

"Oh, right." She let out a weak laugh. "Ha. That was funny."

"Obviously," her sister said drily.

"Well, see you tomorrow morning," she called, heading toward the back hall that led to her suite.

Was it a hundred degrees here? She was perspiring by the time she made it to the door of her suite. Since she'd given her key to Ian, she lightly knocked on the door. Ian immediately answered it.

With a devilish grin, he casually leaned his shoulder against the doorway. His shirt was already unbuttoned and in that second, she wanted nothing more than to run her hands all over his exposed chest. "That was more than five minutes," he practically growled.

"I know. I'm sorry. I ran into Kalinda."

"Loni!" she heard her sister Marise call out. "Hold up a sec!"

With a gasp, Loni shoved her bag at Ian and pushed him back into her room. "Quick! Hide!"

"Hey!" he yelped as Loni slammed the door in his face. Then she whirled around just as Marise came striding down the hall toward her.

"What did you say?" Marise asked her, a puzzled expression on her face.

Loni swallowed. "Uh, I said, *hey...*you."

"Hey, yourself. I've been looking all over for you."

Join the club. "Well, you've got me now. What's up?" she asked, lightly dabbing her moist forehead.

"It's about The Beach Bash. I wanted your opinion to break the tie between me and Kalinda. We're going to have vendors setting up on the beach in front of the hotel and we're also going to have some vendors inside the hotel. It will be a nice natural flow leading them out to the beach. Kalinda thinks we should mix up the food vendors with the store vendors but I think we should keep the food vendors all together. What do you think?"

"Um, I think either would work, but maybe keep all the food vendors together. This way when people are hungry they know exactly where to go."

Marise nodded with a smile. "That's what I thought, too. We have over fifty vendors committed to being here. Can you believe it? I can't wait to see the look on Ian's face when he finds out."

Loni averted her gaze. "Uh, me, too."

"Actually, I haven't seen him around lately. He must be in hiding," she said with a sly grin.

Loni nervously stepped away from her door. "Uh, yeah, probably." *Actually, that's more accurate than you know.*

"It's going to be a big day tomorrow night," Marise said brightly. "I'm going to grab the velvet ropes from storage and then I'm going to hit the hay. You should go to bed early, too."

Loni sent her a weak smile. "Oh, I plan on it."

"Great. See you tomorrow," her sister said, turning and heading back down the hallway.

Loni let out a relieved breath. Then, once she was sure Marise was gone, she turned and knocked on her door again. This time, when Ian answered, he looked so disgruntled, she had to laugh.

"Sorry," she said again and followed him into the suite. "Marise and Kalinda both wanted to talk to me about The Beach Bash."

Ian peeled off his shirt and then climbed onto her bed. Making himself comfortable, he leaned back, resting the back of his head on his hands and crossing his ankles. "Oh, and how's The Beach Bash preparation going?"

Loni kicked off her shoes, then slowly approached the bed. "Um...good."

Ian grinned at her evasiveness, but his gaze remained trained on her face as she stepped closer. For all his relaxed outward posture, he reminded her of a lion watching for movement in the grass. She imagined he was probably that way in business dealings, too.

"Care to share more details than that?" he asked, his eyes glittering with amusement.

"Not particularly," she teased back. "I suppose you're just going to have to be surprised like everyone else."

"Well, then..." Without warning, Ian snatched her hand and yanked her onto the bed with him. "That's perfectly fine with me," he said with a faint smile, curving his lips. "Because I happen to love surprises."

Then he lowered his mouth to hers and proceeded to show her a few of his own.

Chapter Twenty

On Friday morning, Loni woke up later than usual, grateful that Kalinda had been training the hostess to take over table serving. As a result, Loni didn't need to report to the café until ten, but then she remembered she had to get up because she told Kalinda she'd help her with her pies.

With a long, satisfying stretch, she turned to her side, happy to see Ian still sleeping beside her. She had no regrets about last night with him. For all his claims of superficiality when it came to personal relationships, he was a gentle and caring lover. But she reminded herself not to read too much into what they had done. Sex was sex. And even though he was starting to mean something to her, as a friend and now a lover, they had made no promises beyond that.

Loni let her gaze travel over his chest and the sleek expanse of his shoulders. He already had a shadow of stubble on his face and out of impulse, she reached out to run her fingertip over his jaw.

Ian opened his eyes halfway and when he saw her, let out

a drowsy smile. "Loni," he said in a sleep-roughened voice, gathering her close.

She nuzzled into his chest with a sigh, feeling like it was the most natural place to be.

Just sex! she reminded herself sharply. *Do not, I repeat do not, let yourself fall for him.*

Loni would have to be kidding herself if she believed the hotel was working its one-of-a-kind magic on her now. That Ian could ever open himself up to a meaningful commitment with her. But they had so much potential together. Only if she allowed herself to entertain any of those thoughts for more than a nano second, she'd almost certainly end up with a broken heart.

Get a grip, Loni. It was one night of sex.

Besides, Ian was only here to buy her resort. Once her father saw what she and her sisters could do with it, he wouldn't sell. She was sure of it. Then Ian would leave… She knew that, although it didn't make it any easier. To make matters worse, Loni didn't even know where she belonged anymore. At one time, she'd thought it was California, but the more time she spent here in Sunny Banks, the more she wanted to make it permanent. But who would she be if she did stay? She'd been so close to making a partner at a prestigious city law firm. Anything else felt like a step down in her career. And would it even be worth it?

Ian startled her by laying a finger on the notch between her brows. "Wow, you are the only person I've ever seen look more stressed asleep than when awake."

She opened her eyes and forced a smile. "I guess I have a lot on my mind."

He grinned down at her. "No kidding. Solve the world's oil crisis yet?"

She laughed. "No, still working on my climate change proposal."

"Ah, that's good, I'll sleep well tonight knowing you're on the case." He gazed at her for a long moment, his expression turning serious. "However, I'd sleep even better if I were sleeping here tonight. And maybe the night after that."

She blinked, realization hitting her. "Oh, of course you're more than welcome. Like I said, this room is definitely better than yours."

Ian shook his head, his eyes grave. "No, Loni, I wasn't asking to be in your room." He cleared his throat, suddenly looking unsure of himself. "I was asking if I could...you know, just be with *you* tonight and every night I'm here. And before you answer, I'm not looking to complicate things between us. You know that's not me. I just want you to know that I like you. *Really* like you. I'm obviously very attracted to you and want to spend as much time with you as I can. But I'm not trying—"

She placed a finger over his lips. "I'd like that, too."

"You would?"

She grinned, stroking his face with her hand. "I take it you're not used to hearing that answer from a woman. Maybe I was too hasty in my response."

He chuckled and let out what sounded like a relieved breath. "Well, to be honest, I'm not used to asking women if I can stay with them." He frowned as if realizing that for the first time. "Actually, I don't think I've ever *had* to ask."

She felt his forehead. "I'm not a doctor, but I think you'll live."

"Yeah..." he murmured; his brows still knitted tight.

"I promise you, Ian, I'm not even *thinking* of ordering save-the-date cards yet."

Judging from the smile that illuminated his face, that had been the right thing to say. "I'm sorry. Am I being too weird about this?"

"No," she lied, wanting to put him at ease. "But I find it hard to believe that you've never come close to a real relationship before."

"Once." He sighed.

"Once?" She chuckled. "That's all the answer I'm going to get?"

He made a face and rolled his eyes. "I dated a nice girl back in college. She wanted to get engaged after graduation. She and her parents thought it was the obvious, natural next step."

"But you obviously didn't think that."

"No. In my world, where I came from, there was nothing obvious or natural about it. So I broke it off with her instead." He shrugged, his voice turning quietly reflective in thought. "I think I did her a favor. We wouldn't have lasted."

"How do you know that? There are a lot of people who are high school sweethearts, marry, and stay married for fifty years."

"There's no logic to it. I just know," he said, tapping a finger to his temple.

"So you never bothered trying to find the right woman after that?"

"No, not when I'd never seen the benefits of love."

She thought of his upbringing. "Because of your parents?"

"Pretty much." He gave her a weary nod. "Not that I'm against love and commitment for other people."

"Oh! Is that why you're a fan of *Bridgerton*? You're secretly rooting for love to win out in the end?"

He half grinned. "Hell, no. I'm a fan of Bridgeton because

of the gratuitous sex and the phenomenal costume designs. But if you haven't watched season three yet, I'd totally be open to watching it with you after work."

"Can't," she said with a pout. "I need to get ready for The Beach Bash. I'm glad I'm here because there's lots to do."

"Hmm."

"What does that mean?"

He shrugged. "Nothing. Just... What happens after The Beach Bash?"

"We figure out our next steps to keep the momentum going with the resort. Why?"

"Well, you talk about the resort a lot, understandably, but say your father decides not to sell. Do you plan on working here or do you plan on going back to practicing law?"

She frowned, growing a tiny bit defensive. "Why do I need to do one or the other? Maybe I can open up my own practice here. Plus, Kalinda said they could use my help with contracts with some of our vendors and suppliers, especially if we were to expand and do a banquet room. Marise and I already discussed hiring more people, so she wants me to make sure we have some policies drawn up to ensure the resort is operating within the bounds of law."

"Sounds like you've thought about this a lot."

"Yeah," she breathed. "I guess I have." And she felt good about her decision. Maybe her life wasn't such a hot mess after all.

"And if your dad decides to sell...?"

She narrowed her eyes. "Do you know something I don't?"

"Nope. Just curious to know if you'd still want to stay in town even if the resort wasn't here."

"I think so," she said thoughtfully. "You have to admit there is something special about this town."

"Yeah, there is…" He smiled at her. "All right then," he said, rubbing his hands together. "Takeout, popcorn, and Netflix after The Beach Bash. Be there or be a chit," he said in a fake British accent.

Loni smiled to herself. For someone so adamant about avoiding emotional attachments, his actions were proving just the opposite. However, she wasn't so naïve to think she would be the woman to change him. No. But in the meantime, she vowed to enjoy every single moment she could with him.

"I would be most honored, sir." She reached her other hand up and brought his face to hers, taking his mouth with a sudden rush of intensity. "Oh, and speaking of asking for things…" Her gaze drifted to the clock on the side table. "I have about thirty minutes before I have to hop in the shower."

His hands lightly traced a path over her skin. "Sweetheart, in this particular case, and with you, the answer will always be yes."

• • •

After Loni had gotten dressed to go to the café, Ian had slowly made his way back to his room, feeling a little unsure on his feet. It was weird, this feeling of already wanting to see her again. Maybe he'd grab a quick shower and head down to the café and check on her. Just to make sure she was okay after last night. He *had* to eat, after all. Then maybe he'd pick up where she left off on that guest list and see if he could help her narrow down the ever-elusive TJ.

But as soon as he reached his room, Lucille called out to him from down the hall.

"Morning, Ian," she said cheerfully, wheeling a room

service cart his way. "Special delivery for y'all. Coffee and a hot breakfast." She removed the dome of the tray and there was what looked to be a vegetable omelet, two hashbrowns, and a small bowl of fruit.

"Is this from Loni?" he asked without thinking.

Lucille's brows furrowed. "Well, maybe. But doubtful."

"Why doubtful?"

"Sugar, in case you've forgotten, she doesn't like you very much."

Ian thought about all the things Loni had done to him last night and had to suppress a smile. "I think she may be warming up to me."

Lucille shrugged and placed the dome back on the plate. "I also had special instructions to deliver this as well." She pulled an envelope out from the inside of her shirt and blushed. "Didn't want to risk losing it," she said, handing it to him.

"What is it?"

She grinned. "You're moving up in the world. We had a checkout today and I was told to move you to room 1020 for the remainder of your stay with us. That is, if you *want* to move. No pressure. But I guarantee y'all will love it. Has a great view of the boardwalk."

He blinked down at the new room card. A view meant it actually had a window. This was certainly a pleasant switch. Maybe they'd finally realized he wasn't the devil reincarnated. Or at least...he wasn't trying to be.

"To whom do I owe a thanks for this?" he asked. But he'd already had a sneaky suspicion *this* gift at least, was from Loni. After hearing enough complaints about his room, combined with their newfound *friendship*, she'd probably decided to cut him some slack, which he greatly appreciated along with the breakfast. In fact, he was already contemplating all the ways he could thank her in private later tonight.

Lucille scratched her head. "To be honest, I'm not sure which one of the girls decided to move your room. Could have been all three. Personally, I don't ask questions. I just follow orders." She leaned in and lowered her voice. "Remember that if you become the new owner."

Ian nodded gravely. "Will do, and good to know."

"Great. Now, will there be anything else..." she said, looking hopeful. "*Anything* else at all?"

"*No*, thank you." But he couldn't help but grin.

"Can't blame a woman for trying," she said, making a face. "Enjoy your breakfast and see you at The Beach Bash later tonight."

"See ya, Lucille." With a mood that was strangely buoyant and lighthearted, Ian watched her go. It was a phenomenon to be sure. He'd hardly been here a week and was already feeling like a part of a community family. And he quite liked it.

He swiped his key card, then maneuvered the tray into his room with one hand. Although he was grateful for the food, the impromptu delivery did take away his excuse to go and see Loni at work. And even though he knew it was for the best to give them each some space, he couldn't seem to shake the feeling of uneasiness at the thought. Before he could give in to that worry, his cell phone rang. He set the tray down on the bed and reached for his phone. He didn't think it was a particularly good sign to see his boss's name illuminate the screen.

"Hey, Raj," he said, picking up the call on the second ring.

"Don't *hey, Raj*, me," his boss barked out. "What the eff is going on down there?"

Even though he was alone in his room, Ian's posture

automatically straightened. He'd never heard Raj sound so stressed. "Everything is proceeding as planned."

"Bullshit. If it were, I would have those contracts and you would be here meeting with Denali Builders—who are chomping at the bit and have been up my ass all week. What is the problem?" he demanded.

"There is no problem. The resort contracts are coming. I promise—"

"No promises. I want written assurances."

"You'll have them as well."

"Good. Because if *The Predator* can't acquire this land, I doubt I'll have much use for him in the future. Do I make myself clear?"

Ian swallowed. "Understood."

There was a click and then silence.

Despite the threat from his boss, Ian wasn't entirely worried. He knew how Joe thought, and knew he was just trying to give his daughters an olive branch by hearing them out first before doing what he really wanted. Ultimately, he'd sell the resort to Hollavest. In the meantime, what Ian needed was to focus on work. Work would get him back in the right frame of mind while he bid his time. He'd check his emails, tidy up any loose ends, and make sure there weren't any pressing matters at hand and...

He lifted the plate and beneath it found a Chamber of Commerce brochure. Handy. Especially if he wanted more information about the area and businesses. There was also the town newspaper folded in half. When he opened it, he saw the front-page news was that the mayor was putting the new airport project in their capital plans budget, since the rezoning was approved.

Interesting, he thought. Things were moving more quickly than he realized in Sunny Banks. Which meant he had to, too—especially after that phone call with Raj.

He'd be extending his stay for sure—more for business, of course, than to spend more time with Loni. But if he could afford to do both then he didn't see the harm. At least, not right now.

• • •

"Loni!" Kalinda barked. "Wrong table. *Again.*"

Loni looked at the plates she'd almost put down and pivoted to the table next to her. *Dammit.* "Here ya go," she said, calmly placing them at the correct table. "Enjoy."

Gosh, she was a scatterbrain today. Not that she was all that great a waitress on a good day, but still, she was making a lot of stupid mistakes today. Between The Beach Bash and last night with Ian, her mind was all over the place. Before heading over to grab a coffeepot, she glanced at the entrance one more time, hoping to see Ian. It was getting late, and she'd assumed that after last night he'd worked up an appetite and would stop by to see her.

Marise sidled up next to her with a wide cat-caught-the-canary grin. "What's up with you today? I'd say it was excitement over The Beach Bash, but I think it's something else."

"I don't know what you mean," Loni said, grabbing the coffeepot and heading to the counter service.

"Oh, don't you?" Marise asked, practically bouncing on her toes as she followed her. "One, you can't focus. Two, you keep glancing at the door. And three, anyone just needs to look at you to know what's going on."

Loni placed a hand on her hip and turned to her sister.

"How do I look?"

Hazel, who was sitting near the register because of her booted foot, chimed in, "Like you got lucky."

"Bingo," Marise said, grinning.

Loni huffed out a breath. "Y'all are crazy."

"Ooh," Marise said, pointing at her. "And now you're slipping into your accent. Wow, it must have been really good."

It was really good.

"What was really good?" Kalinda said, coming out of the kitchen. "Please say it was my Almond Joy French toast. I toasted the coconut this time."

Marise's eyes widened. "Sounds amazing. But Loni's sex life is still probably better."

Kalinda quirked an eyebrow. "Loni has a sex life? Since when?"

Loni placed her hands over her ears. "Can we not talk about sex right now?"

Hazel frowned. "There's no better time than the day after sex to talk about sex. Details please. I can barely walk with this thing on," she said, gesturing to her wrapped foot, "so I need to live vicariously through y'all."

Loni shook her head, partly amused and partly disturbed that everyone was so interested in her love life. "No one wants to hear details."

An older woman at the counter raised her coffee mug Loni's way. "I sure do."

Marise smirked. "Told ya."

"Not going to happen," Loni warned. Not that she had anything to feel guilty about, but Ian was still considered the... *adversary.* And even though it seemed as though he'd made peace with leaving the decision of selling up to her father, she didn't want anyone to think that she was wavering in her loyalties.

"You can say that again," Kalinda said, motioning to the entrance of the café. "Daddy and Pamela have just arrived."

Marise snapped her fingers. "Dang it all. You got lucky.*"*

Although Loni wasn't entirely thrilled with having to deal with Pamela, she had to admit she couldn't have asked for more perfect timing to avoid talking about Ian. "I'll go make sure they're seated in my section," she said, rushing over to greet them.

"Good morning, Daddy," she said, kissing him on the cheek. She turned to Pamela. "Good morning, hope you slept well."

Pamela took her father's hand and smiled. "Yes, thank you. The cottage is lovely. I so appreciate Kalinda and Marise making room for us both there."

"They're happy to have you. It's not like Daddy visits often."

Her father visibly stiffened. "Could say the same thing about you, darlin'."

Daddy was right. She should have made arrangements to visit more often. She'd been so busy with work, she'd lost track of everything else. Things, she realized, that meant a lot, like unconditional love and support.

Loni forced a smile on her lips. "Touché, Daddy. Follow me. I have a nice window seat open for you," she said, grabbing a couple of menus and leading them across the room.

"Do I want to know why you're helping out in the café here?" her father asked, taking a seat.

"Hazel hurt her foot, so Kalinda asked me to step in."

"Oh? What's her plan when you have to go back to LA?"

Loni glanced around to make sure she wasn't needed at any of her stations, then deciding there would never be a perfect time to tell him the truth, pulled out a chair for herself and sat down. "Daddy, I think you should know, I'm not completely sure I am going back."

His graying brows furrowed deep. "Because of that boy Blaze? Hell, California's a big state."

She shrugged. "It's not just because we broke up. It's a long story that I can't get into now, but there is a chance I could lose my job, too."

Pamela let out a little gasp while her father went strangely quiet.

"You'll get another job," her father finally said. "I'm not worried about that."

"Well, of course, you'll find another job," Pamela offered. "Your sisters have told me what a bright attorney you are."

Her sisters told Pamela that, not Daddy. Loni sighed, wishing she didn't feel like such a failure in her father's eyes. He didn't even think she was a good waitress! But becoming a successful attorney didn't seem to have moved her up the ladder in gaining her father's approval or attention. Maybe that was the real reason why she was so desperate to save the resort. To her, their hotel was the last link, her last hope of salvaging their relationship.

"Do you plan on looking for another job out here, then?" Daddy asked.

"I'm not sure what I'm going to do," Loni said carefully. "I'm waiting to see what happens with the sale of the resort."

Daddy shook his head. "Land's sake, girl, that law firm doesn't deserve you, but that doesn't mean your only option is to run a struggling resort. You could be making a much better living where you are in LA."

Loni swallowed. Put that way, it did sound rather insane.

And like she'd told Ian, why couldn't she do both? Her decision had more to do with family, her mother, this community than it had to do with money. She could get another lawyer position here in Sunny Banks, and in the meantime, she could help around the resort. "I know. But I could still stay and help. I know I could. At least until I get another job. Three heads are better than two and Mama—"

"Enough about your mama," he barked, standing up to leave. "I—" He shook his head. Without another word, he stormed out the side entrance and headed in the direction of the beach.

Pamela watched him go and then turned to Loni with sympathetic eyes. "It's not you, honey," she said quietly. She scooted her own chair back and stood.

Loni scoffed. "I wouldn't be too sure about that."

Pam inhaled deeply before letting out an explosive sigh. "Look, your father and I are in love and as a result, we're privy to a lot of personal things about each other. However, he's got his own demons with regard to this resort that he needs to come to terms with before he'll be able to share them with me." She stood silent a moment, then added, "I'm sure I'm the last person you want to hear this from, but you sound as if you have some of those you need to deal with as well."

Chapter Twenty-One

Once the sun went down and the cooler September night air settled in, Loni was glad she'd borrowed a light sweater from Marise. Some vendors were still setting up, but that didn't keep people from approaching their tables. Marise had hired a piano player and, for the families, a person making balloon animals. It was early yet, not quite six o'clock, but the turnout to their Beach Bash was already respectable. Loni had to give Marise and Kalinda credit for handling all the table and tent setups on the beach as well as the invitations to the various restaurants and vendors in town—each who showed up with their own specialty to highlight and sell.

Her sisters were remarkable women. Women Loni hadn't given enough credit to in the past. She'd been so driven by her own career and success, she'd never bothered to look back and appreciate all that her sisters had achieved as well, and it made her feel small to think how petty and sometimes even materialistic she'd been. Their resort not only served visitors, but served the community as well.

Marise came over and wrapped an arm around her shoulder. "Your face is not marketing this event well at all."

Loni bit down on a grin. "Sorry. This better?" she said, grimacing.

"Better if you want to look like your appendix just burst." Marise eyed her closely. "Hey, don't let Daddy get you down. I had a talk with him this afternoon. Told him my plans for creating a bigger venue here."

"Really? And what did he say?"

Marise bit her lip. "Hard to tell between all the grunting and growling, but I am hanging on to hope. Oddly enough, I think Pamela's in our corner now."

Loni had gotten the same strange feeling about Pamela from their conversation this morning as well. However, she still wasn't sure if she could trust it.

"Well, I'm glad he's listening to *one* of us," Loni said, shaking her head. "Maybe the Grinch's heart is growing after all."

More and more people began funneling through the hotel to access the beach. There were faces she didn't recognize, but Loni was pleased to see so many townspeople among them who came out to support their event. She saw Samuel and his mom perusing the craft tables and waved when she caught his eye.

The boy quickly ran up to her, a big smile on his face. "Hi, Miss Loni! Hi, Miss Marise! Guess what?"

Loni and Marise exchanged amused looks. "What?" Loni asked, enjoying how excited the boy seemed.

"I got two bikes! One for me and one for my mama!"

Marise's eyebrows shot up. "Wow, I can't believe you raised so much money. Congrats, little man," she added, giving him a fist bump.

Samuel shook his head. "I didn't have to spend any of my money. My mama took me to the Hobbyhorse Bike Shop and they told me my money was no good. Someone told Mr. Finkle that I was to pick any bike I wanted for me, and my mama could do the same."

Loni frowned. "Do you know who that someone was?"

"Nope. Mr. Finkle said he couldn't say."

Loni tried to cover her shock with a wide smile. "Th-that's amazing." And just a little bit curious for someone to do something like that out of the blue.

"My mama's waving me back," he said, looking over his shoulder. "Bye!"

"See ya, Sam."

The little boy took off for his mom as Marise turned to Loni. "What a sweet gesture. I wonder who did it."

Loni did, too, although she had a strong suspicion about who was behind the generous gift. She smiled to herself. Maybe Ian wasn't as unaffected by this town as he pretended to be.

More people filtered in around them. Loni glanced around, looking for Ian but didn't see him yet. But to her surprise, Henry Shelton popped into view. The older man carefully made his way over to her, strategically using his cane to weave through the crowd toward them.

"Why, Henry," Loni said, smiling down at him, "I didn't picture you to be a Beach Bash kind of person."

The man scowled. "I ain't. But I didn't want that developer gettin' any fancy ideas. Figured I'd show him that people here do care that this resort is a success." He glanced around and nodded. "Not that my support is very much needed here."

Marise bit down on her smile. "Well, of course it's needed, and it's mighty nice of you to come out all this way."

"Had to take a taxi," he grumbled. "It smelled like cabbage. Now I'm hungry. There better be food."

"Why, yes," Loni said, winking at Marise. "In fact, you go to The White Squirrel Café's table over there on the left and you tell them Kalinda's BBQ chicken platter is on me."

Henry stroked his long beard in thought. "And dessert?" he added.

Loni held in a sigh. "And dessert."

The old man's grumpy countenance lifted. "Ain't that the berries. Anything else you givin' away for free here?"

"Don't push your luck, Henry."

"Righto. See you ladies, later," he said with a little shake of his cane.

Loni watched him hobble away with a smile. "He tries to hide it, but he's a big old softy at heart."

"*Tries* to hide it?" Marise made a face. "The man is as covert as a CIA agent."

Loni checked her watch and was about to go look for Ian but noticed Angela skirting the line and heading their way.

"This is amazing, y'all," Angela said, grinning at them. "Have you ever done an event like this before?"

"Yeah, but on a smaller scale," Marise said, her gaze scanning the crowd. "I wanted to get our feet wet first, then once I figured out the kinks, like making sure part of the beach was roped off and you could only approach the vendors if you came in through the hotel, then I approached the Chamber of Commerce and got their help expanding and finding out who to contact."

Angela and Loni exchanged impressed looks. "Well, thank you for inviting me to sell my shell wreaths. Ansley's here, manning the table for me now."

Marise's face perked. "Ooh, Ansley's here already? I'll

go say hi to her now before things get too busy." Then she maneuvered into the crowd and disappeared.

"You look lovely, sugar," Angela said, admiring her new sundress. "Red is definitely your color and—" Her gaze focused on the pendant Loni was wearing, and her expression softened. "The necklace looks beautiful on you. My word but you look more like your mother than your mother."

Loni chuckled. "That's a very nice compliment. Thank you. I figured if my mama kept this necklace hidden, it must have been special to her, so I decided to wear it," she said, fingering it lightly. "For her."

"Any other particular reason you got all dolled up?"

Thinking of Ian, Loni averted her gaze. "Oh no, not really."

"Are you sure it doesn't have anything to do with a certain tall glass of water parading around looking at you like a wolf in a sheep pasture?"

Loni blinked. "Um, translation?"

Angela elbowed her in the ribs. "Ian is over there, looking like a man smitten."

Loni turned her head to follow Angela's gaze and her breath caught unexpectantly. How had Ian managed to get more handsome in less than eight hours? "Oh," she managed.

"Ian looks a lot more than just *oh*," Angela said, sounding amused.

Loni was saved from having to explain herself when Ian approached them, kissing them each a hello on the cheek. "Nice night," he said, tipping his chin toward the crowd. "It's more than what I expected."

Loni cleared her throat, trying to school in the overwhelming need to get closer to him. "Yes, Marise and Kalinda worked really hard putting this event together. I think they've been planning this since before summer started."

Almost as if he was thinking the same thing, he moved forward, even nearer. "Well, uh, it definitely looks like it paid off for them."

Angela rolled her eyes. "This is pathetic, y'all. Youth really is wasted on the young. I'm going back to my vendor table now and leave you two to have the conversation you really want to have," she said, her eyes sparking with humor. "Come visit me there later on." Then, with a wave of her hand, she was off and heading toward the beach area.

Glancing around to make sure no one was watching, Ian took the opportunity to gather Loni into his arms. "That's a relief, I thought she'd never leave," he murmured into the crook of her neck.

Loni closed her eyes, chuckling. "I don't think we're doing a very good job of hiding this from everyone."

Ian pulled back suddenly and looked at her. "Why do we have to hide anything?"

"Oh. I—" The question caught her off guard, and she swallowed, looking around.

"Loni," he said calmly, taking her by the shoulders, "we're both single, consenting adults. You do realize that, don't you?"

Riiight. Of course, she knew that. However, as foolish as it sounded, she couldn't help but feel that if she put her relationship out there with Ian in the public eye, it would be like she was accepting the fact that he could buy her family's resort and do whatever he wanted with it. And she wasn't ready to give up that fight. Especially not after the success she hoped tonight would be.

"Hey," he said, lifting her chin with his finger so he could look her in the eyes, "this is personal between us. It has nothing to do with business or the resort."

She wanted to believe him. But it was far easier for him to compartmentalize his feelings—to rule out emotions. For Loni on the other hand, not so much. It was much more personal, too. Ian's whole family history didn't hang on this hotel.

But then again, he did have moments when he showed glimpses of compassion and heart.

"I ran into Samuel," she said, gauging his reaction.

"Oh? Is he here selling ice cream?"

"He doesn't have to be. He told me someone not only bought him a bike but bought his mom one, too."

Ian glanced away, looking uncharacteristically uncomfortable. "That's, uh, nice."

"It's more than nice." She grinned, noticing his cheeks growing pink. "It's something a very special person with a good soul would do for another person in need. Someone who may not be as unemotional as he claims to be, wouldn't you say?"

Ian rolled his eyes. "Leave it to you and your keen brain to figure it out."

She laughed, not thinking it was possible to like this man any more than she already did.

"Well, isn't *this* surprising to see," Pamela said, interrupting them as she laid a hand on Loni's back.

Loni quickly stepped out of Ian's embrace and sobered, grateful for the interruption. Uh-oh. She and Ian were probably looking entirely too chummy together in public.

"Hello, Pam," she said, then noticed her father standing awkwardly there as well. They hadn't spoken since this morning. "Daddy."

Joe nodded warily. "You look mighty pretty, Loni," he said softly. Then his gaze shot hard and fast to Ian. "Care to give my girl a little breathing room, fella?"

Ian was startled, then took a step back. "Oh, sure, Joe."

"Joe," Pamela said in a chiding tone, "let them be. Why shouldn't two nice-looking, intelligent people be attracted to one another?" She took hold of Joe's arm with her two hands and grinned up at him. "After all, look at us."

A reluctant smile slid across his lips. "Sorry. Once a parent, always a parent."

Loni watched her father and Pamela's interaction with some bemusement. She'd never seen Daddy rendered so agreeable and so quickly before in all her life. Although Daddy was typically a genteel man, he was also hard-headed and sometimes brusque in many ways, which caused many battles of will at home. Perhaps Pamela had a more positive influence on him than Loni had suspected.

Pamela turned her smiling gaze up toward Ian. "How about us Yankees venture over for some real Carolina barbecue and let these two have a moment?"

Ian sent Loni a concerned glance. "You good with that? I'll grab you a plate."

Loni nodded. "Sure, thanks."

"And you, behave," Pamela whispered to Joe before taking Ian's arm and going off in the direction of the food.

Daddy shook his head. "That woman knows how to drive a point home." He sighed. "I am sorry I lost my temper with you today, Loni. But hearing you go on and on about your mama and this resort just makes me crazy sometimes."

"But why, Daddy?" She flung her arm out, gesturing to all the people about. "Doesn't this remind you of the old times? I remember when Mama needed eight arms because this place was so busy. I learned how to crack eggs because she needed extra help in the kitchen."

Her father smiled sadly. "That's the *only* thing you learned to do in a kitchen."

She made a face. "Probably because cooking seemed more work than fun back then. Funny, how I wish for those days again with Mama, when I thought cracking an egg was grounds for child labor law violation."

"She sure knew how to whip you girls into shape—but in a loving way," he said fondly. "Your mama had a gift for that, which was a good thing because I was so busy running around this place myself, it sure as heck couldn't have been me. I'm sorry about that, and I'm sorry for suggesting you wouldn't want to live here and work at the hotel. But I'm not sure you realize the time commitment especially since you were already spread thin at the law firm. Working as an attorney gives you a freedom you won't have if you're tied to this hotel. I want you to be sure you can do both."

"I know, Daddy. You've given me a lot to think about."

He nodded.

Loni glanced out toward the patio and saw her younger sister directing a couple toward the beach. "Marise told me she talked to you today. About expanding the hotel to add a few venue rooms for parties and maybe even weddings."

Her father groaned. "Yeah, she told me."

"What do you think?"

He gave her a noncommittal shrug. "It's not a bad concept. You'd have to change the name of the hotel, though. Ain't no couple in their right mind is gonna want to have the name The Sandy Bottom anywhere on their wedding invitation."

"Some might." Loni grinned, giving her father a sidelong glance.

He rolled his eyes, but a small grin escaped. "True. Some might."

Loni leaned into her father and pressed her head against his shoulder. This conversation she was having with him felt like a step in the right direction. He was actually listening to her and remembering the good times their family had, running this hotel. It was the first time in a long time that felt as if shadows were lifting from her heart.

"So, what do you think of the turnout?" she asked, gazing around at even more people filing in.

"I don't know why I'm ever amazed at what you ladies can do. But, yes, I am quite impressed."

Loni was tempted to squeal at her father's compliment and what that inevitably meant to his decision to sell the resort. She decided to hug him tighter instead. "I'm so happy to hear you say that. I knew we could change your mind. Marise told me that she already talked to you about making this event even bigger next year."

Her father lightly patted her head. "Marise always manages to put her cart in front of her horse. Too bad Kalinda's not for it, otherwise—"

"Wait, what." Loni lifted her head as shock flew through her. "What do you mean Kalinda's not for it? Not for The Beach Bash?"

He frowned. "No, darlin'. I thought you knew. I'm sorry. She's not for keeping the resort."

"When did she say this?"

He squinted as if in thought. "Oh, I don't know. Last night, I guess, at the house. She and I were sitting on the back porch having a beer. Told me she wasn't so sure of Marise's endurance with a project like that. Marise's enthusiasm for these kinds of things tends to dwindle with time."

Loni narrowed her gaze. "Oh, really? Says who?"

"I do," he said simply. "And of course, Kalinda. Sorry, but to be frank, I have to go by her opinion rather than yours because she has worked with Marise so much longer. You understand that, right?"

Loni shook her head, not quite believing what she was hearing. "No, Daddy, you must be confused."

"Watch it, darlin'." He frowned. "I may be old, but I ain't senile yet."

"No, no, I mean, Kalinda must have misspoken." There was no way that Kalinda could have changed her mind. There was no reason to—especially after such a successful turnout of The Beach Bash.

Loni grabbed his hand and squeezed. "There has to be a mistake. I know she would support Marise's idea one hundred percent. And she wouldn't want to sell the resort, she's told us as much. Let me speak with her. Don't decide anything yet. Please."

He sighed. "Apollonia—"

"Daddy, please. Just wait. If I can convince Kalinda to move forward with the renovations and we all want to keep running the hotel, will you still let us?"

He quirked an eyebrow. *"Us?"*

Loni drew back slightly, her own words surprising herself as much as her father. What exactly had she meant by "us"? But deep down inside she knew. Ever since she came home, it was like a missing piece of her puzzle had been found, and now she'd finally made her decision. "I...I would help them. I'll definitely stay here in Sunny Banks. I could even act as the hotel's legal attorney on top of everything else. I—"

"Honey, I don't think you know what's involved." He shook his head sadly. "Make sure you're doing this for you and you're not chasing some pipedream of your mama's." It was then that he glanced down at her neckline and froze.

Loni reached up and pressed her fingers to her pendant. "What? This?"

"The sun," he whispered in awe.

"Yeah." She glanced down at it. "I think it belonged to Mama. I found it in my room here."

He nodded, never taking his eyes off of it. "I remember it."

"You do?" she said, cocking her head at him. "Did you buy it for her?"

Her daddy's expression hardened as his gaze lingered a few beats longer on it. "No, I didn't," he finally said, looking up at her. "But I can see why your mother liked it. She was like the sun herself: vibrant, warm, a giant star."

Loni tried to hold her tears in check. "She was," she breathed. "Exactly like that."

"She'd be happy to know you saw her that way." He reached out and squeezed her shoulder. "Listen, you talk to Kalinda, and we'll see about this hotel. Maybe there's a future for it after all."

A rush of pure joy swept through her, and she launched herself into his arms. "Oh, thank you, Daddy."

"Easy," he said with a low rumble of laughter. "You still need to talk with your sisters."

"I will. No problem." She was sure it was a misunderstanding with Kalinda.

Daddy reached out and tucked a strand of hair behind her ears. "All right then. I'm going to go find my fiancée now."

Loni stepped aside to let him pass, but something about his

last words about her mother made her pause. "Daddy, wait," she called.

Her father turned to her, an expectant look on his face.

Loni bit her lip. "What you said about Mama," she tentatively began, "about being like the sun and that you were glad I saw her that way. Didn't *you* see her that way, too?"

His gaze turned thoughtful a moment before he answered. "Yes. Yes, I did." Then, her daddy's eyes turned so unexpectantly sad, it made Loni's heart twist. "However, as much as we enjoy being around the sun, too much time in it can lead to a really bad burn."

Despite her enthusiasm about Daddy's offer to reconsider selling the hotel, Loni couldn't get over the confusion about what he'd revealed about Kalinda. She just needed a little time to herself to process her conversation with her father and what to make of it all. It wasn't as if Loni was hiding from anyone. Not entirely. Why would Kalinda try to talk Daddy into *selling* the hotel? True, Marise had a habit of starting projects and not finishing them, but she was young, and Loni was sure that nothing meant as much to her as preserving their mother's memory. It just didn't make sense.

Luckily, she was saved from her thoughts when Ian found her half an hour later nursing a piece of buttermilk pie in one of the loveseat chairs, facing the ocean.

"Hey," Ian said, sliding into the open seat next to her. "I brought you a perfectly good fried chicken leg and here you are eating dessert first."

Chuckling, she took the plate of chicken from him. "Lucille forced the pie on me. It's buttermilk. One of my favorites. Her new boyfriend made it."

Ian did a double take. *"Boyfriend?* Oh, thank you, Jesus," he said to the sky. "This is good news for me."

"You'd think that. However, something tells me that if you gave the word, she'd dump him faster than her panties could hit the floor."

Ian cringed. "You had to go there, didn't you?"

"Here," she said, giving him the rest of her pie. "Peace offering. It should more than make up for that visual."

"I don't know...I'm not much for buttermilk and I'm pretty sure the visual of Lucille is tattooed on my temporal lobe." Ian sniffed at it, then tentatively took a bite. "Ooh. You're right. All is forgiven. This is good stuff." He let out a contented sigh. "A New Englander like me could really get used to the food down here."

Ian was trying to be funny, but little did he know how much his words filled her with melancholy instead. The problem was she was starting to care for this man—a man who would have more of an attachment to food than to her.

Loni forced a smile and then turned her gaze back to the water. The moonlight bouncing over the rolling waves had a calming effect on her mood after everything that had been thrown at her tonight.

"Is everything okay between you and your dad?" he asked, misreading her silence.

"Yeah. I mean, I think so. We were able to have a civil conversation about Mama for once. And the good news is he loved how The Beach Bash turned out." She turned to him, wanting him to see how earnest she was. "You know, I'm glad he met Pamela now."

His brows rose. "You are? What spurned this sudden

change of heart?"

"Well, Daddy said some words to me tonight that made me think he'd been shielding himself from love and affection—even from his own daughters—after he lost Mama. So, I'm glad that Pamela was able to bring him back to the living again. To risk being loved again."

Ian placed the plate he'd been holding aside and studied her closely. "Such wise, mature words for someone your age."

She grinned, bending slightly in a mock bow. "Why, thank you. I'm glad you appreciate my wise, mature mind."

Ian wrapped his arms around her and brought her in close. "I do. It's very sexy," he whispered in her ear. He began kissing a trail of light kisses along her neck. "Along with the red dress you're wearing."

Her eyes closed as she leaned heavily against him, her pulse kicking up. "I was hoping you'd notice my dress."

"Honey, I'd have to be dead not to notice."

"Speaking of noticing, do you think anyone would notice if we slipped off to my room?"

"With this kind of crowd? Not a chance," he said, reaching for her hand and kissing the inside of her palm. "And thanks to you, we can now use *my* room."

Loni pulled back, slightly puzzled. "What do you mean *your* room? The closet?"

"No. Because of the upgrade."

Upgrade? "When did you get an upgrade?" She dropped her hand and gently pushed him away.

"Today," he said with an amused look. Then his smile slowly fell. "I thought after we... you know... Wait. You really didn't know anything about it?"

Stunned, Loni could only shake her head.

He cleared his throat, looking suddenly uncomfortable. "Well, I guess it's time I should come clean about the other stuff as well."

"*Other* stuff? Like what other stuff?" she demanded.

Ian swallowed. "Uh, like all the free room service breakfasts?"

She raised her eyebrows at him. "Free room service? Really?"

"Yeah, and uh, there were the hotel site plans, the Chamber of Commerce brochures, not to mention the article on the new airport being built that were dropped off at my room, as well. But I—"

"Hell's bells," she muttered, feeling nauseated from the emotions raging inside her. "Why didn't you tell me this before? I thought you were going to be upfront with me when it came to the resort."

"Okay, take it easy, Loni. I should have told you, but I figured it had to have been Kalinda or Marise. And I'm sure there's a reasonable explanation as to why they were trying to help me behind your back. I just didn't want to cause a rift between you and your sisters for no reason."

Ian had said the words with an obvious, forced calm, as if he were dealing with a woman who was about to have a major freak-out on him. He was not wrong.

How could they? Actually, not *they*. After speaking with Daddy, she knew it had to be Kalinda behind it all.

Loni had thought she and her sisters were united in their fight to prevent the hotel from being sold. However, one of them was not being honest with her. Worse than that, Kalinda was *helping* the enemy. She gave him the hotel site plans without her knowledge. The betrayal twisted like a hot knife through her insides.

Loni rigidly held her tears in check as she got to her feet. "I'm sure there *is* a reasonable explanation." She looked at him resolutely, mentally gearing herself up for battle. "And I'm going to find out what that is right now."

Chapter Twenty-Two

Loni marched through the hotel lobby, weaving in and out of the crowd before she finally spotted Marise, talking to the pianist. She tapped her sister none too lightly on the shoulder. "Where's Kalinda?" she demanded.

Marise turned to her with wide eyes. "She's in the café, making more sweet tea, why?"

"I'm calling a meeting there. *Now.*" Loni turned and headed in the direction of The White Squirrel.

Marise hurried after her. "Loni, what's the matter? You seem upset. Is it something Daddy said?"

Loni opened the door of the café and flicked on the lights. "Kalinda!" she called. "You here?"

Kalinda emerged from the kitchen, wiping her hands with a dishtowel. "Jeez, Loni, what on earth? Shut the lights. People are going to think we're open."

"Right," she said, folding her arms. "Wouldn't want that, considering you're trying to sell this place anyway."

Marise frowned, gazing back and forth between her two

sisters. "I don't understand what's going on here, Loni. Kalinda doesn't want to sell the hotel."

Loni leveled her gaze at Kalinda. "Apparently, she does. Kalinda's been keeping a secret from us."

Marise shook her head with a half smile, almost as if she was waiting for Loni to tell her the punchline. "No. Who told you that?"

"Daddy. Not to mention Ian. He told me everything you were doing behind our backs. The fancy breakfast trays, the new room with a view, airport construction news, the *site plans*... Am I missing anything?"

Kalinda flinched. "Well, I'm not the only one who's been keeping secrets," she said quietly. "I know you found Mama's letters. When were you going to share that tidbit of information?"

"You knew about them?" Loni asked.

Marise threw her hands up in the air. "See? This is why I hate being the little sister. Nobody tells me anything!"

Loni's fingers automatically went to her pendant. "I didn't want to tell either of you about those letters because I was trying to spare your feelings. Don't you think I was devastated when I found them?"

"*What* letters?" Marise demanded. "Please, *somebody* tell me *something*."

Loni sighed, dreading what her sister's reaction would be. "Ian found love letters that were sent to Mama. Actually, he found the necklace, too. He was in my closet and—"

"Wait," Marise asked, wrinkling her nose. "Why was Ian in your *closet*?"

Loni rubbed her temple. "It's not important to the story. The point is, he found them."

Marise blinked. "Okay... So, what exactly was in the letters?

Were they from Daddy?"

Loni glanced at Kalinda, who nodded once for her to continue. "The letters were written to her from someone I believe she had an affair with over twenty years ago. Someone with the initials TJ, first name Tom."

Marise raised a hand to her mouth. "Mama had an affair. Are you sure? Maybe it was some guy who was just infatuated with her and who'd sent her gifts. Maybe even a stalker."

Kalinda rolled her eyes. "Mama wouldn't keep mementos from a stalker, Marise."

Marise planted a hand on her hip. "Well, maybe she was keeping them as evidence for the police. Did you ever think of that?"

"She was *not* holding onto evidence," Kalinda told her adamantly.

Loni narrowed her gaze and watched as Kalinda shifted in her seat. "Kalinda, how did you know about the letters? What are you not telling us?"

The color in Kalinda's face drained away, then she looked down at her clenched hands. "I'm sorry. I can't say," she whispered.

Marise reached out and placed a hand on her forearm. "Please, Kalinda. You can't hold back on us now. We all need to know everything. No matter what."

Loni could see whatever Kalinda was keeping inside was taking a toll on her physically. She had thought Kalinda had looked worn out from running the restaurant and hotel, but now she knew it was from something else entirely. Something Kalinda was afraid to even share with her closest family.

Loni's anger seeped away like helium out of a leaky balloon. "Marise is right. Maybe it's time we all be honest with each other. I think enough time has passed. No more secrets among us from now on, okay?"

Kalinda's eyes bordered with tears. "Okay. But maybe you all better sit down for this."

Once she and Marise did as they were told, Kalinda took a deep breath. "I know that Mama had had an affair because… she told me."

"Told you?" Marise exclaimed.

Loni let the jealousy that Mama had confided in Kalinda and not her pass before she spoke. "When did she tell you about the affair?"

Kalinda looked up and into her eyes. "On her deathbed. Mama told me all about it. All about *him*. How much she loved him. His name was Thomas Hannigan Jr—which was why she called him TJ. He was the one who gave her that necklace."

Marise gasped. "What? Why would she tell you all that when she was dying?"

Kalinda shrugged. "I don't know. Maybe the guilt weighed on her. But she told me where to find the letters and necklace and told me to get rid of them but… I don't know, maybe I wasn't in my right mind myself, but I couldn't find them. And then I just thought maybe she'd made a mistake and had put them elsewhere. Then, after a time, they'd never shown up and I forgot about them."

Loni thought back on when she'd first shown Kalinda the necklace. How oddly she'd acted, and how Loni had mistakenly chalked it up to her being emotional about Mama being gone. "That's how you knew that I knew about the letters. When you saw I had the necklace."

"I assumed they'd been hidden together." Kalinda numbly nodded. "I just about freaked out when I saw it."

"Well, I don't understand why you didn't say anything before," Marise said, raking her hands through her hair. "You should have told us long before now."

"Mama made me promise," Kalinda said. "It was her dying wish that no one else find out. I guess since I was with Mama the most toward the end, she entrusted me with the secrets. She didn't want that as part of your memory of her."

"And what about you?" Loni asked. "You're mad at Mama, aren't you?"

Kalinda heaved a frustrated sigh. "Yeah. You know, I am a little. I'm mad at her for cheating on Daddy. I'm mad at her for telling me everything. And I'm mad at her for making me keep these little sordid secrets for so long."

Loni's stomach dropped. She could imagine the anger, the resentment, her sister would have holding onto a secret as heavy as this from her family. "I'm sorry, Kalinda. Is that why you were encouraging Ian? You want to sell the hotel because you're mad at Mama?"

Her sister shrugged. "It's not that I *want* to sell. But honestly, I began to understand where Daddy was coming from, wanting to start his new marriage fresh without this reminder of Mama and what she'd done to him. And then I didn't want Daddy to get hurt any more than he was."

"So Daddy *did* know about the affair," Loni said.

"Yes, I did," their father said hoarsely.

They all turned toward where his voice came from. Joe stood at the café entrance, looking worn and weary. He slowly crossed the room to them as if gathering his thoughts and his courage in the process.

"Daddy," Marise said, rushing up to him. "We're so sorry. Mama should have never done that to you. She's a horrible person."

Joe patted her on the back, his mouth as pale as his face. "Easy, darlin', it wasn't entirely your mama's fault."

Kalinda's gaze hardened. "What are you talking about? Of course, it was her fault. My God, Daddy, she even kept the love letters. The necklace, too. The way she would talk about him like the man walked on water. Even the whole time you were the one taking care of her, making sure she got to her doctor appointments. Trying to save her life. We *all* were."

A stab of guilt lay buried in Loni's chest. Not *all* of them helped out. Loni had been in Los Angeles, working her ass off at a firm that didn't even want her anymore. She wished she'd been here to support her family more. Loni had even blamed her father for not devoting more time to her mother while she was undergoing chemo. Oh gosh, no wonder he'd been so distant.

Loni licked her dry lips. "Who was this TJ? The man she was in love with."

"I don't know," his father said stiffly. "Once I found out about the affair, I gave her an ultimatum to either choose him or me. She chose me. And I was thankful she stayed and gave me another chance."

"What?" Marise cried. "Gave *you* another chance? She was the one who cheated."

Her father smiled grimly. "Thanks for that vote of confidence, honey, but I was not the great husband everybody thought I was. I devoted so much time to this damn hotel, thinking that's what your mama wanted most of all. But in the end, I think all she really wanted was attention from me."

"I don't understand," Loni said, shaking her head. "If she stayed, why was she still talking about him twenty years later?"

"As much as we tried to keep the marriage together for you girls, it wasn't working," Daddy said sadly. "We had planned to get divorced once Marise finished high school, but then the cancer diagnosis came. I thought it would be best for her and the family if we just all saw her through her illness together until she got better." His eyes cast downward. "But she never did."

"Oh, Daddy," Loni said, wiping her eyes. "All this time we had no idea that you did that for her."

"I'd do it again in a heartbeat," her father said. "Like I said, your mama was a good woman. Just lonely and neglected. And she loved you ladies with all her heart."

Marise frowned. "Is that why you wanted to sell the hotel, Daddy? To have a fresh start with Pamela?"

Daddy shrugged. "It sounded like a good idea in the beginning. But being back here... Seeing you ladies work together... I don't know what it is about this place. We had a lot of good times, too, as a family. Took me seeing you working all together to realize that I was holding onto a lot of bitterness. It's probably why I stayed so much in Massachusetts. Well, that was *one* of the reasons. The other was Pammy," he said, blushing slightly.

Loni was trying to make peace with the secret her father and Kalinda had been holding, but something her sister had said was niggling at the back of her mind. Then when she looked at Kalinda, she happened to notice that her sister still seemed troubled.

"Kalinda," she said, slowly turning to her, "you said you were angry that Mama made you keep her *secrets*—plural—and that you didn't want Daddy getting more hurt. What else did she tell you?"

Kalinda froze but her eyes traveled around the room, as if looking for an escape hatch. "I don't think now is the—"

"Kalinda," Marise said, pointing a finger at her, "remember what Loni said. No more secrets among us."

Kalinda remained silent for a few beats, almost as if wrestling with her thoughts. "Mama might have been hallucinating from being on so much medication. She wasn't even completely sure—"

"Just *tell* us," Loni insisted.

Kalinda drew in a deep breath. "Well, um, Mama thought that there was a good chance that...Daddy wasn't Marise's... daddy." Her gaze flew to both Marise and Daddy. "I'm so sorry to be the one to tell you."

Marise looked up at Joe. "Is that true?" she asked in a wobbly voice.

Their father brushed it off. "Of course not. It's like Kalinda said. Maybe your mother wasn't thinking straight."

Marise began to do the math, counting on her fingers. "But it could be true." When no one said anything, she raised her voice. "It *could* be true. That man—TJ—could be my father."

Kalinda looked at Loni with a sense of helplessness.

"See?" Kalinda said, waving at Marise. "This is why Mama had me promise."

"Well, she shouldn't have told you," Joe snapped. "If she had questions, she should have come to me first."

"Marise, Daddy," Loni interjected, "let's not get excited about this without any real concrete evidence."

Marise rubbed her forehead in an agitated manner. "I need some air," she finally said, making a beeline for the exit.

"I'll go make sure she's okay," Kalinda offered.

Joe nodded, then looked at Loni. "What do you think we should do about all this mess?"

That was the problem.

Loni didn't know what to think at the moment. She suddenly felt like a child who'd just discovered there was no such thing as Santa Claus. The pedestal she'd placed her mama on—as well as the reasons she'd wanted to keep the hotel—had toppled before her very eyes. Would this hotel still have the same family values after everything that was known now? Would keeping this hotel bring their family closer or slowly tear them apart? Would it be better in the end to erase these memories?

Unable to form a coherent thought, Loni stood and numbly made her way to the side exit door. Daddy might have called her name, but she just continued on, opening the door and then heading out toward the beach.

Loni sought the solace of the ocean. Her favorite aspect of being back in Sunny Banks. Now. *And the one thing here,* she realized, *that couldn't let me down.*

• • •

When Ian hadn't seen or heard from Loni, he became concerned. Since she wasn't responding to his texts, he went in search of her sisters. Luckily, he ran into Kalinda who'd been wheeling out tea in the lobby. She told him that their little family meeting had not gone over well, and that she and Marise had just up and left in the middle of it. She hadn't seen Loni since.

That's when he knew where Loni would be. Ian had a pretty good understanding of Loni at this point and figured he'd find her where he'd found her last week when she'd learned she was in danger of being let go at her job. Purchasing a piece of chocolate pecan pie and then grabbing a bottle of wine from his room, he walked out onto the beach.

Although it was a bit hard to see because of the time of night, he soon saw her silhouetted form several yards away. She was sitting on the sand, her arms resting on her knees, and even though she had to have heard him approaching, she continued to stare straight out into the water.

"Hey," he said softly, dropping to his knees next to her. "I've been worried about you."

She remained almost in a catatonic state, staring straight ahead. So he tried again.

"I, uh, come with cheering-up gifts," he said, holding out the pie and wine. "I wasn't sure which you'd prefer. The pie was the only thing with chocolate so—"

Loni grabbed the wine and took a rather large swig from the bottle.

"Oh, okay, wine it is." He glanced at her half amused as she continued to drink. "I did bring a cup, if you'd like to share. Or we can just pass the bottle back and forth to each other."

Loni shot him a look.

"Or perhaps you'd like me to get my own bottle…"

She finally cracked a smile. "You're being too nice to me."

"Does that mean you'll share the wine with me?"

Loni passed him the bottle. "Thank you," she said gratefully. "I'd like the pie now, please. I haven't had much to eat tonight."

"As you wish, my queen," he said, presenting it to her like his palm was a silver platter. He reached into his shorts pocket and pulled out a plastic fork and handed that to her as well.

Loni took a forkful and sighed with pleasure. "Wow, good choice." She glanced at him with an appreciative smile. "You know, you're perfect to have around in a mental crisis."

He made a show of pretending to polish his knuckles on his shirt. "Not to brag, but my mother used to call me 'The Fixer' growing up. I got pretty good at problem solving for her and Dad." *For a while, anyway.*

Until their problems got too big for a young teen to handle on his own.

"The Fixer," she repeated. "I can see that. You seem to always be around helping me fix my problems. You certainly fixed Samuel's problem. Do they call you that in your company?"

"No. That particular name didn't catch on."

"So, what name did catch on?"

"The Predator."

Loni winced. "Eww. That sounds awful. Why would they call you *that*?"

Ian shrugged. "Some people in my company tend to think I, uh, have a knack for..." He paused, trying to come up with a nicer way to describe himself.

"Just say it," she said. "No one has been holding back on me tonight. Why should you?"

"Um..." He cleared his throat. Jeez, why was this so hard? No woman had ever asked him this before. Then again, he'd never told women he'd been seeing that he had a nickname around the office. "Well, the nickname is because people see me as someone who preys on a business dealing, pounces, and then..."

"Devours?" she said warily.

"More or less." Said out loud, he was surprised she was still sitting next to him.

"Interesting." Loni reached for the wine again and drank. "I like 'The Fixer' better. It suits you more. At least, with me it does."

Ian would rather believe that as well. That he could be more help to Loni than a predator, and that the hotel situation was different. But he knew who he was deep down inside and if push came to shove, unfortunately where his priorities would lie, too.

He needed to acquire her resort. Even though she could very well hate him for it. He'd convinced himself it wasn't personal. It was never personal. Not when business was involved. Maybe he could convince her of that, too.

"Those letters you found were just the tip of the iceberg," Loni said, breaking into his thoughts. "Everything I believed about my mama and daddy's relationship wasn't true. This hotel doesn't have any magic to it. It's all a farce. They tried to make their marriage work for our sake, but she was still in love with TJ. My parents would have divorced but then she was diagnosed with cancer and Daddy took care of her." She turned and gazed at him with teary blue eyes. "That wasn't even the end of it."

"What do you mean?"

"Mama told Kalinda that Marise might not even be Daddy's daughter. So now Daddy and Marise are dealing with *that*." She placed the pie down and shook her head. "Can you imagine keeping all that a secret for so long? From everyone. From us?"

Ian ran a hand down his face. Jeez, no. He could not imagine. But then again, he'd seen his own parents do things that he wouldn't have done either. "I'm sorry, Loni."

"All this time I was blaming Daddy for not having a heart when it came to this hotel and this family. That he didn't care. But turns out, he was the one who kept this family together."

"Your dad is a good man."

Loni smiled sadly. "Yeah, he is. I'm lucky in that respect, at least."

Ian thought of his own dad, and couldn't have agreed more. Joe was pretty much the closest thing he had to a father and Pamela was the closest to a mother. Ian felt himself pretty darn fortunate to know them both.

"I wish I could do something for you," Ian told her. "Fix how you're feeling somehow. But as someone who lived constantly trying to keep my dad's drinking a secret, be glad your mom's secret is out in the open now. In fact, a wise woman once told me that no one should have to face family challenges alone." He swung his arm around her, bringing her close to him. He didn't know how she felt, but this wasn't close enough for him. It was strange, this thing between them. This overwhelming need to touch a woman not only physically but mentally as well.

Loni rested her head on his shoulder and sighed. "I feel a little better already. Like I said, you're good to have around in a mental crisis. And for the free wine," she said with a chuckle.

Ian leaned in and kissed her, a slow, searing kiss that had him wondering if he'd have enough strength left to stand up. "I'm actually pretty good to have around for a lot of other things as well."

"I know." She kissed him again and smiled. "Let's go back to my room and you can show me."

Chapter Twenty-Three

On Monday morning, Ian received two texts. One from Scott, telling him that he had already perused the site plans of the hotel and that he was working on the purchasing contracts. Everything was a go on their end. The other text was from Joe Wingate, telling Ian to stop by the cottage next door where he and Pam were staying. Joe apparently had a lot on his mind to discuss with him.

Great, he thought grimly, as he made his way out of the hotel and onto the beach. This was what he undoubtedly was after. Joe was going to agree to sell him the resort and then he'd have no reason to stay. He'd be packed up by nine.

Not exactly the way Ian wanted to start his day. He would have much rather stayed in bed with Loni and shut out the rest of the world for a few more hours. Put off the inevitable. Unfortunately, she also had to be up early to help out in the café. Just as well. His inner relationship alarm clock was already alerting him to the fact that he was getting a little too involved with her. That became more than apparent last night on the beach and after... Then again, Loni made it way too easy for him. She was a special woman, one whom he cared for and respected a lot. Which was why, for both their sakes, he needed to stop things before they went much further and he hurt her.

So he shouldn't mind that the time had come to make the sale of the hotel official and move on.

Joe's cottage was a short walk from the hotel. It was a small, one floor beach bungalow with a wraparound porch that offered a straight shot view of the ocean. Loni had told him Marise and Kalinda still lived there, which explained the charming and homey look. Ian even noticed one of Angela's homemade wreaths on the front door. Apparently, Joe and his wife had it built next to the hotel when his wife was pregnant with Kalinda, just so that the children could be raised in a real home.

Ian walked up the porch steps, inhaling the fresh salt air. But before he could knock, Pamela threw open the door. "Oh," she said, startled. "I didn't realize you were there, Ian. Come on in. I was just on my way out for a little beach walk."

Ian smiled. "Well, enjoy. It's low tide so you'll probably find some nice sea shells."

Pamela quirked an eyebrow. "Really? I wouldn't have pegged you for a seashell collector."

Yeah, I wouldn't have either. "I'm not," he said simply. "Loni told me about them. We collected them for Angela the other day."

"Loni." Her smile grew wide. "You two have been spending a lot of time together. That's quite a change for you."

"Nothing's changed," he said. "In fact, I'm leaving soon..."

"Uh-huh. Weren't you supposed to leave *last* week?"

"Pam," he warned. Although, he really should be warning himself. Damn, without even realizing it, he *had* overextended his stay. Business or not.

She shoved him lightly in the chest. "Oh, relax. You look and sound just as cranky as Joe this morning. Go have some coffee and get something to eat," she said, fluttering her fingers toward the back of the house. "Joe's in the kitchen waiting for you. Kalinda dropped off some yummy pastries, too."

He drummed up a smile of his, despite his growing concern over Loni. "Thanks, Pam," he said, heading toward the kitchen.

Ian found Joe sitting at the kitchen table dressed in a flamingo and palm tree Hawaiian shirt, looking just as cranky as Pamela had promised. "Morning, Joe."

Joe tipped his mug of coffee to him. "Mornin'. Help yourself to some coffee. Pammy made it good and strong. I think we're both gonna need it today."

Ian grabbed a mug and poured himself some coffee. Once he doctored it to his liking, he grabbed a blueberry muffin and sat down. "So, what's on your mind, Joe?" he asked, getting right down to business.

Joe folded up the newspaper he had spread out on the table and placed it aside. "I'm not gonna play games with ya. I suppose Loni told you about Friday night's family discussion."

Ian hesitated a moment before nodding. There was no point in trying to pretend he wasn't privy to those personal aspects of their lives.

Joe sighed heavily. "Dang it, I should have just told you myself. Would have made things a little clearer for you as to why I wanted to sell the hotel. But it didn't seem right to tell others when my own daughters didn't know. Well, Marise and Apollonia, at any rate. And this whole business with Marise. I know she's my daughter. We don't need no blood test to prove that."

Ian was saved from commenting when his phone chimed. He pulled it out and discreetly glanced at the text. It was from Scott.

Contracts ready for DocuSign.

Ready for me to send over now?

In light of Friday night's circumstances, Ian quickly typed back:

Yes.

"Anyway," Joe went on, "that's why I wanted you to come by this morning, seeing how things have changed."

Changed?

Ian looked up. "Wait. I'm sorry," he said, putting down his phone. "Back up. What do you mean things have changed?" That was a turn of events he was not expecting.

"From the beginning, the girls wanted to keep the hotel. Despite everything that's happened, they still do."

"And does that include Loni?"

Joe gazed down into his coffee mug. "I don't think the hotel matters much to her anymore. She'd held her mama and the memories she had of that old place on so high a pedestal that nothing could ever touch it. It was the ultimate symbol of love and family for her, and it hurts me to know how hard she's taking our mistakes. Sandra and I both only wanted the best for her. For *all* of them. And well, as the old saying goes, time heals all wounds. I know it did for me once I came back here and saw the girls in their element."

Ian shook his head. "I'm not sure I understand, Joe. What are you thinking of doing now?"

"I'm gonna keep the hotel."

Heart racing and mind scrambling, Ian sat up straight. "Seriously? You actually don't want to sell now? That doesn't seem like you. Not to mention after all this time I invested here?"

Joe frowned. "I'm sorry, Ian. I'm just as confused as you are at the moment. Originally, I thought it would be the best to sell, but now, being here with the truth finally out...it's made me reconsider. My girls worked hard with The Beach Bash. Maybe being here with Pammy has me seeing that old place differently, too."

Ian sat back and thought quickly. Like slipping into his favorite shoes, it was easy to convert his mind into business mode. For Ian, it was a logical move for Joe to sell—not just because Scott, Raj, and the rest of his company were counting on him to close this deal—but he'd even convinced himself that it made the most sense for Joe's family. It made the most sense for Loni. Ian hadn't lied Friday night when he'd said that he wished there was something he could do to help her. He'd hated seeing her so upset. Selling and removing those memories and emotions would be the best for both of them.

"You're making a mistake," Ian told him flatly.

Joe's eyebrows went up. "How so?"

Ian leaned in, resting his forearms on the table. "Look, I do want this property, Joe. I won't kid you about that, and I know I can turn it into an investment that would be great for the community as well. But I'm really thinking of Loni."

"Why Loni?"

"Because—" Ian cleared his throat, feeling heat unexpectedly rising up from his neck. "We've gotten close. I care about her. A lot." More than he'd cared about anyone before. "I can't stand to see her hurting, either, which is why it's best to cut ties. Start fresh."

Best for Loni to cut ties with him, too, and start fresh, he realized. As much as that thought weighed on his chest.

"True." Joe scratched his face. "Loni probably does need that."

"From my experience with family, it's best to get rid of the emotional baggage and allow the girls to heal properly."

"That was kind of my thinking from the start of all this," Joe murmured. "Especially with Pammy now in the picture."

"Exactly. And you yourself said the girls will be happy with whatever decision you make. Plus, with the amount of money that each of your daughters will get from the sale, they can decide to do almost anything they want. And isn't that a healthy aspect for them to look forward to?"

Joe furrowed his brow. "I do want them to be able to do whatever they want…"

"I would give you your asking price, plus pay salaries of all employees for three months once the hotel was officially closed. Anything to make this acquisition as painless as possible."

Ian waited, allowing his words to soak in before solidifying their agreement. As much as he wanted this property—needed to make this sale happen—Ian also wanted to make 100 percent sure that Joe felt good and comfortable about selling. Ian would always be The Predator in business, but as a friend, he owed Joe that much.

He owed Loni that much.

"Well?" Ian finally said. "What do you say, Joe? Do we have a deal?"

He waited, keeping his face calm and breathing even, despite how alarmed he felt internally.

Joe met his gaze, direct and unwavering. "We do, son," he said, slapping his hand on the table. "We certainly do."

• • •

"Wrong table!" Kalinda shouted.

Loni looked back and saw Kalinda point to the table she'd just passed.

Oops. She backed up to the correct table and placed the tray down. Kalinda was probably secretly grateful this would be Loni's last day helping out, since Yolanda was back. They had Dana, and Carla was already surpassing Loni in serving skills, and Hazel was much more mobile now and could easily handle the rest of the hostess and cashier duties.

After Loni placed the breakfast platters on the table, she headed back to the kitchen. "Sorry about that," she told her sister. "I wish I could say I have a lot on my mind, but after last night, I'm sure we all do."

Kalinda gave her a tired smile. "No worries. I'm just glad you were here to pitch in when I needed it. I appreciate you."

Loni glanced at Duke, hard at work over the kitchen griddle, but lowered her voice anyway. "I want to say that I'm sorry I wasn't around to pitch in more. You know, years ago, with Mama and everything here."

Kalinda shook her head. "It's okay. Mama wanted you to follow your dreams. The hotel wasn't your responsibility. *Isn't* your responsibility."

Loni frowned. She wasn't so sure if she really followed her own dreams, or if she just went to Los Angeles because it seemed to please her mother so much. Maybe Mama wanted for Loni what she really wanted for herself. Freedom to leave. She had to wonder if Kalinda felt that way, too.

"Did you really want Daddy to sell the resort?" Loni couldn't help asking.

"I only wanted Daddy to sell because I wanted to make it easier for him to let go of any past hurt. That was what noble Kalinda wanted." She let out a tentative smile "Don't worry, selfish Kalinda wants to keep the resort."

Loni let out a relieved breath.

Kalinda placed a hand on her shoulder. "Hey. Are you okay? We were kind of worried about you Friday night. Angela said even Ian was looking for you."

"I'm okay. It was just a lot to process. As I'm sure it was for Marise, too."

"Marise will be okay. She was definitely shaken up, but we're hoping that Mama was mistaken."

Loni nodded. She hoped that was the case, too. "Sorry, if I worried you."

"Well, when I didn't see Ian around, I'd figured he'd found you." Kalinda bit her lip, pausing. "And I'm sorry I went behind both your backs to help Ian, too. I'm kind of surprised he told you about that."

Now that Loni had gotten to know Ian better, she wasn't all that shocked that he'd confided in her. He knew how much the resort meant to her. He really was a decent guy and someone who wanted the best for her and not just himself, which was making it all that more difficult to face saying goodbye to him. She'd wanted to hold onto what was building between them. And part of her hoped he wanted the same.

Loni shrugged. "Let's call it even. You and I *both* weren't honest with one another for a long time. I'm sorry I was so jealous that Mama wanted you during her last days." Loni finally felt like cracking a smile. "I guess she knew I was lousy at keeping secrets."

Kalinda wrapped her arms around Loni and squeezed her tight. "That's for sure." She pulled back, matching her grin. "Now get back to work before I have to fire you on your last day."

Just then Duke came over and placed two plates of pancakes in front of Loni. "And take these orders to table fifteen while you're at it," he barked out.

"You heard the man," Kalinda said, gesturing to him with her thumb.

Loni sighed and picked up the plates. "No offense, but as much as I love you, I won't miss you two bossing me around," she said with a wink, carrying them out of the kitchen.

Loni walked across the room and delivered the breakfast items to table fifteen—what she *assumed* was table fifteen—and perked up when she saw Angela standing at the door, waiting to be seated.

"Hey, Angela," she said, grabbing a menu for her. "This is an unexpected surprise. Will Ansley be joining you?"

"She's Facetiming her fiancé right now, so I figured it was my chance to sneak out of the house and check up on you."

"Check on *me*?" Loni led her to a table by the window and placed the menu down. "Why?"

"Kalinda told me what happened after The Beach Bash the other night," she said, taking a seat. "I'm so sorry, sugar. Just as I just told you before, your mama never breathed a word about any of it to me. I'm stunned."

Loni glanced around the restaurant. The crowd had thinned considerably from earlier in the morning, so since it was slow, she pulled out a seat and sat across from her. "Jeez, Kalinda managed to keep that secret for years, but once she pulled the pin, now half the town knows."

Angela chuckled. "Now, honey, don't be too hard on your sister. Kalinda only told me because she was worried about you and Marise. She said you both looked like someone out of *The Walking Dead*."

"Well, can you blame us? What a mess. And to think this whole time I've been here, I've been wasting all my energy on trying to preserve a myth."

"What on earth do you mean by that?"

Loni swiped at her eyes, feeling her emotions coming to a boil inside of her and unable to combat them. "Angela, I thought this hotel was my family legacy, that my mama was truly happy here, that it kept memories worth holding onto. I even believed that stupid fallacy that the hotel guaranteed a marriage for life." She snorted. "What a crock. Every single bit of it."

Angela's eyebrows went up. "Well. I'm not going to tell you that you don't have a right to feel angry about your mama's affair and that Kalinda and your daddy kept it from you, but we'll never know your mama's true feelings or reasoning why, so I don't think we can quite judge her too harshly."

"That's what Daddy said." Loni pressed her palms against her face. "I don't know what to think," she groaned.

"You can know that your parents loved you. All three of you. Enough to want to preserve the great memories they gave you growing up here. They wanted to keep the family together as best they could up until the very end. I'm sure the hotel might have contributed to your parents' marriage falling apart, but who's to say something else wouldn't have done the same thing? And as angry as you are now, you can't deny that this place held a lot of happy times for you all as well. It did for me and my family."

Loni's shoulders wilted. It was true. As much as she hated to admit it, despite everything she now knew, the hotel was still a source of comfort for her. A place she still idealized. "I feel guilty for not wanting to sell—like I'm hurting Daddy—maybe even my sisters— to want to keep something my mama valued."

"Oh, my dear. Whether they would have divorced or not, your mama still would have been your mother. It's okay to still love her even though she may not have been perfect."

Loni smiled grimly and sniffed. "Some mess our family is, huh?"

Angela grabbed her hand and squeezed. "Most families are."

"Yeah." Loni used a nearby napkin to wipe her nose, then stood. What Angela had said made a lot of sense. And if her daddy was able to forgive, then she might as well try, too. Maybe there was a way to salvage the hotel as well as her family. "Thanks, Angela. After my shift, I'll go and talk with Daddy."

"That's a great start, sugar."

"I'll go grab you some coffee and be right back to take your order. It'll be on me," she added, bending over to kiss her powdered cheek.

Loni headed toward the coffee station, but Marise entered the restaurant and quickly blocked her way. "Code green," she said to Loni.

"Code...*green*?" Loni asked in alarm. "Are you feeling okay? Is that supposed to mean something to me?" She tried to walk around Marise, but her sister put her palm up to stop her.

Marise threw her hands up. "I can't say code red because that was for Ian, and even though Ian isn't really a code level threat anymore I didn't think it made sense to use that same color code for a different person."

Loni drew back. *Different person?* "What do you mean different person? Who's code green?"

Before her sister could answer, she heard a familiar male voice.

"Hello, Apollonia."

Loni turned toward the entrance and her heart dropped when her gaze landed directly on the last person she had expected to see in Sunny Banks.

Chapter Twenty-Four

"Blaze," Loni said breathlessly. "What are you doing here?"

He grinned, and that dimple on his left cheek—the one she used to think made him so devilishly handsome but now only made him look devilish—slipped out. "I was hoping for a happier greeting. Especially since I've come bearing good news, regarding your job."

Loni glanced at Marise. "Do you mind covering for me for a bit?"

"Hey, no problem," Marise said, taking her serving apron from her and placing it around her hips. "Take as long as you need."

"Let's take a walk outside," Loni suggested to Blaze. "I could use the fresh air." Without waiting for a response, she turned and led him out of the café and toward the patio entrance.

The temperature felt like it was eighty degrees already. The sun was shining and a nice cool breeze coming off the ocean ruffled through Loni's bangs as they continued toward the start of the boardwalk, but it didn't stop her heart from beating frantically. What was Blaze doing here?

"Are we actually going on the beach?" Blaze asked finally.

Loni turned to him, surprised at the disgust in his tone. "Yeah, I thought you'd want to, since you flew out all this way."

He looked down at his expensive suede loafers. "I'm not really dressed for the occasion."

She resisted the urge to roll her eyes. "Just take them off, Blaze. Come on, it's a fantastic grounding technique," she said, kicking off her sneakers and then peeling off her socks. "Trust me, there's nothing better than the feel of the sand between your toes."

"I suppose it's better than sand in your bottom," he grumbled, doing as she suggested.

Loni chuckled as she stepped onto the beach. Blaze followed suit, his expression looking as sullen as a child who was denied ice cream. *Had he always been like this? So stuffy and tense?* Then again, she was first drawn to him because he'd felt so similar to herself. Maybe she was the one who'd changed. It had only been a few weeks and already she and Blaze seemed like two puzzle pieces that didn't quite fit together as perfectly as she'd once thought.

Was that how Mama had come to think of Daddy? The thought gnawed at her.

"You should have told me you were coming," Loni said, trying to keep her hair from blowing into her mouth. "I would have made sure I was off from work."

Blaze snorted. "Work? Babe, what you're doing here is *not* work."

"Of course, it is. In fact, it's hard work." She felt her defenses rising and it annoyed her further that she was even allowing him to put her in that position. "My sisters really needed the help, too."

"Yes, I know." He sighed. "I'm sorry. That was very kind of you. But if you weren't around, they would have figured something else out. I'm talking about *real* work, Loni. Your career. More specifically, your career at the firm."

Her stomach clutched, and Loni stopped walking to look at him. "What about it?" she asked warily. "When I last spoke to Mark, he said they wouldn't be done with the investigation until the end of the month."

"Well, that's why I came all this way," he said, his smile growing. "To give you the good news in person." He paused for what seemed like an exaggerated dramatic effect. "Your suspension has been completely lifted. Congrats. The firm wants you back ASAP."

She blinked. "When? How did this happen?"

"The investigation ended yesterday. You're cleared." He stepped closer, taking her hand in his. "Not only does the firm want you back, but *I* want you back ASAP as well."

"What?" Loni flung his hand away, and Blaze flinched. She didn't mean to react so strongly, but his unexpected declaration after everything else she'd experienced this week threw her for a loop. "Blaze, I'm sorry, but that's not what I want."

Blaze's brows furrowed together, looking more frustrated than confused. "What don't you want? Your job back or me?"

"Both." The word came straightaway out of her mouth. But as it settled and landed between her ears, it also settled firmly in her heart. It was the truth. She *didn't* want her job back. Not in Los Angeles, anyway. Not far away from family. And she certainly did not want Blaze. "I'm sorry," she said again.

Blaze placed his hands on his hips and turned to look out

into the ocean. "This is unexpected. I can't believe you're turning this down."

"Turning what down? An opportunity to come back to a firm that doesn't trust me? How do I even know that this kind of thing won't happen again?"

"It won't happen again." He let out a mirthless chuckle that made the hairs on the back of her neck stand up. "It's actually kind of funny and a little embarrassing what we found out during the investigation. Turns out it was a big miscommunication. We tracked that it was me who accidentally sent that email to your client."

How Loni was able to keep herself under control she'll never know. She stood there, shocked and shaken. Her reputation and her job had been on the line and all this time, it took an outside investigation to uncover the truth when it could have been easily discovered.

"I must have been using your computer while you were at lunch and accidentally sent the email. I feel so horrible about what I must have put you through," Blaze went on. "I even offered to have the partners give you a bonus for returning to make it up to you. Out of my own salary, of course."

"Is that why you wanted my computer passcode after I changed it? To hide your *mistake*?"

"Of course not." At least Blaze had the decency to blush. "I really needed to access your files for work. And I really am sorry. If I had known I had caused the whole mishap, I would have apologized sooner."

Blaze's remorse seemed genuine, so she nodded in acceptance.

"Does this mean you'll come back to LA with me?" he asked.

"No, I can't." Her mind flew to the resort and everything

that was on the line with it. "Not right now."

"Loni," he sighed, throwing his hands in the air. "You can't throw this opportunity away. Do you want a formal apology from the partners? Is that what this is about?"

"No, it's not about an apology from them, but considering that I have been wrongly accused despite my past performance with the firm, yes, I think Mark or one of the other partners could have picked up the phone to call me personally. I was owed that much."

He huffed out a breath. "Well, that's my fault, too. I thought you would have preferred the news coming from me directly. Or at least…I had hoped. That's the real reason why I came out here."

She blinked. "Real reason?"

"I've missed you…"

Loni shook her head. "Blaze, you were the one who initially wanted the break."

"Not for real. Just for show, so the partners wouldn't think anything untoward was going on. But then you hung up on me and it scared me to death. We love each other. We belong together. And now that you're back in the firm's good graces, we don't have to hide our relationship. We can move forward."

"Move forward how?"

"Well, now we can be out in the open. In fact, we should set a date as soon as possible. What do you think?"

"I—" Her mind was whirling. She didn't know what to think, where she belonged anymore. Los Angeles, her relationship with Blaze—they were sure things. What did she really have in Sunny Banks? No job and soon, Ian would be gone from there, too. But something still had her hesitating. Suddenly the thought of leaving town—leaving her family—and making her mark on the world in LA law wasn't as appealing as it once had been.

Taking her silence as affirmation, Blaze smiled. "It's going to look great to the partners once we come back together and announce our engagement, too."

"What?" Loni rubbed her forehead as she fought her own battle of personal restraint. "You mean it would be especially good for *you* for us to come back together. I mean, how could the partners be mad at you for accidentally sabotaging one of their best attorneys if that attorney is willing to marry you, right?"

Blaze frowned. "It's not like I didn't want to marry you in the first place. I love you."

"You don't love me," Loni said calmly. "Love involves sacrifice and trust."

Blaze swallowed. "But what will the firm think if I come back alone?"

She shook her head sadly. "I don't care. But I'm sure they can figure that one out on their own."

Loni couldn't believe how blind she'd been. Although maybe part of her problem stemmed from all the encouragement she had received from her mama. Loni had felt so lost and unloved while Mama had been dying. Daddy had pulled away from her for his own reasons and her mama, unhappy with her own choices, encouraged Loni to leave Sunny Banks and have a different kind of life from her sisters. A different kind of life than *she* led. Unfortunately, that decision only left Loni unhappy and wanting. And she wasn't going back to it.

Loni turned away and began heading back toward the hotel.

"Wait," Blaze called out. "That's it? You're not even going to help me? You're just going to throw away your career?"

"I'm doing no such thing. I'm just going to take some more time to think about what I want to do and what truly makes me happy. Right now, it's being in Sunny Banks and helping out my sisters while they need me."

"Loni, you're talking crazy talk. What do you think you're going to do, wait tables at a three-star resort until you find yourself? Come back to Los Angeles. You're too good an attorney. It's where you belong, even if it's not with me. Where your mother thought you belonged," he added.

She sighed, weary of arguing with him. "No, Blaze. I don't belong there. I used to think so, but being around family can change a person's perspective. Years ago, I went to Los Angeles for my mama. But today, I'm staying in Sunny Banks for me."

• • •

Ian knew Loni's shift at the café would be ending soon, so he headed down there, hoping to tell her about the hotel sale before her father. Better coming from him first. Ian knew that even though Loni's feelings about the hotel weren't what they once were, that didn't mean she wouldn't still need some mental support.

The café crowd was sparse. There were a few people at the counter stools and at a far table by the window, he saw Angela sitting by herself. She looked up and waved when she saw him, so he walked over.

"Good morning, sugar," she said, smiling up at him. "Are you hungry? Kalinda gave me so much food. I couldn't even touch this slice of chocolate espresso banana bread."

Ian took a seat across from her and eyed up her plate. "I had breakfast with Joe this morning, but I'm sure I can give this banana bread a good home."

Angela chuckled. "So what brings you here then? Looking for Loni?"

"I was," he said, breaking off a piece of the bread and popping it in his mouth. "I had some—" Whoa. If taste buds could sing, his would be belting out "Chandelier" by Sia. Ian took another bite of banana bread and swallowed. "Holy crap, that's delicious."

"Yes, Kalinda is a magician when it comes to food combinations."

"She should be doing other things with her talents." Once Ian shut down the hotel, he pictured her getting a job just about anywhere, or even opening up a standalone restaurant or bakery.

Angela took a sip of her coffee. "She likes what she does here."

Ian frowned. "But she doesn't have to be here. Kalinda could be anywhere." *Loni could be anywhere.*

Angela cocked her head. "Why are you so concerned with what Kalinda should or could be doing?"

"I'm just trying to—"

"Sugar, let me tell you. Kalinda could have hightailed it out of Sunny Banks years ago. But she chose to stay. Marise, too. Personally, I think if their mother hadn't pushed Loni into leaving, she would have stayed, too." She patted him on the knuckles. "It's probably good Loni left, though. Time away makes you appreciate what you had, right?"

Ian looked away. He couldn't relate to having appreciated something more after time away from it. He'd simply learned to move on and adapt, whether it be with family, friends, relationships, or work life. And soon, he'd have to move on from Loni.

He pushed the half-eaten bread away, no longer hungry.

"Oh, hey, Ian," Marise called. She wore her typical business attire of a sleeveless blouse and gray skirt but had an orange White Squirrel serving apron overtop of her outfit. "Kitchen is closing, but if you want me to tell Duke to throw something extra on the griddle for ya, I will."

Ian smiled. "You are too good to me, but as I was telling Angela I already ate."

Angela pointed to the picked-on banana bread. "And then some."

"Are you looking for Loni, too?" Marise asked.

Ian narrowed his eyes. "What do you mean by *too?*"

Marise's grin fell. "Oh. Uh, I thought you knew."

Ian glanced at Angela and noticed she'd suddenly become tense. Oh, he didn't like the looks of this one bit. "I don't know anything," he said with forced calm. "Is something going on with Loni?"

"Well..." Marise swallowed. "Maybe I—"

"Oh, for heaven's sake, just tell the man," Angela huffed out.

"Blaze Clemson is here," Marise blurted. "That's Loni's fiancé. I mean, *ex*-fiancé. He flew in from California this morning to surprise her."

Ian looked down at his hands, which were clenched in two tight fists. He forced his fingers to relax and took a breath. "It certainly is a surprise," he murmured.

Marise flipped her hair off her shoulder and quickly sat down. "Look, I wouldn't worry about them getting back together. She's completely over him. From what I overheard— and don't judge me, I'm her sister—I have a right to snoop. I think he came back to tell her she had her job back at the law firm. Which I'm sure will be a complete relief to her."

Ian sat back, trying to quickly put together what this all meant for her. For them.

For them?

Wait, there *was* no them. Loni knew from the start there wouldn't be a *them*, not in the long run, anyway. He and Loni had long before discussed that he would eventually be heading back to Boston, and she would most likely be heading back to California. But, still, he'd thought—hoped—they'd have more time.

"Ian?" Angela said, breaking into his thoughts. "Isn't that great news? Loni's a wonderful attorney. There should have never been an investigation to begin with, in my opinion."

Ian rubbed his forehead, distracted by the chatty happiness from the women before him. Loni would be living across the country. Too far for even the most casual of long-distance relationships. Not that he wanted that or even had promised that. Their relationship was getting tricky to maneuver as it was, so the timing of this news couldn't have worked out more perfectly. He could simply chalk up the numbing sensation that floated through him to be mere... *Relief?*

"I'm sure gonna miss her, though," Marise said with a sigh, placing her chin in her palm.

I'm going to miss her, too, he thought sullenly. That's when he realized he needed to get a grip. It wasn't the first time he had to part ways with a woman he genuinely liked. He'd move on, like he normally did. Starting right now.

Ian abruptly stood, scraping the back legs of his chair against the hardwood floor in the process. "I've got to go."

Marise's brows shot up. "Go? Aren't you going to wait for Loni? She and Blaze should be back soon."

Ian shook his head. "No, I'll talk to her later. I have some things to take care of that can't wait."

. . .

After her discussion with Blaze, Loni called the firm and explained to Mark Becker personally that while she appreciated their offer to allow her to stay on with a bonus, she would not be returning. She wanted to stay where she was needed. Where she was respected. And most of all, where she was appreciated and loved. There was no doubt she'd probably have to take a pay cut at whatever job she took around here, but in her estimation, no amount of money could ever compete with those other things anyway.

The café had already closed by the time Loni sent Blaze on his way back to the airport, so she went to Marise's office to thank her again for covering for her. When Loni walked in, Marise was at her desk, looking like she was working on some kind of graphic design.

"Hey, what's that?" Loni asked, pointing to her computer screen.

Marise jumped and quickly turned her screen around away from view. "Nothing."

Loni cracked a smile. "Then why do you have the same expression as you did in tenth grade when you were smoking pot and Daddy asked you what that funny smell was coming from your room?"

"Hey, that really was nothing. It was a regular cigarette."

Loni rolled her eyes. "Sure, it was."

"Is there another reason you're here?" she asked, folding her arms. "I mean, besides wanting to harass your sexy little sister."

Loni took a seat. "Yeah, actually, I just want to make sure you're okay. If you want to talk about all this stuff about Mama and Daddy or—"

"Honestly, I don't know if I want to know if it's true or not. I could be making things worse for me and for Daddy."

"How so?"

Marise chewed her lip. "Well, what if we find out that I'm not a Wingate, that I'm a Hannibal or whatever his name is? I'm afraid Daddy won't want me in his life anymore."

"Oh, honey," Loni said, coming over to put her arms around her sister. "That would never happen. He didn't abandon Mama even after Mama's betrayal, so he certainly wouldn't abandon you now. Besides, relationships aren't just genetic connections. They're made up of emotional ties of love, support, and shared experiences. All that doesn't get erased because of a blood test. And you will always be my sister, so you never have to feel alone in all this."

Marise sniffed into her shoulder and Loni could feel the wetness of her sister's tears through her tee shirt. "I wish you weren't leaving."

Loni pulled back and looked at her sister. "Who told you I was leaving?"

"Well...no one. Blaze—"

"Left for Los Angeles already."

Marise frowned. "But I thought Blaze was here to give you your job back."

"He was. He did. And..." She took a deep breath. "I turned it down."

"What?" Marise took her hands in hers. "Oh my word, why on earth did you do that? I thought you were dying to get your old job back."

"I did, too," she said wistfully. "But I suppose things change. *I've* changed. As crazy as it sounds and after everything we learned, I want to stay in Sunny Banks."

"You're brave. I can't believe you turned your old life down. I'm still trying to find where I fit and now I don't even know who I am."

Loni smoothed the hair away from Marise's face and smiled. "Look, I'm struggling to find my place here in this family and at the resort, just as much you are. But we'll all figure out our way through it. Together. At The Sandy Bottom."

Marise nodded then hugged her tightly. "Best news ever."

Loni hugged her sister back, her eyes growing misty. All she could think—feel—at that moment was *home* and it filled her with such peace. "I'm glad you think so. Otherwise, my announcement could have been really awkward."

"I still don't know what I want to do about the DNA test, though. I need more time to think."

"Well, whatever you decide, just know that we have your back and love you."

Marise smiled. "Love you, too."

"And if you need to talk about this some more, you'll have plenty of opportunity since I'll probably need to move in with you until I find a job."

"No worries," she said with a chuckle. "Plus, I think Ian will be thrilled with this news, too."

"Ian? Oh, but my decision—"

"Relax," Marise said with a wink. "I know you staying here has nothing to do with him. But, still, it does make things a lot more convenient with you both being on the east coast."

Loni shook her head, her heart heavy. "I could be living in downtown Boston, right next door, and it wouldn't matter to

Ian. He's not into long-term."

"Well, I didn't say he had to propose. Although, he totally should, and I'd support it one hundred percent."

Loni chuckled. "I guarantee you, Ian will never propose."

"Which is a dang good thing," Kalinda said, standing in the office doorway, her arms folded and eyes blazing. "We already had one close call with Blaze. Ian's not any better."

Marise frowned. "What are you talking about, Kal? Ian is a great guy."

"No, he most certainly is not." Kalinda dropped her arms and took a step farther into the office. "And I know this because I just spoke with Daddy. He told me that he's decided to sell the resort after all—and Ian was the one who convinced him to do it."

Chapter Twenty-Five

As Ian was packing, Scott sent him a text message to say that Joe had signed the DocuSign seller's agreement already and had sent it back to him. Scott also told Ian that he would set up a meeting with Denali Builders for next week to see how they wanted to proceed with the property. In Ian's mind, there was a good chance the hotel would be bulldozed and either a retail storefront would be built in its place or high-end condos would go up. Either way, Ian's company stood to gain a good amount of profit from the deal and more importantly, reestablish their relationship with a well-respected builder. Plus, he had an advantage over Alex Winters.

The best yet?

The Wingate family could finally move on. Ian could move on and feel good about the situation, too. Loni could go back to her law firm and not look back, either. A triple win. Everything fit into place perfectly.

So why the hell was he walking around like the wind had been knocked out of him?

Ian placed his laptop into its case and had just zipped it closed when there was a knock on his hotel door. When he opened it, Loni was standing there. Almost immediately, he knew something was wrong. She looked as if she just learned someone had died.

"Loni," he said, reaching for her but she recoiled back.

"May I come in?" she asked instead.

"Of course," he said, stepping back. "Are you all right? Marise told me your ex is here."

Loni walked in, rubbing her arms in the process as if there was a chill in the air. "Yes, he was here earlier. Blaze wanted to tell me I'd been cleared of any wrongdoing and that I could come back to work."

Just as Marise had suspected. He should have suspected it, too. But for some reason he had to drum up enthusiasm for her news. "Th-that's great. I'm so happy for you." He then peered at her closer, not liking the bleak look in her eyes. "It *is* good news, isn't it?"

"It would be if I *wanted* my old job back. But I've decided to stay in Sunny Banks instead, where my sisters are. Where my family home is. Well, where my family home *was*, no thanks to you."

"Right. About that—"

"How could you?"

For the first time in his life when it came to business, he had to grope for words. "Loni, your dad thought it best for everyone in the family. You could all move on."

"Please save your explanation. I've heard enough of them today," she said, turning away.

"Hey, wait a minute." He reached out and took her arm so she could see how earnest he was. "I'm not Blaze. In fact, I was hoping to tell you about the sale myself so you would know that I didn't set out to hurt you. I saw how upset you were with your mom the other night. I was only trying to help."

She raised an eyebrow. "Help? Really? You mean yourself? I mean, this is what you do for a living, right? This was what you wanted since you came to town. And The Predator got what he wanted." She huffed out a mirthless laugh. "I've been so blind."

"Look, I never tried to hide who I was or what I wanted from you. I've been honest since day one about wanting this resort. But this decision helps your whole family. Selling is best for everyone." He raised a hand when he saw her incredulous look. "Okay, and yes, selling is best for me, too. But I never would have done it if I'd known you felt any differently about the hotel."

Loni snorted. "Well, that's kind of the whole point, Ian. You *didn't* talk to me about it first. But I guess that's just your way, isn't it? See a problem, look at it unemotionally, fix it and move on. Well, that's not how families work. Emotions are always involved. *People* are involved. And you can't just expect to tear down a building and think the feelings and memories will disappear along with it."

A tear escaped her eye, and Ian stepped forward to wrap his arms around her, which she allowed although her body was stiff. Okay, he'd messed up. He realized that now—a little too late. But he couldn't back out on the agreement with the builder. Not now.

"I'm so sorry, Loni," he said, against her hair. "I never wanted to hurt you further. You just seemed so miserable after learning about your mom's affair. I wanted to fix it for you."

"I know," she murmured. "But you can't always be the fixer. Sometimes people need to fix things themselves."

"You have to believe me. I honestly thought a clean break would be best."

"A clean break, huh?" Loni pulled out of his arms, then glanced down at his duffel bag, half packed on the bed. "Yes, I can see that."

Dammit. This day was getting worse by the second and like a moving freight train, he was unable to stop it.

"Okay. This isn't how I wanted to tell you," Ian said, running a hand through his hair. "I do need to head back to Boston, today, but this is bad timing. I don't want to leave you upset like this."

Loni sent him a brittle smile, tears glittering in her eyes that made him want to reach for her all over again. "I'll be fine," she told him. "You and your company can enjoy your little victory lap all you want, but at least I still have my family and friends, which is more than I can say for you. I value people over business. I guess, that's where we differ and why we knew it would never work out in the long-term for us. We knew it'd be ending eventually anyway. So what difference does a day or two make, right?"

Although her words were nothing but truth, they still gave Ian an unfamiliar burning in his chest.

"I should go and let you finish packing," she said with a satisfied nod. "Goodbye, Ian."

Loni turned and with the kind of stoic resignation he'd only ever seen in himself, left his hotel room without so much as a glance back.

Slowly, Ian sat down on his bed, thinking he might just puke. Maybe Kalinda had poisoned him with the banana bread after all. It had to be that. He couldn't think of any other reason for the sickness. He made deals like this all the time. He broke up with women all the time. Anticipated it. Besides, she would eventually get over it once she saw he was right about selling. And really, he should be glad that Loni was upset with him. Right now, he was doing them both a favor by making his leaving that much easier.

But if that were truly the case, why did it feel ten times harder?

• • •

Kalinda had decided to make an old fashioned "Sunday supper" on Wednesday night, as part of Daddy's and Pamela's send off. But Loni imagined it was also a way to finally lure her out of her hotel room.

Loni hadn't been much in the mood for company since learning about the resort and breaking up with Ian. There wasn't much to say anyway. Even just thinking about either subject left her with a hollow feeling in the pit of her stomach.

The thing was that Loni had really come to care for and trust Ian. They had shared so many aspects of their lives in such a short amount of time. She thought things were different with him. *Could* be different with him. She certainly hadn't experienced the kind of loss she was feeling now when she had broken up with Blaze. So, out of self-preservation, if she continued to act like a hermit, so be it.

Personally, Loni felt she was a little more than due for a self-pity party anyway. It's not every day a person lost a job, lover, and family resort all in the span of a day. Quite exceptional, when she thought about it. She could possibly enter herself in a World Record title.

However, as depressed as she was, she was proud of herself with regard to one aspect of her life. She had submitted her resume to two law firms in town and had started the ball rolling in settling into her new life in Sunny Banks. A life that would be on her terms and her wants. She'd even called Catherine to ask her to put any personal items on her desk in a storage box for her, which she'd pick up in a few weeks.

Loni grabbed an umbrella behind the front desk that they kept on hand for unprepared guests like herself. It was a light drizzle, but enough to drench her on the walk to the cottage. When she arrived, Daddy was sitting alone on the porch, nursing what looked to be a bourbon or scotch.

"Daddy," she said stiffly. She shook out the umbrella and was about to enter the house when he quietly called her name.

"Sit with me, darlin'," he said, gesturing to the rocker next to him. "Please."

The added *please* and the sad look in his eyes got to her, despite how frustrated she was at him for selling the hotel, she did as she was told.

"I'm so sorry, Apollonia. I made a mistake," he said quietly, staring into his drink.

Loni sighed. Daddy was never one for apologies—at least, not to her—so hearing it come from his lips snuffed out her anger like a gust of wind to a candle flame. "It's okay, Daddy. What's done is done. Kalinda and Marise did say they would abide by whatever you decided to do with the resort, so I'm outnumbered anyway."

His head sprung up and he looked at her. "Huh? I wasn't talking about the resort."

She blinked back at him. "You weren't?"

He shook his head and put down his drink. "No, I was talking about how I've been acting. I've made a mistake pushing you girls away for so long just because I was upset at your mama. Heck, if I hadn't done that maybe I wouldn't have felt so compelled to sell the resort in the first place."

"Why did you, Daddy? When Mama was sick and even after she passed, I needed you. We all needed you."

He dipped his chin. "Honestly, I don't think I realized what I was doing. I was just so angry at your mama. I was angry that she had the affair, I was angry at myself for allowing it to happen, I was angry she was dying, and then I was angry that all those memories we made here were tarnished because of all that."

Loni reached over and grabbed his hand. "Oh, Daddy, is that why you left so suddenly after she passed?"

"Yeah. It hurt to be here, to be around you girls." He frowned into his glass and then lifted his gaze to Loni's. "It especially hurt to be around you."

Loni flinched. "Me?"

"It's not your fault that you are the spittin' image of your mama, my dear Apollonia. Even act like her. I was a damn fool to push you away because of that."

Loni closed her eyes, allowing her subconscious thoughts to surface. So many years Loni had tried to earn her father's love and attention, thinking there was something lacking in her. Something unlovable. When in reality, it never had anything to do with her at all.

"But you have to believe me that I thought selling the hotel would make it easier for you all to move on," he added. "I wasn't trying to hurt you. Ian even thought—"

"I know what Ian thought," she snapped.

Her father sighed. "Deep down he's a good man, darlin'. But Ian said the contracts are already in place. He felt really bad about it. He didn't want to hurt you, either."

Loni looked away. Oh, she was sure that Ian was convinced he could erase any bad memories for her by destroying the resort, but ultimately, Ian was a successful businessman for a reason. Things were never personal with him. And it hurt her further to know that business still took priority over friendship—even over love.

Love.

She supposed that was the true crux of the matter: Ian didn't love her. Loni wasn't even sure someone who could shield himself from emotions like Ian could was even capable of love. And that thought depressed her even more.

"Yeah, well, emotional attachments are not Ian's forte," Loni said. "So he doesn't understand that although he can take away the hotel, he can't take away the fact that she was my mama and that we all had some wonderful memories here that will never go away even though she did a bad thing. She hurt all of us, but the resort was starting to represent something more than just Mama to me. It was starting to represent family. And that's why I really wanted to keep it in the end. Not for her." She reached out and took his hand in hers. "For us."

His face went grim. "I'm damn sorry I took that away from you girls."

She sent him a small smile. "Luckily, the resort isn't family. Family is family." She paused. "Even when family becomes new family."

His eyes went wide. "You mean Pammy as new family?"

She rolled her eyes, amused at how delighted his tone was. "Yes, but I'm not calling her Pammy—or *Mom*. I draw the line there."

He chuckled. "'Pam' would be just fine with her and me. I'm just tickled pink you're finally giving her a chance."

Loni smothered a smile. "Pam's okay. Besides, it's selfish of me to not want to see you happy."

"Thank you, honey. That means the world to me to hear you say that."

"You certainly *do* seem happy." *Someone in this family deserves to be.*

"I am." Daddy suddenly cleared his throat. "Look, speaking of happy... I want my daughters to be happy, too."

"Even Marise," she hedged.

"Of course, Marise," he said hotly. "I don't care what doubts your mama had. She was and always will be my daughter."

Loni patted his hand. "Marise needs you to tell her that."

"I will. Has she decided about the DNA test yet?"

"No. As you can imagine, it's a lot for her to take in right now."

"You're telling me," he muttered. "She shouldn't have to deal with this. I just want her to be happy."

She could see how much the topic worked up her dad, so she let it drop. Besides, that situation would have to remain between him and Marise.

"I want you to be happy, too," he told her in a gentler tone. "As worried as I was about Ian and you being together, I am kind of surprised he left in such a hurry. He seemed different to me. Changed."

I thought so, too.

Loni snorted. "It's unfortunately not the first time I've been duped by a man, if you recall."

"Hey, now, Ian is *not* Blaze."

"No, he's not. But Ian isn't the settling down type, either. He's already married to his job." She straightened, hugging her arms to herself. "Ian and I had fun while he was here. We liked each other, but it was good it ended now. Before anyone really got hurt."

And maybe—*just maybe*—if she said it enough times out loud, she'd actually start to believe it.

Her father nodded and then picked up his drink, draining his glass. "Kalinda said you're staying in Sunny Banks now."

"I am. It's what I want." *What I need.* "Besides," she said, cracking a smile, "if you're staying in Cape Cod with Pam, somebody has to keep an eye on Kalinda and Marise."

Her daddy's face creased into a sudden smile. "I don't have to worry too much about you girls. Your mama did a fine job raising you all. Can't ever take that away from her. She loved you with all her heart."

"She was a good mother. But you were an even better father."

He squeezed her hand. "Thank you for saying that. I may not have been the best husband but I sure as heck like to think I got something right."

"You did." She leaned over and kissed him on the cheek. "I love you."

"I love you, too. Even though you're a terrible waitress."

"Hey, but I'm a great attorney," she said with a grin.

Her father shook his head. "You're more than that, darlin'. You're a great daughter, and that's more than any parent can ask for."

Chapter Twenty-Six

"Based on Ian's evaluation of the area," Scott said, passing out the notes he'd composed on Sunny Banks to the rest of his colleagues at Hollavest, "the best bet would be to level the hotel and build a high-rise luxury condominium. Zoning allows it, although we are capped to a certain height requirement that I marked on the sheet. I think they'd be easy to sell, too. Especially with those sweeping views of the ocean and being so close to the downtown shopping."

Ian sat at the table in the meeting room, pretending to listen, but really studying the pen in his hand as Scott continued on with what they'd agreed to propose to Denali Builders. It had been five days since he'd left Sunny Banks, and he'd been walking around nauseous, his bones aching to their very core. Ian had convinced himself he was suffering from food poisoning, but Scott had dismissed it as a stress ulcer and had tossed him a packet of antacids before their meeting.

It hadn't helped.

Ian was tempted to but purposely did not text Loni. Instead, he'd called her father to fill him in on minor last-minute details regarding the sale. Things that could have easily been done via email or text, but Ian had been hoping for a crumb of information about Loni. How she was doing, where she was going to live, if she had found a job. Anything really. He'd just been desperate to hear her name mentioned. However, Joe was tight-lipped when it came down to his daughter, which Ian supposed he couldn't blame him for. Ian had no right to know anything about Loni. He gave up that right when he'd given her up.

"Ian?" Scott said, poking him in the shoulder.

Ian blinked, then looked around the room at the expectant, curious faces. "Uh, sure," he murmured without knowing to what he was agreeing.

Judging from Scott's scowl, it was the wrong response.

"Let's take ten," Scott suggested to the rest of the room. There were some murmurs of agreement and then one of the men stood and reached for a bottle of water. A few others made their way to the restroom.

Scott's gaze dropped to Ian. "Can I have a word with you in my office?" he asked in a low tone.

Ian shrugged and followed his partner out. As soon as they were safely behind closed doors, Scott whirled around. "What the hell is wrong with you?" he demanded. "I'm out there doing a one man show. At this rate, you might as well have stayed in Sunny Banks."

Ian dragged a hand through his hair. "I told you before. I'm sick."

Scott's eyebrow raised in amused contempt. "You are not sick."

"I *am*," he insisted. "My appetite is shot. I ache all over. My chest hurts. I can't concentrate…"

Scott snorted. Then his lips slowly parted in surprise. "Oh no," he breathed.

"What, *oh no*?" Ian asked.

"Oh no, you *are* sick." Scott's mouth twisted.

"Told ya."

"Not that kind of sick. Lovesick," Scott said, taking a step back.

"There's no such thing." Ian gave him a mocking glance. "It's the flu."

"You have no fever. Which means it's worse than the flu, man. Much worse. How many days have you had this *sickness,* anyway?"

Ian thought back. "About five or six days."

"Okay," Scott said, folding his arms like he was cross-examining a witness. "And when did you break up with your little southern fling?"

"Her name is Apollonia," Ian snapped. "And we broke up about…"

Panic like he'd never known before welled in his throat. "*Oh no.*"

Scott nodded. "Mmm-hmm. Prognosis does not look good for you, my friend."

Ian began to pace the room, suddenly feeling like his skin was too tight for his body. "No. I don't let emotions in. This isn't supposed to happen to me."

Scott slapped him on the back. "Hey, sometimes even predators fall victim to their prey. For humans, it's a delicate symbiotic relationship that ensures the creation of families and ultimately the survival of mankind."

"Well, Dr. Darwin, what the hell am I supposed to do about

all that?"

"Depends."

"On what?" he asked warily.

"If you think you're capable of blocking out this emotion and moving on like you normally do. Or...you're willing to let go and ride that feeling and see where it takes you."

Ian frowned. For so long he'd carefully erected and kept a wall around his heart so that he would never be touched by emotions. By love. So that he would never go through what his mother went through with his father. But by doing so, he'd built himself a cage. His past had kept him a prisoner from feeling—*really* feeling—and trying to love anyone. But Loni had found a crack and slowly touched him where no woman had before: his heart.

Would she want him back? Probably not. Not now. He'd allowed himself to fall into his usual business practice and tried to keep things impersonal. But Loni—the town, and even the ridiculous people there—seemed to have wormed their way in and created a bond he couldn't shake no matter how hard he tried. And they felt like home.

He whipped his gaze to Scott. "We can't build those condos. We need to preserve the resort."

Scott rolled his eyes up toward the ceiling. "Dear Heavenly Father, please let this be the virus talking."

"Sorry, man," Ian said, grinning as he added, "You're actually right for once. It's not the flu."

"I was afraid you'd say that."

"I know it's not what you want to hear, or what Denali Builders is going to want to hear," Ian said, taking out his phone. "But destroying something that the woman I love wants is not the best way to embark on a new relationship. Let's take another look at those contracts. I think I know a way for Joe to get out of it."

"Mother eff, I was afraid you were going to say that, too," Scott muttered. "And how would you know a way to get out of the contract?"

Ian shrugged. He'd always lived by the rule that emotions don't belong in contracts. But in this case, for the first time ever, he had made sure there was an out for Joe in case he'd had a change of heart. Or in this case, Ian had a change of heart.

"You do realize that this may not be the smartest business move you've ever made, right?" Scott asked. "Raj will not only fire you on the spot, but you'll have to claw our reputation back and hope it's even a tenth of what it was."

Ian exhaled a long, contented sigh. "Yeah, I know. But I really don't care. And you know why?" He walked over to Scott and patted him on his jaw. "Because it's personal this time."

• • •

Loni was exhausted by the time she pulled back into The Sandy Bottom parking lot. She had planned to spend a week in Los Angeles packing up her belongings, but ultimately cut it down to six days. The city was just not as appealing as it once was.

While she was there, she managed to grab lunch with Catherine in between packing and tying up loose ends at work. She wanted to make sure Blaze hadn't sold her Nespresso machine and her bike—the two major things that she owned. She was able to retrieve them from Blaze's apartment and pack a few more boxes of clothes, as well as another bag to carry on the plane with her. Funny how she didn't really have all that much to send back to North Carolina. It was as if her subconscious hadn't allowed her to put down any serious roots there. At least she didn't have so much stuff that it would overcrowd the cottage when she was ready to move in. She planned on sharing it with her sisters till she found a place to live. In the meantime, she decided to remain at the resort before Ian and his company could officially kick her out.

Loni parked and checked the time. The café had closed over an hour ago, but if she were lucky, there would still be some leftover pastries from breakfast. As soon as she wheeled her luggage into the hotel she'd shoot over there and see what she could scrape up to eat. But once she'd gotten within three feet of the front door, it swung open and Lucille's smiling face greeted her.

"Howdy, sugar!" Lucille belted out. "Welcome back!"

Loni gave her a weary wave.

Lucille pouted. "Bad flight?"

Bad life.

"The flight was fine. But you have to give me a few hours to get the LA out of me before you toss around your niceties and southern charms on me like a bowl of confetti."

"Wow, Ian sure did a number on you, babycakes," Lucille said, holding the door for her. "If he were here, I'd give that man a piece of my mind. Talking your daddy into selling and then hightailing his Yankee ass back to Boston like he did. Shame on him. Like jobs like this grow on trees or something. The nerve! He's ruder than a telemarketer the day after Christmas."

Loni had to smile. "I'm sorry about everything, Lucille. Thanks for the support, though."

"My pleasure, honey." Then she cupped her hands around her mouth and screamed, "Knox!"

Knox bounced up out of his chair and gave her an impressive military-style salute. "Yes, ma'am," he said.

"Don't just sit there like a bag of potatoes. Take Miss Apollonia's bags to her room," she ordered.

In spite of how rotten she'd been feeling lately, Loni couldn't help but be amused. "That's okay. I can take them myself, Lucille."

"Don't be silly. We're all carrying out our jobs here to the bitter end. Whenever that end will be. Isn't that right, Knox?"

Knox nodded solemnly. "That's right. And I promise I won't literally take your bags. I will deliver them right to your suite. Just like Lucille said."

Sternly suppressing a grin, she nodded. "That's very good, Knox."

Knox reached for the rim of his baseball cap and brought it farther down on his forehead. "Like I said. I'm on it," he said, taking both her suitcases from her.

Loni felt reasonably sure both pieces of luggage would be waiting for her in her room but gave him a ten-dollar tip for insurance's sake.

"Wise move," Marise said from behind them. Her sister was leaning against the doorway of the back office with a smug smile. "And good to have you back, Loni."

Loni walked over and hugged her. "It's good to be back. Permanently, this time."

"Hey, now, what's all this?" Kalinda said from the other end of the lobby. "Nobody told me there was a family reunion going on."

Loni and Marise opened up their hug to include Kalinda, and the three held onto each other tightly. "You guys are acting like I've been away for a month," Loni mumbled into Kalinda's shoulder.

"Aww…" sighed Lucille. "This is the sweetest. It's just like the picture."

Loni pulled back and asked, "What picture?"

Grinning, Marise pointed to a ten by fourteen framed picture hanging by the check-in desk. "Kalinda was moving things to the attic to make room for your stuff. She found that wrapped up in Christmas paper."

Loni blinked, then moved closer to get a better look. It was a photograph their mama must have taken of the three sisters on the beach, hugging like they'd just done. Only, in the picture, Loni couldn't have been more than six years old.

"Maybe Mama meant to surprise us with it at Christmastime," Kalinda said, coming up to stand alongside Loni. "But by then she'd gotten pretty weak and probably had forgotten about it."

Loni heaved a sigh. "Probably. It is a sweet picture, though."

"Marise almost drowned that day," Kalinda murmured.

Marise came to stand on Loni's other side and looked up at it. "Yeah...good times."

"We should probably hang it in the cottage now," Loni said, turning to her sisters. "Seeing as we don't own the hotel anymore."

Kalinda cocked her head, still eyeing the photograph. "No, I think it should stay." She glanced at Loni with a grin. "After all, Ian hasn't shut us down yet."

Loni shook her head. "No, but he will."

"Are you sure?" Marise bit her lip. "It seems so *un*-Ian-like."

Loni would have thought the same thing a few weeks ago. After all, she'd come to trust him. Thought that she'd meant more to him than a business deal. Had hoped, anyway. "People aren't always what they seem. Or relationships, for that matter," she added.

"You can say that again," Kalinda murmured.

"Are you okay?" Marise asked.

Kalinda nodded. "I'll be fine."

"I meant *Loni*," Marise said. "Ian broke her heart."

Yes, he did. As much as she'd tried to convince herself that they had ended things at the perfect time, it wasn't. It was already too late. "I'll be fine, too."

"Are you sure?" Kalinda asked. "I feel terrible encouraging you with him. But I really thought... Well, men just suck, don't they?"

"They sure do," Loni said, wiping her eyes. "Thank God I won't have to see him again."

Marise worried her lip. "Well, that might be a teeny problem. Daddy told me that Ian's company is flying in the day after tomorrow."

"Sheeze Louise, that was fast," Kalinda commented hotly. "Maybe you're right. We better take down the picture before the wrecking ball comes through without warning."

"No," Marise said, stomping her foot. "No. If Ian and his crew are coming, we need to stand up and make sure our voices are heard loud and clear. They may own the resort, but we still work here. Maybe we can convince them not to knock it down. Maybe Ian's had a change of heart and misses Loni."

Kalinda rolled her eyes. "Hell's bells, this is not the ending of a Julia Roberts rom-com, Marise. This is big business. Money talks and is much louder than three southern sisters."

"I'll help," Lucille offered. Loni and her sisters turned to her. "Everybody in town knows I have the biggest voice."

"Biggest *boobs*," Kalinda corrected.

Lucille waved a hand. "Whatever. Marise has a point. Any

good developer has to listen to the community. We can have our own impromptu town hall when they get here. Tell them they need to keep this hotel *as is* because it's not just what the former owners want but what Sunny Banks wants."

"Maybe not *as is*," Marise interjected, wrinkling her nose. "I think we need a banquet hall. Plus, a little sprucing up wouldn't hurt."

"I'll call Dana and Duke," Kalinda said. "And Hazel and—"

"Henry Shelton," Loni added.

Lucille squinted at her. "That old coot is still livin'? He's meaner than dirt, which he'll soon be under."

"Yes," Loni said, amused, thinking of her and Ian's run-in with him downtown. "However, I saw him the other day at The Beach Bash, and Henry told me he loves our old hotel."

"Oh," Lucille said with a sniff. "Well then, he's my favorite mean old coot."

Kalinda looked at Loni. "If we're going to do this, we probably should have an attorney there. You know, just to make sure everything is on the up and up."

Loni looked at everyone, suddenly overwhelmed by the torment she'd gone through this past week and shook her head. "I'm sorry. I can't be there."

"Why not?" Marise asked softly. "We can't do this without you. Remember, the sunshine sisters are finally back together again."

She shook her head regretfully. "You don't need me. You never needed me, really. You two did a great job managing this hotel on your own while I was off in California. Besides, I might make things worse for you if Ian is there. I'm sorry." She turned away and began heading toward her room.

"Loni," Kalinda called. "Marise is right. We need to be all

in this together. Ian will listen. He does care for you. Give him one more chance."

"I can't," Loni said sadly. "It hurts too much. And if country living has taught me anything, it's to not only know when to hold 'em but know when to fold 'em as well."

Chapter Twenty-Seven

As Ian and Scott pulled into the hotel parking lot, Ian noticed an unusual number of cars and bikes in the area. He had to wonder if there was some kind of event going on that Marise had failed to mention to him when he alerted her he was coming down.

Scott dipped his chin, looked above his sunglasses, and let out a slow whistle. *"That's* the hotel? You threw away your career for this? Are you sure you know what you're doing?"

No, Ian wasn't sure. He wasn't sure about anything—except his feelings for Loni. And if the resort was important to her, it was important to him. Was it too late? He rubbed a hand over his face, feeling nervous and uneasy like he was about to jump out of his skin. Did Loni even want to see him again after what he'd done?

Ian looked over at Scott and shrugged. "I have to try."

Scott shook his head and stepped out of the car. "I guess for the sake of love, I don't need that new Tesla Roadster I had my eye on," he mumbled.

Ian grinned. "Aww...you old softy."

"Yeah, yeah."

The hotel door swung open, revealing a frowning Lucille. "Well, well, look what the cat killed, batted around, chewed up, spit out, and then dragged back." She crossed her arms with a defiant glare.

Scott's brow rose. "Southern hospitality is portrayed differently in the movies," he murmured.

"Shut up," Ian said, elbowing Scott. He then sent Lucille his most winning smile. "Lucille, it's lovely to see you again."

Her eyes went wide. "It is?" Then she shook her head and frowned. "I mean, wish I could say the same," she said tersely. She turned her back on them and disappeared into the hotel lobby.

"This should be interesting," Scott said, holding the door for Ian. "I'm glad I get to witness this town handing you your ass on a platter. It'll make what I went through with Denali Builders almost worth it."

Ian rolled his eyes, then entered the hotel. The lobby was jam-packed with people—locals he recognized from town— including Angela, Dana, and Duke from the café, and Henry, the older man he'd met that day shopping with Loni. Man, he missed them. Unfortunately, the one person he didn't see in the crowd was the only person he truly wanted to see.

People pushed and shoved to get closer to him, and Ian raised his palms up in surrender. "Whoa, I, uh, didn't expect such a homecoming."

"This ain't no homecoming," Henry grunted, throwing up his hands in two fists. "This is an unarmed militia session. Ain't no Northerner going to change our land without our say so."

Although Henry looked ready for battle, Ian's shoulders

relaxed somewhat when he heard Henry say *unarmed*. "I'm not looking for a fight, Henry."

Henry scowled, then spat on the floor in front of him.

"I saw that, Henry," Lucille called, wagging a finger at him. "No spitting inside the premises. You clean that up or no tea and cookies."

Henry's expression soured as he pulled out a handkerchief from his back pocket. He dropped it to the ground, stepped on it, and began wiping the floor with it, grumbling something inaudible all the while.

Marise and Kalinda weaved their way through the crowd until they reached Scott and Ian. "We, uh, told a few people you'd be coming," Marise told Ian. "They're a lot of people who want a say in what your company does to this resort. Daddy may have signed the papers, but we're not going down without a fight."

Ian glanced out into the sea of people, his heart dropping. Still no Loni. "I'm not surprised. Ladies, this here is my partner, Scott Simpson. We're actually anxious to hear all the input you have and then tell you some of our own."

Kalinda eyed Scott with open skepticism. "Oh, great, because *two* Yankee minds are so much better than one."

Scott shrugged. "Hey, I'm just here for the tea and cookies. And to see Ian get his ass whooped by some angry southerners."

"Well, then." Kalinda smirked, amusement lighting her eyes. "Right this way," she said, leading him to a table filled with pitchers of sweet tea and refreshments.

Marise glanced at Ian. "We should probably start this forum before the crowd gets restless."

He cleared his throat. "Is, uh, Loni coming? I wanted to talk with her first." He couldn't help but ask.

Marise gave him a sympathetic look, then shook her head.

"Right. I probably deserve that." Ian swallowed the despair in his throat. He could only hope when he did see her—after she learned about what he wanted to do with the property—she'd hear him out and give him another chance. "Let's just start then. I think you'll be pleasantly surprised."

Marise nodded and then turned toward the townspeople. "Thanks for coming, everyone," she said, raising her voice to be heard over the talking.

Some hushes went through the air and the murmuring died to silence. Marise smiled. "As I was saying, I can't tell you how much we appreciate you all coming out to our little town hall meeting." She gestured to Ian. "As some of you may know, this is Ian Hollowell from Hollavest. He's technically the new owner of The Sandy Bottom."

Boos and hisses came from the crowd and Ian was pretty sure he heard himself referred to as an *egg suckin' dawg*. Thankfully, he'd been called much worse in his lifetime and had thick skin as a result.

"We'll let Mr. Hollowell speak and then maybe he'll take some questions from the audience." Marise nodded encouragingly for him to address the people.

Ian glanced across the room at Scott, who shoved a cookie into his mouth and then gave him a thumbs-up.

Here goes nothing. "First of all," Ian began.

"Speak up!" Henry scowled.

"First of all," Ian repeated, louder, "I just want to say how much I admire this town. And all of you. I think it says a lot about a community when people give up their time to come out to preserve even just a small piece of it."

Ian paused, looking out upon all their faces—Angela

throwing an arm around Marise's shoulders, Kalinda and Lucille sharing a smile of support for each other, and something tugged at his insides. Emotion. The hotel—the whole resort—did mean a lot more to this town than he'd ever imagined. Not just memories, but history as well. Friendships and relationships. As a result, this business transaction *had* become personal. It had come to mean more to him than what it could mean to his wallet.

Before he could say anything else, movement way across the room caught his gaze. Ian saw her then and his heart stopped. Loni stood in the back, her blond hair hanging loose against her tanned shoulders. Her arms were crossed, and her chin tipped up as if she were ready to defy everything that was about to come out of his mouth. His little fighter. A force to be reckoned with since the day he'd first laid eyes on her. God, she never looked more incredible to him.

Marise cleared her throat loudly. He turned and she made the wind-up gesture with her finger for him to continue.

He swallowed, his gaze swinging back to Loni. "Anyway, the company I worked for had some big plans for this area."

"It better not be a casino!" someone called out.

Ian frowned. "Uh, no, it won't be a casino."

"I like aquariums!" a woman shouted.

Henry shook his head. "Why on earth do we need an aquarium, Ethel? All you need to do is take twenty steps east and you can swim in a natural *aquarium* for free."

Ian scratched his head. "I think you're all getting ahead of the point I was trying to make."

Loni slowly made her way through the crowd until she stood before him. "What do you mean by the company you *worked* for?"

Ian took a deep breath as he gazed into her beautiful, tear-flooded eyes. "I mean that I don't work for Hollavest anymore. Turns out they didn't really appreciate the way I handled the contract...specifically the loophole in the contract. Apparently, there are grounds to nullify the sale of the resort, if you want."

Her lips parted in wonder. "B-but why would you do that?"

"Because I was wrong. Wrong about everything. This hotel, this land, your family...you. It is personal. And you were right. This place is special." He cracked a smile. "It's not perfect, but it's home."

Loni's breath hitched. "Home?"

"Yeah. You've come to mean something to me, Loni, and I want to see where we can go. I want us to be together, in a real relationship, exclusively." He let out a rush of air. "For as long as you'll have me."

Loni smiled through her tears. "But you don't do commitment."

"I've changed my mind. I do contracts all the time and they're commitments. The only thing missing in them was the emotion part. But you made me realize that emotion's the best part, because what is the point of anything if it doesn't mean something? And to prove that point," he said, taking out the seller's agreement he and Joe had signed, "I want to make this contract more personal."

Ian held the papers up, then ripped them in half to some gasps in the crowd. "That's why I brought Scott down here with me. We're starting up our own development company together. And I'd like to draw up a new agreement with me as part owner. One where all parties involved can have some ownership and have a say, where we *all* can benefit." He looked over at Marise and Kalinda. "That's if you both agree, too."

The sisters smiled and nodded happily.

"I can't believe those words are coming from The Predator," Loni said with a watery chuckle.

Ian gave her a gentle smile. "It's your fault. Because of you I'm feeling all kinds of things. Feelings that feel a lot... A lot like love." He stepped closer, taking her face in his hands.

Loni looked at him in a way no one ever had before, with such tenderness that his breath caught. "Me, too," she whispered.

"That's good because I *do* love you, Loni. I love you, and I'm just so sorry that it took me this long to figure it out. You told me a while ago that people—family—aren't tied to things. They're tied to what's here," he said, pointing to his head. "And they're tied to what's in here." He reached down and took her hand, gently placing her palm against his heart. "I want to buy the resort. Not because it's great, but because we can make it great together by adding new memories."

A collective "Aww," came from the crowd, along with one "worthless as gum on a boot heel" that Ian had no doubt came from Henry.

"Yes!" Marise and Kalinda high-fived each other. "I can still get my event room," Marise gushed out. "We're so going to start doing weddings and private events."

"I'd love a bigger kitchen and some outside table space," Kalinda added. "Maybe even start serving dinners."

"Don't forget the aquarium!" Ethel shouted.

Ian closed his eyes with a sigh. "Please tell me the aquarium won't be in the new contract."

Loni chuckled. "You're safe," she said, wrapping her arms around him.

"I haven't been safe since I met you." Then, Ian covered her mouth with his in a kiss he prayed conveyed to her all the emotion he'd been bottling in for the past week. When they finally broke apart, he rested his forehead against hers as they each struggled to catch their breath amidst the applause and hoots.

"You should know, Mr. Hollowell," she said, smiling up at him, "I happen to be a really good attorney, so there won't be any loopholes in this new contract. And don't think you're going to be getting off cheaply, either. It's the price you pay when you let emotions become involved with your business dealings."

"Darlin'," he said, with his best exaggerated southern twang, "between us, I wouldn't want it any other way."

Epilogue

6 MONTHS LATER

At sundown, Marise and Loni walked out onto The White Squirrel's renovated patio to check out the new outside seating. Comprised of bistro-style tables with little umbrellas, it provided a lovely view of the water as well as their mama's garden.

Loni sighed when she saw it. Kalinda had already filled the planters with flowers, giving the area a kind of romantic feel. "Wow, the architect Ian provided outdid himself," she said in awe.

"It looks amazing, but I don't understand," Marise said with a pout. "Why does Kalinda get her restaurant renovation before I get my private club expansion?"

"Because," Kalinda said, her head popping out from behind a trellis, "the expanded restaurant will be more of an immediate revenue maker." She then flipped her hair off her shoulder. "Plus, I'm older and get first dibs. Sibling rule order and all that."

Loni chuckled. In the last six months, she hadn't stopped feeling happy to be home again. Back in Sunny Banks with her sisters. Back at the hotel. She couldn't wait to start creating new memories.

Shortly after the new contracts were drawn up on the hotel, Ian and Scott were able to secure Denali Builders to do the renovations for their new company and not his old company Hollavest, despite the fact that the money wasn't nearly as much as they could have been making. Fortunately, Ian managed to secure the old bank building downtown and already had big plans to create more space for another retail shop, several offices, and even a few condos on the top floor that Denali Builders was all too pleased to also renovate for him.

Loni planned to open up her own law office there, too. In fact, Ian promised her first pick once completed. The exact rent amount was still under negotiation. But she had a feeling he'd come around and meet her terms. Seemed as though "The Predator" didn't quite have the same ruthlessness in business he once had. At least not with her.

"Speaking of the new restaurant," Kalinda said, looking at Loni and waggling her eyebrows. "I will need some help during the dinner service, just until I can get all my new hires trained."

"Ready and able," Loni told her with a short nod.

Kalinda cracked a grin. "Not so sure about the *able* part."

"Hey, I got better at table service." She bit her lip. "Eventually..."

"I love the stage." Marise pointed behind them to where an elevated platform had been set up. "Having some live entertainment is going to be a great addition. Daddy sent me the number of a local band to check out, too. Said he'd love for me to book them for when he and Pamela come back in June for Ansley's wedding."

"Ugh," Kalinda muttered, rolling her eyes. "Hopefully the restaurant will be so busy, I'll have to miss that wedding."

Marise frowned. "What do you mean miss the wedding? You're my plus one."

"Can't Loni be your plus one?"

"I have my own plus one," Loni informed her, hand on her hip.

"One plus one at your service," Ian announced from the gate entrance. He was grinning ear to ear, and even though the darkness from the setting sun half hid his eyes, Loni knew his gaze was directed at her.

He rushed up to Loni as if he couldn't bear one more second away from her and took her face in his hands. "Hello, darlin'," he murmured before bringing his lips to hers in a sweet yet searing kiss.

"That's a piss poor southern accent," Kalinda commented once they pulled apart.

"No, it's not," Ian tossed over his shoulder, still gazing at Loni. "At least, no one else here has complained."

Loni let out a giggle. "It is terrible." She kissed his frowning mouth. "But it's very cute."

Kalinda made a gagging sound while Marise hushed her.

"What are you doing here anyway?" Loni asked, lacing her fingers with his. "I thought you'd still be in Boston until the end of the month with Scott."

He grinned down at her. "I just missed you and wanted to come home early to show you the new designs for the banquet center."

Even though they had mastered the art of the long-distance

relationship, Loni was thrilled to hear that he still missed her. And perhaps, even more pleased to learn that he now considered Sunny Banks his home, too.

"The banquet center?" she asked. "That's great. Did you hear that, Marise?" She looked behind her, but her sisters had quietly disappeared. "That's weird. I wonder why they left." Before she could turn back to Ian, twinkle lights lit up all around them.

"Just a hunch, but they probably left so I could give you this," he said, pulling out a ring box from his jacket pocket.

Her heart swelled, as she stared at the beautiful diamond ring he presented. Catching the lights above them, it sparkled like a star. "Oh, Ian," she whispered.

"What did she say?" a male voice grumbled in the distance.

"If you'd shut your pie hole, we'd all hear," came another voice, sounding a lot like Lucille.

Startled, Loni looked up and had to chuckle at the annoyed expression on Ian's face.

"There's nothing to hear because I didn't ask her yet!" Ian called back.

"Well, hurry up!" Kalinda shouted. "The champagne is getting warm."

Finally, Ian let out a chuckle of his own. "You heard your sister." He took a deep breath. "Apollonia Wingate, will you agree to marry me in the presence of your nosy sisters and some impatient Carolina knuckleheads who apparently can't keep a secret?"

"I definitely will," Loni said with a breathless laugh.

She couldn't imagine agreeing any other way.

Ian gathered her into his arms, his eyes shining with both humor and affection and her own smile tugged at her lips. He leaned in to kiss her but before he could, a crowd of people came bustling out and onto the patio, popping bottles and yelling congratulations.

"You're a little early," he grumbled to Marise who suddenly appeared at his side. "We were still having a moment."

"Plenty of time for that later, kids," she said, nudging a tray of champagne between them. "First we celebrate."

"I thought you said first we eat," Henry grumbled, shaking his walking cane at her. "I haven't had my supper yet."

"Hors d'oeuvres are coming up," Kalinda promised. "Right after I toast my sister."

"We *both* toast her," Marise corrected, raising her glass. "To Ian and Loni. May their love be as sweet as Mama's sweet tea and their passion be as hot as Kalinda's pepper omelet." A few chuckles emerged from the crowd.

"To family." Kalinda winked. "As messed up as we are, you're both stuck with us."

"You're stuck with *us*, too," Lucille and Knox said together.

Ian leaned in. "You're lucky I'm so in love with you that I'm ignoring all that," he muttered from the side of his mouth.

Loni's eyes filled with tears of happiness as she looked out into the crowd of family, her dear friends and then into the smiling eyes of her future husband. "To coming home," she added.

She then clinked glasses with Ian, and as they drank together, for the first time in a long time she felt she was exactly where she belonged.

Acknowledgments

The author may write the book but it takes a village to get it into the reader's hands. I am truly fortunate to have been surrounded by so many wonderful people in its journey.

First and foremost, I want to thank my BIGGEST cheerleader and supporter, my agent Lesley Sabga. You took a lot of the stress out of the process and always make me feel like I have your undivided attention and time. I appreciate you! Thank you so much to Nicole Resciniti and everyone at The Seymour Agency as well. I'm definitely in good hands.

Huge thank you to my critique partners, especially Nina Croft, Jus Accardo, Debra Dennis, Jerri Drennen, and KT Roberts. I appreciate all the time you gave me in reading and your thoughtful feedback.

Thank you as always to Liz Pelletier and the entire team at Entangled and Macmillan Publishing who had a hand in shaping this book, especially Stacy Abrams and Jessica Turner for their thoughtful brainstorming sessions, Elizabeth Turner Stokes for such a beautiful cover, and editors Jen Bouvier, and

Alice Jerman for making this book so much stronger. You were all a pleasure to work with!

Lastly, thank you to my husband, Jeff, for giving me not one but THREE spaces in the house where I can work and for offering me the freedom to give up pharmacy so I could stay home and write. You always tell me life is too short to not do what makes you happy. But—as I'm sure you know—you also make me happy.

Resorting to Romance is a sun drenched romantic comedy about two workaholics on opposite sides of a deal. However, the story includes elements that might not be suitable for all readers. Parent death, cancer, alcohol abuse disorder, car accidents, job loss, and misogyny are mentioned, referenced, and discussed in the novel. Readers who may be sensitive to these elements, please take note.

*Don't miss the exciting new books
Entangled has to offer.*

Follow us!

 @EntangledPublishing

 @Entangled_Publishing

 @EntangledPub

AMARA
an imprint of Entangled Publishing LLC